A Brighter, Darker Art

Halli Starling

For contact information, please visit hallistarlingbooks.com

Book design by Halli Starling

Cover design by Ilaria Romani

ISBN: 9781737323488 (hardcover)

ISBN: 9781737323495 (ebook)

First edition: 2023

10 9 8 7 6 5 4 3 2 1

Contents

Praise for Halli Starling's Books

Praise for *Ask Me For Fire*

"Every once in a while, we stumble upon a book that just knocks our socks off (please excuse my choice of words here). This book just swept me off my feet." – Goodreads reviewer

"Wow. This book was wonderful. It's a trope you don't see very often, two grumpy loners finding their way through a lot of ups and down, through their pasts, building something to last. There was so much potential that these stories and their histories becoming something angst ridden and dark but instead you're left with a heart warming story of two complicated men that ended up living away from everything so they could find peace. Which they find, in time, with each other." – Goodreads reviewer

Praise for *When He Beckons*

"Sometimes it's nice to read a story about two people whose weird works together, and they acknowledge it and are happy together, with no contrived plot points. This is that. (With spice!)" - Goodreads reviewer

Acknowledgments

This book, like all of mine, are labors of love. I think most authors and artists of any strain can relate to that. But that labor is never done alone.

My deepest thanks to:

- Agu, for the name Silvan and for yelling at me about Raf so many times, I began to believe he was real.
- Allison, for all her love and support and everlasting encouragement.
- Cayla, for always being my FIRST reader and for finding the joy and love in the story.
- Anna and Jen, my early readers who brought me such joy and helped me with rough spots in the draft.
- To everyone who read *Ask Me For Fire* and realized that genre books do not have to adhere to every convention and trope in order to build a genuine, realistic story.

Author's Note

While you do not need to read *Ask Me For Fire* in order to enjoy the novel, this is its direct companion. Ambrose, Raf's best friend, and Ambrose's boyfriend, Barrett, are the main characters in that novel. This book begins after the destruction of Alpha firewatch tower in *Ask Me For Fire*. Alpha Tower is destroyed at the end June and this book picks up a few weeks later.

Content warnings: language, explicit sex, drinking (not to excess), discussions of relationship parameters (one MC has a friends with benefits agreement before any relationship with the other MC); behavior by an ex that is questionable/borderline obsessive.

Chapter One

"That is the ugliest shade of yellow I've ever seen. It's not yellow, actually. It's essentially a shade of jaundice and completely hideous."

"I agree." Arie cocked her head and squinted at the bare wall. "And worse, all the sunlight coming in makes it look kind of puke green."

Raf pointed to a spread of paint swatches. "And those are no better." He frowned and leaned back in his chair, reaching for the beer bottle cradled between his knees. "Awful," he said after taking a swig.

Arie laughed. "The paint or the beer?"

"Both." For some reason, the paint swatches were bothering him. It really shouldn't be difficult to pick a color for the walls of the new gallery. But everything needed to be *right* and the pale yellows and greens Arie had brought over simply weren't the way to go. "Truly terrible," he said, taking another swig.

"Spoiled."

"I am not."

"You absolutely are. It's a grave of your own making, my friend."

He swiped a hand down his face and tried to push away the creeping sensation of inadequacy he always got when things didn't go as planned. Picking paint should have been easy and it wasn't Arie's fault he was being stubbornly particular. But Raf had dreams for this space. He'd envisioned a bright, sunny place with light yellow paint, but his imagination and cruel reality weren't matching up. Fickle mistress, reality, casting doubt on his pristine plans. "Ugh." When Arie snickered but said nothing, he glanced at his friend and watched her fiddle with the end of her long blond braid before saying, "All right, scratch the yellows and greens. Let's see that swatch book again."

By the time they'd picked out a deep navy, so dark it felt velvety on the eyeballs, the sun had long set and Raf could see the glow of the streetlights in the nearby park. The newest gallery was in a quiet part of St. Augustine, a town with a reputation for perfection in a cozy seaside kind of way. It was a strange shift from the bustling streets and flickering surrounding his other galleries. His best friend, Ambrose, had teased him when Raf talked about this most recent move.

"Cottage-core seaside isn't quite your vibe, Raf," Ambrose said with a laugh.

"Maybe I'll start wearing hemp, just to prove you wrong."

There was a clang on the other end of the phone, and then Ambrose cursed. "Keep forgetting how heavy that damn pan is. Barrett says hello, by the way."

In the background, Raf heard Barrett's deep baritone and smiled. Barrett was easily the best thing to ever happen to Ambrose, and even though he'd visited them earlier in the year for Ambrose's birthday, Raf felt their absence. A lingering ache deep in his bones. Ambrose was his brother, his friend, his closest confidant; and he lived across the country and now had the sweetest bear of a boyfriend in Barrett. If Raf could have, he would have moved Ambrose and Barrett to St. Augustine, set them up in a house on the coast. But those two weren't beach people, preferring dense forests and the call of birds high up in a pine tree canopy.

They'd be in town in late autumn, but he missed them.

"Well, I should have everything by the end of the week," Arie said, rising from her chair and offering a hand down to Raf. "That timing still okay?"

He gave her a small smile, head still clouded with thoughts of Ambrose and Barrett. "You know me. Always ahead of schedule to keep from being behind."

She chuckled and hauled him to his feet with a firm grip. "We good?"

"We're good." Raf helped her scoop up her swatch books and the various notebooks and pens and pencils that always rattled around in her bags. Arie was an artist at heart; it was how they'd met, at her first exhibit years ago. Even then, she'd had several pencils jammed into her messy bun, more in her overall pockets, and a big canvas bag slung about her tiny frame. Raf had immediately liked her, so calm and collected and very *laissez-faire* about the number of snobby rich folks who swarmed around her. They felt the same way about art - it should be interesting, different, and accessible to anyone and everyone. It was partially because of Arie that he'd opened up that first gallery on the east side of nearby Balmer Bay, in an "undesirable" part of town.

Art was for everyone and should never be gatekept. That was, and would always be, the mission.

"All right, you. Be good, I'll see you in a few days. And I'll text you when I've got all supplies so me and the crew can get started." Arie looked down at the dusty marble floor. "You got lucky with this one. Clean it up good and you're going to have this place rockin'."

Raf accepted her cheek kiss and warm hug with a grateful heart, and then watched her leave, bag swinging at her hip. He sighed and sat back down, draining the last of the beer. There was a lot to do to get this place up and running for the opening, but all that work would be worth it. It always was, but this one was special. He eyed the shadowed corner where his showstopping opener sat. Waiting.

It was tempting to flick through those canvases; to let the soft purples and deep greens soothe his jangling nerves. Perry Bourdet's illustrations of the flora and fauna of the far northeastern coast were so lifelike they practically begged to be touched. As if they were a check on one's senses to ensure they really were just illustrations.

To say *just illustrations* felt like a grand disservice to the art. And that wasn't only because Raf knew about Perry through Ambrose and Barrett. Perry had been Barrett's neighbor before he passed away, and Ambrose had bought Perry's home. Ambrose and Barrett fell in love. And Barrett had trusted Perry's illustrations to Raf. Raf had to make sure Perry's art, and the gallery's feature for its first show, got the praise it deserved. Especially after all the grief and trauma Ambrose and Barrett had been through. Ambrose had been in an accident involving the firewatch tower Barrett had been assigned to for part of the summer. A saboteur had been caught. And while Ambrose was healthy and on the mend, it only made Raf more determined to make this gallery opening better, bigger. More deserving of Perry's art, and Ambrose and Barrett flying out to attend.

He stood there, halfway between the rickety chair and the canvas stack, undecided. He knew there were beers left, but they were terrible. Arie was an amazing person, but she had truly horrific taste in all alcohol, not just beer. This was also the woman who thought shot gunning Fireball was still a good idea, long past any of their college days.

Raf's lip curled at the thought of the beers and other cheap alcohol. And standing here, indecisive as all hells, was a little sad. The night air would clear his head for sure, and then he could stumble home and sleep. He cleaned up their bottles, flipped off the lights, and refused to look back at those goddamn ugly paint swatches. It didn't have to be perfect quite yet.

The Lash and Rose only *sounded* like a dungeon but in reality it was a bar with a dance floor and plenty of seating. Previously the building had housed a sex shop by the same name, and the new owner decided to keep it for their club. Despite the Mod sixties vibe inside the bar and club, St. Augustine was a more *knitted blanket and boats in the bay* kind of place.

Raf dug the bar, from the floor to ceiling lava lamps and deep pink and orange leather sofas, to the heavy beaded curtains that partitioned off the private booths for high rollers. He hadn't been to L&R in a while, and he was mildly curious if one of the bartenders, Matteo, was on staff tonight. They were friendly acquaintances after Raf had recognized Matteo at another gallery's show and struck up a conversation. Talking to people had always been easy for him.

Raphael could charm the money out of a bank vault, making it follow him down the street as if he were the Pied Piper.

Even now, those words bothered him. It had been a remark on a professor's grading sheet he'd received after a massive presentation for his thesis. The professor had likely meant it as a compliment, since "so few people have such natural speaking abilities" and "you'd make a great politician" had been slung at him previously. But Raf couldn't deny that he could talk to anyone about anything, but it had nothing to do with oozing charm or sophistication. He simply liked people.

So when he'd spotted Matteo across the gallery floor, he'd thought nothing of heading over with a friendly smile and a wave. They'd spent the rest of the show shoulder to shoulder, discussing the mixed media pieces on display. And since then, Matteo always kept a look out for Raf on his shift nights at The Lash and Rose.

Head still too full, Raf rounded the final corner before the bar, fingers itching to straighten his collar. He was rather casual today, next to his usual slacks, sweater, and jacket, but the bar didn't have a dress code. And he certainly wasn't trying to impress anyone tonight. This was a *drink and toddle on home* kind of evening.

The bouncer at the door, a woman with a scowl on her face at the line forming, motioned him forward. "Good to see you, babe," she said as he passed, both of them ignoring groans and protests of those in line.

Raf patted Sara's arm absentmindedly then strolled inside, hands dug into his jean pockets. Past the main door, the hall split into two pieces. The much shorter end led to an elevator, which was where Raf was headed. The other created a long walk to the main floor; the rotating spotlights dashing rainbow colors against hard concrete and faux wood paneling. Anywhere else, it would have been a horrific combination but here, it transported back decades to when wood paneling and those spotlights were cool. He couldn't help but grin. The bass from a popular dance floor song from the sixties thumped through his ears, making him glad for the solid soundproofing in Marianna's office.

At the elevator, he swiped his key card, waited, then took the sleek metal box a floor up, walking out into a sumptuous office decked in vibrant jewel tones. Marianna wasn't one to shy away from velvets and leather. As he entered the room, Marianna looked up from peering at a record in her hand. The rubies in her ears glinted in the soft light overhead. "I'm feeling nostalgic tonight. Some Joni Mitchell?"

Raf grinned at her. "Nostalgic for you usually means Chopin. What's going on?"

She smiled at him, dark red lips in a wide bow. The lipstick drew the eye to follow her angular face and the severe lines of her bob. "Raf, darling cousin of mine. Do not tell me you forgot."

He felt his eyes go wide with panic. Shit. What had he forgotten? He rarely forgot anything anymore, not with his detailed note system and in-depth calendars and alarms. His memory problems weren't getting worse, were they?

"Whew okay, I did not mean for that to be so stressful." Immediately, Marianna was at his side, her warm hands gentle as she directed him by the shoulders to the sofa along the far wall. They sat down, Raf's mind reeling. "Raf. When you signed the lease on the new gallery! It's been six months, and when you called me, you were playing Joni Mitchell!"

Raf hung his head in relief. "No problem. I just...it's been a day."

She hummed sympathetically and hugged him close. "And a week and apparently a month. Sorry again, totally didn't mean to do that."

He was so relieved to not have forgotten something genuinely important, he almost missed understanding the bigger picture. It had been a trying few months and it wasn't going to get any better. And the fact that time had gone by so quickly and he'd barely noticed the pass of a full *half year* since that call? He looked up, feeling despondent. "Just makes me panic when I think my memory's going the way of roadkill."

"I think you mean the way of the raisin. Left out in the sun to dry slowly."

"I was going for smashed under the weight of a car tire - aka reality - and then left for the vultures, aka my shitty brain."

"Well, we know it isn't like that and since the smartest person I know should be celebrating..." Marianna gave him one last squeeze and he caught a whiff of herbal shampoo as she stood and went to the liquor cabinet. "Tell me what you're feeling."

Marianna's cabinet was stocked with the best L&R had to offer and Raf wasn't one to say no, especially not tonight when he'd come to the bar *for* drinks. "Please tell me you have some of the Pappy left."

"Good choice, cuz." Marianna was quick to pour two healthy fingers of the aged bourbon for each of them and then handed Raf his glass, settling on the couch to his left. "So, we're celebrating. But you look like someone's been kicking the back of your seat the entire flight."

Despite his despondence, Raf chuckled. The sip of bourbon he took immediately warmed him, so he leaned back into the sofa, turning slightly to better look at her. "Just the usual. *Poor me who has to have everything perfect.*" Raf frowned as he said it, knowing it sounded pathetic.

To Marianna's credit, she never laughed or teased when he was stuck in his head like this. Instead, she put a hand on his knee and said, "Want to talk about it?"

Raf fixed his gaze on the gift he'd given her years ago; his first purchase from Arie. Marianna liked dark, gothic-inspired pieces and Arie had done amazing work, sculpting a raven's head with top hat and monocle, a whip dangling from its beak. Whatever she'd used in the finish on the sculpture cast an iridescent gleam over the bird's feathers, and the monocle was glass and gold, the top hat coated velvet. It was just the right amount of kitsch and dark glamour, and Marianna had promptly named him Sven and declared him the mascot of the club.

"I'm all right," he finally said, grateful for her patient silence as his wandering mind settled. "I'll head down to the floor in a bit. Is Matteo working?"

"He's off this week. His sister just had another baby so he's watching his nephew."

"Oh. Right." But he hadn't known that. He hadn't even known Matteo's sister was pregnant. Raf flashed back through his various conversations with Matteo. For someone he chatted with regularly, he didn't know much about the man. And that realization made him a tad upset. He should have been asking Matteo more about his life, getting to know him better. It felt like a tiny failure.

"Why don't you text him next week?" she suggested, nudging his leg with her own. "I'm sure he'd like to hear from you."

"Yeah, good idea," he replied softly, refusing to look up at her. He felt ridiculous, to be upset at his own little social snag that meant nothing in the long run. But he couldn't shake the feeling he should have known and offered Matteo and his family congratulations.

"You can't keep track of everything and everyone, babe. Go easy on yourself."

"I know."

"Yes, and you say that every time and yet." She nudged him again. "Go downstairs. Find someone pretty to chat up. Or just sit in the corner and brood."

"Am I bringing down the vibe in the office?" he teased, managing to smile at her again. "I'll go, I'll go."

Marianna blew him a kiss as he got to his feet. Raf took himself and his very nice bourbon down to the main floor. The drink was helping his self-aggrandizing pity party, and hopefully the unrelenting bass thump of dark techno would, too.

Chapter Two

"Downsized? You gotta be shitting me."

Silvan knocked back the last of his beer and set the bottle down hard. Harder than he meant to, but the slight reverberation of glass on wood felt good, like a throb in his fingertips. He shifted on the hard booth seat as he replied, "They didn't need us senior people anymore. Me, Anita, Daman, LaTisha. Just gone."

"Jesus Christ. Did they at least give you a severance? Isn't that a *thing* when you're that high up the food chain?"

Silvan winced. "Yeah, yeah they did. It'll cover Bonnie's next couple of semesters but Ivy Leagues aren't cheap."

"Damn." Yusuf's gaze was fixed on the scarred oak tabletop on which their beers sat. Durham's wasn't a coaster kind of place, so the oak was covered in dents and dings, scratches and the ghosts of thousands of cold or sweating bottles from over the years. "So you're unemployed?"

Despite the roiling ball of stress in his gut, Silvan had to laugh. "That's usually what it's called when your job boots you."

"I thought it would be something fancy like *I'm a gentleman of leisure now.*"

"That doesn't pay the kid's college bills. Or my water and electric."

"Fair." But then his friend lit up like the sun, his face cracking into a grin. Lucky bastard didn't even have visible frown or smile lines. Silvan swore Yusuf was de-aging, but given how good his mom looked at nearly eighty, the smoother skin and thick brown hair must just be all genetics. He scratched at his three day old stubble with bitten fingernails. Damn. He was already letting things get to him. "But! But! Now hear me out."

"Oh no."

"Yeah, yeah." Yusuf leaned forward, bony elbows evident through his thin plaid shirt. "But! You've talked for ages about writing a book. You could work on that while looking for jobs."

It wasn't completely mad. "Okay, so just take one of my many, many drafts and...do it." He could feel his frown deepen. "That sounds depressing. Sitting alone in my boxers, staring at a blank document."

"It doesn't have to be! If you'd take your pasty ass outside every now and then, you might find some inspiration." Yusuf leaned in more, grinning widening like a wild, mad river. "Come on, S. We know you've got cash socked away. Take a month or two, see what happens. You constantly bitch about -"

"I don't bitch."

Yusuf was undeterred. "Constantly bitch about not having time or focus to work on those drafts. Do it! Go nuts! Self-publish them, do something, man." All pretense dropped from his face. "I gotta admit, I'm a little worried about you."

"I don't know about publishing them myself, Yusuf. That's maybe a tad too aspirational for me." Silvan stared hard at his friend. "Don't worry about me, please."

"I'm serious. You've been..." Those warm brown eyes he knew so well were firmly fixed on Silvan's face. That ball of stress in his belly grew; almost out of control now, desperately swirling into a void. "You've been distant lately."

"I know." Silvan reached out and put a hand on Yusuf's arm. "I'm sorry. I've been too in my head lately and the kid's gone now and I guess it just fucking sucks."

"What does?"

He shrugged, helpless against his next two words. "Being alone."

Yusuf didn't say anything, he simply came around to Silvan's side of the booth and threw an arm over his shoulder. They sat like that for a few minutes, people-watching from their little corner, as it faced the side door popular with regulars. Silvan watched a few couples enter, followed by one guy he recognized as a regular from the shiny silver belt buckle in the shape of a bear head. Finally, he said, "Thanks."

"Any time. You know that." Yusuf nudged him with a narrow shoulder. The man was paperclip thin and tall and absolutely had the pointiest goddamn shoulders. "I should head home. The twins will be back from practice soon and Irene's got a contract gig she'll want to work on."

Silvan said his goodbyes to his friend, getting another shockingly rib-crushing hug before he was left alone, standing on the street. He had options. Walk home, be alone, maybe drink too much. Or find another bar, drink, stumble home. The problem with that plan was there were no other decent bars in the area; at least not ones he liked hanging out in. Silvan stood in the cool air and let his mental map wander over the city. Jake's Den was several blocks away, but on a Friday night it would be packed with college kids. And considering he had a kid *in* college, that sounded like torture.

A fuzzy memory, strained through the haze of maybe one too many beers, blossomed in his mind. The Lash & Rose wasn't too far from Jake's but it was a certain type of crowd. He would be walking in wearing chinos and a button-down, straight from work like a total *dad*. And worse, he'd probably look like a desperate fool trying to pick up some strange.

Damn.

Well, maybe he should. Maybe someone wouldn't mind an older man.

Fuck.

Silvan pulled out his phone and looked up the club's website. It had been a few months since he'd been there but he remembered its' funky retro vibe. The website bore that visually and he noticed the offerings had been updated to include custom cocktails. It at least sounded fun, and maybe no one would notice his sad dad vibes. At the very least, he'd get a good, stiff drink out of this little adventure.

"So you and me." Raf tried not to wrinkle his nose at the man seated to his right. The guy was coming on way too strong, from his pharmacy-counter cologne to the blatant up-and-down looks he'd been shooting Raf's way for the last ten minutes. They'd made some idle chatter but this guy had no subtlety and it was getting on his nerves. He was also leaning into Raf, his breath heavy and smelling of gin. Massive turn-off.

"Sorry, pet," he said, having to almost yell over the music thumping around them.

The man frowned but, shockingly, shrugged and got up to wander (slightly unsteadily) across to another empty seat. He and Nina, the bartender, watched the man go. "He's here every Friday night," she said, cocktail shaker in hand. "I was gonna warn you away."

Raf waved her off. "No worries. He wasn't my type."

"Don't blame you." And she went back to her work, leaving Raf with a fresh martini and a friendly nod. He took the drink and spun on his stool, bracing his back against the bar so he could watch the early birds filter in. It was usually an older crowd that came to L&R before ten pm and now, just barely past eight, he was surprised at the number of people filing in. They weren't the boisterous, half-drunk young things looking for sweaty dance floor action and the occasional groping. With age came wisdom and all that, and now he could use the temperance of that age and wisdom to enjoy people-watching. When he was younger, he had no patience. No appreciation for the slow, dripping passage of time. He had been so eager to not live in his own mind that he sought relief in the usual. Alcohol, drugs, sex; seemingly carefree and pretty and ready to take flight at a moment's notice.

He'd learned the hard lessons, the expensive and stressful and painful ones, and by the time he'd changed his habits, he signed up for college courses. He found a job in an art gallery. He fell in love with art and expression and the idea of *passion* articulated in safer, saner, quieter ways. So as Raf sat on his stool and watched people move about, ordering at the bar or joining the growing throng of dancers, he saw the passion in those people. He saw the linked hands and swift kisses, the care in unwrinkled shirts and understated but expensive jewelry. And he noticed, with no small amount of jealousy, how easily some of the couples moved about each other, as if they'd been doing so for years.

Raf was so wrapped up in his people-watching that he didn't notice the stool to his left become occupied. "Do you still have the ingredients to make an aviation?"

It was the voice that had him looking in their direction. There was something *cultured* about their delivery, reminding Raf of some of the students at a boarding school his frustrated mother had sent him to when he was ten. He was kicked out of the school not two weeks later for "mischief and the disobeying of rules". They were from places like Lithuania and Denmark and Raf enjoyed listening to them speak, even as a child.

"Yep, got it all here!" Nina said as she swung around, showing off a bottle of creme de violette. "I'll have it up for you in a minute. You good, Raf?"

Raf raised his still mostly full martini at her, then turned to the stranger at his left. "Don't let the owner catch wind you order aviations," he said with a smile, getting in a look at the man beside him. "She's partial to them but hoards the good gin for her private stock." He was sociably practiced enough to not openly gape at the man beside him but he realized very quickly it wasn't his smoothest line. It hadn't meant to be *butter smooth*, in a pickup artist kind of way, but Raf considered himself a well oiled machine when it came to talking to people.

This man made his brakes malfunction. Funny, he'd never been particularly partial to the salt-and-pepper hair crowd, but liked it no less than any other shade. But on the stranger, it fit him perfectly. Distinguished, coiffed, and dangerously handsome. In a perfectly pressed button up in light pink with sky blue check, grey chinos, and pointy-toed black patent leather boots, the man looked like he'd stepped out of a luxury ad. Understated watch, gold studs in his earlobes, bright blue eyes, and pale skin stretched tight over high cheekbones.

Raf thought he might swoon.

"Perhaps I know the owner," the man said.

Now he laughed. There was no way. Right? But Marianna moved in a lot of business circles, and if this man wasn't a lawyer or some C-level executive, he'd eat his Prada boots and walk home barefoot. Gladly. "Well, if that's the case..." He put out his hand with the most charming grin he had in stock. "Raphael Lutz. I'm the cousin."

"Silvan Diedrich. I'm the now former marketer for your cousin." The man squeezed his hand, not too much but just *enough*. But all Raf could focus on was the tidepool of his eyes and the laugh lines and dimpled chin. There was such a thing as infatuation at first sight, surely. Because Silvan was *stunning* and he smelled far too good and Raf was just reluctant enough to drop the warm hand wrapped around his.

He took a steadying sip of his martini before saying, "Former?" And he let Silvan's hand go.

Nina handed over a purple cocktail and Silvan took it with a grateful smile. She was quick to whisk away whatever bill Silvan slipped across the bar, but Raf wouldn't have been shocked if it was a fifty. "My firm let me go in the middle of a meeting for a new account. Fired their four most senior employees and marched us out like we'd been caught stealing pens." Silvan held his drink aloft, studying the color before taking a small sip. "My compliments, Nina."

She tossed him a wink that made the pink glitter on her eyelids shimmer. "You know I always got you, S."

"I'm so sorry. That's horrible." Whatever flirting he'd been concocting evaporated from his mind. "And I assume there's no recourse?"

"I've got a call in to an attorney but honestly..." Silvan sighed, putting his drink down. "I've seen how those fights go. They claim they had standing for the firing, the ex-employee argues otherwise. The company has infinite resources, the employee little. And even if the ex-employee wins, they're drained of all money and life by the end of it, and that's usually after years." His small, sad smile turned into a full grimace. "I just don't have the wherewithal for it. So thank you, and apologies for dropping all that on you."

"I'm sure my cousin would consider retaining you on her own." He winced as soon as he said it. Marianna would *kill him* if he somehow made this man think he spoke for her. "I mean, that's just my guess. I don't mess in my cousin's business and nor she in mine."

Silvan waved him off and Raf caught sight of the glint of gold on his right index finger. An oval signet ring of some kind, though it was far too dark to see more detail. "She couldn't, even if she wanted to. Clients of my old firm sign contracts for years. She's locked in for a bit yet. And I have a noncompete."

"Just for customers of the firm."

"For most of the city, really. They handle all the middle-sized and large clients around here. Kind of a monopoly. Plus..." Silvan sighed, sipped more of his drink. "Truth be told, I don't know if I want to go back."

"Damn." Raf truly didn't know what to say but he was so struck by those eyes. He watched a curl of grey hair fall onto Silvan's high forehead and had to resist the urge to brush it away.

"Yeah." Silvan's blue eyes widened slightly, face becoming more expressive. "You don't know anyone who needs a marketer? Hell, I'll take part-time bookkeeping, just to keep the skills sharp."

The idea hit him like a ten pound mallet between the eyes. "As a matter of fact, I do." Raf leaned in, heart pounding wildly in his chest. "What do you know about art?"

Fuck, Marianna was going to *murder him*.

Chapter Three

It wasn't flirting if they were talking about his sad sack of a situation, right?

Silvan knew he was lucky, knew being able to send his kid to a top tier school and pay for it out of pocket was an incredibly privileged position to be in. He knew all of that. And yet anger still burned. He'd helped make the firm what it was. He'd been expecting an offer of partner, not a pink slip.

But then again, he'd certainly not been expecting the incredibly charming, handsome man to his right. Silvan's mind whirled, trying to figure out where Raf was going with his question.

"What do you know about art?"

Apparently it was a night of strange expectations, or lack thereof. "Some, if you count a pottery class years ago and my many, many trips to the museums up in New Amsterdam."

"I love it up there. The coast is stunning, of course, but the museums..." Raf drifted off. "Ah, ignore me. I tend to get a little dreamy when someone starts talking about art culture."

"The passion is nice. It feels like it's rare these days." His mouth was suddenly dry and Silvan wondered if he should lean in a little. Maybe display some kind of visible interest? Is that how people flirted now? He'd been out of the game for so long. Maybe drawing the conversation back to ground would be better. Silvan felt a little off-kilter just being in Raphael's presence. "But what's this about a job?"

"My god, I really did get off track. I run four art galleries. Well, almost five. The fifth's due to open in a few months." The other man smiled proudly. "I find myself in need of more guidance on the marketing side of things. It's getting to be too much for me to handle and do the day-to-day operations."

Silvan blinked. "You handle your marketing on your own?"

Raphael shrugged. “I was fine up until now. But if you’re interested, send me your resume and we can set up a time for you to swing by one of the galleries. I have a rotating schedule between locations, so it’s fairly predictable.”

Raphael seemed smart and capable, and given Silvan had worked with his cousin for years, it was a promising opportunity. But if age had taught him anything, it was that jumping in feet-first usually spelled disaster. Or maybe that was just his own track record. So caution stayed his hand. “Do you want me to email it over?”

“Sounds perfect.” Raphael gave him a work email address and as Silvan was typing it into his phone, Raphael said, “This was possibly not the smartest way to make a business contact.”

“At a bar?”

“At a bar. With a man I was about to flirt with.”

He froze, thumbs hovering over his phone screen. When Silvan looked up, Raphael was giving him a coy little smile. “Funny,” he said, throat gone completely dry, “I was trying to figure out how to flirt with you. I’m a little long in the tooth for the bar scene.” Silvan gestured at himself but Raphael just shook his head. “Don’t agree?”

“I don’t, actually.” And then the smile dropped and something neutral replaced it. Gone was the tingle of warmth and familiarity. His expression was still polite but Silvan could see a solid gate slam into place. “But that’s not important. Shoot me that resume and we’ll find a time for you to drop by for a chat.”

“Sounds good.” Silvan internally panicked for a moment. A resume? He had an old one, could probably touch it up and send it over tonight. If he didn’t fall asleep at his computer.

Raphael stuck out his hand and Silvan shook it. “Very nice to meet you, Silvan. I look forward to talking to you.”

“Yeah, same.” Left with nothing else to do, he finished his drink, waved at Nina, and with a nod to Raphael, left the bar, shoving his arms into his jacket as he went. It wasn’t until he was back outside that Silvan had a chance to process the whirlwind that had happened. He’d gone to the club looking for...*something* and walked away with a job interview opportunity.

Strange fucking day. Fired hours ago. Now slightly tipsy. Alone on the sidewalk wondering what the hell he’d just gotten into. Silvan sighed and pulled up a rideshare app so he could get home.

"You did *what*?"

Raf put his hands on his hips, accidentally mimicking Marianna's pose. "You never told me your marketing guy was...*like that*!"

"Like what?"

"You can't be serious right now."

"I'm being very serious!" Shit, she was. Marianna wore every expression on her heart-shaped face and now she was looking at him with a mixture of bafflement and amusement.

"Deeply attractive!" Raf scrubbed at his face with his palm. "And I kind of hit on him and then offered him a job. Fuck, I am an ass grab away from a lawsuit."

Marianna snorted. A tiny laugh escaped her and she clamped down on it. "One, no you're not. And two, Silvan's his own man. And apparently up for grabs."

"I hate you."

"No, you don't." She started chuckling. "I can't believe you stole my marketing guy!"

"He's not yours anymore," he protested but it was helpless. Marianna was biting her lip, indenting that dark red with a perfect white tooth. He felt laughter bubble up in his chest. Jesus Christ, what a day.

"You still....stole him," she wheezed out between bursts of laughter. "You're so dumb. Oh my god. This whole thing is so stupid."

"Fuck me." Raf flopped down on the couch in her office. Right back where he'd started the night. Except now he had a line on someone to handle advertising.

He'd talked to Silvan with the intention of flirting. But he was a professional and could easily whisk away any troublesome attraction to the man. Compartmentalize and move on.

"Aw, Raf." Marianna plopped down beside him. "I know. He's a hottie but he really is a good ad guy. I hate that Longbeach & Stymer let him go. It's kind of stupid, getting rid of your senior people like that."

"Not if you're more concerned with profits over people and quality."

"True." She patted his knee. "So, looks like you have a choice. Hire him or date him."

The groan building in his chest released like steam from a valve. "Mar, *come on*."

"I'm being realistic. You need someone to help you keep track of all the marketing for the galleries. He's good at what he does." Marianna waggled her dark eyebrows and he couldn't help but laugh. "Or you can pretend he's not what you need and then ask him out to dinner."

He really did need a marketing manager. He could always find someone else to flirt with. Decided, he gave his cousin a grateful hug and left the club. It was easy to let his thoughts drift as a cab drove him home, but he kept coming back to Silvan's practicality. The man had just been fired and if it was throwing him for a loop, he hadn't shown anything but normal frustration over the situation. Raf was sure there was more to the story and he was, admittedly, curious. It wasn't *only* because Silvan was incredibly good looking. He seemed interesting and apparently liked art, or the thought of art, and that was a plus in his book.

When he arrived home, Raf put his shoes on the rack and his coat on one of the hooks in the closet, then made a beeline for his bed. His curiosity about Silvan was waylaid by the jaw-cracking yawns that had interrupted his trip home. Sleep was hard to come by of late, so he figured he'd best take the opportunity to collapse now, and worry about his potentially bad business decision in the morning.

And eight hours later, the sleep scrubbed from his eyes and coffee in hand, Raf sat down at his laptop. Might as well do his homework like a proper business owner and see to whom he'd offered an interview. As he was typing Silvan's name into a search engine, his email alert dinged. Speak of the silver fox.

He couldn't think like that. Silvan was a potential interviewee.

And attractive. Raf frowned. *Dammit. Curb your lust.*

Raf opened the email, scanned the polite, business-like language. Saw the just personalized enough cover letter and resume. But there was a second attachment, the file name simply "project". Okay, Mr. Diedrich, he'd play along.

It was a set of five images with captions. Each one an art piece, with a few sentences on why the piece spoke to Silvan and when he'd first seen it. And in those words, it was like Silvan had opened up a gate to who he was. He learned Silvan had a college-aged daughter and a love of local art. And by sharing these stories with him, Silvan had revealed quite a bit about himself, and Raf was touched. And intrigued. Replying so quickly was probably passe, but he didn't care. He'd found himself curious before; now he absolutely wanted to know more. To pick Silvan's brain, to hear about his life.

But first things first, a job interview.

Chapter Four

Two days later

"Definitely the lilac. It makes your eyes look even bluer."

Silvan held up the lilac dress shirt again. "I don't know. This pattern might be too much."

"Paisley is never too much, and this one is understated. Wear it with silver cufflinks you wore to my wedding." Becca smiled at him in the mirror before hooking her chin on his shoulder. "Trust me on the lilac, dear."

"Lilac it is." He sighed and she stepped back so he could lay the shirt on the bed. "Thanks, Becca. I didn't want to bug the kid."

"Silvan, you can always call me, you know that." She ran a finger over the sleeve. "And you've always had good taste. Why are you doubting now?"

She was teasing him and he shook his head, smiling. "Maybe for the same reason you gave me the lilac one to begin with, knowing it's my favorite."

"So, who is this mysterious man you're trying to impress for a job and simultaneously blind with your blue, blue eyes?"

Silvan sat down on the edge of the bed and Becca perched beside him. "You can't tell Bonnie."

"You *do* have a crush!"

He groaned and dropped his head into his hands while she laughed delightedly. "None of it. Not a word." When he looked back to meet her gaze, Silvan fixed her with a hard stare. "Especially not about the job thing. She doesn't need to worry about her tuition. And you and Shaleena covering the room and board and supplies is a huge help. Besides, Bonnie's got to-"

"Focus on her studies, I know. But if you don't tell her and she finds out..." Becca grimaced. "I would not want to be you. And Shaleena and I will be clearing the blast radius if that happens, so a little head's up would be wonderful."

"Oh sure, leave me to die in the fire of our daughter's wrath."

Becca clicked her tongue at him. "You should be more scared of her disappointment. You taught her that steely gaze, after all."

His head felt too full and too foggy at the same time and he was left staring down at the floor. Worry had been choking him since he'd been laid off and he was running on little sleep and too much caffeine. Silvan was pretty sure he'd bleed black tea at this point.

Becca's phone dinged, pulling them back into focus. "Shaleena just got home and wants to know if you would come to dinner with us." Becca's long, thin hand landed on his knee and squeezed gently. "Come out with us, dear. It'll be good for you."

"I don't know." He was always welcome and he knew that. But it was hard to shake the feeling of being the third wheel when out to dinner with your ex and her partner. Even though Becca and Shaleena had been married for two years and together longer than he and Becca's entire relationship, Silvan never wanted to crowd. He knew he was lucky, having a congenial - even friendly - relationship with them, and having a co-parenting arrangement that worked so well. It was a dream scenario for most people.

"I won't push," Becca said softly. "I know you always feel like an outsider."

Silvan gave her hand a squeeze and let go. "I appreciate it. I'm gonna take tonight to prep for this interview."

"With the handsome man." She grinned. "So, how handsome?"

How the hell could he categorize someone like Raphael Lutz? Yes, physically he was attractive; anyone with eyes and the inclination to find others appealing could see that. But there was an air about him, an ease, that Silvan liked immediately. To strike up a conversation at a bar the way Raphael had, to smooth over any bumps, to sincerely apologize for Silvan's misfortunes? That took an awareness of the self and others to make work, and Raphael seemed particularly clued in on body language and word choice. Maybe it was that, the emotional intelligence, that was really driving his attraction.

"Very. But he's also got a great eye. You should see the pieces he puts into the galleries. Not a single painting of fruit or a pasture to be had."

"Good taste is always attractive, as is uniqueness. And I know you're quite unique, my dear." Becca stood and held her hand out to him, which he took to pull her into a hug. "But this is a job interview."

"It is. Tomorrow at eleven."

She gave him a swift kiss on the cheek, making sure to swipe her lipstick off his skin. "Then best of luck and I'm sure it will go wonderfully. You know what you're doing, Silvan. He'll see that immediately."

"I sure as hell hope so." He had other job opportunities shimmering on the horizon, but the idea of doing marketing for a set of art galleries appealed to him on a deeper, more personal level. And it had nothing to do with Raphael's attractiveness. He could put aside his little crush to have a good job.

He walked Becca out to her car and leaned into the driver's side when she put the window down. "Tell Shaleena I said hello and that I owe you both a dinner."

That got him a grin, wide and open, and he was reminded once again of how beautiful she was. Becca had always been a stunner, but it was her mind and her wit that had made him fall in love. Years and years ago, when they were in college and the future looked bright and full of possibility. But it hadn't worked and they'd split amicably, each going their own ways after the heartbreak of losing that spark between them. There'd been no big betrayal or set of arguments. They'd fallen apart, distant, like many couples did. Except when it happened, Bonnie was three and her wellbeing was paramount for them both. Co-parenting worked well for them over the years and now Bonnie, so smart and resourceful and a force of nature like her mother, was poised to take over the world. At least in his opinion.

Silvan looked down at Becca's dark brown hair and deep set eyes, the cupid's bow mouth, and realized again how much she and Bonnie looked alike. Bonnie had gotten his eye color and his tall, slim build, but she was otherwise a dead-ringer for her mother. "I'll do that," Becca said. "But you worry about you, my dear. And let me know how it goes."

"I will. I promise."

She blew him a kiss and put the car in gear, moments later disappearing down his long drive shadowed with tall pines. Living on the outskirts of Dexter had been an unexpectedly smart move when he'd purchased the house years ago, before the housing market busted then boomed again. He was more than content to stay a little off the main roads, his Cape Cod down a cool, dark lane that a lot of people missed when trying to find his place for the first time.

But standing in his driveway now, alone with just the breeze and birds for company, an old ache rose up in his chest. Silvan didn't do well alone, and most of the time his job kept him from feeling the ache too deeply. Consistently working sixty to seventy plus hours a week would keep loneliness at bay, even if it meant sacrificing sleep. And in the free hours he had, he was always with Bonnie; homework and bowls of mac and cheese in blanket forts slowly morphed into movie nights and driving lessons over the years. He missed his kid a lot but that was part of being a parent: helping them grow up, then letting them go.

It still hurt, though.

Silvan gathered the mail from the box, grimacing at the rusty door that didn't shut all the way. He really needed to get a handyman out to fix all the little bumps the house and property had taken on over the years. All things he'd been too busy to handle himself while he was working.

You're unemployed. Do it yourself.

But maybe he wouldn't be unemployed for too long. This interview with Raphael had him nervous and, despite his insistence with Becca that this was all business, he knew he was going to be distracted. At least in the beginning.

So with a sigh, Silvan turned back up his drive, determined to buckle down for this interview. He needed to nail it. Something about this felt *right* and he'd never been one to ignore his gut. But the loneliness was a constant thing, so he pulled out his phone and fired off a text to Yusuf.

His phone rang immediately and Silvan chuckled. "That was quick."

"Hey, when my friend needs me, I'm there. Sorry, hold on, the kids are outside with the dog."

Chuckling, Silvan went back inside, sank down on his sofa, and leaned back, listening to the sound of his friend tell his children to give the dog back his ball.

"How's that look, Mr. Lutz?"

"Mike, truly. Call me Raf." He shot the young man a comforting smile. "You're on Arie's crew, you can use my name."

Mike flushed and ducked his head, and Raf heard Arie snort in the background. He gave her a pointed look and she just shrugged. "Well, okay but uh...is the painting okay?

Cause if it is, we'll mark it and keep going." Mike tipped his head back, gaze darting in a quick scan over their heads. "We doing the ceiling, boss?"

"Nah." Arie grinned. "Unless Raf's changed his mind."

He waved them on. "Leave the ceiling and if it becomes a problem when you're hanging the globes, then let me know."

"Can do." Mike moved down the wall, pencil and laser sight in hand.

"I never said flirt with the crew," Arie whispered as she passed. "You got Mike all flustered!"

"I didn't!" he hissed back. There must have been something in the air today, because it felt like everyone from the barista at the coffee shop to the cashier at the farmer's market and now Mike were being a little flirty with him. Normally, Raf would enjoy the attention, the coy bantering, the fluttered looks. Flirting was fun and he was rather good at it. He enjoyed making others feel good, too. But Mike was college-aged and on Arie's crew; two massive hard stops for him.

He thought back over the morning and his interactions with others. A lightbulb went off. Raf quickly walked over to Arie and pulled her to the side. "Am I suddenly looking older to you?"

She drew back and gave him a clinical once-over, but he saw the edges of a smile tugging at her mouth. Okay, maybe he hadn't worded his question the best. "You look like a distinguished, successful man on the other side of thirty-five."

He huffed. "My attire is stuffy. And old. That's what you're saying."

"No, I said *distinguished*." Arie motioned at him. "You look like a professional with a modicum of taste."

"Rude."

"It was a compliment. And clearly the clothes had an effect on Mike."

"I'm serious, Arie." Raf leaned in to whisper, "Please don't tell me I've fallen into the trap of gay sugar daddy." He shivered. No kink shaming but that lifestyle was not for him.

"Ooo, hate to tell you this, my friend but uh..." Another wave at him with a flick of her hand, her silver and gold bracelets jangling. "Perfectly pressed gray slacks, black turtleneck sweater, square rimmed glasses, tasteful silver jewelry. You look responsible, smart, and rich. And a lot of gay and pan and bi young men would be drooling all over you if you walked into certain places looking like that."

"I wanted to be the picture of your first sentences, not your last."

"Maybe change if you go out tonight."

"Good idea."

Arie glanced at her phone. "What time is your interview?"

A thread of nerves wound its way through his stomach. "In thirty minutes."

"I'll make sure the hammering is done before then."

Raf kissed her cheek. "Thank you."

She made a shooing motion at him. "Go do whatever. And I hope this guy's more than just good looking." Aric gave him a knowing smirk. "He's older, right?"

"Don't you start. "

"I'm just saying!"

Raf left her chuckling softly to herself and took the right hallway, leading him back to what would be staff areas. He'd debated if asking Silvan to come interview at the new gallery was the better move. Would seeing a new, expensive space put Silvan in the mind of Raf getting too big, too quickly? Would it make him think Raf was desperate for marketing to drum up buyers, in some kind of final breath attempt to save his business? But those fears had been mislaid, because as soon as he'd asked Silvan to come by the new gallery, the man had expressed excitement at viewing it. It had *sounded* like honesty, but time would tell.

Thirty minutes felt like both eternity and the blink of an eye. Raf spent most of it preparing what would be his office. It was a converted conference space with a desk, two chairs, a massive worktable, and a floor lamp. Very spartan with none of his plants or crystals, but with truly the best view. The wide, double windows opened to the distant, shimmering line of ocean and beach and he opened one of them now to pull in the soft autumn breeze. Fussing with the coffee cart helped his nerves but so did remembering he was the one in charge of the interview.

So far, Silvan had shown both an impressive resume and an eye for the creative. After he was done with the coffee cart, Raf took a moment to flick through Silvan's digital portfolio again. The other man had a flare for the one-two: catchy taglines or bright colors, but with a pointed message and obvious call to action. He was particularly a fan of a series of advertisements Silvan had done for the local farmer's co-op, picturing modern farmers and their lives instead of illustrated fruits and vegetables or all white men on tractors. Real people, real lives, impacted by growth in the co-op and investments in local farmers. That was the kind of insight and focus he wanted for the galleries; a spotlight on the artists and the value of their creations. Not what the galleries could *sell*, not a flimsy excuse to drum up business and put more money in his pocket. Raf knew for everyone to succeed, the artists had to be the focal point. As they should. Art gave back to everyone, a labor of love without which society would have never flourished.

His phone buzzed with a message from Arie: *I think your eleven am is here.* He gave himself one more moment, then strode out to the main room, bypassing the workers and Arie with a wave, and opened the front doors. Focusing on greeting Silvan was important, because then he wouldn't be staring in open-mouthed shock.

Because the man looked *good*. Really good. Three piece business suit in a deep navy, lilac paisley shirt, perfectly shined shoes. But he didn't look *too* perfect, and Raf knew that took skill. The pocket square was neatly folded but off center just a touch, and the sapphire studs in Silvan's ears were probably a little too gaudy for any kind of serious, professional setting like lawyer or brokerage manager. Thank the gods Raf wasn't in the business of serious.

"Silvan. Good to see you, thanks for coming out." Raf motioned the other man in and moved to shut the door and offer his hand, but Silvan was staring up at the gallery's high ceilings, big windows, and the few pieces of art hung up on the western wall. "Test pieces to make sure we get lighting placed right," he explained.

"It's a beautiful space. I bet you can't wait until it's finished."

"I really can't." Silvan turned to look at him and offered his hand, so Raf took it. His grip was firm and sure. "Thanks for coming out here. I know it's a bit of a drive."

"A drive along the coast is one of the joys of living out here, honestly."

Raf couldn't agree more. He moved them down to his office and got Silvan settled with a cup of coffee before opening his laptop and sitting on the other side of the table. He took a deep breath, smiled at his prospective marketing manager, and said, "So I'm curious about something."

One of Silvan's dark eyebrows twitched but he otherwise kept his face neutral as he replied, "I'll answer anything to the best of my abilities."

A smart answer, leaving Raf the one to drive conversation. He wondered if Silvan would be like this the whole interview. That would be a pity. Raf pulled up the set of images Silvan had submitted with his resume and spun his laptop so Silvan could see it. "I've never had someone submit a portfolio of their favorite art as part of their resume. Your resume itself is almost beyond the pale." He tipped his chin up and gave Silvan a calculated smile. "But you know that, I think. Given your experience in advertising. It speaks for itself. But this..." He tapped the mousepad a few times and let the images flick by. "This is unique. It's interesting. It told me a story."

It also gave me more insight into you than you intended. But Raf immediately admonished himself. Be professional, be courteous, be curious. Do not flirt.

"That was my intent." Silvan's answer was confident, easy. The man himself sat in the chair as if he belonged there, blue suit and lilac shirt and salt-and-pepper hair and stupidly blue eyes. It was *distracting*. "I know it's not typical to include something like that with a resume but I had a sense it might be appreciated."

"Observant is good. Very good, in fact, because I need that. But I also need someone who is proactive, not just reactive." Raf crossed one leg over the other and clasped his hands on his knees. The movement drew Silvan's attention and *that* he certainly didn't miss. One more tweak to his psyche before he mentally slapped himself and fully dropped into professional mode. "When it comes to marketing, what do you think that means for an art gallery?"

Silvan smiled and Raf's heart melted a little. Shit. "I've a few thoughts on that."

Chapter Five

It was unlike any interview he'd ever been a part of, but ten minutes in, Silvan knew he wanted this job. Raphael - Raf, as he preferred - was sharp-minded, ambitious, and had an awareness of himself and his business Silvan had never encountered. The man looked thirty but seemed to carry the wisdom of the world with him. Such a demeanor, a standing, was deeply attractive on a lot of levels. As an employer, Silvan could only see good things. Raf would let him be more creative, more daring (within reason), and try new avenues of marketing and advertising he hadn't been able to at his old firm. There they'd been focused on "If it isn't broke, don't fix it" and that mantra had driven away some customers looking to stand out.

But here, as part of Ablaze Galleries, he could stretch himself. The appeal of that was almost incalculable. Raf himself was a contrast of stickler and dreamer; he offered flexible hours, good pay, and solid insurance coverage. But he expected meetings and portfolios, progress reports and proof of concept. Those normal things would help Silvan set a rhythm, a kind of baseline, to use should his more creative endeavors need grounding.

And what really sold him on the job and the galleries and Raf were the *opportunities*. There was a solid website and social media presence but nothing to spark joy and wonder. Raf had an assistant answering emails and website inquiries, but a lot of that wound up on Raf's desk. He could help there. He could make Ablaze Galleries part of the social and cultural awareness outside certain circles. Raf and his galleries traded in the unique and sometimes bizarre, but always fascinating. And from what he'd seen of past exhibits, the creativity displayed was incredible.

"Everyone should know about Ablaze," he said as they stared at the freshly painted, deep navy walls where the newest exhibit would hang. "Everyone. Not just fussy art critics and those who are involved in the arts center of St. Augustine. Your galleries should be a movement. A voice for those who believe art is meant to be shared. I can help you with that, Raf. I know I can."

Raf turned slowly to pin Silvan with a stare he felt go right to the center of him. Beyond simply hitting him in the heart or looking through some part of his soul. He felt as though Raf could peer into his mind and suss out his intentions. It was intimate; a vibration through his body and like nothing he'd ever felt before. The man staring at him was powerful and beautiful and Silvan wondered if he should drop to his knees.

"I like what I hear, Silvan. Quite a bit." Raf stepped closer. It wasn't enough to put him in Silvan's space, but it made his breath catch a little. "I've got a few more people to interview, so if you'll send over references by midday tomorrow, that will help speed up the process."

And his potential employer was back to business. Gone was the soul-searching hazel gaze behind black rimmed, square glasses. It was impressive how quickly he adapted. "If you don't mind paper..." Silvan pulled out an envelope from his satchel and held it out. "Four references and four letters of recommendation. If you need more, or different contacts, just let me know."

"Perfect." Raf took the envelope and tucked it under his clipboard catch. "I do like how prepared you are."

"I try."

"I've no doubt."

They shook hands and Silvan ignored how warm and smooth Raf's fingers and palm were. It would do him no good to moon over the man. The job was paramount. He could feel the clock ticking down to when Bonnie's new semester tuition would need to be paid and he didn't want to miss a dime of it. He had the cushion for a few semesters, but that money was a rainy-day fund. Panic welled in him at the sheer thought of anything going awry for his kid.

Instead, Silvan focused on the large center display wall. "You said nature illustrations are part of the gallery's opening. If a sample of the marketing pieces I would make for that would be helpful, I can send those over in a couple of days."

"A generous offer." Raf seemed to mull the idea for a moment, then motioned to the wall. "This opening is rather special. My best friend's partner lost a neighbor and good friend recently. The neighbor was quite the artist, and his illustrations are what we're displaying in this room. They remind me a little of Beatrix Potter mixed with Victorian botanical drawings. There's something whimsical there, but also detailed and almost intense." He drew his phone out of his pocket and quickly made a note. "When I get back to my computer, I'll email you a draft copy of one of the illustration compilations. See what you can do with them."

Silvan quietly breathed a sigh of relief. An assignment would let him focus and settle the fleeting, flitting part of his brain that always worried. He hated that feeling of helplessness, with his fate in the hands of someone else. But he could ground himself with this work, this thing Raf asked of him. "I've never had an employment test quite like that. It's good, it'll let me stretch some stiff muscles, so to speak."

That got him a grin. Another punch to the heart he had to ignore. "I look forward to what you send back."

Raf escorted him to the gallery's front doors, shook his hand once more, and said, "I should have a decision made by the end of the week. No later than Friday afternoon. I don't like to keep people hanging."

"I appreciate that. And I'm looking forward to hearing from you."

Raf smiled at his hopeful cheek. "Have a good afternoon, Silvan."

"You, too."

The door closed and Silvan walked out into the early autumn sunshine, feeling quite a bit lighter than he had since he'd been laid off. He ambled around the corner instead of going straight to his car, thinking a coffee and pastry at the little coffee shop he'd seen on the way in would cement his good mood.

He held the door open for two teenage girls, their hands full of recyclable cup holders with several drinks, and slipped inside. Steamy Indulgences had all the boho-chic charm he'd come to expect from a city like St. Augustine, decked out in white-washed wood, beaded curtains, crystals, and posters with mantras like "Be the you who is content and not perfect". And there was no coffeehouse jazz here; instead chillhop played on the discreet speakers overhead. He took a moment to watch a man and a woman in the far corner flashing what looked like tarot cards at each other, his eye caught by the bright geometric shapes on the cards.

"It's our newest deck. *Shapes in the Moon.*" The woman behind the counter grinned at him. Her dark red beehive was threaded through with beads that caught the light and it bobbed slightly as she moved down the counter toward the register. "New in town?"

Silvan laughed. "No, I live in Dexter. I just haven't been in downtown St. Augustine lately." He made note of the name *Desiree* written neatly on a tag at her left shoulder. "Glad I found this place. It smells heavenly."

Desiree chuckled and motioned to the big menu board behind her. "Feeling anything in particular? If it's not up there, I can probably make it."

Silvan realized the handwriting on the menu board and on her name tag was the same neat block print, with tiny swoops on the ends of the Ts and Ps. "Something in lavender, maybe?"

"Good choice!" Desiree beamed at him and he watched that beehive bob again. "I make a mean lavender latte, or I've got lavender cold brew on nitro."

"Surprise me."

The look she gave him was assessing, sturdy. It lingered on his lilac shirt and blue eyes. "Hmmm, all right then."

As Desiree began making his drink, Silvan watched two more people enter but, instead of going to the counter, they walked by him and down a long hallway. A slight scent wafted toward him; the very particular, unmistakable funky perfume of patchouli. Desiree saw him looking and said, "It's our rotating art display. We borrow pieces from this art gallery's storage and put them out either for exposure or for sale. Always local artists." Desiree nodded at the counter where a messy stack of postcards lay. "And we do a monthly showcase, which the art gallery sponsors." She moved to the large machine on the other end of the counter. "Raf's opening up a gallery here in town at the end of October. I can't wait to see what he's got planned. His other galleries are gorgeous."

Steam curled up in the space between them and Silvan lost sight of her for a long moment. The explosion of steam from the machine died down and Desiree put a recycled paper sleeve on a cup and handed it to him. "You know the gallery owner, then?" he asked. There was no way he could resist hearing about Raf and the galleries from someone else. As good as he felt about the interview, a little perspective from something or someone other than a search engine would be helpful.

"Oh yeah. Met Raf several years ago, when he opened the first gallery in Balmer Bay. It was already quite the scandal before it even opened."

He gave the cup a sniff, then a cursory sip. It was perfect - frothy and light, with a smattering of lavender and honey buoyed on a perfect little lake of pale brown latte. "Scandal how?"

"Well, he had the gallery open with a show focused on the human body." She leaned in, eyes glittering. "So, lots of anatomically correct paintings and sculptures, which no big. You get that stuff in classical art all the time. But he did an after-hours event in the back half of the building, which was a display of some pretty lewd photographs along with talks on sex and sex education. Raf donated the gallery's portion of the proceeds to a sex education group that works with queer youth. Safe sex, consent, that kind of thing." She grimaced. "Cause, and pardon me here, but that abstinence-only bullshit only hurts young people. I grew up during the AIDS crisis, and being closeted was the only thing that probably helped me then."

Silvan remembered that time, too. His parents immigrated from Denmark before he'd been born, and despite being raised bilingual and bicultural, he'd always considered himself an American first. And America in the 1980s had not been kind to gay men, people of color, or anyone outside the "lines" drawn by the Regan administration and the evangelical right. He hadn't been old enough to fully understand the societal, political, and cultural ramifications then, but he remembered the names he'd been called in school and the sight of his uncle in a hospital bed, a mere skeleton of his formerly effervescent self.

Silence lay between them for a long moment, and then he said, "Has the gallery ever shown those pieces again?"

Desiree shook her head. "I think they were all auctioned off. Pity, cause they were really beautiful in a raw kind of way."

The doorbell jingled again and two men in chinos and polos stepped up to the counter. Silvan smiled and waved at Desiree, who grinned back, and he took the hallway to the small room at the back of the building. The hallway quickly opened up into a large, bright room with exposed brick and more kitsch-witch crystals, macrame, and dried herbs on the walls. But on four small pedestals, encased in glass, were strange sculptures of wood, metal, and what looked like raw gemstones. He paused before the first case, leaning down to peer at the twist of copper wrapped around birch bark. It was pretty from this angle, but when he shifted to the right, he saw a jagged piece of smoky quartz tucked inside the sculpture. Behind the stone were teeth, installed to look as if they were floating in the middle of the stone.

Silvan was instantly curious how the artist had put the piece together. With no screws, nails, or clamps discernible to the naked eye, he marveled at the intricate construction but kept going back to that quartz and those teeth. He held his own gaze in the crystal for a long moment, then moved on to the next piece. A few people came and went from the gallery, and as he was leaving, he noticed the sun slowly sinking behind the horizon. The last few sips of his latte had gone cold but he downed it anyways, unable to let it go to waste.

As Silvan walked out, he glanced behind the counter but Desiree and her red beehive were nowhere in sight. In her stead was a young man probably Bonnie's age, and he was hurriedly making several drinks at once. Silvan didn't want to bother him by asking about Desiree, so he dropped a ten dollar bill in the tip jar and left. The drive home was contemplative in the kind of way that made his head feel fuzzy; maybe the stress of the day had finally rung his bell. He always felt like this before a migraine came on, so he hurried home, knowing pajama pants and leftovers and a call with Bonnie were the things to look forward to as night fell. He needed to put the job interview and Raf's hazel eyes out of his mind for a bit.

Raf celebrated potentially finding a marketing manager with Thai food and a glass of Riesling. He followed that up with the sight of Henry leaning against the frame of his front door as he swung it open.

"It's no fun when you have that damn camera doorbell."

Raf grinned but didn't move to pull him inside. Staring at Henry was fun, especially when he was wearing leather. Naked was always, always the best but leather was a close second. Maybe he had an unexplored leather fetish. "Didn't your mother ever tell you it's rude to sneak up on people?"

"And why would I sneak up on you..." Henry advanced on him, blue eyes burning. Raf barely managed to push the door shut. "When I can only get this when you're fully aware and willingly participating?"

No matter how many times they did this, no matter how many times Henry leaned into him, teasing Raf's body with his own, Raf wanted to melt. Henry looked like the grown version of the bad boy your mother told you not to date at sixteen. The man *smoldered*, and that was not a verb Raf used lightly. The first time they'd met, at Raf's first gallery opening years ago, he'd been too nervous to do much other than notice the supremely attractive man making eyes at him all evening. And by the time the final few patrons had filed out, leaving him exuberant but exhausted and several thousand dollars wealthier, the stranger was throwing back the last of his drink and tipping the bartender.

In the moment, Raf had found himself blatantly staring. Everything about the man was *right* and there had been a flitting, nervous energy in his stomach. Comedown from the adrenaline of the night, happiness at having pulled off a massive gallery opening, maybe a little too much champagne.

(Definitely a lot of champagne but he'd tried to space it out.)

The man had walked over to him, put out his broad hand, and said, "I'm Henry Claudette. Congratulations are in order, Mr. Lutz."

They were up in Raf's little loft office five minutes later, with Henry's fist in his hair while a set of warm lips sucked at his neck, leaving Raf pinned against the wall and loving every second.

"Got something in mind?" Henry asked, snapping Raf back to reality.

"I'm flexible tonight." He toyed with the silver chains nestled in the vee of Henry's black t-shirt. Henry smelled like warm leather and sunshine and ocean breeze and some needy thing in him surfaced for air, gasping. He'd been *so busy* that anything not involving the gallery or basic human maintenance like sleep or sustenance was sent spiraling from his mind. But tonight had been slower, easier, and earlier he realized he'd missed a few texts from Henry days prior. That's how fucking busy he'd been.

"Dealer's choice, huh?" Henry softly kissed his cheek and let the touch linger while he deftly undid the buttons on Raf's shirt. "Lucky me."

Henry knew about the sensitive spot under his jaw and was making it his job to turn Raf's knees to jelly. "Sorry about the texts," Raf whispered.

"Not a bother." Henry pulled back to look at him and Raf wanted to push his face back down. Half his shirt was undone, leaving a wide target for Henry's warm fingers. "This is the busiest I've ever seen you."

"You weren't there that first year. This isn't that bad, but it's high on the scale." He reached up to brush dark brown hair off Henry's forehead, but Henry caught his hand, nosed into his palm. Heat flared in Raf's belly at the simple touch. "I'm wondering if I picked the wrong city for this one."

"Can I help keep your mind off it for a bit?" With the barest line of a smile, Henry sucked Raf's first two fingers into his mouth. Gripping Henry's shoulder tighter seemed like the appropriate response. The whimper he let out in accompaniment was just greedy.

Eager, he pulled Henry to the right and through the massive doors that led to his bedroom. The space was ridiculous for one person, but his years of investments in art had provided a comfortable livelihood. There were some days he wondered if it was worth the stress, but tonight was not for that line of thinking. Henry was here for sex on Raf's massive bed and cold Thai leftovers and more sex, maybe on the couch. Their agreement dictated sex as the keystone of their relationship. It wasn't the only thing between them, but he'd never ascribe the word *love* to it. Fond affection, certainly. Henry had, over the years, swung by to help at the other galleries or bring him food when Raf had a week-long flu. He'd had Henry stay with him for a week when Henry needed tendon surgery. It had been a week of Henry napping most of the time and Raf working from his balcony to give the man space to rest. And Henry came to gallery shows and they went dancing from time to time.

Fond affection and spectacular sex. And the mouth now pressing against his and the hands wandering his body made *fond* go out the window, replaced instantly with bone-melting desire. Like himself, Henry got better with age and closer to forty than thirty meant they both knew what they liked, and how to express those desires. Raf tugging Henry to the bed was a sign he wanted to be pampered (*pressed into the mattress, lavished with attention*). And given their history, Henry knew precisely how to do what Raf needed and find his own pleasure.

Henry also had a bit of a forceful streak in him and nights like this one were made for being wrung of every drop of physical lust. Raf wanted to be unable to walk for a while.

When his thighs hit the bed, Henry pushed him down, one hand on Raf's bare chest. Raf reached for him but Henry teasingly pinned his wrist to the bed. "Now, if you want me to take care of you, you need to be good."

"How good?"

"Thinking of shirking my orders already?"

Raf clawed at the air, helpless in Henry's grip. It was perfect. The man could read him like a goddamn thermometer. "Maybe just a little."

"I'd never expect you to go down without a fight, Raphael."

He huffed. "You think you know me that well?"

Yes, yes he did. Henry and his goddamn blue eyes. He'd seen bluer recently, though. And this was not the time to think about that. Him. Never was rather the time to think about Silvan that way. He didn't even know the man.

Henry answered him with a slick, biting kiss and hands busy on the rest of his shirt buttons and Raf sighed into that familiar, warm touch.

Chapter Six

Silvan was nodding off in his chair when his phone buzzed. He'd sat it on the armrest and it rattled toward the edge, so he grabbed for it. "Hey, kid."

"Dad. Did I wake you up?"

"No."

"Uh huh."

"Forgive your *old man*. I had a long day." Shit. He cringed at his slip up. He wasn't supposed to make any kind of motion that today had been different from any other.

Bonnie made a sympathetic noise. "Tough day at the office?"

"Something like that." Silvan sat up in his chair, shaking his head to try to wake himself up. "How's things?"

"Project, project, paper." She paused, dropped her voice. "Group project."

"Ouch. Sorry."

"I'll survive. Not all of them in the group are useless."

That was his kid, all right. She sounded so much like her mother it was uncanny. "Glad to hear it. And oh hey, I saw this thing today." Silvan pulled up the photo he'd taken of the strange, druidic sculpture at Steamy Indulgences and sent it her way. "Don't laugh at your dad's taste."

"Oh. What...are those *teeth*? Wicked." Of course she would love it. Bonnie still collected rocks like she had when she was four, but her emo phase as a teenager had added bones, feathers, crystals, and other strange ephemera to shelves that groaned with trinkets and books. Most of it was at Becca and Shaleena's house, but Bonnie's room at his place had its own cabinet of curiosities. He wandered there now as he talked to her, idly dragging his fingertips along shelves and pausing to stare at battered paperbacks displayed as though they were priceless. To Bonnie, they were. "I think it's like a witch light."

"What's that?"

Bonnie hummed in thought for a moment. "You know, a fairy lantern? To ward off evil spirits. But with the teeth...maybe the message is something like embracing the inner wild spirit, or freeing it."

Silvan remembered all the myths and legends he'd read to her as a child, the way her little face had lit up as they journeyed together through tales of tricksters and sun gods and swamp-dwelling spirits that protected lost children. She'd taken her favorite books with her to college, safe and sound in their own little box. Bonnie had been adamant about them, and Silvan was so proud of her for not eschewing the childhood things she loved.

"Tell me more about the art, Dad."

He told her about the coffee shop, thankful she hadn't asked why he was in neighboring St. Augustine. At the end of his story, he was left trying to stifle his yawns but one must have slipped through, because soon Bonnie was saying, "I think you're up past your bedtime."

"I'm afraid I have to agree." Staring at her neatly made bed, Silvan remembered she'd be home in four weeks. If he got this job at Ablaze, he could tell her about it during her visit. Hopefully Raf would understand he'd need some time off to spend with his daughter.

"Okay, you sleep. I have two more pages of this damn paper to write and I'm procrastinating hard."

"I swear I won't tell your mother."

"You better not."

"Idle threats, kiddo."

"Don't challenge me. I'll find something to torture you with. Adopt a puppy while I'm with you and leave it there."

"How is a puppy torture?" Honestly, that didn't sound half bad. Maybe the house wouldn't feel so empty; though a cat was probably more his speed. Silvan's path took him back out to the living room and his laptop on the coffee table.

"Because I'll find the most energetic, noisy thing that just wants to lick you and will grow to like, a hundred pounds."

"How did I raise such a spiteful daughter?"

Bonnie was laughing now, the sound echoing in his bones and filling up the hollow spaces that had settled there when she'd gone off to college. She still came home, still spent time with him and Becca and Shaleena. But his mourning period was now, not when she'd turned five or sixteen. Becca had been the one to get a little sad when she and Shaleena had stood with him in his driveway, watching Bonnie drive off in her first car for her sweet sixteen. Adult Bonnie, smart and vivacious and steely-eyed as her mother, wasn't his little girl anymore.

No one had told him being a parent meant letting go. He was better at it now, but it still ached, left empty like her bedroom in his too-big, echoing house.

"You better get to that paper, Bon-Bon."

"I'll let that one slip cause I know you're tired." Bonnie was still laughing. He never lost Bon-Bon privileges, no matter how much she teased. "Night, Dad. Love you."

"Love you too, kid."

The phone clicked in his ear, the screen went black, and Silvan sunk back into his chair, knowing he'd fall asleep there and hate himself in the morning.

Two days later

Raf's assistant caught his eye over their computer screen. Camilla was a person of many, many facial expressions, but their annoyance showed only in the firm line of a mouth glossed with lavender. And then he turned, following Camilla's eyes, and saw her.

The Matriarch

Judy Thoreaux. Matriarch of Bangles Bagels. The kind of wealthy that never looked it unless you knew what to look *for*. Her silver hair was slicked away from her finely-boned face, letting the eyes catch on lime-green frames and filigree silver earrings. She wore a dark blue jacket, white slacks with subtle embroidery at the cuffs, and a white shirt with tiny floral print in blue, green, and yellow. Her painted nails matched the lime green of her glasses.

Raf could have written sonnets to the way she dressed.

"Keep staring and your eyes might fall out."

He shrugged, grinning. "I've yet to hear you complain about being stared at."

Judy turned, gave his simple red cashmere sweater and grey slacks a warm nod of approval, and said, "Too true. Though I don't court it on purpose."

He gave a mock gasp, fluttering hand to chest. "The lady either doth protest too much or she accuses me of something."

"I'm quite sure it could be both."

Raf gave her a hug, knowing the scent of eucalyptus would be something he smelled the rest of the day. He couldn't smell it anywhere without immediately thinking of her. "You always make an appointment before coming over. Unless it's an emergency."

She sighed. "It's an emergency."

"Tell me."

Judy pointed to the east wall, where big white canvases sat, waiting to be filled by a local mixed media artist during live shows over the next few weekends. Today Raf was at the gallery in Tangine, the furthest south on his route. Tangine had been the second gallery he'd opened and it was the kind of city that earned its "weird" label. Though *weird* was harsh; eclectic, quirky, and funky were better adjectives. The entire town was full of artisans, and while he'd wanted the first gallery to be there, he couldn't afford the real estate at the time. So he'd worked hard to build up the funds and clout (the clout very much needed to court investors). And one purchase of an old church later and he had a second gallery, one that split between showroom and performance art room. More than a dream, almost unbelievable reality that still left him reeling sometimes.

"Are you handling the show this weekend?"

He shook his head. "April's doing the whole series."

"Ah, very good." That was a very Judy response. "Well, then I'll get down to it. One of my brunch guests backed out and I have an empty seat."

Most people would kill to do Sunday brunch at Judy's house. It was an honor, according to Tangine gossip mills, to sit at one of her tables. Tarot and tea leaf readings accompanied the free range omelets and generously libated Bloody Marys, and five thousand dollar suits were eschewed for hemp linens in white, off-white, bone, cream, and ivory. Maybe a light blue or pink if someone was feeling daring. It was a faux hippie slash cottage witch white party. Definitely not his vibe. And Judy knew that.

"I know, I know." She held up a hand decked in silver rings. "And if not, I understand. I would never push."

"And I know that, Judy." Judy understood that after talking all week with artists and agents and customers and vendors, Raf enjoyed the soft, domestic silence of his home. But a little voice in the back of his mind, the one that echoed with both his mother and his cousin's practicality, said that this would be a chance to drum up interest in the new gallery. Tangine and St. Augustine were practically sister cities, even though they were less than two hours apart. St. Augustine had less of Tangine's uber-weird and more a refined quirkiness, but residents often matriculated between the two.

"I can see those wheels turning, Raphael." She smiled at him, motherly and kind but her eyes flashing with calculation. "Darcy and Veronica will be there. They've so wanted to talk to you for ages."

Shit. The Smitherton wives were monied, prestigious, and deeply involved in the arts scene in St. Augustine. He had to straddle a line between courting artists and courting the money to back the galleries, and if he wanted *Ablaze St. Augustine* to be successful for the artists, the Smithertons had the clout.

He could survive one Sunday morning for the sake of the gallery and the artists. "Consider me your seat filler."

In a rare show of surprise, Judy's eyebrows shot up. "I'd make you my guest of honor but I don't want you to go running for the hills."

He laughed. It was one thing to garner attention by dressing or standing a certain way. He'd been told more than once that his presence tended to draw the eye, and he wasn't above courting stares if those developed into conversations about art. But *guest of honor* would be a bit too much; too proactive, too grasping for attention. "I appreciate it but no thank you. Shall I bring anything?"

"Just you. Though if you want to get them going..." Ah, so there was the cunning he'd seen on her face moments ago. Judy Thoreaux did love riling up her guests. After all, she and Raf had met during one of his first "after hours" showcases and one comment from Judy got the rumor mill going. A rumor mill that, once churned up, liked to use their wealth to craft influence. Raf had no problems motivating the wealthy to buy art from the galleries, since almost all of it went back to the artists. "It's not a strict dress code like usual. Surprise me?"

Oh, he had a few lovely items in the back of his closet that could really get them going. He was starting to warm up to the idea of this brunch. "Are we at full 'Miami spring break', or more 'I drove down the coast just for this martini bar' vibes?"

"I'm thinking *windswept starlet out for a drive, and oh, I just happened by for cocktails.*"

"Provocative but not scandalous. Understood." Raf thought about what he had in storage that could sell. One part of the contract between Ablaze and any artist was that pieces not sold after a showcase could go into gallery storage. If it was sold at some point in the future, the artist cut was split more evenly with the gallery. "Well, if we're going all in, shall I bring something to pique interest?"

She put up her hands, rings glinting in the sun streaking through the tall windows. "If you happen to show up with something, I'm sure we can find space."

Looks like I'm going storage diving. I should take Silvan with me as part of his first week. Give him a look at the gallery's past. "I'll bring something and hopefully my new marketing manager, if they're available. That's the deal. If you want me and a piece..."

"So an extra seat for your presence and a bit of art." Judy narrowed her sharp brown gaze but he wasn't fooled. She was over the moon and they both knew it. "You're bargaining with me?"

"Maybe I am."

Judy waited a beat. "Fine. I'll see you and this new person next Sunday. If they can't come, we'll just extend the invitation to a later date."

Damn. She was good. Even with his deal, she'd found a way to hook him into another one in the future. The Matriarch of Bagels didn't fuck around. It would be much easier to attend the brunch with a friendly face in tow. Maybe that would be Silvan's first test as marketing manager: charming the people of Judy's little entourage in exchange for some donations.

"I will see you in just over a week." Judy dashed a kiss across his cheek and bustled out, waving to Camilla on her way.

"You were beat before she even spoke." Camilla waited to speak until after Judy was gone.

"I'm afraid so."

"Are we taking bets this time on how much you can wring from some self-righteous assholes?"

"Cam." Raf pressed his palms into his forehead. "The walls have ears."

Cam wasn't impressed. Their lavender lips stretched wider, smile growing. "They're your walls, boss."

"Why did I hire you again?"

"Because you're an easy mark for Marianna. And you're the best." Cam was the younger sibling of Marianna's best friend, Rhys. Rhys used to manage the bar at Lash & Rose but now worked overseas and was the closest thing to a brother, outside of Raf, Marianna had ever had. Even at a young age, Marianna and her sister Lily hadn't gotten along; there'd been no change in the present, either. So the four of them, Cam being the youngest, were rather tight growing up. Cam was trouble, but Raf could handle trouble just fine.

He put on an unimpressed air and waved them on. "Don't you have emails to answer?"

The gallery phone rang. Cam cleared their throat, and in their best polite, professional voice, answered. "Ablaze Gallery in sunny Tangine. What can I do for you today?"

With an eye roll, he was walking back down the hall to his office. He'd realized after Judy left that he'd already involved Silvan in his plans, and he'd yet to call the man to offer the job. It hadn't been any real competition once he'd met Silvan. The man's eye matched or complimented his aesthetic for the galleries, he understood the passion behind art, and most importantly, he was damn good at his job. Raf had interviewed a few people earlier that week, and he'd been considering one woman, but Silvan was what he needed. What the galleries and the artists needed.

He reset his shoulders, sat down at his desk, and dialed Silvan. It was Thursday afternoon and he'd promised an answer by Friday. But as the phone rang and rang, doubt crept in. He could be in another job interview or doing some other important task -

"Raf. Hey. Apologies, I was in the garden, didn't hear it at first." Silvan was a little out of breath but Raf could hear the happy note in his voice. "Trying to get the spring bulbs in."

"No apologies needed. I know you're busy."

He laughed. "More like procrastinating. Gardening is my zen moment."

"Well, perhaps I can help out there." He hesitated, then said, "Can we do this over video? I prefer seeing people when I offer them a job."

There was a long pause, and then Silvan's name showed up again, asking for a video call. "I got excited and couldn't talk and hit the button at the same time," Silvan confessed. "Also, please don't let this be your first memory of me as your employee."

There was a smudge of dirt on his cheek, another on his high, lightly lined forehead as Silvan pressed the back of a dirt-covered glove there. Those blue eyes sucked him in and Raf shook his head, trying to be very serious. "Though admittedly, it is a unique memory. Hard to shake those."

"Damn." But Silvan was smiling and Raf felt himself do so in return. "So, what's this about a job?"

If there was relief in the man's voice, Raf heard it behind the excitement. "Turns out I'm in need of a marketing manager. If you're amenable."

"Well, I believe I am."

"Very good." Raf leaned back in his desk chair, propping the phone on a little stand by his keyboard, and said, "Let's talk specifics."

Raf had been afraid the sticking point would be the salary. Hiring someone with as much experience as Silvan Diedrich came with a cost, usually quite a high one. But Silvan didn't try to negotiate.

"I know where you're coming from," the other man said. He'd sat down at his little wrought iron patio set and Raf could see weathered brick and ivy behind him. Immediately a picture of an old, but well cared for, home came to mind. Something with sturdy walls and drafty windows but a ton of character. Scratched but clean wood floors, lots of light, maybe some potted plants in the kitchen. "Honestly, getting laid off might have been the best thing for me. It's made me reevaluate some things. And one of them is how I'm living."

"I admit to some surprise." He watched Silvan smile slightly and bring his gaze back to focus fully on his phone screen. "But you can negotiate up until we sign the employment contract." Silvan's brow furrowed and he held up a hand. "There's no non-compete. I'm not looking to oust other galleries. Most of us work well together. One of the things we'll be talking about during your first week is our 'network'. A bunch of the gallery owners have banded together to make sure we go to city council meetings and such to talk about arts funding."

"I can help there." Silvan was immediately leaning forward with an intensity that hit Raf in the gut. *No, not again. Not that entirely unhelpful flare of attraction.* "I used to be on the Dexter library board and frequently went to city council meetings."

"That wasn't on your resume."

Silvan flushed, pale skin going pink around his jaw. "I didn't do it for a resume-builder, like most people do. I really enjoyed that time, and we managed to get some extra funding passed. I can definitely help there."

It was easy to talk to Silvan. Raf had to admire the way the man was settled in his bones; he knew who he was and what he wanted. Something like envy rose up in Raf's chest. He put on a good front but there were days where Raf doubted everything he'd ever done. He wondered if Silvan had those days, too. "Well good, then we're in agreement so far. I'm sending over the offer now, so look it over, take your time, and ask me any questions that come to mind."

"I'm sure it's more than generous."

"That may be." And it was, in his opinion. Silvan was taking a salary cut but by his own admission, it wasn't the money he was after. Satisfaction in one's work was so often hard to come by. Raf understood that intrinsically. "But take the time you need. Please. I don't want you to have regrets on something I could have answered or helped avoid."

Silvan turned those blue eyes on him and Raf almost swore. Maybe it was just the color of his eyes but in that moment Raf felt his heart jump a little. "Understood. Well, then, you have my verbal agreement and hopefully soon the physical one."

"One more thing, Silvan. This is going to be an adjustment for me, so I ask for patience. I won't overstep but I'm so used to handling everything on my own and I'm certain I've some bad habits I need to break. I'll be deferring to your expertise, of course."

"Bad habits? I doubt it."

"Maybe I'll avoid introducing you to my assistant, Camilla, on your first day. I'm sure they've got a list somewhere."

Silvan laughed. "You realize you just tattled on yourself and gave me excellent blackmail potential."

His newest employee wasn't flirting with him. He was being funny and charming. It *wasn't* flirting. Just like it wasn't flirting when Raf replied, "Well, shit."

When they hung up, Raf felt lighter than he had in months and at the same time, new worries cropped up where he'd razed others. The galleries needed a marketing strategy more than what he'd been doing in the last few years; and to be fair to himself, it had been quite a lot. The flyers and postcards, the digital media campaigns, the social media that Camilla handled deftly but hated every second of. Raf could get back to focusing on connecting with artists and setting up showcases, and Silvan would be there to help guide marketing and art direction.

New beginnings. He could work with that.

Chapter Seven

The following Monday, Silvan's first day at Ablaze

"You're fussing."

"Is that a bad thing?"

Camilla shrugged. "Depends on if it's helping or not." When Raf moved the coffee pot once again, Camilla put their hand on his. The early morning sunlight hit their many gold rings, nearly blinding him. "I don't think this is helping."

"Definitely not." He patted their hand. "Thank you."

"It's just me trying to offset the next time you threaten to fire me."

He huffed but Camilla had got him smiling. They were good at negating his anxiety and helping him reign in that churning need for everything to be perfect. "You accuse me of something I've never done?"

"You did it twice on Friday."

"You started it by eating the last Belgian cream donut."

Camilla waggled a finger at him. They'd changed their nail polish from lavender to sky blue and it looked even brighter against their tawny skin. "I didn't see your name on it."

"Dammit."

"It's working, isn't it? I am a professional distractor, after all."

Raf wanted to say, "Professional procrastinator, maybe," but it wasn't true. Camilla was a fantastic assistant and no matter how much shit he gave them, they'd stuck around for years. Family wasn't just blood, after all, and Camilla had been a part of his life for decades. He remembered pigtails and a preference for the color green and them constantly sticking their feet out the back window as a teenaged he and Marianna went on winding, aimless drives up and down the coast.

Raf pulled Camilla into a tight hug. "Thank you for saving me from myself."

Camilla gave him a cheeky wink. "Always."

The front door opened and Silvan walked in, blue eyes immediately landing on them. He was pressed and polished, with slicked back hair and a hint of stubble, his light blue pants, navy loafers, and white shirt with bold blue and pink zigzag lines making him look right at home. Silvan had a messenger bag slung over his shoulder, the dark grey leather worn but sturdy. Raf suddenly felt underdressed and he was wearing his favorite embroidered vest.

"Not too early, I hope," Silvan said as he held up his hand in greeting. "I have an awful tendency to show up before people are ready, so I've learned to wait."

"You're perfect." Raf kept his face neutral but inside he was groaning in agony. *You're perfect. Jesus Christ, Raphael.* Camilla kept a straight face but he heard their tiny snicker. He gave them a warning look, which of course they ignored in favor of waving to Silvan and bouncing back to their desk. With a shake of his head, Raf stepped over to Silvan, shook his hand, and said, "Ready? It'll be a lot of information so you have to tell me if you need to stop. I tend to bullrush forward until I hit a wall."

"I'm ready when you are."

The exuberance and excitement in Silvan's voice helped dislodge some of the stress in his belly. "Then let's go."

Raf had Silvan come to the Tangine gallery since it was where the latest showcase was happening, but they had a schedule of tours for the full week. Tangine, Dexter, Hades, Balmer Bay, then St. Augustine. Silvan lived in Dexter and had familiarity with Tangine and Balmer Bay's art scene, but had stressed he wanted to learn more about all the cities in which Ablaze galleries had been established.

Thirty minutes later, as they were sipping coffee and looking over old marketing pieces for each gallery, Silvan turned that blue gaze on him. When Raf looked up, Silvan gave him a small smile. "I'm wondering something." He gestured at the various posters and flyers strewn about the concrete conference table. "Because these are really great. Are there certain advertisements you weren't fond of, or that you felt didn't properly convey their message? I'm a firm believer in learning from mistakes."

And I hate making them, Raf thought. *I can't stand making mistakes. It's why I agonize over each piece as if it were the first and last one I'll ever do.* "Quite a few, honestly. Though don't tell anyone else that." He got up and moved to a file cabinet where Camilla had neatly organized every example of print marketing they'd done over the years Tangine had been open. He had a few that, upon reflection, weren't great, but there was one that really bothered him.

When he handed Silvan the poster, the other man gave it a good, hard stare. "No need to be gentle. I can take the criticism." Raf kept his voice soft, The look of concentration on Silvan's face was quite a sight and he didn't want to break the man's thought process.

"No, it's not that." Silvan put the poster on the table and ran his index fingers over the words *Sky So Blue, Planet So Green*. "This was for this gallery's opening?"

"Earth Day. It felt appropriate. Tangine's very big on community gardens, tree planting, that kind of thing."

"Smart." Silvan mulled more a few more seconds, the time everlasting in Raf's mind. "I love the theme. You're appealing to the city's heart, drawing them into something that they can look at the poster for and say, 'That looks great, I need to go to it.'"

Raf leaned on the table, his head bent over the poster. He wanted to look at it through Silvan's eyes. "I'm waiting on the *but*."

The older man chuckled. Raf watched as Silvan circled the sketchy outline of a planet high up on the left side of the poster. His new marketing manager seemed to be the kind that created a chain link between touch, thoughts, and feelings and while Raf had kind of figured that out during their interview, seeing the process before his very eyes was doing things to the part of his brain that *wanted*. "No *but*. Just a note. There's a lot of information on the poster, and it's hard for the eye to take all that in, much less the brain." Silvan drew a line with his fingertip from the planet outline to the time and date on the poster. "Somehow I'm not shocked you're the wordy sort."

Raf wasn't one to blush but he felt heat in his cheeks. "Caught me."

"I figured."

"Camilla helped me edit on subsequent posters, but I agree." He sighed and stared down at the poster once more. "This was a great show. Packed to the rafters, to the point I was afraid the fire department would check me for code violations. Sold almost every piece, put the rest in storage." His gaze flicked down to Silvan's neatly pressed and tailored clothes. "I do hope you took my advice and brought other clothing, since we're going storage diving today."

"I did. And I can't wait. You were rather mysterious about it on the phone."

"I think you'll enjoy it."

The moment they stared at each other stretched, leaving Raf caught in a swell. Silvan was entirely too handsome and he absolutely had to shake this little crush. He should probably message Henry later. Maybe they could go dancing.

Silvan cleared his throat. "So I have ideas, lots of them. I don't want to overwhelm anything or anyone or get too far ahead of myself. But this is helpful. It'll start giving me a direction in which to go."

"Good, good." Raf leaned away, eager for a bit more space between them. Silvan even smelled good and it was making his head swim. Right, professional. Business. Just a gallery owner and his marketing manager having a meeting, talking strategy. "Do you want some time to go through the old campaigns? The biggest thing right now is getting the marketing done for St. Augustine. We know what the show is, but I'm stuck between designs and could use a fresh eye."

"That would be great." The smile Silvan shot him sent a ripple of awareness through Raf. Damn it all.

"Everything's in the file cabinet and while you comb through, I'll go get your laptop and some paperwork. Logins, that kind of thing. You'll have full access to the stock photo and font libraries, the image software. And you can work from wherever." He gestured to the conference room, a frown on his face. "Unfortunately we don't have space here or at Hades gallery for offices. Mine's basically a closet. Which you're welcome to! I'm rarely in there."

A dark eyebrow went up and Silvan's mouth twitched. "I'll keep that in mind. Granted, I haven't been in the closet in about three decades."

Jokes were good. That made Raf feel like he was back on solid ground. He could joke and volley with the best of them, had built a career partially on that ability to charm and make people genuinely laugh. "Surely not. I think the baby blue kind of gives it away."

"And here I thought it was the earrings." Silvan touched the sapphire stud in his left ear.

"How very 1980s of you."

Silvan did laugh then and it made Raf feel better. With a nod, he ducked out of the conference room, avoided Camilla's wink, and set about gathering the items he'd promised Silvan. A quiet morning of establishing procedures would do a lot to settle his mind and teach him some fucking restraint. He couldn't crush on the man he'd just hired, and putting a big "NO FUCKING WAY" sign on Silvan was the easiest way to handle it.

As far as first days went, this was the best one in his entire career. Raf had an archive of the old marketing posters and flyers, progression and story boards that showed the thought process of each campaign, and tons of unused ideas, some nearly complete. It was a treasure trove and already Silvan could feel that urge to *create* rise up. The potential was even more than he'd originally expected and he wanted to make that clear to his new employer (his very handsome new employer who was decidedly *off* the table and had to stay that way). But even as he poured over folders and stacks of posters and other advertising flotsam, Silvan caught himself tracking Raf's movements. They were simple, casual things like bringing in more coffee or passing over papers, but he swore everything Raf did was elegant. Hard not to think that when those hands danced as he talked, flashing silver rings dotted with smoky quartz and turquoise. Not the choices he'd expect of anyone but Raf. Unique. Interesting. Off the beaten path.

When had he started thinking of him as *Raf*? The thought startled him and he dropped his pen.

"All right there?"

"Got lost in thought." Pen back in hand, Silvan finished his note and studiously didn't look Raf's way for a moment.

Silence comfortably blanketed them again as they worked and some minutes later, Raf's phone lit up, the buzz of it a slight vibration through the table's surface. "And that is our cue to head out. Up for some storage diving?"

There was a glint in Raf's eyes Silvan found he liked. "I have strangely been anticipating this all day."

Raf chuckled and stood, holding the door open for him. "I might have played it up a little but honestly, the storage unit is a good excuse to get out for a bit. " When Silvan nodded, Raf motioned for him to follow. They said goodbye to Camilla and to April, Raf's second in command of the Tangine and Hades galleries. She was in the middle of a discussion with what looked like a wealthy client - perfectly tailored suit, perfectly shined shoes, subtle watch.

"She's the best salesperson I've ever had," Raf had said when he'd introduced him to April. When the woman rolled her eyes with a fond smile, Silvan could instantly see how easily Raf handled people. It was a remarkable thing to watch him shift, chameleon-like, to adapt to whatever situation he was in. Few people had that kind of skill, and if they did, they weren't as genuine as Raf. No wonder the galleries were popular, outside of the incredible art, of course.

Raf drove them to a warehouse about twenty minutes away from the Tangine gallery, making idle chatter and triple checking that Silvan was comfortable. "I'm good. More than, truly." Without thinking, he reached out and patted Raf's arm. The younger man didn't flinch or move away - tough to do in the confines of a car - but Silvan noticed his breath catch a little. Shit, he'd overstepped.

He opened his mouth to say he was sorry but Raf got there first. "I apologize. I tend to fret and when I do so, it makes me a little jumpy. If my dear friend Ambrose were here, he'd tell me to stop worrying." Raf spared a glance his way and Silvan caught sight of a slight smile. "Which, coming from him, would be rich, considering Ambrose is a gold medal champion of worrying."

Silvan saw the opportunity and latched onto it. "You two are close?"

"More than. He's essentially my brother." Raf gestured to himself. "Only child, raised by a single mother and constantly pestered by Marianna. Surrounded by amazing women in my family but when I met Ambrose, it was though something clicked. Something I'd been missing."

Raf told him the story of how he and Ambrose met, set up by kind-of mutual friends on what turned out to be a blind date. With no physical attraction but an intellectual one, they tried to kiss but it wound up so bad they laughed and then sat on the beach and drank themselves stupid until sunrise. "One of the best nights of my life," Raf said with a sigh. He turned the wheel and gestured toward the plain brick building looming through the windshield. "And here we are."

When Raf got out of the car, Silvan felt a bubble burst; as though reality had cracked through and now he had to leave the quiet safety of the car and Raf's easy conversation. It felt a little hollow.

His new employer navigated them down wide, dimly lit hallways until he came to a rather large steel door with a padlock the size of Silvan's fist attached to it. "Now, with any luck we'll find a piece worthy of the company it's to be displayed in and we won't get a speck on us." He frowned, glancing at Silvan's pastel and white clothes. "I probably should have recommended you change before we left."

"What about you? I can't imagine you want to ruin any of that." And it would be a pity if he did, because Raf had on an unassuming pair of black, form-fitting slacks (very distracting how they curved around the man's thighs and ass) and a slightly billowy pale green shirt, while the vest he wore was heavily embroidered with blue and silver. It looked like the kind of expensive that only custom-made clothes could pull off.

"Oh, the vest is coming off, trust me." Raf grinned and pushed hair out of his eyes. "Now, I know I've been secretive about this whole thing but I'm doing something I only make room for when it comes to Judy. The Matriarch of Bagels."

His eyes went wide. "Judy Thoreaux? That Judy?"

"That Matriarch." Raf pulled out a set of keys, plucked one out of the ring, and began to unlock the door. "She's having one of her infamous brunches soon and she's looking for a piece to auction off for the gallery." The look Raf shot him over his shoulder was of the grinning devil kind. "And she's invited both of us. It's not normally my scene, but she's willing to send some money our way for the new art studio at St. Augustine."

"Why would she want both of us there? Surely you're the -" He stopped, unable to come up with a good metaphor that didn't sound vaguely insulting.

But Raf only laughed. "Oh, Judy loves having me there but she knows I'm the kind that has to recharge on the weekends. But having both of us there, particularly the new blood, will send her minions into a titter." His smile dropped and Silvan felt its absence like a wound. "You are not obligated, just so you know. I would never, ever hold that against you."

Had it come from anyone else, Silvan would have severe doubts. But in his short time around Raphael Lutz, he understood the man's nature was wholly genuine. And from the snooping he'd done - namely reading newspaper articles about Raf or the galleries - that impression was only made stronger. "Honestly, if you give me a goal for the brunch, I can meet it."

"Like?"

He shrugged. "Like chat up this wealthy donor or just make myself a presence. I'm good in small crowds like that."

"I'm sure you are." The look he got was appraising. Clinical but with an edge of warmth. "Then I'll let Judy know we'll both be there. Just watch out, because Judy's mimosas are the stuff of legends." He leaned in. "Legends that lead to the deputy mayor puking in her box hedges."

With a heave upwards, the door slid noisily into the slot above their heads and Raf dusted off his hands. "And *voila*. Ablaze's little dragon horde."

The lights kicked on with a buzzing flicker that filled Silvan's ears and he blinked against the sudden filmy light. "It's like out of a heist movie," Silvan said as he stepped forward. "Did you rob a museum?"

"Maybe a very strange one," Raf replied but there was pride in his voice. Silvan could only imagine the years of careful negotiation and cultivation it would take to build a bulwark of art like this. There were neatly labeled boxes lining the three walls, wrapped canvases stored on racks, and more covered and wrapped lumps on thick metal shelves.

"Your own little cabinet of curiosities," Silvan marveled as he slowly walked the perimeter. The scent of dusty linen filled his nose and he sneezed.

"Here." A dark blue handkerchief was thrust into Silvan's view. "It's clean, I promise."

"Thank you." Before he could note how charming it was that Raf carried actual handkerchiefs, the other man was shrugging out of his vest and gently setting it aside. "There's really nowhere to change in here but if you want..." Raf gestured to a bank of shelves where the shadows clung deep and black.

Silvan glanced around again and saw dust but no real grime. The entire scene vaguely reminded him of an abandoned parlor in a wealthy home; everything covered in sheets and awaiting the time when their stories would be unveiled once more. It was a sacred space, and a haunted one. Reaching into his satchel, Silvan pulled out an old t-shirt and a pair of athletic pants. "I'll just be a minute."

Raf nodded and reached into his own bag for what looked like a different shirt in a dark grey. It would be pretty with his black hair and hazel eyes, even if the shirt was old and worn. Instead of focusing on the depths of Raf's eyes, Silvan ducked behind the shelves, turned his back, and began to unbutton his shirt. But it felt strange, the intimacy of the moment, and he found himself talking just for something to *do*.

"I didn't want to pry but...what made you want to open an art gallery? Or five, as it is now."

Raf's little thoughtful hum made the hair on Silvan's neck stand up. "My mother," he said quietly. "She was always painting. It's one of the first things I remember clearly, her smiling down at me, putting a paintbrush in my hand, and letting me go wild on an old canvas. Painting brought her joy, but she gave a lot of her art away instead of selling it. Said she couldn't spare the time it would take her to do up a painting she'd be proud to sell, since she had a kid to take care of and a job and a million other things going on with her sister and my cousin." Something about the volume of Raf's voice made Silvan think Raf had turned his head just a little toward his bit of shadow and shelving. "And when I was a bit older, she sold her first painting at an art faire and she was *so happy*. Because she loved that painting, and was thrilled when it went to someone she thought really wanted it."

There was a rustle of cloth, and then Raf sighed. An echo of it snaked down Silvan's spine. The passion drenching Raf's voice. The love. The clear adoration for his mother and family. Changing was abandoned so he could *listen* and *focus* on how Raf sounded right then. "She taught me to love art, especially its weirdness and flaws. Its lumpy clay and caked brushes and canvases that stayed empty until the muse struck."

"She sounds amazing." His voice was a little rough but he hoped Raf thought it only from a drop of emotion, not the tidal wave sweeping through him.

"She is. I wasn't exaggerating when I said I was raised by amazing women. It all starts with my mom." Raf's voice was now more distant as his footsteps carried him away from Silvan. The moment broken, the tidal wave crashed upon the rocks, Silvan shook himself into moving faster. "When you're ready, we can start with the easy to reach stuff. Canvases and the like."

"Do you know what you're looking for?"

"Not yet. Though I was thinking you might want to pick it out. With my guidance, of course."

Silvan laughed, pulled up his pants, and neatly folded his other clothes before stepping out. "Of course."

Chapter Eight

The canvases in storage were a bust. A few items had potential for Judy's party, but a third of them were new enough to likely be recognized by another party guest. Raf still wanted that *something* alluring, enticing...

"What's in here?" Silvan asked as he tapped a crate toward the back of the massive storeroom, hidden by shadow and drapes. There was a piece of straw in his hair, dust on his cheek, and a streak of dirt down the front of his black shirt. But those eyes, blue as anything, sparked. Raf blinked hard, then leaned over to peer at the label. The writing had faded, but he could make out *Dexter* and what looked like a date four years back. And if his memory served, he'd had a horrible assistant about that time; one who half-assed everything. Including, apparently, proper labeling.

"Good question." Raf held up a crowbar. "Would you like to do the honors?"

"Absolutely."

Silvan was rather proficient with the crowbar and soon had two sides worth of nails pulled out. Raf watched Silvan's biceps flex, his forearms bulge, and tried not to sigh. He failed.

"You all right?" There was sweat on Silvan's brow and it glistened in the harsh overhead lights. Maybe he should give Silvan his other handkerchief.

"Very much so. Simply wondering if the *Glass Triad* we set aside is good enough for Judy's party."

A few more nails undone. "Well, in my non-expert opinion -"

"Pish. You know more about art than most people." Raf gestured to the room. "You're an aficionado. An admirer. Admiration doesn't come easily."

The third side was now undone and Silvan paused, a look of raw curiosity on his face. "No?"

"I think admiration is earned."

"A curious thing to form an opinion on." Still no judgment there, simply wide blue eyes, a relaxed jaw, and strong hands frozen in place on the crowbar. There was a soft intensity about Silvan and Raf found he liked it.

"A side effect of being around artists all the time." But Raf had to smile. "Honestly, they're like everyone else in some ways. Some think they're giving selflessly of themselves to the world, others think they're God's gift. Some create because it fulfills them. Others because it quiets the demons." Raf slid his gaze away from Silvan to stare down at the four nails left. "And while people are worthy of respect, only a few come into our lives worthy of stronger, more passionate emotions. I think admiration is a step above fondness and a step below love. Intense enough to allow for the remittance and forgiveness of errors." Raf paused, gathering his thoughts as easy as trying to pick up confetti. "I admire art and artists. I wouldn't be doing business with them if I was simply fond. I learned to admire art for its beauty and inspiration, but for its flaws, too. You look at art like you understand it in the same way. It's part of why I hired you."

Raf looked up again and had to catch himself on the lid because Silvan was staring at him hard now, knuckles tight on the crowbar. This was bad. He needed to shake this off. And he was *definitely* calling Henry tonight. When Silvan finally nodded and handed Raf the crowbar, disappointment whispered through him. He'd been hoping for some kind of response, but Silvan appeared distant. Removed.

"Apologies," Raf said, focusing on the last few nails. The scent of old straw rose in the air, choking him. "I didn't mean to be so intense."

Together, they lifted off the lid and set it aside. Raf ran a hand through the straw and other packing materials, but his fingers grazed over something. A memory rose up, fleeting and distant, and he pushed his hand down into the straw, grasping. *Impossible.*

"What's wrong?" Silvan hovered a hand over the straw. "Radioactive spider?"

He tried to laugh but it came out more like a scoff. "No, I...I forgot we had this still." Under his fingertips were the very distinct curves of a statue Raf knew well. "Help me lift it out? It shouldn't be too heavy."

As the straw fell away, sticking on their clothes and dropping to the concrete floor, what they pulled out was a statue roughly two feet high and three feet wide. The thick base on which it sat added weight, but the artist had insisted on a classical look to help pull the viewer in more. "*The Dual Sisters*," Raf said softly as they carefully set the statue down. "It's by an artist named Kareem Jonas. Every artist showcased creates at least one feature piece for that night. This was his."

Silvan was circling the statue and when he saw the back, his eyebrows shot up. "Not what I was expecting."

"Nor anyone else who first saw it. It's what drew you in to the show."

Silvan was now kneeling, fingers hovering over the face in the middle. The carved woman was flanked by two others, all of them identical save a few details. The woman on the left held a skull in her outstretched hand, and the woman on the right had a snake wrapped around her forearm. The one in the middle bore no accompaniment, but when you looked at the back of statue, you would see her head was bald and a horrific face was carved there; its mouth open wide, eyes stretched in terror, cheeks sunken in at a strangely disturbing angle.

Silvan stared up at him. "What's the story?"

Thankfully, Raf had a quick answer. "I don't know. Kareem is very 'death of the artist' in his mindset."

"It's stunning."

"I agree. I wish I could give Judy this, but it's not right for her brunch."

When Silvan got to his feet, he did so slowly, as if he were loath to take his eyes away from that Janusian visage. "What should we do with this?"

"I'm not sure yet. But I think it deserves some kind of permanent home, instead of sitting here." Raf's mind reeled with possibilities.

Silvan moved closer but didn't touch him. "What can I do?"

"Think of some really good options for this piece. There's no rush but..." He cast his hand over the statue's right head. Not touching, simply hovering.

"I would love to."

Silvan was at his side, warm from their work and looking at him as though Raf could have asked anything and he would have given it. "Right. Okay. Thank you."

"Of course."

Now Raf put his hand on Silvan's shoulder, dragged his gaze up until they crashed together. "Thank you. I mean that. Some first day. I swear I didn't plan to be this mysterious."

Silvan's shrug was easy. "Maybe I don't mind a little bit of mystery. It's like looking at a little piece of your gallery's history."

The confidence in Silvan's voice helped him breathe a little easier. "Thank you. Truly."

"You don't have to keep saying it. But I appreciate it." Silvan motioned to the statue. "Ready to get it back in the crate?"

"Yes. Out of sight but not out of mind, for now." Raf shivered in the dry air of the storage room. That piece had always bothered him on an animalistic level, but at the same time, he loved it. "We should do something dark. Gothic, maybe. Haunting."

"And I'm assuming we don't want to be obvious and host it around Halloween."

He laughed. "Definitely not. Though winter might be a good time."

"Agreed." Silvan paused, gaze distant. "I'll think on it."

"Excellent."

"That's all we have, Raf."

"Shit." Raf sounded despondent, even though Silvan couldn't see his face. That rich, cultured voice drifted down the hallway to him, through the open door of the conference room from where he sat with his laptop. Raf had been right; *Dual Sisters* spoke and when it did, everyone listened. He couldn't get his mind off of the piece and had decided, since no other source of inspiration was striking as hot in the moment, to start making lists of themes for a showcase centered around it. It was good work, the kind of dug-in creativity he adored. But as happy as Raf had been to see the statue, now he sounded a little upset. Silvan wanted to creep closer to the door but decided against it. Eavesdropping on his boss wasn't the smart move. Now or ever.

Raf came back in to the room roughly five minutes later. "Apologies. I was asking Camilla to pull up records of past artists based on theme - a list they're very good at keeping - and we don't really have anything in the same vein as *Dual Sisters*." He sat with a heavy sigh. "With that kind of darkness, I mean. I was hoping there was something I missed."

"And that bothers you?"

That got Silvan a quick smile. "You're good, I'll give you that. It does, on a weird, selfish level. I remember every piece I've ever hosted. We've done everything from landscapes to portraits, to all glass or all concrete. The perfectly mundane to wildly sexual. But nothing dark or deep. I don't know why, but that bothers me."

Silvan saw Raf very clearly in that moment. Tall and lean and handsome as sin. Perfectly poised, dressed elegantly but with little whimsical touches, like the multi-colored stitching on his vest and the silver and turquoise rings that would have fit well on a tourist in the desert. On Raf, all of it looked *right*. But there was a flicker of something vulnerable, something needy, and it spoke to Silvan. Nearly knocked the breath from him. He saw Raf in all his perfectionist glory, and a moment later, could see him willingly open to a different kind of vulnerability. One that made him feel safe and loved and cared for, but one that Silvan was in charge of.

"I understand. I think we both have a bit of a perfectionist streak but I will say, I'm more than willing to get messy."

"I sensed that." Raf leaned forward and peered down at the scattered posters and flyers. That gaze slid back up. "It's part of why I hired you." The moment stretched, thin like an old rubber band. Just waiting to snap. It made Silvan's teeth itch to look at Raf and see the man for who he was, and who he wanted to be.

But the moment snapped when Raf stood quickly and smoothed down his vest, bejeweled hands flashing. "I'm going to make a couple of calls and then we should probably call it for the day." The smallest smile graced his elegant face. "Thank you for not running for the hills."

He was truly baffled. "Why would I? This is the best job I've ever had."

"I...right. Good." Raf motioned to the door. "Please, don't feel as though you have to stay until I leave."

"I'll stay."

"I'll try to keep it quick."

Raf sucked in a breath, straightened, and left the conference room with a nod. Silvan tried to keep working but his mind was reeling, so instead of staring aimlessly at the files, he began making a list. Lists eased his mind when things felt too upside-down and tossed about.

- *Review past showcase marketing campaigns, both print and online*
- *Establish contact with community stakeholders*
- *Check with Raf about what spokesperson responsibilities stay with him vs go to me, if any*
- *Work with Camilla on sorting digital stock image folders into*

CRASH

Silvan shot to his feet, pen skittering across the table. Heart hammering, he looked around and then remembered he and Raf were alone in the building after Camilla had gone home about a half an hour ago. The gallery was a long building with tile and concrete floors, and he still wasn't used to the way it echoed. He bolted out the door and looked both ways before taking off right, toward locked double doors leading to the staff bathroom and supply rooms. There was also a door leading to a postage stamp sized, walled-in courtyard. Raf might be taking calls outside, so maybe the door slammed shut?

Silvan wanted to call out but didn't want to interrupt Raf's call or make him think something was wrong, so he yanked his new employee badge from his pocket and scanned it, then kept going down the hall. The overhead lights down here were on, as the wide open windows of the gallery didn't carry back to the more boring areas.

Both staff bathrooms were empty, as was the kitchenette. Concern growing - what if he'd come down the wrong side of the building - Silvan raced forward, hand on the supply room door handle when he heard Raf's voice up ahead. Around the corner was a short hallway, a janitor's closet, and the door to the courtyard.

"No, don't worry about that. I don't need anything else tonight."

Raf's voice was low and Silvan could feel a faint wind tickling his face. The courtyard door must have been propped open somewhat. He froze, stuck in place with his fingers wrapped around the door handle.

Raf laughed quietly. The velvety sound twisted something up inside his belly. "Henry. I swear. You don't have to pamper me." A pause. "Well, if you must twist my arm, you know what I like. And since I like being held down by pretty men, I'm afraid my only request is that."

Oh *god*. He was accidentally eavesdropping on his boss. That was bad enough. But he was accidentally eavesdropping on his boss having *that kind of conversation*. And despite his own preferences and tendencies in the bedroom, he felt his cheeks go red. Of course Raf had someone. A man that intelligent and successful...

And deeply, unfairly attractive, his out-of-control libido screamed.

He sighed. And that deeply, unfairly attractive wouldn't be alone if he didn't want to be.

"I'll see you soon. Preferably with no shirt on under that jacket when you show up? Let's give the neighbors something to waggle tongues at." Raf laughed again, sounding delighted and flirty, but at ease. He probably knew this person well, then. Someone even as unshakeable as Raf needed a little stress release, right? Or maybe it was something more serious? "I still have some of that red you like. Maybe we can drain the bottle this time, instead of getting *distracted*."

Hells. That shouldn't have been attractive but hearing Raf sound so....was *dark* even the right word? It was like velvet rubbing inside Silvan's skull. But he needed to move. That realization was quickly reinforced when Raf said, "Bye, darling."

Shit. Shit. Silvan whirled, saw the open staff bathroom, and dove into the darkness. He shut the door as quietly as possible, flicked on the light and fan, and turned on the water just as he heard Raf's footsteps growing closer. The bathroom smelled of apple cinnamon air freshener and he wrinkled his nose. And as he looked down, Silvan saw a few bottles of cleaning supplies had fallen to the floor. The source of the crash, apparently.

"Silvan?"

Oh gods. He gripped the edges of the glass bowl sink, refusing to look at his own reflection. "Uh, yeah. Be out in a minute."

"No worries. I had to leave a message for Arie. Knowing her, she's stuck at another job and I'll hear from her later. Ready to wrap up?"

"I think so." He was having this conversation like nothing was wrong. Everything was fine. Totally fine. Silvan turned off the water, grabbed a paper towel, crumpled it, and then opened the door. Then he put on a slight smile and said, "Calling it for the day?"

Raf looked a little mussed, which shocked him. Another button on his shirt was undone, showing off thick chest hair, in which was nestled a single gold pendant. He'd scooped his hair up into a messy bun, leaving tendrils of brown-black hair brushing his neck and jawline. Silvan couldn't make out the pendant's details (not without leaning in *very* far), so he jerked his eyes up as Raf said, "I think that's wise. And I'm grateful you decided to stay."

"Of course." Silvan's response was automatic but not unenthusiastic. But it made Raf's mouth thin a little. "Sorry, I just uh...yeah, it's been a whirlwind. But I'm here to help."

Raf let his frown drop. Surely he heard the sincerity in Silvan's words, right? "Thank you. Again. We really should get you home before the night starts."

They went back to the conference room and left the posters and flyers on the table in neat stacks. With bags slung over their shoulders, he and Raf left the gallery through the small loading dock and he waited while Raf locked up. "Have a good night, Silvan," Raf said as they went to their cars. "And again, I very much appreciate you staying. I promise things around here are rarely quite so exciting."

"Guess we'll have to make our own excitement." Silvan smiled but kept his gaze soft, unassuming. The conversation he overheard (the heat and purr in Raf's voice, remembering the way it went to his cock) should be a thing he put out of his mind. Just act normal. *He never heard anything*. "Drive safe, Raf."

"You as well."

Silvan waited for Raf to leave before lowering his window, blasting some oldies rock, and heading to the Thai takeout place he loved. He was going to need something to take his mind off of this weird, wonderful, admittedly slightly frustrating day. And his beautiful boss.

Chapter Nine

"Hand me the onion, love."

Raf passed over the container of chopped onion but otherwise didn't move from his stool at the kitchen island. He barely looked up at his mother, who gave him a smile as she stirred one of the many pots on the stove. "Sorry, Mum."

"You don't need to apologize to me. You've got a lot going on." Francia swapped her wooden spoon for a spatula and moved to the container of fresh hummus Marianna handed over.

"Yeah, Raf, give yourself a break. Even as soon as you got here, you were outside in Auntie's garden." Marianna slung a long arm over his shoulder and he leaned into his cousin with a sigh. "It's Saturday lunch, take it easy."

Saturday lunch was the one thing he always looked forward to, no matter what else had happened that week. At least the St. Augustine gallery was chugging along on schedule, but Raf was just waiting for the other shoe to drop. Even Henry - lovely Henry, with his firm grip and perfect mouth - couldn't soothe his anxiety completely.

"I was hoping you'd be in the mood for slow," Henry said as he pulled Raf tighter to his side. In the quieter, fuzzier moments after they'd been together, Henry liked to talk. Soothingly, nothing too loud or frenetic. And after being taken so hard his limbs still trembled, Raf could do nothing but melt against him and let his words tumble forth; a slow rockfall of thoughts with no second-guessing or concern about how he would be perceived. Because Henry was good like that, and their long-standing agreement had never, ever taken a turn away from getting what they both wanted and needed. Bachelors, the both of them, with high libidos and a solid understanding of their own and each other's desires. It was the best possible arrangement.

"I am. Especially tonight. I just...with everything swirling around me, I feel kind of scraped thin." Raf dug the heel of his palm into his forehead. "You don't want to hear all of this."

"You seemed distracted tonight. I wanted to see how you were." Henry turned to his side and let his fingers glide, almost worshipful, over Raf's bare torso. "And I'm afraid I can't stay. Early meetings tomorrow and I cannot show up with bed head and pajamas."

If Henry was trying to make him laugh, it was working. Raf gave him a playful shove and together they hauled out of bed, slowly dressed, and then Raf walked Henry to his door. "Thank you for the assistance, as always," he teased as he played with the buttons on Henry's jacket.

"You know me. Can't say no to a handsome, intelligent man." Henry kissed him goodbye and left with a wave. That man always made him feel better but tonight, after everything that had happened, Raf couldn't find peace in rumpled sheets and empty wine glasses.

The doorbell rang, followed by the sound of squeaky hinges, and then Camilla was there, bright blue nails and lips and long, curly hair with the ends tipped with deep purple. "I like it," he said as they came closer, shrugging off their jacket and flinging it over a chair. Francia huffed and rolled her eyes at their casual messiness. "The purple, I mean."

"I know. It looks good, right?" Camilla grinned.

Marianna hid her laugh in her wine glass and Raf and his mother exchanged a *look*. Camilla seemed oblivious to all of it as they swanned through the kitchen to give Francia a kiss on the cheek. "Oh, paella? You spoil us."

Francia shooed them away, wooden spoon in hand. "I cook for me and my son. You two freeloaders got adopted out of luck and pity."

No one in the room took her seriously. As much as she liked to grouch about Camilla raiding the fridge and Marianna taking up precious kitchen island space, his mother wouldn't have it any other way. Saturday lunches had been like this for years and when a rare one was missed, Raf felt it like a hole in the heart. And he knew his mother did, too. Her soft eyes and little smiles gave her away.

"So, Raf. How's Silvan working out?" Marianna was eyeing him curiously. "Anything exciting on the horizon?"

"He's great. More than, actually." A wine glass was pressed into his hand, the sparkle in Camilla's nail polish catching his eye. "He's been digging through the old marketing campaigns to see what might be revamped. Part of the plans for St. Augustine is to, after the opening, do a few throwback shows. I've got some artists chomping at the bit to do revisits on old themes."

"I like the ideas he had for the Coastal Wayfarers revamp," Camilla said as they sat at his right. "Like a chill retro vibe on the posters and flyers. Very cool after the nature illustrations for the gallery opening."

Raf couldn't agree more. Despite the hectic back-and-forth of his first few days, Silvan had proved to be a font of ideas and inspiration. He'd found himself frantically taking notes while the other man talked. Mostly to keep up with Silvan, but also to ignore the day-old stubble gracing his sharp jawline. Apparently his little crush was going to have to die out on its own, and he didn't want to rely on Henry all the time. Maybe it was time to try dating again. Gods, Ambrose would have a *field day* when Raf told him.

"I'm glad you found someone, dear," his mother said. "Coming in hot, hold that thought." The bubbling cast iron pan came out, bowls and ramekins shifted, and then his mother was setting aside her heat gloves and slipping onto the stool across from him. Francia waited until everyone had their food to lob the question he knew was coming. "So, how cute is this man?"

Raf managed to duck the question until an hour later as he sat with Marianna and his mother in the garden behind her little Cape Cod. Camilla had taken off for her apartment, something about a date with whatever reality show was new and hot. His mother's house was like all the others on this side of Dexter; small but tidy and owned mostly by busy singles and empty nesters. The yards were also small and well-tended, but his mother had everyone beat with her incredible garden. The gift of keeping greenery alive seemed to miss every third cousin or so in their family, and it had definitely skipped him. But not his mother. She was sitting beside Marianna on the porch swing, trailing her fingers over a deep green leaf as she said, "All right, no more delaying, Raphael. Marianna says your new marketing manager is a looker."

So many replies sat on his tongue, most of them only slightly sarcastic. His mother was lovingly teasing him and would drop it in a heartbeat if he asked. But the gleam in his cousin's eyes made him say, "You get five minutes and then I'm not talking about Silvan anymore."

"Oh, I like the name. It's kind of...Nordic?"

"His last name's Diedrich."

Francia's gaze narrowed. *Oh no.* "I've met a Ansa Diedrich, years ago though. At some artist gathering. It can't be a very common last name. I wonder if she was related to him."

Silvan hadn't mentioned any family outside his daughter yet, and it had been in passing. The man seemed private when it came to family, so Raf hadn't pushed. Not everyone had a set of cousins and aunties and great-uncles like the sprawling tangle he'd grown up in.

Marianna practically read his mind. "Not everyone's like us, Auntie. The wife of a cousin of a grandchild blah blah blah." She nudged Francia with an elbow. "How many of us were there at the last family reunion?"

His mom groaned. "Don't remind me of that disaster. We're lucky something didn't get caught on fire."

Seeing conversation had diverted, Raf jumped at the chance to leave talk of Silvan behind. "Yes, but what about when Uncle -"

"Great-Uncle," Marianna corrected with a grin.

"Great-Uncle Pieter took the mic and started singing?"

Francia snorted into her tea.

Kareem let out a quiet whistle as he, Raf, and Silvan stared at *Dual Sisters*. Raf had Arie and her crew move the statue to the St. Augustine gallery, locked up behind keycard scanners and deadbolts in the back of the building. And two days later, Kareem had been able to peel out of work a little early and swing by. "Gotta admit, man, I really thought this had sold."

Raf scoffed. He was trying to look affronted but it wasn't working. Kareem was the kind of person who projected calm even in the strangest of situations. He watched Kareem lean in and narrow his eyes as he inspected the statue, so he backed up to give the man some room. That put him squarely beside Silvan against the wall. "I'm waiting on a call back from the St. Augustine Chamber of Commerce," Silvan said softly, turning his head so Raf could better hear him. It also let Raf stare without being weird or creepy. The man's impeccable taste had been displayed over the last few days and today was no exception. Slim fit trousers in heather gray, thick pine-green sweater, salt-and-pepper hair slightly ruffled, as though he'd been running his hands through it. "Betsy Myers said you'd reached out once but she was thrilled to have a new gallery in town."

Raf smiled slightly. "Betsy seems genuinely interested in the arts, which is more than I can say for the bulk of those in the chamber."

"Like most of those groups, sadly."

"True."

"I've got a meeting with her next Monday. Should I take a packet of flyers and such?"

"I would. Handing them directly to someone seems to work best."

"Sorry to interrupt. But if you're wanting another piece like this, I'm afraid I can't help you. I moved away from these themes a while ago." Kareem gave them a small smile. "Sorry about that."

"It's all right, Kareem. I figured it was worth a shot." Raf replied, pushing away from the wall to stand beside Kareem. "Thanks for coming in. Camilla's got some paperwork for you on the way out. If you're still serious about signing it over."

"Yeah, I'm sure." Kareem shivered. "Honestly, this feels like an age ago. I was in a weird, dark place when I made this. Happy to let you all have it."

He and Kareem shook hands and the artist walked out, leaving Raf and Silvan alone. After a long pause, Silvan gave Raf a once-over he felt down to the soles of his shoes. "So, the statue belongs to the gallery now?"

"It does. Kareem didn't hesitate for a moment when I called to talk to him about it. It is a strange piece, but I ..." Frustration welled inside him. He hated not being able to put voice to his thoughts. Because for all the impression he gave of being charming and collected and always in-the-know, he certainly felt unmoored of late. "But no matter what, it's an opportunity."

Silvan hummed for a moment. "You'll have to excuse my forwardness, Raf. But I think you need a break."

He couldn't stop his huff. "I think I need to open my damn gallery."

Slowly, Silvan laid a hand on his shoulder. The touch was electric and Raf suppressed a shiver. Ridiculous, really, to not put his attraction to bed. It wasn't as though Silvan felt the same, their first meeting at the Lash & Rose notwithstanding. Because Silvan was the consummate professional and Raf had come to realize that this thing he felt when around the other man was truly one-sided. "No, I understand that. And I wish there was more I could do. But I mean right now." He gestured to the window on their right, where afternoon sun splashed through. "Take a walk, get some coffee or a scone. Go stare at the ocean. Take a moment. You need it."

He didn't say, "I think it would do you good" or "Maybe it will help". It was the command in his words, the thing that brooked no questions and no leeway, that made Raf swallow hard. Best not to think *like that* right now. Ever, actually. Ever, ever about Silvan. Gods, he was a mess. "You're right."

"I am." Silvan's smile was gentle. "In this instance, anyways. My daughter has other opinions on such statements."

"I can imagine."

"Go on. Get outside for a bit."

Raf wavered. Warm sun and the ocean breeze sounded...well, rather pleasant right now, as mired as his head was in all the bullshit that was going on. "What about you?"

"I'm fine. I've got a bit left on the new flyers to finish. It'll be done when you come back."

And for whatever reason, Raf couldn't say no to those blue eyes and that unshakeable tone. "Okay. But twenty minutes."

"Thirty at least. Have you even eaten today?"

"I did."

"Hmmm."

He fought not to squirm. "I'm an adult, I can handle myself."

Silvan chuckled and backed up, giving Raf room again. The vise on his lungs loosened. "I know. But some of us tend to be pretty bad about taking care of ourselves when we feel like other things need our attention more."

Raf couldn't argue with that. But he had to get one more dig in, for good measure. "And here I thought I was the boss."

Silvan's expression remained a frustrating and attractive mix of slightly amused and deadly serious. "You are. And even the boss needs a breather now and again."

Silvan watched Raf leave, waiting to slump against the wall until he was long out of sight. That man was dangerous. There was something quietly, softly vulnerable about him that made Silvan want to bundle him up and take care of him. He could see the bags under Raf's eyes, the deeper lines around his mouth. He was thirty-seven and in great shape, but stress knew how to mess with a body *just so*. And all that went into getting the gallery ready to open was clearly more than enough to cause tension.

Something about Raf left him prickling in all the right ways. Taking care of someone who wanted and needed it (*his hands on their body, the sound of silk and leather rasping and sliding against their skin, the ripple of pleasure down a supple spine)* hadn't been something he'd indulged in for a very long time.

Raf called to him, pulled those desires up to the surface, and Silvan had to fight against it.

His boss.

His very attractive, very stressed boss.

But...he'd look so good spread out wide against dark sheets, that black hair sticking to his forehead as he moaned and thrashed and begged.

Silvan ran a hand down his face. Fuck.

He was so wrapped up in his head that he didn't hear the footsteps approaching, so the sight of Raf's head around the door made Silvan jump. "Come with me."

"What?"

Raf smiled, wide and bright, and it set Silvan's heart thumping harder. "If I need a break, so do you. You've been here every step of the way. I'm grateful." Raf motioned to the door with an elegant hand. "Come on."

Silvan couldn't help but say, "Boss's orders?"

"Something like that."

Was that a glimmer of mischief in the man's deep-set hazel eyes? Silvan didn't get the chance to linger on that thought as he followed Raf down the hallway and out the gallery's back door. They passed by some of Arie's crew as they hauled in new light fixtures and cans of paint. Arie herself looked a little frazzled, blond hair tied up in a messy ponytail, her face red from exertion as she and another staff member moved a ladder to one of their work trucks.

Raf waited to speak to her after the ladder was secured. "Arie, call me if something comes up? I'm taking a walk. My new marketing manager is a real hardass."

The woman laughed and swiped the back of one hand across her brow. "Well, the painting's done except your showcase wall. I want to make sure that blue dries right before we fuck with the big wall. Get out of here, Raf. Enjoy yourself." She shot Silvan a look. He felt it rattle through him; as if he were under inspection. But he didn't know the verdict, because she nodded politely, smiled, and set about helping another one of her crew with a table.

"Apparently I'm off the hook," Raf joked as they rounded the side of the building, cutting down the alley separating the gallery from a dry cleaner. "Lucky me."

"Arie seems like she's got a good head on her shoulders. Good to have in a contractor."

"I've known Arie a long time. She was one of the first people I met when I moved out here. Years and years ago." A grin, and then it dropped. "I'm glad to have her around. She's...steady but easy, if that makes sense."

"Predictable and reliable aren't bad things." Any bit of Raf Silvan got to know made him want more, and yet he couldn't resist poking about that mind. From what he had seen so far, Raf had an unquenchable curiosity and yet managed to maintain a level-headedness he admired.

"Oh, not at all. Especially when it comes to the art world. And *artists*," Raf replied with a grin.

He waited for Raf to pick the direction down the street, and when the other man turned toward Steamy Indulgences, he had to smile a little. Maybe Desiree was working today. Maybe that little art exhibit with the strange, druidic-like sculptures of crystal and branch and teeth was still there and they could walk around the glass cases together, discussing their meaning. Maybe they would spark inspiration in Raf.

With the salt air and sunshine boosting his mood, Silvan broke the silence. "I realize this might be out of line, and please say so. But we should probably get to know each other a little bit more."

The response was immediate. "Trying to take my mind off current events?"

"Maybe. But I do enjoy getting to know those I work with." Silvan gave Raf a curious but open look. Daring him to ask. "Or, work for, in this instance."

Raf put his hands in his pockets before taking a deep inhale. "I think that's fair. Outside of April and Camilla, you're the one I work closest with. And normally I would have had more of a chance to do that very thing but..."

"This past week hasn't exactly been boring."

That got him a laugh, a genuine sound with a tiny snort at the beginning. It was rather charming. Like the handkerchief and Raf's vests. The one Raf sported today was a simple dark green that matched his slacks, but the buttons were abalone shell that glinted in the afternoon sun. "Both a massive understatement and yet completely true." Raf pointed to the coffee shop up ahead. "Have you been to Steamy Indulgences? It's an adorable little place."

"I have, actually. Right after I interviewed with you."

Raf looked delighted. "Please tell me you met Desiree. Red beehive?"

"Hard to miss."

"Most definitely." Silvan noticed Raf's shoulders relaxed a little bit more. "Let's get some coffee and chat. What do you want to know?"

That was a very good question. Relationships like the one between he and Raf were built over time, colleague to colleague, employee to boss. But Silvan *liked* Raf; his charm and air of mysteriousness, his adaptability, his love of art.

His vulnerability. The softness he sometimes saw at the edges of those hazel eyes.

Silvan hedged a bet. "You mentioned your mother a few times, and I know Marianna. Any other family around?"

"A few cousins and aunties. My mother's family is rather matrilineal." Something flirted at the corners of Raf's smile. "We do big summer get-togethers up north, where most of them live. But Mom and Marianna are in Dexter, so there's always someone close by."

"Oh? I didn't realize. I'm going to laugh if somehow I've lived near them for years and not known."

Raf gave him a smile. "Mom's lived in Eastern Hills since before I was born. And Marianna just moved to the south side, close to her."

Two kids on skateboards buzzed by, their laughter caught on the wind. "I've been in Geneva Park since Bonnie, my daughter, was five. Bounced around a few spots but I've been in the same place for about ten years."

"You have roots." Raf's expression was softer now, more open. "Are you from here?"

"Are we quid pro quoing right now?"

They rounded the final corner and came upon Steamy Indulgences. The smell of fresh coffee and sugar was on the air and it made Silvan's stomach rumble. Raf chuckled. "If you want. Though we should take care of that empty stomach before exchanging more."

"Agreed." Silvan motioned Raf forward before following. Desiree and her beehive were behind the counter and she grinned wide and bright as they entered. As she passed a carafe of coffee to another staff member, they stepped up to order.

"It's like you never move from this spot, love." Raf had switched again, now teasing and charming as anything. Silvan marveled at how smoothly he did it, without a word of it insincere. Raf might be the most sincere person he'd ever met. He couldn't help but wonder if the man simply collapsed when he went home, hollowed out by everyone else's emotions. As if he had to build a new cocoon every night.

"I do too! And I could say the same for you!" Desiree gave Silvan a conspiratorial look. "He works too hard, doesn't he, Silvan?"

What could he do but agree? "He does."

Raf gasped. "Traitor."

He and Desiree laughed, her louder and heartier. A few heads turned toward them. "And here I was going to buy some of your delicious scones for my friend and I," Raf continued unabated, "but now I find myself in need of one of Shana's cookies."

"Like that's supposed to hurt my feelings. Raf! I never thought I'd see the day."

Silvan listened to them play-bicker for a few moments, but he kept looking back the hallway to where the art exhibit was housed. He started to drift that way when a hand on his arm stopped him. "Did you want anything to drink?"

Raf was looking at him earnest, expectantly. Silvan's fingers twitched against his thigh; he wanted to reach out and try to wipe away the bags under Raf's eyes. This man was speaking to every bit of his being that enjoyed taking people apart, then spoiling them rotten. "Desiree, can you make that -"

"Lavender latte? Of course."

She whirled away with a smile, leaving Raf to shake his head. "I think she likes you."

Silvan flushed a little. "She's nice."

"Hmmm."

"That was a rather pensive *hmmm*."

Raf shrugged. "I'm always thinking."

"I'm getting that."

They were smiling at each other and Silvan had to turn away slightly before he was pulled into Raf's orbit once more. While they waited, he busied himself looking at the community notice board on the wall opposite the door. Maybe it was his imagination, but he swore he saw approval splash across Raf's face.

Most of the notices were for yard sales, one person businesses making candles or blankets, but a couple caught his attention. Silvan took pictures of them with his phone and was just putting it away when Raf came over, two cups in hand and a cookie for Silvan. As the first time, his latte was perfect and Silvan gave Desiree a wave and nod to let her know.

"She likes you. That's a good thing." Raf slowly sipped his own drink before continuing. "She's been a good community partner for a bit now. Getting the gallery into St. Augustine was a....let's say an endeavor of not only effort but time. Desiree was one of the first people I met."

"So I should put her at the top of my contact list for advertising."

"You know you should!" Desiree said as she handed the next customer a massive drink in a clear cup.

Silvan had to laugh. She was as bodacious as her hair and he liked that. "I just want to peek back there again." With a nod to Raf, Silvan wandered past the counter and back the hallway to the art exhibit room. Not much had changed since he'd stopped in a few weeks back, but now there was a small wood table on the left wall, between two of the glass cases. On it was a rectangular case, the glass lid almost as tall as it was long and wide, and inside was a coiled snake skeleton.

Fascinated, Silvan leaned in, peering into the case's corners. Hoping it, like the druidic statues behind him, contained some little secret. As his eye caught on the glistening stones in the snake's skull, Raf spoke up from his side. *Shit.* He hadn't even noticed the man slip in next to him. "I know this artist," he said softly, also leaning down for a better look. "They do incredible work."

Raf's voice dropped; almost hypnotic. "Beautiful, but lush. Darkness sitting at the center, if you'll just take the time to stare into it and see it for what it is. It's the kind of work I'd love to host sometime. Another after-hours event, perhaps." Raf was even closer now, voice dipping into a range that made something clench low inside Silvan. "Maybe we can discuss that in the future. Something befitting the new gallery."

The whisper-silk of Raf's voice was curling within him, coiling like that snake skeleton. Patient. Waiting. Silvan gripped his cup harder, the heat from his drink nearly searing his palm. He jerked up a little too quickly and latte dribbled onto his hand. "Shit."

"Here." Raf handed him a napkin he pulled from gods knew where. As Silvan mopped up his hand, Raf wandered over to the other cases, occasionally bending down to peer into them. Silvan saw introspection - real thought, real consideration - flicker over his boss's face.

His boss. Remember that, asshole.

"As loathe as I am to return, I'm afraid we should. Heaven help me if I leave Camilla in charge for more than about thirty minutes."

And there he was again. Chameleon Raphael. Master adapter. "Sure. Thanks for the invite. It was nice to get out."

"Occasionally taking one's own advice is a rather grand idea."

"Too true. The problem is, I'm shit at it."

"So am I." The smile Raf gave him could have powered the building. "So that's why I took yours. And not to inflate your ego, but I'm thinking we take the long way back. Across the boardwalk."

"Ah. So if I agree, I'm taking your advice and not my own. I like it." Silvan tapped the side of his head. "Very smart."

"I do, on occasion, have a good idea or three."

"I'd say more than on occasion."

"Keep inflating *my* ego, and you'll talk yourself into a raise rather quickly, Silvan."

Silvan laughed as they left Steamy Indulgences and walked out into the sunshine and sea air, drinks in hand and the beach ahead of them. And then it dawned on him they had never quid pro quo'd.

"I'm originally from up further north, " Silvan said as they walked along the boardwalk, the weather-beaten wood creaking under their feet. "But the jobs were better down here, so my father moved us to Dexter. I've floated around some but I always seem to wind back up there." Silvan motioned to the slow waves lapping up on the shore and the few people and dogs who were on the sand. "I find it hard to give this up. Even with the traveling I've done, I come back here."

"Our origin stories are somewhat similar." Silvan couldn't see Raf's eyes behind his sunglasses but the smile was hard to miss. Raf leaned back against the railing and Silvan mimicked his stance on the opposite one. They stood with a pathway between them, but somehow Silvan felt closer to Raf in that moment. A bond forming, perhaps? It would be good if that was the case, because then he could put his crush to rest once and for all. "I'm also from the area originally. My mother moved as her job demanded, so we picked up every few years. And then I went off to university on the other coast and so much changed while I was there."

Raf trailed off and Silvan watched him turn toward the ocean. He knew that pull as well, to the water and the sand and the smell of salt on the air. "But my mom and cousin and some friends are here, and I'm not built for living in the woods. My best friend, Ambrose, loves it. I would kill to have him closer, but he's happy and that's what matters." Raf pushed his glasses up into his hair and some of the dark strands went awry. It was charming instead of messy, black hair against tawny skin and bright silver in his ears. "I take it you're more of a beach person, since you've remained here."

"I am. I actually learned to surf before I could ride a bike." He smirked. "My father was adamant that I learned to appreciate the ocean the way he did."

Raf's expression went soft in the moment and the sun hitting his face just right made something clench in Silvan's chest. "Single father?"

"Yes. I actually never knew my mother."

"Ah, so we do come from something alike. I never knew my father and my mother is possibly the best person on the planet."

Oh, didn't that go right to his gut. "Next to my father, of course."

Raf grinned. "Of course. Is he still..."

Silvan shook his head. "No, he passed when Bonnie was ten, so it's been a while."

"I'm so sorry."

"Thank you." He sighed, remembering his father's crooked grin and weather-beaten skin and how he always smelled like sea air. Time had bandaged his heart with sure hands, but that didn't mean the loss was any less painful. It was simply muted. "I miss him. And I know Bonnie does, too. They were bonded at the hip from the moment she was born."

Raf was looking at him now, lips firm, brow creased. Silvan wasn't sure if he was weighing his confession or thinking about a loss he had experienced. But the sympathy rolling off him was honest and sweet. Raf was sweet. This was not helping his crush *at all.* After another long moment passed, Raf finally said, "Well, as much as I'd love to stay out here, I'm afraid we've extended our break and now I have to be the big, mean boss."

"Consider me thoroughly chastised." It rolled off his tongue so easily, and was worth watching Raf blink rapidly. "After you."

Chapter Ten

The day before Judy's brunch

Henry's text read, "Can we talk?", and for whatever reason, it made Raf nervous. He didn't even have the breath or headspace to think about the text until much later in the day, when Silvan gently shoved him outside for some fresh air. The man was relentless about ensuring Raf took breaks, and while some part of him chafed at it (he was a grown adult, wasn't he?), he also knew Silvan was only looking out for him. It was sweet. Most of the time, Raf grumbled good-naturedly and then did exactly as Silvan suggested. Even ten minutes helped him re-sort the jumble of thoughts constantly invading his brain.

When the day was over and Raf was home, staring at the contents of his fridge and feeling uninspired, Henry called. "Apologies for not giving much of an answer, hell of a day," Raf said when he picked up. "What's up?"

But Henry's usual velvety voice wasn't there; instead, he sounded anxious. "Can I come by?"

"Certainly." Something like tension knotted his gut. "Is something wrong?"

"Not...like that. But it involves us."

Another knot. He'd just been de-stressing, staring into the void of the fridge. "Well, I'm home now."

"I'll be there in fifteen. See you soon."

Raf stared at the screen. Stared at the fridge. Shut the fridge and walked out into his postage-stamp backyard to wait. It took Henry ten minutes to get there, and he looked as good as always: tight jeans, button-down open at the throat, dark hair swept away from strong, aquiline features. For once, Raf was in no mood to get the man naked as quickly as possible. "Saw you out here," Henry said as he opened the garden gate and walked over. "Sorry about this. I just...Raf."

There was something like sorrow in the man's eyes and it sent his heart plummeting. Consciously, he knew the days with their specific arrangement were highly numbered. Most of Henry's partners were like them; not caring that they weren't the only one. Henry would describe himself as polyamorous, but Raf tended to shy away from labels. He enjoyed relationships, but with the way his life had turned into a beehive of activity the last few years, it had simply been easier to be one of Henry's partners.

"You've found someone serious," he said softly as Henry approached. "Somehow, I had a feeling."

"I have." He reached out and Raf came to him. Hard not to, when he knew Henry's touch and its warmth and steadiness. But he kept his hands on Henry's biceps, away from any more tempting areas. "And we're looking for someone else. A third. They want to meet you, Raf. To know the person I've been with the longest, the one I trust the most." Stunned, he watched Henry swallow hard. "They're open to the idea, if you are. It can't be just anyone. And they know how I...how I trust you."

That was *not* what he'd been expecting. Not at all. It was too much at once; the dizzying sadness that his suspicions were about to be confirmed, and then the shock of hitting unknown, uneven ground after plummeting from a height. This was *not* anticipated. And yet it somehow felt worse, as though a bit of his reality had shifted. Everything was jumbled up in his brain and Raf couldn't *think.*

"I...I don't know what to say." He leaned into Henry's warmth, still freely given. At least for right now. "Knocked the wind out of me a little, I think."

Henry guided them to the wrought iron bench, and the cold, biting metal made Raf suck in a breath. He faintly registered the heavy aromas of dirt and sea breeze, the sound of cicadas in the distance. But Henry - lovely Henry, darling Henry, whom he had known for *years* - was watching him closely. There was a hopeful desperation on his face and Raf was loath to disappoint or sadden him. But he must. "I'm sorry to spring this on you," Henry said as he pulled Raf close, almost cradling him. "And I know you need time to process. And of course meet Kate."

He froze. Henry must have felt him stiffen but he stayed silent. It wasn't who *Henry* slept with, but their lack of discussion in who *Raf* slept with. It had never been about the physicality of their other partners, as long as everyone got tested and had sex safely. Raf didn't simply prefer men, like Henry. He was exclusive in his partners; something that came to him early on in his teenage years and had never wavered. He was only attracted to men, and while polyamory wasn't something he was interested in, he couldn't claim to be monogamous. "Kate."

Henry nodded. "She's eager to meet you."

Oh gods. What had Henry told her? Were there now *expectations*? "Henry. I'm not sure how to say this without truly sticking my foot into my mouth."

Henry smiled softly at that. "Impossible."

"Oh, well...here goes. The big issue is you don't have much of a preference when it comes to presentation, and I do. *Exclusively*."

"I know."

"Do you?" Somehow, in all the years they'd been sleeping together, this had never come up? Was his memory that bad? Had Henry, in his rush of endorphins and excitement, forgotten Raf's preferences? "Then fill me in, cause I'm lost here. On top of the fact that you're assuming a fair bit at the outset."

Henry frowned. "But I'm not."

Raf sat up, pulled upright by an invisible string of confusion and, yes, a bit of anger. "Henry. I care for you deeply. Adore you, even. And while I will be sad to lose you, you deserve anything that makes you happy. I would never stand in your way. You must know that." When Henry nodded, Raf continued. "But this arrangement you want to bring me into is not for me. I'm going to assume you were excited and again, I'm honored you thought of me. But you and I...shit." He wiped a hand down his face, agitated. He wanted to tell Henry exactly how strange and unmoored he was feeling, how affronted he was that Henry had jumped to several conclusions without asking him. How he'd pulled Raf into an arrangement that took no consideration for his feelings.

"Okay, long and short of it is, what you're talking about is not for me." Raf gave Henry's forearm a squeeze but Henry pulled away. The man's expression had gone sour, brow furrowed and lips pursed. "It's not. And again, I'm honored - touched, even - that you thought I'd be a good fit for something so personal. And if you need to break it off with me, I completely understand, though I will miss you."

"But Kate's -"

"I'm going to assume a woman?"

"Yes."

"I've never been interested in women, darling. I'm sure she's lovely."

"But she -"

Something dawned on him in the moment. Henry was a bit of a people pleaser and maybe this wasn't all his idea. "Is this what *you* want, Henry?"

Henry snatched his arm away and leaned back. Away from Raf. "Of course it is. Why would you think otherwise?"

Raf held his hands up, placating. Disappointment, that he'd been expecting. But this flash of anger marring Henry's beautiful face was...disturbing. The faster this conversation ended, the better. Otherwise his panic would set in. Already Raf could feel it clawing at his throat, his lungs. "I'm only asking, as a friend. And now you know where I stand. I hope you can respect it."

"I really thought -" Henry got to his feet, trailing off while looking anywhere but at Raf. It wasn't a breakup, but that didn't mean it was easy. He was going to miss Henry a lot. But the smart play here was to let him cool off, to pull back and *think*. He could have been more offended at Henry's strange leaps of logic, but he was tired and wanted dinner and a drink and his bed. Finally, Henry said, "I'm sorry, Raf. Maybe don't call me for a while?"

Wow. Okay, well then. "Consider me a ghost."

"Okay." He dipped his head toward the street and said, "I'm gonna go."

"Take care, Henry."

Henry left without another word and Raf was alone with the dying sunset and a wind that turned bitter cold. Not how he'd expected that conversation to go *at all*. The urge to hide away warred with the urge to vent. What if he went out, sat at a bar with a book and some food? But that took effort and Raf was loath to get back into his car and drive downtown.

Raf sighed and stood up, resigning to his fate of rewarmed soup and decent wine, but he also texted Ambrose. They talked all the time, texts during the day and weeknight calls to joke and catch up. He wanted to hear about anything, anyone, to take his mind off Henry. And Ambrose had Barrett now, and their bond was growing stronger. Ambrose wasn't one to move quickly; in fact, he often took things at such a slow pace a snail could beat him to the finish line. But Ambrose and Barrett seemed fated. It almost made Raf jealous.

From Raf: *Are you busy?*

From Ambrose: *Just pulling the kettle off the stove. Give me five.*

Ambrose called as Raf was pouring a second glass of wine. Gods knew he needed it. "Hey."

"Oh, my friend." Raf sank back on his couch. "Do you have time for my drama?"

"Always. Oh wait, hold on." Ambrose's end of the line became muffled and then he came back. "Sorry. Barrett was just dropping something off." There was a bark in the distance and Ambrose laughed. "And Dandi has things to say about that."

Raf was a sucker for all animals, but he'd grown up with Bull Mastiffs and that bark on the other end of the line made him, even for a moment, want to bury his face in a dog's fur. "I so love that dog."

Ambrose laughed. "I think everyone who meets her falls a little in love."

"How could they not? She's the best there ever was. Except for my Rudy, of course." Rudy had been his best friend growing up and had followed Raf everywhere. He missed that dog so much.

Talk of Dandi made things easier, made the swirl of anxiety and worry in his stomach slow down enough to let him relax and listen to his best friend talk. After a few minutes, Ambrose said, "So what's going on? You don't typically need a distraction."

He sighed before gulping more wine. "Henry."

"What happened?"

"Ugh."

"Words, Raphael."

"I'm trying, my dear. It's just...fucked up."

"Start at the beginning."

Raf closed his eyes and sank further into the couch. "It's a fucking mess."

"Are you ready for this?" Raf asked, a teasing smile on his beautiful face.

Silvan fought the urge to fuss with his signet ring. It just felt like the right thing to do, instead of shoving his hands into his pockets. Last minute nerves, and the pressures of his own expectations for this brunch, were severing his self-control.

Also severing his self control was Raf's outfit.

When Raf's sleek black car pulled into his drive, Silvan had anticipated his boss (remember, his boss, and maybe his friend, but even that was dangerous) would be dressed to the nines. Some perfectly tailored jacket with a breezy button down and slacks on the right side of too tight. Something very Raf. And it might be on the edge of autumn, but this was middle California and the sun was still warm, so Silvan had opted for a combination of business and playful. And since Becca had given the outfit her blessing, Silvan had felt confident when opening his front door to greet Raf. Dark green slacks with a soft herringbone print, light green shirt, scarf done up in swirls of blue, green, and gray. Demure but striking.

Raf stood on Silvan's front steps, lifted his head as the door opened, and said, "My, my. You look fantastic. Judy's going to eat you up."

All his witty remarks popped like soap bubbles in the wind. There was no excuse for Raf's outfit. His white pants were very standard in appearance from the front, if he turned a little to the side, Silvan got eyefuls of muscular legs. Because the sides of the pants were cut out in a zigzag pattern, those open spaces covered with a fine mesh netting in rose-petal pink. His shirt was the same shade as the netting, and on any other man it would have looked ridiculous. On Raf, it looked like he'd ripped it from the pages of a fashion magazine, decided he liked it, and immediately put it on. The slouchy, tucked-in silk button down shone softly, but its bright silver buttons winked at him in the morning light. And Raf was utterly decked out in silver everything else, from the hoops in his ears to the choker at his throat and the bangles and rings on both arms and hands.

And while Silvan was gaping, Raf lowered his sunglasses to show off kohl-rimmed hazel eyes. Silvan seriously considered proposing marriage right there. "Judy's brunches are spectacles," he explained as he gestured to his clothing. "It's a bit - no, a lot much. I know. But you will look like the proper businessman and I'll flit around. As they all expect."

"There are expectations?"

Raf's smile was only a little bit bitter. "Of me, yes."

Really, the man looking like that was a crime against sexuality in general. Since *looking at him* made Silvan want to lay Raf out on his bed, tie him down, and gently break him until he *sobbed for it*, all he could do was fuss with his ring and try not to let his jangling nerves take over. They stood in the foyer of a ridiculous manor, the kind he figured could only match the infamous Matriarch of Bagels.

"It's quite a lot," Raf murmured as the valet handed him a ticket while a waiter swooped in to offer mimosas in delicate glasses decorated with elaborate swirls of citrus peel and fresh orchids. "And I mean *a lot*. But this is why we planned."

"I'm glad we did," Silvan replied as he plucked up two glasses and offered one to Raf. Anything to keep him from staring at the amount of chest visible. Raf was leanly built, sinewy and long like a runner. A lot of runners shaved their chests. Raf very much did not and Silvan was having a very difficult time keeping his eyes away from thick, curly chest hair and the layers of necklaces on top. The glint of gold deep in that nest of jewelry made his teeth itch.

If he were a smart man with no compulsions about keeping his job, Silvan would have cornered Raf somewhere dark and quiet a long time ago and taken delight in tasting every inch of him. Hell, that other Silvan wouldn't have taken the job at all and simply begged to take Raf home. Fuck.

FUCK.

The first sip of mimosa made his eyes pop open wide and Raf chuckled. "She makes them strong. There will be more than one incident today. They'll be discreet about it, but still."

They weren't fifty feet past the marble foyer when Judy swooped in, bright orange jumpsuit and five inch espadrilles giving her sight and height on most of the crowd. "And there's my star, my favorite art curator," she said with a kiss on Raf's cheek. "Along with his newest acquisition."

Silvan had dealt with people like Judy Thoreaux before. A lot of money, privilege, and power, with the cunning to wield it to her advantage. Money only played so far, and it was also easy to lose. To run a big, successful business like Bangels Bagels, keep herself in the news as a positive community influence, and be whispered about as utterly cutthroat, Judy had to be a master in a lot of arenas. It just so happened Silvan was quite practiced in those same arenas.

After Raf introduced them, Judy immediately said to Silvan, "I'm stealing you to make some introductions," and left. Expecting Silvan to follow. Ah, the game had already started.

Raf, for his part, looked a little surprised. "I'm so sorry. I didn't think she would -"

Silvan decided to make a small wager. Just a little one. Just to see what would happen. Because it was growing more evident by the day that his attraction to Raf wasn't dying down; hell, he'd given it the mental and spiritual equivalent of a tranquilizer and it wasn't shutting up. So daring it was. He put his hand over Raf's and squeezed, then let go. "I've got this. Trust me. I've been in this business a long time, and Judy's not the first of her kind I've tangled with." Then Silvan winked and wandered off, only sort of following Judy and unable to suppress his grin when she turned and saw he was admiring her artwork instead of directly falling in line.

He was very good at this game. Raf had no idea how well he played it, or that he played to win. And since the end goal was to garner more donors to the gallery's community projects, Silvan was aiming for nothing but the best by the time they walked away from this cursed brunch.

Two hours later

If Raf had to answer the same three questions about the piece on auction, he was going to scream. Question one wasn't so bad, asking about the artist's inspiration. He knew that answer by heart, since *Glass Triad* was one of Benecio DePonte's finest pieces, and the man had been delighted to send it to the brunch. Benecio was a master glassmaker and the purple, clear, and orange glass shone with every bit of his attention to detail.

To most, it looked like an inverted top, or an overly large Christmas ornament (some of the jokers at the brunch thought that was the highest form of hilarity, questioning why anyone would want something that looked like it belonged in Rockefeller Square at the holidays). But, in Benecio's words, he was representing the finest colors of a day: the orange of a sunrise, the brilliant clearness of a beautiful day, and the deep velvet purple of twilight. It wasn't anything particularly philosophical, but Raf saw the beauty in its purity. As did many of the people who walked by, noted the starting bid of an eye-watering six figures, and then immediately went over to the auctioneer. It was a silent auction, so no big dramatics of paddle raising and fervent whispers to mysterious buyers on the other end of a phone. Thank fuck for that.

But the other two most common questions were starting to grate on him. *If I win, can I have it delivered?* (That was part of the gallery's service, so clearly his messaging needed work - a job for Silvan.) And then his all time favorite: *If I win, do I get a special visit from such a handsome man like yourself?* That one made him grind his teeth. And of course, the more they all drank, the flirtier they became. Although flirty wasn't perhaps the correct word.

Borderline obscene was more like it. As if he were some pretty thing Judy hired to play as art tour guide, and not the owner of four - almost five, hopefully - very successful art galleries and a name in those communities. Raf could feel his enamel wearing down every time he had to smartly shy away from anything so much as a pass.

Raf was very close to the end of his tether when Judy approached, a big smile on her face. "My god, your Silvan is a fucking miracle worker. He's got the Smithertons eating out of the palm of his hand." She handed him a water glass and he gulped from it eagerly. "How bad is it this time?"

How could he answer that honestly? Judy wasn't friends with most of these people. He didn't fault her for continuing to court influence. He couldn't even fault her for using him the way she did; he was using her, too. Theirs was an exchange of money and power, except for Judy it was all about social clout and for him, nothing mattered but the galleries and the community programs and artists. But this brunch, right now? It rankled. The comments, the looks. But then again, wasn't he courting them in the name of the gallery and the artists?

There had to be another way to raise money and not feel so debased, so stretched. Every smile Raf gave these people made him feel a little dirtier. This had all been fine when galleries were opening and projects needed funding; in those earlier, more desperate years, when it was a handful of artists and one building and one big opening night on which he'd staked everything.

But Ablaze was successful now. Known. Part of the communities in which the art lived and breathed and *gave back*. There had to be another way.

"Not great," he finally admitted. "I'm thinking this is my final brunch."

Judy gave him an assessing look and then, very slowly, nodded. Raf let out a silent sigh of relief. "I understand." She waved a hand at the slightly inebriated crowd. "But I'm always here for you. You know that, right?"

He leaned in conspiratorially. "Are you going soft on me, Matriarch?"

Judy's laugh cracked open in the space between them. "Never. But you've been playing this game for years, Raf. And I know these..." She waved a hand at the crowd. "Faux bacchanals aren't your thing. The auction wraps up soon and then you'll be free."

He laughed, the sound dry. "I hate to tell you you're right, but you are."

"I know."

He glanced past her to where *Glass Triad* sat on display, drawing more lookers with every passing minute. These people always loved an auction, a chance to show off their wealth and one-up their neighbors and friends. Raf hated all of it. He'd grown up squarely middle class, with a single mother who fought tooth and nail to provide for him. She'd taught him about working hard but also enjoying life, and she was the reason his galleries even existed.

The realization hit him square in the jaw. He'd been growing distant to his past, to who he was. Hell, even carrying on with Henry was a distraction. Raf sucked in a deep breath, nodded his thanks to Judy, and strode past everyone. Head held high, newfound determination in his chest. It was time to go back to who he was. And he had five art galleries to do it with.

Swinging past the near-groaning tables of food and drinks, Raf let his feet carry him out into Judy's topiary gardens and to a bench. It was well hidden in a corner, so he could avoid all the eyes and questions. Then he sat down, pulled out his phone, and started making notes. Notes on the illustrations he'd taken charge of on behalf of Barrett and his friend Perry. Perry's drawings were things of delicate beauty, so the plan was to make those illustrations and the book he was helping to arrange the stars of the St. Augustine gallery opening. But Raf wanted more.

More beauty, more inspiration. To go back to looking at the world with an artist's eye and see the delicate fold of a waxy green leaf, the awe in a night sky dotted with stars. He knew artists who used the natural world as inspiration, of course, so Raf immediately made a list. Some of them could churn out pieces with short notice, and others had items in their own lofts he could borrow. The opening of the St. Augustine gallery was suddenly looking a lot different, and a lot more hopeful. But he still wanted *more*. He wanted to speak to the darker side of nature, too. Bone and blood, teeth and dirt. Lust and sex and power. Antlers rising out of a black pond.

"Raf?"

Raf looked up quickly and saw Silvan approaching. Gods, the man looked good enough to eat. He'd been so stunned by Silvan just....looking like *that* today that he'd foolishly not given him any compliments.

Maybe Silvan didn't need him to. Surely he knew how good he looked, right? The salt-and-pepper hair slicked back, ends a tiny bit untamed; the slight scruff drawing the eye to a sharp jawline; and those fucking blue eyes. They matched the blue in his scarf perfectly. Something silver glistened at his throat and Raf wanted to peel that bit of fabric away to see it better.

"Enjoying brunch? I know it's a bit much." He gestured to the topiaries around them. "I needed some air. And...sanity, I suppose."

Silvan didn't answer. He walked over and sat down on the bench, the tight space leaving them in constant contact from knee to hip, elbow to shoulder. Something buzzed over Raf's skin; a gentle hum of awareness that had him gripping his phone tighter.

"No apologies needed. I haven't been in such a crowd in a rather long time. It's overstimulating." Silvan chuckled. "They're definitely not the kind of people I enjoy keeping company with. But I know it's necessary." Silvan motioned to Raf's phone. "Something wrong?"

"No. Yes." He sighed and slumped back against the hard concrete bench. "I don't know. My head is full of what I want to do versus what I've been doing and I just feel...pulled in all the wrong directions. Stretched too thin. And when that happens, I can't focus. But I had an idea."

This was perhaps one of the dumber things he'd done in some time, but fuck it. Raf leaned in and watched with a curl of pleasure at how Silvan tracked him. Eyes steady, posture relaxed, but the very air around him simmered with something. Raf was drawn in.

This was very stupid. It could end very badly.

Raf simply didn't care right now. He'd always been so careful.

Fuck it.

"I want to make the opening of the gallery a focus on the natural world. Wood, sea-tumbled glass, bone, feathers, flowers. Anything we can get. I've got a list going. But I want more." Raf slid his hand down his knee and watched Silvan track the movement. "I want to pair it with an after-hours show. Two weeks for the first show, all beauty and science and everything that makes the sun brighter, the sea air better. And then the next week, we reopen after regular operating hours. We get pieces like those ones in Steamy Indulgences. Photographs, sculptures. Vivid, startling, raw things." He paused to swallow the little spark of reluctance rising up. "I want people who attend to feel claws down their spine and lust in their soul."

Silvan's response was so immediate, Raf was taken aback a little. "I think that sounds divine. And I know a few photographers who specialize in the kind of thing you're looking for."

So his instincts about Silvan hadn't been wrong, perhaps. Was there a darker, more sensuous side to him? Was there something else beyond the even-keeled demeanor and willingness to help, the steady hands and kind eyes? Raf had seen the barest glimpses of *something else*, something held at bay. And his instincts about people were rarely wrong.

"Will you introduce me to them?"

"Definitely. Mika's in Balsam Bay, so it's a bit of a drive. But there's another she works with near there. I bet we could meet them at the same time. Two birds, one stone. Mika does what she calls 'raw nature' photography, mostly nude models in the woods. And the other photographer, Sasha, does a little bit of everything. I've seen some of her work in a few places, it's very dark and sensual."

"I think that could be what we're looking for." Raf forced himself to take in a breath, to force out the words that might snap the moment in half. "What I'm looking for."

Silvan was so still, his gaze so focused, that Raf found himself leaning into Silvan even more. If the other man cared, he didn't say so. And he certainly wasn't moving away from Raf. This closeness felt *right*. The breeze pulled something like smoky moss and cedar into his senses; it set the pit of his belly roiling with indescribable yearning.

"Is that you?" he asked, inhaling deeply once more.

Silvan didn't look the least bit startled in Raf's sudden shift of attentions. One eyebrow arched ever so slightly. "Depends on what you're talking about."

The urge to press his face into Silvan's neck was leaving him on a cliff's edge. Raf wanted to jump. "That scent. Like...I can't even describe it."

Silvan gave a little hum. They were inches from each other now and Raf had no doubt that the older man was *interested*. He was looking at Raf with open curiosity, but the darkness lingering at his edges pulled Raf in. Sucked him under, made him want to roll them to the ground and bite along that sharp jawline and let everyone watch.

"Like a dark pine forest at night where wolves howl from their hollows and the things in the trees watch as you pass under them. So yes, that's me, if you're referring to the scent." A smirk grew on Silvan's face and it was the sexiest thing Raf had ever seen. There was wisdom in it, and playfulness, but also a promise of darker, secret things. "May I?" Silvan reached out to him with lean fingers.

What could he do but agree?

At Raf's nod, Silvan gently plucked up the gold medallion that lay below his collarbones. That single brush of warm skin nearly had him groaning. "I thought I recognized this earlier. It's a one hundred *lira*, right?"

Fuck. He was fucked. *So, so fucked*. Silvan was worldly and brilliant and handsome and Raf could feel the urge, that *need*, to be taken by someone willing to give in that way. He'd settle for a quick fumble in a closet but that would only quiet his want for a little bit. "It is." Gods, his throat was dry. "My mother gave it to me when I was eighteen, before I went off to university. It was one of the few things she had from her father."

"It's beautiful." Silvan rubbed his thumb over the coin's rippled edge. "Wearing a bit of your family's history around your neck. Keeping it close." Silvan's gaze dropped to his mouth as he let the coin go, and Raf swore the world *stopped*. "This was my grandmother's." Silvan held up his right index finger where the gold and labradorite signet ring he always wore sparkled. "Bonnie already has her pearls. She got arrested during Prohibition and was wearing them in her mug shot. My kid said she didn't want to wear them until she'd done at least one thing worthy of that kind of badassery."

"I think your daughter sounds like a total badass already." His heart was pounding in his ears and his skin felt like it was on fire. Silvan was keeping him balancing on a knife's edge.

"She would agree. As would I." Something like pride shot across his face. "She's way braver than I was at her age."

"I'd think that's partially to do with you, Silvan. Don't forgo that credit."

"You're sweet."

"Hmmm, not what I usually hear."

That thick air between them began to settle. Which was, truly, for the best. Raf didn't want to think *again* on ways to handle an interoffice affair and not become the instant source of all gossip in the art world along the coast. It would probably do wonders for his reputation, which was sparkling but a little *too* clean for the likes of some of the grittier artists and groups.

"What is it you usually hear?" Silvan asked , looking genuinely curious

Raf straightened and crossed one leg over the other, adopting a regal pose. "That I'm the consummate professional. Today's fashion notwithstanding, of course."

"Of course. This is an exception, a rare one."

"You have no idea."

Both of them turned to see Judy headed straight for them, sealed envelope in hand, so they got to their feet. "Auction's over, my dear. And you are the proud owner of a very generous check, plus a few donations gathered up thanks to your lovely Silvan's charm." She grinned at Silvan as she handed Raf the check. "Well done, you. You handled them like an old pro. It was extremely impressive. If you weren't Raf's, I'd be offering you a job right now."

"That's very kind of you, Judy. But I'm wholly dedicated to the galleries and Raf's community missions." Silvan's answer was so smooth, it made the hair on Raf's arms stand up. The man was a born charmer, yes, but also very good at the kind of speech that instantly relaxed you. A born orator, on top of a born charmer. Silvan threw him a glance over his shoulder. "It's the best job I've ever had."

"Too sweet for his own good. Well, Raf, I know you're itching to get out of here." She put a hand up when he started to protest. "We both know it. Denial is a river in Hell, my dear. Take this handsome man home and enjoy your afternoon."

There was a weight in her words and it set Raf's stomach tumbling. *Take him home*. If Silvan heard the same implication, his perfectly neutral expression didn't flicker to show it. They said their thanks and goodbyes, slowly making their way out of the party; stopping to congratulate the auction winner, managing to pick up a few more donation checks on the way out the door as envelopes were quietly pressed into their palms.

When they reached the valet line and a jacketed staff member had picked up Raf's keys, Silvan broke the silence. "Judy's quite the character, but a good host. Thank you for trusting me with today. I know these kind of events are...stressful, to say the least."

"Stressful is the tip of the iceberg. But no need for thanks." Raf gave a wan smile. "You are getting paid for today, never fear."

"Raf." Silvan's touch was light but Raf turned toward it anyways. Pulled by an invisible, secondary hand, as if Silvan had taken him by the shoulders to bring him near. "I wanted to be here. For the gallery. For you. I wasn't joking when I told Judy it's the best job I've ever had. That's because of you."

"I...well, consider this a win. You've left me, however momentarily, speechless."

"I do enjoy winning."

He gave a playful scoff as his car pulled up. "Then may I take the winner home?"

"Is that part of my winnings?" Silvan slipped his sunglasses on and smiled.

Raf's heart could have leapt out of his chest, that's how good Silvan looked at that moment. Added to the moment in the garden before, and Raf's nerves were a tangled pile of yarn and about as useful. "I suppose it wouldn't do me much good to leave you stranded, would it."

"It would be rather unsporting, since you gave me a ride here. To a brunch." Silvan leaned in and mock-whispered, "With a bunch of uptight rich people."

Raf chuckled. "Has anyone ever told you you're terrible?"

One dark eyebrow rose. Challenging. "On occasion. Usually it's thanks and praise. Even when I'm a little rough."

Silvan was flirting with him. Granted, the whole medallion thing in the garden had *definitely* been flirting as well. But this was with words and a coy little smile. Maybe it was a challenge, to see if Raf would rise to it.

Well, Silvan, challenge accepted.

Chapter Eleven

Home felt both too far away and not enough. The long, quiet moments on the drive back stretched out and Silvan felt a wariness bloom in his belly. He'd made a move - several, in fact - on his boss.

His boss. He'd *flirted* with his boss. Touched him outside of casual contact in a workplace. Had made comments about being thanked for occasionally delivering things *a little rough*. Silvan wanted to hide forever.

What the ever-loving *fuck* had he been thinking?

And right or wrong, he needed to apologize.

Now.

"Raf."

Raf cast a glance at him but studiously went back to focusing on the road. "Yes?"

Time to bite the bullet. "I wanted to apologize. I may have made some remarks that weren't entirely professional. And I shouldn't have -"

"I'm going to stop you right there." With ease, Raf steered the car into a parking lot for a smoothie shop, put it in park, and then turned in his seat. "All right. This isn't my favorite thing to discuss, but I had a feeling we'd get there sooner or later." To Silvan's shock, Raf reached out to let his hand hover over his arm. "May I?"

Silvan could only nod, but it made Raf smile. "Thank you." He put his hand on Silvan's forearm. Skin to skin. Such a simple thing and it made him shiver anyways. "You and I met at a bar. In my cousin's club, where go-go dancers in thigh highs and fishnets wiggle for tips. We were going to flirt with each other." One side of Raf's lovely mouth drew up. "Or, at least I was going to try to flirt with you. I had every intention of, if it went well and you were interested, taking you home."

And didn't that confession go right to Silvan's cock. But Raf kept *going*. "But fate had something else in store for us and here we are." Warm fingers danced down his arm. "Things are complicated now."

Silvan swallowed against a dry throat. It was suddenly rather warm in the car but he didn't want to break the spell between them to put the window down. He clung to the intensity in Raf's eyes, the knowing little smile on his beautiful face. All he could manage was, "They are. As much as I hate it."

"Agreed." And then Raf lightly pressed his thumb against Silvan's pulse and the world tilted. "So I'm wondering what we're to do here."

His mind whirled. It wasn't as though he hadn't thought about negotiating certain scenarios with Raf. The man was practically *built* for being spread out on dark sheets and made to beg sweetly. Something about him made Silvan's entire being respond, and as badly as he wanted to find out how Raf liked to be treated. *His boss* was right.

Things were complicated.

But that touch on his wrist was distracting.

Silvan cleared his throat and Raf gently withdrew his hand. "I can't say I have an answer. But I do know that working together can cause...interesting revelations in personal relationships. Maybe we use it to our advantage."

"How so?"

"I'm thinking out loud here, so keep that in mind. Option one, we keep flirting with each other."

Raf let out a snort. "That will end only one way."

"How's that?"

"I've never been good at resisting temptation."

Silvan ducked his head in acknowledgment and that seemed to hit home for Raf; the way his eyes darkened behind his glasses made Silvan's blood heat a little more. Oh, the things he would do to this man given the right situation and an entire weekend alone.

"Option two," Silvan continued with a throat suddenly too tight, "we go the other way and keep things strictly business."

"Also not my speed."

"Nor mine. Some people go to work to do only that; I enjoy getting to know who I'm spending so much time with." He glanced down at the coin resting on Raf's chest. "I would, for example, love to know more about your family. Your mother sounds remarkable."

Wonder of wonders, Raf flushed. "She is. My favorite person on the planet. Always has been."

Gods, that was attractive. He didn't even have the words for why it was so. But to see a smart, successful, creative man like Raf still adore his mother and hold that love close was sweet. He'd viewed his father in a similar light, and he'd raised his daughter with the lessons he'd learned from his *far*, the influence of Becca's more rigid style of parenting, and the understanding that all he could do was give Bonnie the tools to become a solid adult and then let her go. It was hard, it was rewarding, and now he was sitting in a car beside a man Silvan was coming to understand, piece by piece. Raf's family history, his adoration for his mother, his perfectionist streak dappled with the color of joy in art and life and wine and food. Raf was one of the most dynamic people Silvan had ever met. It was more than a raw, physical attraction. There was a lot more to the man he wanted to know about, to explore.

And Silvan had the sense that his option three might be enough to help them find an even keel. "All right, so option three then.

"Why do I feel as though this is the one that will be agreeable for both of us?"

"Because in some ways we're alike." Silvan let a slow smile spread across his face. "We don't mind finding a safe, solid middle ground that works for all."

Raf hummed a little under his breath, his own smile growing. "Safe, huh?"

"Safe enough."

"Now you're speaking my language." Raf leaned in. Close again. Close enough that Silvan would barely have to reach out for that gold coin. "As long as there's a little danger."

The danger is working around you day in and day out. "We set some kind of deadline. A chance to work as colleagues and figure out if this is more than...physical."

"Keep going."

Oh, to hear those words in another context, one defined by taste and scent and touch; a tongue along a stubbled jaw, fingertips mapping muscle and sinew and skin, the sound of soft moans filling his ears. "The gallery opens in just under three months. By then, we'll have had more time to get to know each other."

"Hmmm, interesting. So if say, by the end of the show we meet up, then we confess where we stand?"

"Maybe. If that sounds like the right idea."

Raf's smile dropped and Silvan mourned its loss. He wanted it back, bright and big, or soft and secretive. Snarky, smirking. Any of it. He sounded a little sad now, and Silvan's heart twisted. "And if we're not on the same page?"

Here was the gambit. Silvan took a deep breath and said, "Then I quit."

Raf was immediately upright, so quickly did he move that he smacked his arm into the steering wheel. "Silvan. No. I would never -"

"You're not asking me for anything. But I'm being selfish here, to be frank. I can't work with someone I'm attracted to for long. It's too complicated, too messy." Silvan ran a hand along his jaw. "I'm not a fan of messy personal relationships. I've lived a quiet life so far, I'm not looking to suddenly introduce drama."

"And I'm not drama?"

"No, you're not." *You're a lot of things, but not that. And you're far too beautiful and interesting to look so sad.* "I can't believe anyone would think you're dramatic. But this is one of a handful of times you've made that comment, so I'm wondering who told you that so often that it was embedded in your mind. Because it's not true."

Raf *choked*. "Shit." He coughed, eyes watering. "Okay...Christ. You are far too observant for your own good."

That got Silvan laughing. "I've been told that before."

Raf was quiet for a moment, still recovering from his shock at Silvan's words. Once he wiped his eyes with the back of his hand, leaving Silvan to stare at slightly smudged eyeliner, Raf managed to say, "But I get it. I would never, ever want to drive you away. Shit, maybe we should just take option two."

"I'm afraid I can't. It would be too hard for me."

He was about to make another gamble. Very slowly, Silvan touched his thumb to a bit of smeared black eyeliner on the high edge of Raf's cheekbone. "I'm deeply attracted to you. I look at you now and I see someone who feels *everything* and has learned to shut most of it off. But when you let the floodgates open....I bet you're magnificent." Silvan pressed on that bit of skin ever so slightly and Raf's eyes fluttered shut and his lips dropped open. Lust roared through him, claws out, teeth bared; eager and ready and willing. "Fuck. I know how good you would look."

Maybe he imagined it, but Silvan swore he heard the other man whimper. The leather steering wheel squeaked under the force of Raf's grip and Silvan let himself have one small, satisfied smile before dropping his hand. "So you're serious about this?" Raf finally asked. He sounded a little breathless and by the gods, Silvan wanted to hear it curling into his ear instead of across the interior of a luxury car. "Obviously I can't tell you what to do when it comes to remaining with the galleries. But Silvan..."

"I've thought a lot about this of late. And it was the best middle ground I could find."

"And it's also got a fail safe, for both of us." Raf tapped the side of his nose. "I see you, Silvan Diedrich. If the attraction burns out and we both agree, then we continue forward as colleagues. And hopefully friends. And if we don't agree by that night, then we part ways professionally. I'd still like to be friends, though. If that's all right."

"I think I can manage that."

"Oh, how magnanimous of you."

Silvan laughed. The tension popped. His hands went back into his lap, Raf's back into his. Not a wall rebuilt between them; more like they'd retreated to their ends of the field and were simply waiting for the ball to be dropped.

Silvan was a patient man, he could wait.

And while rejection from Raf come the gallery opening would hurt, he was old enough to know there were other people out there. But he was also fine on his own. What he couldn't tell Raf was that he doubted that night would roll around and he'd be the one changing his mind. Everything about Raf was fascinating. But the man was over a decade younger. Never married, no kids, but plenty of family and friends. Already in the middle of a life very well lived. And had at least one partner on the side, even if it was casual. Raf could have anyone he wanted. Silvan had long ago decided to pick his battles, and his partners, carefully.

Alone wasn't bad. He had his own circle of loved ones and friends. He had Bonnie, who always called or visited. He had the dream of writing a book. Perhaps he'd see it through if he had to leave the gallery and Raf's side.

"If we get to that night and we're on different playing fields, that's okay, Raf. I promise. If I have to leave Ablaze, it doesn't mean we can't be friends."

"You say that now. But I'll admit I was never the pining type."

What could he do but shrug? "And it might come down to that. But we've no way of knowing that now."

Raf studied him then slowly nodded. "All right. Gallery opening is in ten weeks as of tomorrow. So should we say midnight that night, as it rolls into the next day?" He smiled, a soft, secretive thing that Silvan wanted to wrap up and hold close. He liked the way Raf's smile promised things he could never dream of on his own. "Our very own Cinderella story."

"How very mass market paperback of you."

Raf barked out a laugh and fussed with his hair. A nervous gesture, but Silvan was feeling something similar. “Clearly I’m reading the wrong kinds of books. But honestly....all right. We’ll do this. Ten weeks to get to know each other better.”

One more gambit. Why not go all in? “But I don’t want to cross boundaries.”

“I would never expect you to.”

“Is flirting off the table for these ten weeks?”

There was that smile again, sure and bright. “I certainly hope not. I flirt with lots of people. It’s ninety-five percent in good fun, as long as everyone’s on the same page.”

“Glad to hear it. I’m a little out of practice but I suspect you don’t mind being admired.”

“Depends on who is doing the admiring.” Raf batted his lashes playfully. “And since you’re managing to make this conversation a little flirtatious, I don’t think you’re too far out of practice.”

It was some kind of level field now, Silvan figured. Raf seemed to relax in his seat and he felt himself do the same. Whatever tension lay in the air between them settled. But Silvan had to laugh and say, “This might be one of the stranger situations I’ve ever been in, but it has its appeal.” And he shot Raf a pointed look, getting a chuckle in return.

“Agreed. And I work with artists. Quite a lively bunch, as you can imagine.”

“I can.”

Raf put his hands back on the steering wheel. “Then shall we? If you feel as though we’ve come to an agreement.”

Silvan nodded. “I think we have.”

The rest of the drive to Silvan’s house didn’t feel as weighted. The air between them no longer hummed with tension and the tightness in Raf’s stomach eased. He shouldn’t have been surprised by their smoothie shop parking lot conversation, but by the end of it, Raf had decided that Silvan was much more wily than he’d realized. Something about the older man’s stability and even-keeled personality spoke to him on a certain level, but deeper than that was Raf’s shiny new realization of who Silvan was under all those good dad vibes. Granted, good dad vibes were hot, but Raf liked it when people had layers. And

Silvan had those in spades. He was clever and well-spoken, charming and efficient. But there was a thread of something else, something darker. It made him want to know more. The question was how to draw that part of Silvan out.

Silvan's adorable Cape Cod was nestled in a bundle of tall pines down a long drive. Raf had been so focused on being on time when he'd picked Silvan up that he hadn't noticed how pristine the place was. Everything was pin neat; straight out of a home decor catalog. "This is lovely," Raf said as he turned the car down the lane. "How long have you been here?"

"Around a decade. I moved when Bonnie was in fourth grade." Silvan made a small noise, one that sounded a little sad to Raf. "She's twenty now, going to school on the east coast. Engineering and architecture." Then he suddenly leaned forward, peering out of the windshield. "And she's sitting on my front stoop. Her and Becca." But he didn't sound anything but surprised, delightedly so. "What in the world..."

"Here, let me get it in park." Raf stopped the car short of the stone walk leading to Silvan's bright turquoise front door. The two women seated on Silvan's little porch were nearly identical in appearance, with long, dark brown hair, deep set eyes, and narrow noses. They even had the same dimple on the left side of their mouths. But even from here, Raf could see the younger woman had Silvan's bright blue eyes and thick eyebrows. The older woman was wearing a tasteful peacoat and grey slacks and she was looking at them with a curious little smile on her face. Bonnie seemed to only have eyes for her dad.

As Silvan pulled his satchel from the floor of the car, he said, "No pressure but would you like an introduction? I uh...Becca knows about you. Bonnie doesn't." Silvan looked away and something like guilt crept over his face. "I haven't told the kid about my new job yet. Didn't want to make her worry. She's got enough on her plate."

"What if we just say I'm a friend?" Raf smiled at him, trying to reassure his suddenly nervous marketing manager. And friend. It wasn't a lie at all.

"You sure?"

"Positive. I wouldn't out you in front of your family."

"Oh, Becca knows about the job. She helped me pick out that lavender shirt you kept eyeing."

Goddamn, the man was observant. He had to laugh at how matter-of-fact Silvan was when talking about his ex. "Fabulous lavender shirt aside, shall we?"

Silvan looked hesitant for a moment, then nodded and opened his door. As soon as Silvan was out of the car, Bonnie was launching herself at him. Raf had to smile at the obvious delight on both of their faces, and when he glanced at Becca, he saw quiet happiness on her face. She gave Raf a nod and he waved back, unsure if he should introduce himself or wait until Silvan was ready.

And there was no way he was interrupting the touching father-daughter reunion happening twenty feet from him, their laughter spreading out around them all on the slight autumn breeze. But Becca walked over and stuck out her hand, her gaze assessing but not unfriendly. Apparently forthrightness ran in the family. "You're far too well dressed to be anyone but Raphael."

She delivered the line so smoothly, it startled a laugh out of him. Raf liked the gleam in her eyes and the playful edge to her smile. Silvan had spoken fondly of his ex and while he'd been momentarily surprised (and he shouldn't have been) at the mention of such a person, the old saying of *everyone has a past* rang true. Hell, he'd been friend fucking the same man for years and now he found himself strangely alone when that same person wanted to pull him into a relationship dynamic he wasn't interested in.

Everyone has a past, indeed.

So Raf turned on the charm, smiling widely, and gesturing to himself as he replied, "I don't know about 'well dressed', considering a fourth of my outfit is pink mesh. I look like an aging spring breaker who forgot he's not a drunk coed anymore."

That got him the laugh he wanted. They shook hands while Bonnie and Silvan ended their hug by Silvan spinning his kid around as if she were eight years old and pigtailed. "They've always been like that," Becca said softly. "She looks like me but she's definitely more like him in the personality department. Humor as dry as a bone but a mind so sharp you could splinter your face on it."

"That is...yes, that's Silvan for sure," Raf managed to reply. "Good to know, thank you."

"Of course." Another look, this one a bit more disconcerting as he felt it go *through* him. "Business attire, then?"

"Boozy brunch. For art."

"Did someone say boozy brunch?" Bonnie was looking at them now while Silvan smiled fondly at her. Fuck, he looked good like that, all moon-eyed for his daughter, his arm tight around her shoulders. Raf had never considered himself particularly attracted to parents but in the moment, he could see the appeal. It was a Silvan thing, not a parent or father thing. "That sounds incredible" Bonnie turned to Silvan. "Did you go to a boozy brunch without me?"

"You were supposed to be on the other side of the country, Bon-Bon. And besides, I went with a friend." Silvan gestured to Raf. "Raphael, my daughter Bonnie. And vice versa."

Bonnie was probably a little too young and shiny to have her mother's discerning eye, but he didn't feel the need to pour on the charm *too* much. Raf stepped up, gave a short bow, and then held out his hand. "Raf is just fine. A pleasure, Bonnie."

Oh but the look she gave him - ever so brief but it saw more than he'd been expecting. Maybe Bonnie did have her mother's eye, after all. But she took his hand and said, "Okay first, nice to meet you. Second, your outfit is *amazing*. And third, what kind of boozy brunch did y'all go to wearing that?" She smacked her father in the shoulder with a playful hand and Raf saw the wink of silver jewelry. "I'm completely jealous."

"It was an art thing," Raf said with a smile. "Your father has a good eye and I happen to know some people on the inside."

Silvan quickly pulled out his phone to show Bonnie and Becca the glass sculpture that had been auctioned off. Raf saw it was for what it was - an out. He was more than happy to take it. As pleasant, even delightful, as Silvan's daughter and ex were, Raf felt like he was intruding. And given he and Silvan were trying to find their footing around each other, Raf didn't want to butt in where he didn't belong.

After a few more minutes of small talk, Raf gestured to his car. "I'm afraid I need to get going. I owe my best friend a video call, something we try to do every weekend. Bonnie, Becca, a genuine pleasure. Silvan, thank you for letting me drag you to that brunch today. The company was appreciated."

Raf thought for sure he'd be able to hop into his car and scurry away, leaving him to untangle the knotty, thorny vines of his thoughts once he got home and called Ambrose. The video call date wasn't a lie or even an embellishment; it was as routine every weekend as the egg scramble and mimosas he made for himself on those mornings. But as Becca and Bonnie waved goodbye (and Raf caught a knowing gleam in both of their gazes), Silvan gestured him to the side. The women disappeared into Silvan's home, apparently understanding something Raf was missing.

"Thank you again," Raf began, but Silvan shook his head. "Am I not allowed to thank a friend for a massive favor?"

Silvan's little smile was gentle and he stepped closer. Close enough that Raf could feel his warmth and smell the remains of his cologne. Nerves already a little frayed, the combo of sensations forced a shiver through him. "I could say it was part of the job, which is true. But you and I both know more than a work engagement happened today."

Raf wanted to let out a hard breath but kept it reigned in. He could decompress at home, have Ambrose help him sort out all the wild, tangling thoughts. "I do have to admit something happened." Gods, what was it with this man? All his steady composure, his easy charm and teasing simply fled for other pastures around Silvan. "And we're still agreed on our little...arrangement?"

"I hope so." Silvan was *right there*. Kissing distance away. Something electric and needy shot down Raf's spine. It would be easy to give in. Buut he wouldn't. Not now. "I enjoy having things strung out a little. Anticipation is fun."

When Raf looked at Silvan head-on to reply, the words died on his tongue. Silvan was tall and lean and gorgeous, yes, but whatever had shifted in his demeanor now made Raf *want*. He was always looking for that someone to let him flee his mind for a bit, to find that someone to take over so he could melt into rumpled sheets, his spine liquid, his body on fire. Why did he think, right now, that Silvan could offer him that? His posture was relaxed, his back straight, hands loose at his sides. But Silvan commanded his attention.

Dangerous. He's dangerous and you like it and you want to know what's living under that calm air he radiates. You're so curious, so willing to bend to whatever he wants and you don't understand why.

After a few seconds that felt like an eternity, Raf worked up the courage to say, "What is it about you? For once I find myself a little...I don't know, lost perhaps."

Yes, lost and deeply turned on and a little confused and it's all jumbled up in my brain that's too worried about this goddamn gallery.

"I'm pleased you find me alluring." Silvan's smile grew, he leaned closer. Raf shivered again. "I think it's fair to say you spark something in me. Unexpected, but wholly welcome."

With the breath he'd been holding, Raf slowly stepped back, reclaiming his air and his space. "And now that we have an agreement in place, you'll have to forgive me for needing time to process all of this."

"Of course." Silvan's face settled into a softer expression; the darkness at his edges receded. "To be honest, I put up a good front. Don't think for a moment that I won't be awake tonight, wondering what I've gotten myself into."

Now Raf laughed and some of the tension between them eased. It was like the scenario in the car was repeating, but Raf felt completely under Silvan's spell this time. He wasn't used to having someone commanding so much of his attention. "So we're on even ground. Look at us. Negotiating like proper adults."

"And now this proper adult has an ex and a kid to go see."

"And I have a friend to call."

Silvan bowed his head. "See you on Monday, Raf."

The urge to touch Silvan won out. Slowly, Raf reached out, put a hand on the other man's shoulder, and gave it a small squeeze. "See you on Monday."

Becca and Bonnie were making tea and chatting when Silvan went inside. The sight of them, heads bent over his various tea tins and matching glazed cups at their sides, made his heart ache. It wasn't sadness, but an acknowledgement of how lucky he was and how he should make his love known more.

In an ideal situation, he would have gathered them close and let them pepper him with questions about Raf and this brunch they went to over the scent of honey and rose petals. But this was his ex and his daughter, both too canny for their own good. Besides, he wasn't sure if he had the brain space to answer questions right now. Raf had riled him in a way no one had ever before. His entire body felt alive, *electric*. But that made sense. Raf was a fucking live wire of energy, even as tightly as he reigned it in.

It made Silvan want to unravel him and see what was underneath.

"He seems nice," Becca said as he entered the wide kitchen with its big windows and few plants he managed to keep alive. "Interesting choice of clothes."

Bonnie snorted and elbowed her mother. "Mom. He looked great. I know several people who would love to pull off an outfit like that." She speared Silvan with that gaze he knew too well. "So. Dad."

Silvan held up a finger. "No interrogations. I know how you both are."

"I never." Becca arched an eyebrow at him but she was smiling. She knew the deal, and knew how he didn't want Bonnie to worry over his sudden shift in employment.

So Silvan walked behind Bonnie and wrapped his arms around her shoulders. "Want to tell me how you're here three weeks early?"

To her credit, she flushed and craned her head so he could see her grin. "So, this TA in my program up and *left*. Disappeared into the night. So her lecture was suddenly off our schedule, the professor was baffled, and the university swears everything is fine. But my true crime senses are tingling."

"Oh boy. I think that is my cue to plug my ears." Becca pointed a bejeweled finger at Silvan. "This is your fault, you know. You started her down this path and now she thinks every weird thing is a murder in a field or a back alley."

While Bonnie protested, the kettle whistled and Silvan took the out gratefully. "I recommended one podcast to her. I didn't make her listen to all the others."

"*She* is right here!" But he knew his kid was all bluster when it came to their teasing. Silvan poured the water and pulled out a bottle of honey while the women he loved the most playfully bickered. The house felt better when Bonnie was home, but he also knew that was a selfish thing to think. She was twenty and smart and such a force of nature and if he didn't learn to let go, he would wind up heartbroken. "So yeah," Bonnie continued. "We have this side project now that's going to make up the rest of our grade and since I can do it all online, I thought I'd surprise you and come back a few weeks early." Her face dropped. "I hope that's okay."

"More than." Silvan found himself in a rush to relieve her. "Just uh...warn your dad next time, maybe."

Becca held back her snicker by saying, "Because of company?"

"Ugh." Silvan could only shake his head.

Bonnie's next question pulled him back into focus. She was stirring her tea and eyeing him closely from her perch on a stool at the kitchen island. "So, Raf. Raphael...?"

"Lutz. He's a gallery owner." He could admit that much.

"And you met him where?"

Becca's face was a mask of mild but detached interest. Goddammit. She wasn't going to save him, was she? Truth time again. "At a bar. As much as I hate to be a cliche."

"You're not a cliche, darling. It might be different if you were an old gay rolling for some young stud."

"Ouch." Silvan feigned hurt but Becca laughed and Bonnie rolled her eyes at them. "I don't know what your threshold is for *old* but I can guarantee I'm not there yet."

"He's just sensitive about turning the big five-oh next year."

"Says the woman only six months younger than me."

"Ah, but those six months make a big difference."

"I'm trying to remember why I came home now," Bonnie shot across both their bows, making them laugh. "Mom, I'm kicking you out."

Becca took her daughter's demand with the grace she always carried herself with. She kissed Silvan on the cheek, then Bonnie, saying something about lunch over the weekend to give Silvan "breathing room".

Once Becca had left, Bonnie rounded on him and Silvan braced himself. "You know what I'm going to ask," she said as she stirred honey into their second cups of tea.

"I do?"

"Dad."

"All right." Silvan gripped the counter. "I'm ready, go for it."

"You're ridiculous. But yeah...so you and Raf?"

He wanted to squeeze his eyes shut and sigh but that would give him away. Bonnie, like Becca, could read him like a book. "He's a friend."

"Who looks like that."

Another question he wasn't sure he should ask, but out it came anyways. "Like?"

She scoffed, as if his question was the dumbest thing she'd ever heard. "Like a model. Like a goddamn fashion model come to life out of a glossy magazine. Dad, he's *beautiful*." Bonnie gave him a keen look and it ripped right through him. "And, I'm assuming since you're friends, there's a lot more going on with him than just looks. You are not patient with people who need explanations for every little thing." She ticked off the items on her fingers as she went. "He owns art galleries, which is very cool. He's very charming. He's -"

Silvan held up a hand. "Raf is incredibly smart and yet quite modest. He's interesting. I'm enjoying getting to know him."

"So you've not been on a date yet."

"No."

"*Yet*."

He bowed his head. "Correct. It's a process, kid. I'm not going to jump into anything feet first." Silvan wrapped her small, slimmer hand in his. "Raf and I have kind of an agreement. We're going to take it slow, get to know each other. And if the attraction is still there after a while, then we'll figure out the dating thing."

Bonnie seemed content to scrutinize his expression, then his words, before nodding. "That's really reasonable. And you know what I'm going to say. I just don't want you hurt." She bit her lip. "He's younger."

It wasn't a question, and the weight in her words hit him in the chest. "He is."

"Like...thirty?"

"Like thirty-seven."

"Oh." She straightened and the tension in the room popped. "Okay, that makes me feel better. I'd never tell you what to do, Dad, I just worried."

"That I was dating someone closer to your age?"

"Maybe."

"Fair enough. And I wouldn't do that. Too creepy."

"Ugh." Bonnie sipped at her tea. "Okay, yeah this is getting cold. I'll top them off."

Silvan watched her bounce around the kitchen and silently breathed a sigh of relief. He'd held off the storm for now, but at some point he'd have to tell her about the other stuff. The job, the gallery, and with that came the tangled web he'd woven between himself and Raf.

Another time. Not now.

Chapter Twelve

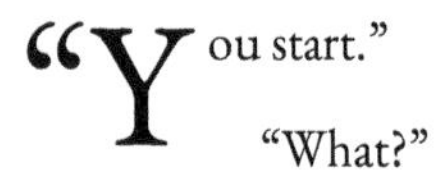

“You start.”

“What?”

“You’ve got more gossip than I do.” Ambrose waved a hand at his surroundings. “I live in the woods, Raf.”

“I don’t see how that matters since you have an incredibly hot forest ranger boyfriend.” He grinned. “Barrett knows he’s hot, right?”

“Nope. He refuses to hear it, even when I shout it across the house.”

He chuckled. Ambrose was clearly enjoying himself, as they could both hear Barrett mutter somewhere in the background. “So...hmm.”

“I don’t think I’ve ever seen you at a loss for words.”

“It’s not as though they’re lost, they’re simply...confused.”

“Then unconfuse them.” Raf watched Ambrose lean back on Barrett’s low slung, grey couch. “Let’s start with an easy one. How’s the new hire?”

For once in a very long time, Raf let himself ramble. He told Ambrose everything anyways, and it wasn’t as if the brunch was a secret. What had happened afterwards was a little harder to wrap his head around what he’d done.

What he’d agreed to.

No regrets, certainly not. But the uncharted ground under his feet left Raf feeling a tad unmoored. Talking to Ambrose made things feel right again.

When he was done, Barrett had joined Ambrose on the couch. “Not that it’s my business, course, but uh...what the hell did you get yourself into, Raf?”

“I don’t know.” He moaned only semi-dramatically and put his head in his hands. “But I know he’s worth it.”

There was a long beat of silence before he heard Ambrose mutter, as if an aside to Barrett, “Well, that’s new.”

"That I'm so into someone I'd leave myself hanging out to dry?"

"A bit." Raf lifted his head and watched as his best friend and his best friend's boyfriend gave him twin stares of concern. "You sure you're all right?"

"More than, honestly. Aside from the stress and the gallery and probably not eating enough."

"I can tell your mom about that."

"Oh god no, please do not. She'll never let me leave her house again."

Barrett began laughing and once that barrel-rolled over them all, Raf couldn't help but join in. "You might be fucked, friend," Barrett said.

"Obvious dirty joke aside, I...I think I'm caught in some maelstrom that just sprung up out of nowhere. But I like it. I like him."

Raf watched Ambrose curl into Barrett, as if his friend's instincts were to seek warmth and safety within the semi-circle of Barrett's left arm. The sight left him both happy and a little sad. Ambrose had the thing he needed, and some part of Raf wanted the equivalent for himself. He'd flitted around for years, city to city and lover to lover, up and down the coast. But the single life had been such a part of his everyday that he hadn't stopped to consider what it might mean to find a partner.

Maybe Silvan wasn't a partner. Maybe he was another person meant to be in his life and Raf would have to enjoy what he could get, for whatever time was available to him.

But his instincts told him otherwise. Or maybe it was just fleeting hope.

After a bit longer, he signed off with Ambrose and Barrett but instantly regretted doing so. There was so much he *could* do. He could continue down the list of artists Silvan had given him for approval, but that felt sort of wrong, since they had been approaching it together. He could again go over the portfolios of the photographers they were visiting mid-week. But again, that was a project they were both involved in.

As his gaze settled on the door to his little reading nook-slash-office, Raf realized all his planning was currently focused on the after hours shows that would be the second part of the gallery opening. But the opening itself, in all its science and nature glory, he was treating as if it were already set in stone. Finished. No need to further think on. And that wasn't like him at all.

The centerpiece of the first gallery show, the opener, was Perry's illustrations, yes, but they still needed *something* to welcome the crowds (hopefully there would be crowds) into the building itself. St. Augustine's building had a massive, cathedral style ceiling with a rotunda. Something had to go there. Something elaborate but sophisticated, worthy of attention. Worthy of time and effort and love. Raf pictured color, but almost a waterfall of it, or a downpour.

Water and nature. Water moved in so many ways, taking the shape of its container, filling space. But he didn't only want to fill space, he wanted to create one. One wholly unique to the gallery and the show and the entire meaning behind what he was doing. Art and beauty, grace and power.

What was more powerful than water? Nature herself.

Before he had a firm grasp on that thought, Raf was digging out colored pencils and a sketchbook from his office desk and settling down in the chair. He wanted Silvan involved in all things around the galleries, but this was *his*. A stretching back to roots he'd never fully let go of, but hadn't reached for in some time. With a grin, he cracked open the pencil tin and got to work.

Silvan dreamt of faces in stone. Soft lines, the kind only a master sculptor could force from cold, unforgiving rock, with flowing hair and bright, wide eyes. Drapes of fabric and scales that looked real, touchable. And then a face, maw gaping, eyes wide not in delight but some mockery of terror, overtook him. Panic welled in his chest and he turned to run, only to feel cold fingers on his arm.

When he opened his eyes for real, the only thing staring back was the tiny light of the smoke alarm above his head.

He was prone to nightmares when his mind was unsettled, and clearly it was all focused around the gallery. And Raf. His new job. His lying - omitting some truths - to Bonnie. The shock of seeing her morphing into delight. Soft contentment knowing she was fast asleep just down the hall.

Silvan sighed hard. It was barely two in the morning and he was adrift on a tide of restlessness, the kind only the dark could bear witness to. Getting up meant leaving his warm bed, though tea would likely settle his nerves. Staying in bed meant fighting to get back to sleep; he'd certainly done the insomnia dance enough over the years to know that was the only other option here.

There was a third option.

Ah, fuck.

With a slow slide of his palm down his thigh, Silvan made a choice.

Besides, maybe if he did this, he could fall asleep and not arrive at work with red eyes and a constant yawn. It wasn't as though he didn't get himself off from time to time, but even in his younger years, he'd never found nearly as much pleasure in the solo act. But taking the edge off wasn't a bad thing right now. In fact, it was probably sorely overdue.

He rustled around until his clothes were on the floor and there was a second pillow under his head. The room was slightly chilly, so Silvan yanked the sheet up to his waist. The slide of worn cotton made his skin prickle in anticipation. He bit his lip, shifted his hips up a little, and slowly wrapped his fingers around his cock.

It wasn't like you forgot *how* to get yourself off, so Silvan expected to do it fast and get a little relief. Maybe it was the feather-light sheet on his body, maybe it was the knowledge that this was the fastest way to get back to sleep.

Or maybe it was seeing Raf's face as soon as he closed his eyes.

But something made him suck in a breath between his teeth as he gently stroked himself. It certainly wasn't only because of a pair of deep-set hazel eyes and artfully messy black hair. It wasn't the slinky glint of delicate piercings up a right ear or the way lean fingers tangled in the chain Raf always wore. The chain on which a piece of the man's heritage lay against supple skin, dark chest hair teasing the v-necks he favored.

Silvan's heart kicked up a notch and he moved his hand faster. This felt...better than he'd expected it would. Shit. He really was going to jerk off picturing Raf. His *boss*. Hell.

He let out a shaky breath, enjoying the way it felt leaving his lungs. Everything felt so *good* right now. He wanted to string that feeling out, ride the sensations as much as he could. So he brought his right hand down, sliding over his thigh, touch teasing. Doing that reminded him of all the ways he enjoyed teasing lovers.

Would Raf like being teased? Something about the man screamed at him, begging for a firm hand to deny him exactly what he wanted. He could picture Raf in dangling jewelry and leather. On his knees, put there by no one. Raf would be there because he *wanted it*. Silvan would play the firm hand, but they'd both know...

Silvan gasped as lightning raced through him. Fuck. It hit hard and fast and lust burned in his veins. The mere thought of Raf on his knees almost made him come. And maybe that was what he wanted a few minutes ago, hard and quick, but now, that yearning ache in him wanted to draw it out. It stayed on the floor, like the Raf in his mind, and begged for more.

Raf on his knees. Raf tied up, cursing Silvan's name, every inch of him straining. Pleading.

Silvan opened his eyes and imagined Raf in his lap, using a softly swollen mouth to suck marks into his neck while Silvan grabbed his hair, his hip. That beautiful creature would be bottomed out and sweating, swearing, holding onto the headboard for dear life. And he'd get to be wrapped in that tight heat, watching as Raf fell apart. Then later, after, Silvan would take care of him and hold him close.

That did it. The image of Raf - sweating, moaning, shaking - then bundled up in Silvan's arms tipped him over. It slid over him, curled into him, and sank fangs into his veins. He didn't even have enough warning to yank the sheet out of the way and he didn't *care* because he was floating. The intense heat slowly turned into sated, sticky relief, the kind that lingered and left him a boneless puddle on the bed.

Silvan lay in the dark, listening to the fan and the rain soundtrack he always played for white noise, and he realized he was going to fall back asleep. And be left with a mess in the morning. He cleaned up as fast as he could, washing his hands, leaving his shirt on the floor and yanking shorts back on before tossing the sheet into the bathroom hamper and throwing a quilt from the closet over his bed. He'd worry about the laundry in the morning.

His phone lit up with an email from Raf.

Well, shit.

Apologies for the ridiculous hour, but I know what we're putting in a rotunda for the gallery opening. And then I have an assignment for you related to that. Again, apologies it's so late but this is what happens when inspiration strikes! Please do NOT reply to this, we'll chat about it at work in the AM.

Silvan had to chuckle at the last line. Raf was still worried he was overworking his newest employee, and it was darling. Silvan always liked someone who wanted to watch out for others, who took their duty of care seriously.

That little personality trait was also rather good in his particular brand of bed partners. It made them very obedient.

He read the email again and then realized there was an attachment. Curiosity won out over his sudden tiredness. A few seconds later, he was texting Raf.

From: Silvan I'm awake. Tell me everything.

Chapter Thirteen

A few days later

"This is mad. Right?" Raf looked at Silvan as Arie's crew carried in twenty foot ladders, spools of thick silver wire, and more toolboxes than they'd ever seen outside of a home improvement store.

"No." That was the easiest *no* he'd ever given. Maybe second easiest, after a disastrous at-home dye job by Bonnie when she was thirteen and she'd asked if she should call her mom. They never did tell Becca about the ruined shirt and stains it took him three weeks to scrub out of the shower. Or the emergency hair appointment he took Bonnie to the next day.

Silvan waited for Raf to scoff, a thing he noticed the man did a lot when he was uneasy or nervous. Most people made the noise haughty or contemptuous. For Raf, it was if his breath could expel his nerves. But Raf finally gave him a pointed look, nodded, and then was called away by Arie. Which left him to deal with the artist.

Desiree walked into the gallery on kitten heels as her beehive bobbed. "Holy shit. Look at this place." Her jaunty walk brought her over to Silvan, but she waved to the rest of the people in the room. Not shockingly, Desiree seemed to know everyone and they all were glad to see her. "Silvan! Oh, I'm so excited, I could just puke."

"Good to see you. Hopefully no puking will be involved today."

"Bah, not at all. I'm just funnin'." Desiree craned her neck to look at the wide expanse of the rotunda. "I absolutely am floored I get to do this. Floored. Chuffed, even. My gods." Then she clapped her hands and said, "All right, I've got my people working on the bottom layers. They're the heaviest, course, with all the wire. But that'll weigh the piece properly so we can let the lighter stuff kind..." She wiggled her fingers in the air, razor sharp, deep orange manicure perfectly matched to her hair. "Float. And I'm ready when y'all are, cause this is exciting!"

When Raf said he knew people, he wasn't kidding. After their frenetic two am conversation a few days back, they'd worked nonstop to make Raf's dream a reality. Silvan had thrown everything he had at the project, knowing they were up against time and resources. So that's when he called in the cavalry. Every time he stopped into Steamy Indulgences, he and Desiree chatted about art. And when he'd found out she made floats for the local Pride parades, he knew he'd found the answer to Raf's sad, "I want to do this, but where the hell will I find someone this close to opening?"

The last thing he wanted was for Raf to be denied anything, especially not when this gallery opening was clearly special. Little pieces of Raf had been revealed to him over the last days and weeks, and what Silvan observed was a man who *gave gave gave*. Who never rested or stopped when he had his teeth sunk into a project. Who felt a duty to everyone around him.

And then add in the fact that Raf's friend, Ambrose, and Ambrose's boyfriend were flying in. That Barrett, the boyfriend, didn't know his deceased neighbor's illustrations were the main focus of the gallery opening. And that Raf, with his big heart, wanted to make that experience special. He'd shown Silvan the news article about the firewatch tower sabotage and Ambrose's accident. The sadness on his face that he couldn't be there for his friend nearly ripped Silvan's heart from his chest.

So he was working extra hard. Keeping paperwork off Raf's desk, helping Camilla answer the increasing amount of inquiries about the gallery opening. Shooing away the curious and tourists. Making sure Raf ate, drank water, and went for walks on the boardwalk.

More often than not, Raf asked him to come on those walks. They talked, they laughed, they moaned about the calluses on their hands and how oxfords were not proper footwear for moving artwork around. There had been at least a dozen of those walks, but the most recent one stuck out in his mind. It had been a shift, a small one, but small didn't mean unimportant.

When Raf met him at the gallery's front doors, Silvan was busy taking pictures of the sunlight hitting the Ablaze logo being installed. It was perfect, low-effort, high-engagement social media fodder.

"Do you ever shut off?"

Silvan didn't even have to look Raf's way. "Do you?"

"Touché." Raf chuckled as they began walking to the beach. "And no is the answer. I'm afraid I can't help myself and neither can you."

Silvan had to smile at the flirty tinge to the other man's tone. Raf was always professional, charming, and ever-ready to shift his demeanor based on what crowd he was in, but with Silvan, on these walks, Raf lowered some of his guard. And today, Raf was in an extra-good mood because they'd just finished unpacking boxes of beautifully printed books featuring Perry's illustrations. He understood the significance of those books on a business level, but Raf hadn't talked much about Perry and Barrett outside of the fact that Barrett was his best friend's boyfriend, and Perry had been a good friend of Barrett's.

As they approached the beach boardwalk, Silvan said, "So I'm curious. You've told me a bit about Ambrose and Barrett. I want to know about you and Ambrose."

"Oh really?" That teasing edge never left, but it added to Raf's little eyebrow raise. Gods, the man made that simple expression look devastating. "Well, I told you we met at uni."

"Hmm, yeah, friend of a friend of a roommate or something?"

"Yes. And we met formally on a blind first date."

As Raf told the story of how he and Ambrose were set up by mutual friends on a date that failed spectacularly on every level except a friendly one, they came to their spot. The one they always stood at. Leaning against the railing, watching the waves, talking. Today the wind blew in unseasonably cold and in short, sharp bursts and Silvan let his gaze trail over Raf as he talked. His black hair was curling at the ends, growing longer by the week and flirting with the tops of his shoulders. The man would sweep it aside with a hand decked in rings and then give that sweet grin as if to say, "You watch me and I see it. And I know you're keeping your hands to yourself by the barest margins sometimes."

Silvan tried very hard to not see an invitation in that smile, that particular one that made his heart race and his insides tremble in anticipation.

The wind blew hard just then and Raf shivered; the dark maroon fleece he wore resisted little of the ocean air. So Silvan unwound the scarf from his throat and laid it over Raf's shoulders. He stepped back to let the man tuck it around his throat but Raf caught his hand and pulled him close. "Better finish the job. I don't wear scarves too often. What if I put it on and look a fool, Silvan?" Another smirk and it made Silvan suck in a breath. "Surely you wouldn't let that happen."

They'd been careful. Very, very careful. Little remarks here and there, light teasing. Neither of them sought out heavy physical contact but they didn't avoid each other, either. It was a delicate dance, but a fun one. Silvan had all but forgotten how fun flirting was.

This was something else.

One dark eyebrow went up. "You won't keep a man waiting, will you?"

Carefully, slowly, Silvan pulled up the end of the scarf and made a loose circle around Raf's neck. He would have left it there, but the expectation in Raf's gaze sent a shot of adrenaline through him. Maybe it was bravery, or stupidity. Whatever it was had Silvan plucking up the scarf's loose end and wrapping it the other way around Raf's neck. He straightened the ends, tugging slightly. "Better?"

Raf's eyes had never left his, except to flit down to his mouth as he replied. "Much. Very kind of you, Silvan. I'll be sure to give it back."

"It looks better on you."

"Does it?"

There was no suppressing his smile. "You know it does, Raf."

"Mmm. I'm not entirely sure. You have such an air about you. So refined, so regal but laid-back." Raf reached out and rubbed the lapel of Silvan's peacoat between his fingers. "Every single part of you so perfectly put together. I wonder what it looks like when you get a little messy."

And then Raf was rocking back on his heels with a mischievous grin, leaving Silvan to shake his head. "You're a horrid tease. Don't deny it."

Raf motioned him forward before starting the walk back down the boardwalk. "I would never."

That moment, just two days ago, had played over and over again in Silvan's mind. A reel of teasing, longing, yearning. Watching Raf now, as he and Desiree directed Arie's crew, was like looking at a different person. So in charge, almost domineering, but still smiling and laughing, his cheeks pink with delight as the crew moved around like migrating butterflies.

"He got to you, didn't he?"

Silvan nearly jumped out of his skin as Camilla popped up behind him. "Jesus Christ."

"Sorry." But they were smirking at him, their dark pink lips curled in satisfaction. He liked Camilla a lot, but they were frighteningly silent on their feet. "Shouldn't you say something about not scaring an old man?"

"Age is just a number, and I've never felt nearly the age that it says on my ID."

Camilla laughed and patted him on the shoulder. "You're almost too good for us here, Silvan."

"Almost?"

"Hey, no one's perfect."

Silvan let out a snort, which made them laugh again. "Hey, I've been meaning to ask you. My daughter's in town for a few weeks and she really likes St. Augustine, but I haven't had a chance to take her out anywhere for a nice meal. Raf says you're quite the connoisseur. Any suggestions?"

It was exactly the right question. Soon Camilla had a list of restaurants over to him in a text message, along with links and recommended entrees. "Does she like Thai? Cause if so..." They leaned in, eyes glittering. "I know a place. It's kind of a pop-up and you gotta *know someone.*"

"You're the someone?"

"Damn right." They pointed a yellow-lacquered fingernail at him, mock threat hanging in the air. "Don't spill the beans, Diedrich. I can't lose my eatery clout."

His phone dinged again and soon he had a strange line of numbers and letters, like an auto-generated password, along with a link. "Are you accusing me of not being cool?"

"Not at all. But your daughter's going to think you're the fucking best with what I just sent you. Trust me on this." And with a wave, they bounced away, curls flying as they offered an extra set of hands to one of Arie's crew who was untangling a box of massive parade float petals.

"Haven't you learned to duck when Cam comes over?"

Silvan watched Raf approach, unable to stop from swallowing hard as the man pushed his hair out of his eyes with a graceful hand. "I apparently missed the memo," Silvan managed to say.

"Not very like you." Raf slipped in beside him and passed over one of the gallery's tablets. "Well, your lack of Camilla radar isn't the issue here."

Silvan frowned. "What happened?"

With a mean lean-in that left the scent of cinnamon lingering on the air (*it always lingered around Raf because that's what he always smelled like and it drove Silvan wild*), Raf tapped the tablet screen a few times to bring up the email app. "Nothing but good news, my friend."

Raf's voice was practically a purr of delight in Silvan's ear. It made his insides tremble a little. He read over the email twice before responding. "Holy shit."

"Precisely." Raf pulled back to lean against the wall with a sigh. "Both in the 'holy shit this is incredible' kind of way, and in the terrifying, shit-your-pants sort."

Silvan's mind was already reeling. The email was an invite from a major news station and they wanted to do a big feature on the galleries, the opening, and of course, on Raf. "You've done news pieces before, right?"

"Newspaper and online magazine kind of things. Blogs." Raf's face dropped and now a frown marred his features. "Never major news like this."

"You have to accept."

"You sound so sure."

Silvan shrugged. "This is a *golden* opportunity. Once in a lifetime, maybe."

"Well, fuck." Raf looked so deflated and it made Silvan want to wrap an arm around him for comfort. Instead, he put his hand on Raf's shoulder and when the man didn't pull away, he dared to scoot a little closer. "So we have to do this,
Raf replied quietly.

"Absolutely." He shot Raf a smile he hoped was reassuring, confident. "I can coach you."

"I don't..."

"Raf."

"Apologies, I meant I want you there with me."

"Why?"

That earned Silvan a scoff so abrading, it was like sandpaper on his skin. "You can't seriously ask me that. You're the expert, for one. Two, you're so charming, we'll be lucky if the reporter doesn't faint. Three, again...you're the expert." The look Raf gave him during his little pause sent a flicker of awareness through Silvan. It was like looking an open-ended invite in the eye and begging it to come closer. "And four, I trust you. You're as much a part of this as I am. You got us those photographs from Mika and Sasha. You found those sculpture artists." Raf gave his arm a squeeze. "You've been with me every step of the way these last weeks. I need you there, with me."

So many times in the last several weeks, Silvan had wondered.

How would Raf's lips feel against his?

What would he taste like?

Would he grip Silvan's shoulders or press their hips together?

Would he sigh or moan?

And right now, in front of a dozen people, all Silvan wanted to do was press Raf into the wall and have all those questions answered with a single kiss. The man was a terrible, beautiful distraction, but one who was looking rather vulnerable at the moment.

"Of course I will. Anything."

"Okay." Raf sighed and slumped more, as if the wall could fuse with his spine. "Thank you."

"Were you worried?"

"Never."

While Raf answered the reporter's email and Silvan dashed over to help Desiree and some of Arie's crew, they both missed the door to the gallery opening.

"Dad?"

Surely he was imagining Bonnie's voice echoing through the rotunda. Surely.

"Hey, Dad!"

And then there she was, sunglasses high on her head, olive messenger bag swung around her torso, battered Converse and jeans topped with a thick sweater the color of lilacs. "Bonnie?"

"Hey!" She grinned and started to come toward him, but stopped as she took in all the ladders and coils of wire. "Okay, wow. I...should have probably texted, huh?"

In the kind of bad movie slow motion way, she backed up just as Raf came around the corner, a box balanced in his arms. And there was no way to stop the collision. Bonnie bumped right into Raf, who stumbled. The box crashed to the floor. And Silvan watched as Raf caught his daughter as her feet gave out from under her. He raced over, handing Camilla the tablet as he went. "Are you two okay?"

Bonnie was as red-cheeked as Raf was pale, both of them surprised and embarrassed. "I'm so sorry," she said, her words tumbling out over themselves. "I just saw you were here on that tracker thing and thought I'd surprise you but..."

"Here." Raf got her to her feet and then gave Bonnie a once-over, as if checking for cuts or bruises. "Well, now that's my heart attack for the day."

"I'm so sorry, Raf!"

"No, no, I'm just glad you're all right." Raf's smile wasn't for her at all; it was shot right at him, point-blank range. "Can't be damaging my marketing manager's daughter. Wouldn't want your dad to think I'm irresponsible."

It took a moment for Silvan's mind to catch up with Raf's words, but the shock on Bonnie's face said enough. As did the guilt on Raf's. "Wait, what?" Bonnie asked, looking between them.

Silvan couldn't stop his grimace. "It's a story I was going to tell you later, Bon. Sorry."

And just like her mother would have in a similar situation, Bonnie raised her eyebrows and said, "Must be some story. I think you owe me dinner for that."

In the background, Camilla said, "You've got the deets, Diedrich."

Silvan watched Bonnie's attention divert - at first a little, then completely when she got a look at Camilla - and he heard Raf whisper, "I think you're in trouble, darling."

In more than one way, he thought while Bonnie and Camilla shook hands, Camilla's ear-to-ear grin making Bonnie go pink in the cheeks once more.

Watching Silvan and Bonnie together was *fascinating*. Raf saw the bond, the love, the care. It was hard not to; they clearly got along and were more alike, personality-wise, than either seemed to understand. He was quickly learning about this other side to Silvan - the doting father, the worrywart, the easy sense of humor. Sure, he'd seen flashes of it at work, like the obvious pride on his face when he spoke about Bonnie. But sitting across from them in a tiny booth in a refurbished warehouse over steaming bowls of noodles was an entirely different experience.

It was also intimate in a way he hadn't been expecting. Then again, he hadn't expected the invitation at all. From the way Silvan had grimaced at his slip-up, Raf had figured he was sunk. He'd inadvertently let the proverbial cat out of the bag, but instead of anger or confusion, Bonnie had simply said, "Dad, you should have told me." And on the walk over to the restaurant, Silvan had drawn Raf aside to whisper, "Please don't worry about it. It was my fault for not telling her."

And now he was being peppered with questions from a very smart twenty year old college student whose bright eyes betrayed her enthusiasm.

"So you started Ablaze when you were...thirty?" Bonnie caught some noodles in her chopsticks and slurped them down before continuing. "That's incredible."

Pride coursed through his system. "Ah, well, thank you. The dream, and the word, started before that, but yes. It was right after my thirtieth birthday, in fact."

Silvan shot him a grin. It was a warm, wonderful thing that curled up in Raf's chest in response, so he held tight to that sensation. Those blue eyes knew too much, and at the same time, promised something secretive, enticing. "You celebrated a milestone birthday by opening a business. So what happens at forty?"

Raf groaned. "That is the last thing I wish to think about. Give me some credit, I'm a few years away from that."

"Better start planning. Trip of a lifetime maybe?" Silvan turned to his daughter. "Remember mine, Bon?"

"Dad took me to Scotland," she replied. A waiter dressed in tight jeans and a crop top bustled up to refill their waters and give Silvan a beer he'd ordered. When they left, Bonnie said, "It was really fun. Though I wish you'd done something more for yourself then."

"I did what I wanted to," Silvan countered with a pat to her hand. "I took you with me."

Bonnie rolled her eyes playfully. "I tell everyone I have the best parents but I don't think most people believe me."

"Well, I certainly do," Raf said after another bite. "Just like I believe I owe Camilla a favor for introducing us to this place. It's astounding."

"So...Camilla." Bonnie was biting her lip and toying with the end of her napkin.

Raf tried very hard not to laugh at the way Silvan's eyebrows went up. "Yes?" he replied.

Bonnie was going for subtle and failing hard. So she didn't have her father's smooth charm, but she was young. There was time to learn. "They're uh...a family friend?"

"Family, actually." Raf shrugged. "Blood has never meant much to us. Marianna, my cousin, has been best friends forever with a man named Rhys. Since they were practically babies. And Camilla is Rhys's younger sibling." He sighed, remembering a lot of really wonderful days with the four of them doing whatever the fuck they wanted and getting scolded for coming home late. "Camilla and Rhys are family. Rhys moved to the east coast several years ago, but we see him a few times a year for the holidays. But Camilla decided to stay here after college." He leaned forward, intrigued by Bonnie's interest. "But you really should get the story from them. They talk all the time, I'm sure they'd love a new audience."

To her credit, Bonnie didn't flush this time; simply nodded and slurped down more noodles. But the look Silvan was giving him spoke volumes. Silence fell over the table as they tackled the last bits of their food, only to be interrupted by Raf's phone ringing. He glanced at the screen and frowned when he saw Henry's name. *Not now*, he thought before hitting the silence button and putting the phone in his pocket.

"You okay?" Silvan was now locking that blue gaze on him once more.

"Yes." Raf sighed and poked a chopstick into a limp noodle. "An old flame, kind of. We were never together but I have no desire to speak to him right now."

"Exes aren't fun to deal with. Sorry about that." Silvan's words were kind, as was his expression, and it helped relieve some of the worry in Raf's gut. The last thing he wanted was to have Henry get in the way of this thing blossoming between he and Silvan.

When they finished up, Raf swiped the bill from the waiter over Silvan's protests. "Absolutely not," he said, holding up a finger. "You can fight me later, if you wish." He swore he heard Silvan retort with, "Maybe I'll take you up on that," while Bonnie laughed into her hand.

This man was going to kill him. The way he looked, the way he smelled, his professionalism and intelligence, his wry humor, his obvious deep love for his family...Raf wanted all of it. Every bit of Silvan he could get.

Maybe their little deal was getting in the way of the natural course of things.

Maybe they should try something different. He wondered if Silvan would be amenable to that. And then he wondered if he should dare, just a little, and see what happened.

After dinner, Bonnie had planned to meet up with some friends, leaving Silvan and Raf alone. "Oh, go on," she whispered while Silvan meandered near the entrance to the restaurant. Raf was answering an email from Arie and Silvan didn't want to up and leave him, but also felt, strangely as if he were intruding.

"Go on what?"

"I don't know! Go...walk with him. Go to a bar. Something." Bonnie pinned him down with her trademark stare. "You two are obviously dancing around each other. Just...go."

"I'm not taking *dating advice* from my kid." If he was lucky, a hole would open up in the sidewalk and swallow him. It was one thing to sort out his feelings about Raf on his own; it was another thing entirely to know his kid - his grown daughter, but still his kid - could see what lay between he and Raf. Was it so obvious? Was everyone in their orbit simply watching their awkward swirling about, as if they forgot half the steps to the delicate waltz that was flirting?

Damn.

Silvan shook his head, gave Bonnie a hug, and said, "Okay. Okay. I get it."

When Bonnie darted off with a wave to Raf and a kiss to Silvan's cheek, Raf soon put away his phone and walked back to Silvan. "So. You and I are, once again, alone." There was a playful twist to Raf's lips and that little thing made Silvan *ache*.

"Very astute observation." His teasing hit the mark, from the way Raf's eyes lit up. "I find myself stuck, however."

Raf leaned against the wall, hands in his pockets, looking all the more like a model at a photoshoot. Every detail about him was perfect, from the slightly mussed dark hair to the curious tilt of his chin to the slim fit slacks, sweater, and overcoat. He looked *edible*. "Stuck, how?"

"That strange crossroads between not wanting to go home quite yet, but unsure where to proceed."

Now Raf was giving him a look Silvan could only classify as *expectant*. "Ah, yes. I've been there many times."

"What about now?"

Raf pushed away from the wall and came to stand before him. Silvan had a few inches on Raf, and the way Raf stared up at him made Silvan itch to touch. That molten gaze had gone from expectant to desirous and honestly...was their little deal worth all this torture?

Couldn't they simply try it?

Silvan wanted to take Raf home and *take him apart*. But he'd settle for something softer, sweeter. As long as it promised teeth later.

"Now," Raf said softly, "I'm wanting to be a little bolder than I have. If that might be all right by you."

He was so close.

Too close. Not close enough.

Silvan's entire focus, from his senses to the tingle in his limbs and the heat racing through him, came down to the man in front of him. If he hesitated now, he'd spoil the moment. So instead, with a deep breath, Silvan leaned down, stared Raf right in the eyes, and whispered, "I was hoping you'd say something like that."

Gods, his lips were *right there*. Raf was *right there*. Flashing hazel eyes and a soft mouth and a body arching toward him, as if pulled by an invisible tether. He was compelled, surely, by the spell that Raf wove, to trace the line of that angular jaw with his palm.

That ache under Silvan's skin pulsed with need. He was aware of nothing except for Raf and his smile and the way he smelled. His instincts screamed to *take*, but he needed Raf to acquiesce. To bend.

"This is such a bad idea," Raf whispered. "But I can't...gods, I can't find my footing with you."

"What do you mean?" A stupid question, maybe, since Silvan knew exactly what Raf was saying. He felt off-kilter any time they were close.

There was that little smile again, on the edge of knowing and flirty and something else that beckoned Silvan even closer. "You throw me off," Raf said softly. He turned his face into Silvan's palm, prickling sensitive skin with day-old stubble. "And every single time I think I have my...fucking schoolboy crush under control, you do *something* to make it even worse."

"Should I apologize?" Silvan kept his expression as neutral as possible but Raf was staring at him *hard*.

"Don't you fucking dare." Raf sighed and slowly took Silvan's hand in his own and pulled it away from his face. "But I don't know what to do about this. We made an agreement."

"We did. But agreements can be amended."

Raf snorted. "Better rewrite the damn contract at this point." He reached up and gently pressed his thumb against the corner of Silvan's mouth. "We made that agreement to avoid this little complication." Raf's gaze flicked away. *Hesitation? Regret?* Silvan's heart dropped into his stomach. But Raf looked at him once more and whispered, "Do you remember what you said to me that day? When we made the agreement?"

Silvan had said *a lot* of things that day in the car while they stared at each other and tried to navigate their work and personal relationships. "Which part?"

"*I'm deeply attracted to you. I look at you now and I see someone who feels everything and has to learn to shut most of it off. But when you let the floodgates open....I bet you're magnificent.*" Raf swallowed hard, drawing Silvan's eye to the movement of his throat. It made him want to stroke that skin and feel Raf tremble. "I remembered it. Verbatim. I've thought about it so much since that night." Suddenly Raf was gripping his hand again, tightly now. Then, with a line of urgency threaded through his voice, Raf said, "Do you still feel that way? I have to know."

Silvan blinked. Of course he did. Maybe more so. "What? Yes, of course -"

With a soft groan, Raf leaned up and kissed him.

Chapter Fourteen

Raf expected hesitation. Perhaps even Silvan pulling away to catch his breath or realign some gray matter.

Raf didn't expect Silvan to kiss him back.

Hard.

With fingers curled in his coat lapels, bringing them close. Closer. *So close.*

Silvan used his entire body when he kissed; mouth, hands, legs, oh god *his hips*. Raf could feel the strength, the coiled desire. Silvan's hands shook as he steered Raf back against the wall while his lips explored. A leg slotted between his. A body pressed against his own.

Raf had control of their kiss - their first kiss, god what a horrifically *brilliant*, *beautiful* thing it was - for all of five seconds. Five seconds too long, according to the fine, firm line of Silvan's mouth.

No, he'd lost control the moment Silvan had put himself back together to *take*. Anything, everything he wanted from Raf. Because he knew he'd get it. Willing, eager, ready. Raf felt fingers in his hair, then his attention fritzed, solely focused on the tongue sweetly begging for entrance into his mouth. Permission he readily granted.

He made some kind of needy, deeply undignified noise. But what Silvan heard, he liked, because the kiss grew teeth. Specifically Silvan's teeth in his bottom lip and Raf swore his vision went white.

Silvan's kiss, his touch, promised more. And Raf had never felt his walls crumble so quickly.

"Too much?" Silvan's voice was a rumble that went straight to Raf's cock.

"Gods, no." Raf pulled Silvan forward that last, final, most precious inch and snarled, "More. All of it. *Please*."

He was not supposed to say that. It should have been *yes, but no*, then a gentle disengagement from Silvan's warm hands and delectable lips. A return to some kind of normalcy.

"I'm going mad, aren't I?" Raf laughed. His head felt too light and too full at the same time.

"Who said a little madness was a bad thing?"

Oh, fuck him. Fuck them. And fuck Silvan in particular for that purr in his voice, so knowing, so confident. Fuck him for those eyes that sucked Raf in every single goddamn time. Fuck him for that body and that mind and...

He reclaimed Silvan's mouth and sought to learn it, understand it. Kissing was an art so few mastered but Silvan was the goddamn gold medal triple-axle kisser of them all. And Silvan's kiss was the very revelation Raf hadn't known he needed.

Everything dropped away. All Raf knew was the man to whom he clung.

"I think..." Silvan's murmur against his lips was soft and it made Raf sigh. Finally, Silvan pulled back to carefully eye him with what looked like satisfaction. Raf knew he was probably a mess, flushed and flustered. "I think we should renegotiate."

Raf couldn't agree fast enough. "Do tell." He refused to let go of Silvan as he said it, far too caught up in the little smirk that appeared on those feline features.

"Let's get a drink, talk it over."

"Nothing bad, I hope."

"Not at all." With gentle fingers, Silvan traced the line of Raf's jaw. "I've a thought on something more exciting."

As much as he wanted this - wanted Silvan and everything those finely cut clothes hid - his mind couldn't hold back on his anxieties. "Not to turn this negative but...I'm still your boss."

He got a chuckle for that. "I'm not planning on ravishing you in front of clients."

Oh gods. There was an image. "So professional during work..."

"Yes. Very much so." Silvan eyed him carefully, as if looking for any signs of hesitation. "We're a good team. And there's a gallery opening staring us all in the face."

"Also very true." Raf sighed and let his head thunk back against the wall. "I'm guessing I should hear you out before I let my fears and worries out of the floodgate."

"I'd recommend it." The smirk was back, but with it came Silvan straightening Raf's collar, then brushing the hair off his forehead. The combination of confidence and gentleness - the same thing he'd witnessed with Silvan over and over again - was enough to send a ripple of awareness through him. "I know it feels...dangerous. This thing between us. I would never put you in a spot where what's most important is on the line."

Raf laughed, the sound dry. "Other than my sanity, you mean."

Those long, agile fingers curled around the hinge of his jaw once more, fingertips stroking his skin. "Art isn't sane or insane, mad or not. It's an expression of something deeper, more human, pure and messy at the same time." Silvan leaned in and took Raf's breath away with a soft kiss. "The only other expression like art I can think of is attraction. And like art, physical attraction can be enough. It can be enticing, exciting." Silvan leaned into him and Raf couldn't resist. Couldn't resist running his fingers through salt-and-pepper waves, feeling the silky strands slip over his skin. Silvan hummed in appreciation.

"Is this all we have? The physical attraction?" It hurt to ask, but he had to. He had to know, to hear it once more from Silvan.

"You know that's not all."

"Do I?"

"You tease, but I think you're also wanting some reassurance." Silvan's touch ghosted over the shell of his ear, teasing. Raf refused to groan but some sound must have escaped him, because Silvan then grinned, all teeth. Those same teeth that had claimed Raf's lower lip not moments earlier. "And I can give it. So, how about that drink?"

Did he dare? Did he dare let slip the thing that instantly came to mind the first time Silvan had asked; only now it was reinforced by a jolt of courage that made him feel less like the ground was tilting under his feet. "Not a bar. Too impersonal. But I'm not far from here."

"I'd love to." No hesitation in Silvan's answer, only smoldering delight tempered by a touch to his cheek that left Raf's knees shaking. "But no further physically than we've gone already. I want to be clear about that. Permission and consent aren't far apart, but I'd never take advantage in any form."

Something about the shift in Silvan's tone left Raf's mouth dry. His head buzzed. He really, *really* hoped whatever lay insinuated beneath those words meant something Raf had never allowed himself. He liked a little rough and tumble, to be touched on the edge of *too much*. But that took trust between partners, and he'd only ever given that part of himself over to Henry. Such trust also required a base of vulnerability and if Raf had learned nothing else from his tryst-hopping days, it was that he had never truly felt vulnerable with anyone. Not romantically or physically. The vulnerability he shared with his family, his friends, Ambrose? That was on some higher plane, where he knew he could talk and laugh and cry and confess and he wouldn't be judged.

The kind of vulnerability needed for rougher, darker things was too fragile. As easy to shatter as a toppled glass; and even with Henry, he hadn't felt fully *available*. He'd always held back. And yet, Henry hadn't been the kind to do more than bind his wrists in silk and tease him.

Something about Silvan made Raf wonder if he could find that trust, and that vulnerability, with him.

"Understood," Raf said softly, letting his hands drop away. Silvan immediately got the hint and stepped back, leaving Raf to suck in a deep breath. "Shall we?"

Silvan wasn't sure what to expect from Raf's abode. The man's wardrobe twisted and turned as much as his chameleon ability to adapt to any situation. He imagined sleek furniture and stylish colors. Polished chrome or sparkling granite, maybe. And from the outside, the condo was precisely the kind of place that seemed to beg for such an interior. Raf's home had an artistically sloped roof, long on one end and short on the other, meaning there was likely a loft space overhanging an open-air first floor. The garage was easy to drive directly into from the short driveway off the quiet suburban road, and exterior stairs led to a bright red front door. It was a nice contrast to the pristine white siding and black roof. The small yard was mostly open, but he saw the rise of a few birch trees over the line of the roof. And window boxes exploding with the dark purples, oranges, and yellows of autumn mums made him smile.

Silvan parked on the right side of the driveway while Raf was exiting his car, and when he popped open his door, Raf gave him one of those heart-stopping smiles. The kind that always hit Silvan right in the chest. He paused, looking up at Raf's home. "Your place is incredible."

Raf ducked his head. "You haven't even been inside. What if I'm a slob?"

"Impossible."

That got him a chuckle. "I've had my days."

And with that Raf motioned him inside the garage and they took the few steps up to a door. Keys jangled as Raf unlocked it. Being this close after the kisses they'd shared made Silvan's senses spike with awareness and it made him *want* all over again.

"Hold on, let me..." Raf flicked on the lights. "Apologies it's a little scattered in here, I haven't had much energy after work."

But Silvan didn't see clutter or a mess. He saw lush velvets, deep, bold colors, and elegant decadence. Instantly he realized his mistake; Raf might be a chameleon in public, but at home, he had a different side. Something playful but sharp, refined with a touch of whimsy and almost gothic infusion. As Raf motioned him forward, Silvan's gaze flitted from the emerald green velvet couch to the tasseled throws, the neatly arranged, packed bookshelves dotted with candles and crystals. The far wall was done up in elegant smoke-colored wallpaper that was likely hand painted, each soft-petaled flower on it glinting in the overhead light. And the other walls were painted a soothing slate gray and covered in framed art. Silvan wanted to run his fingers over every bit of fabric and shining little knickknack.

He curbed his impulse by joining Raf in the kitchen as the other man turned and said, "Wine? Or the bar is stocked, if you prefer something else."

"Wine is more than good." Silvan didn't want to get too close, lest he crowd and make Raf uncomfortable. "Can I help?"

But Raf already had a bottle of red in hand and was digging in a drawer. "You can settle wherever you like and let me bring you a glass of wine." Those hazel eyes raked over him and Silvan saw appreciation - and a fair bit of desire - there. "I'll be just a moment."

Silvan left Raf's side and drifted into the rest of the open space of the main room. He let his hand float over the back of the couch as he wandered to the bookshelves, his curiosity begging to be fed. It was easy to spot some bestsellers, far up on the right, as if they had been read and filed away, no need to be within easy reach. The shelves at eye-level, however, were full of well-thumbed classics. Not the pretentious ones, but the writers with poetry and art and fire in their veins. Marlowe, Baldwin, Shaw, Camus, Shelley, Hurston. Even Rochester and Crowley, as *scandalous* as they might be; but they sat beside Jackson and Wilde, Vonnegut and Morrison, Rovelli, Sagan, Le Guin, Plath, and so many more. Their titles were not pristine, but dog-eared, ragged even in some cases. Their covers faded or even unstylish, corners with bites out of them and pages ranging in color from hardback white to clearance bin yellow.

"I'm partial to the classics," Raf said, appearing at his side with two glasses of deep red wine in hand. "And I hope merlot is all right."

"It's perfect." Silvan accepted the glass gratefully, letting his mind file away the little flush high on Raf's sun kissed cheeks. "Somehow both the Rochester and Sagan don't surprise me."

Raf lead him a few feet away to a pair of blue-green armchairs facing the bookshelves. "My mother used to read me Carl Sagan. Not only Sagan, mind you. I got plenty of age-appropriate stories, too. But she's always been a firm believer in appreciating the natural world. Sagan's one of her favorites."

"I think your mother has excellent taste," Silvan replied as he leaned back. "And that I may never leave this chair. I might be trying to figure out how to steal it from you when I leave."

That got Raf laughing over the rim of his glass. "Does it count as stealing if the person knows you're stealing it?"

"Not a lawyer, I'm afraid."

"No, and thank goodness for that." When Silvan gave him an inquiring look, Raf shrugged. "I prefer knowing you this way. As marvelous as you must look in five thousand dollar suits."

"I have a good suit at home. Not in that price range, but over four figures." Silvan let himself slouch a little, then with a calculated shift, let his legs fall open. "I get quite a few compliments when I wear it." He swore he heard the audible *click* of Raf's throat. Teasing him was far too fun.

But still Raf surprised him. What Silvan figured would be a coy look followed by a gentle side-stepping was...not. Raf stared him down hard but his posture was relaxed. Calm. Collected. They were on his turf, after all. If Raf couldn't fully be himself here, then where? "Wear it to the gallery opening and let me be the judge of this suit."

Silvan sipped his wine, let the comment hang in the air between them for a moment. "And speaking of the gallery opening, perhaps we should talk about this idea I had."

"To business, then."

"No, Raf. This is strictly pleasure." Other than a slight widening of the eyes, Raf betrayed nothing and that excited Silvan to his core. Now he needed to be willing to voice aloud what he'd been mulling over since they'd talked after Judy's brunch.

Since he'd gotten off thinking about Raf's eyes and hands and that lean runner's body.

"We agreed to hold back and at the night of the gallery opening, we'd figure out where the other man stood."

The sip of wine Raf took left his bottom lip stained and Silvan wanted to lick it off. Christ, he had it bad. But if Raf noticed him staring, it didn't keep him from saying, "Right. But tonight..." He shoved a hand into his hair, mussing what was now turning into loose curls. "Gods, where did you come from?"

"Is this the part where I make a Dad joke about being from Dexter?"

"Oh lord help me." But Raf was smiling.

Silvan chuckled. "Tonight wasn't planned. But you..." He sipped his wine again, trying to reorganize his tangled thoughts. "You delight me in the strangest, most wonderful ways, Raf." With liquid grace, the kind that he'd had since his ballet days, Silvan set aside his wine and got to his feet, only to drop to his knees before Raf. He didn't touch the other man but he *wanted to.* Raf's eyes had blown open wide in shock and he opened his mouth, but Silvan said, "Just wait. Please."

He stared up at Raf and saw art, living and breathing and looking at him like he needed to be cared for. Silvan could think of a dozen things to do to this man while never leaving their spots, and he was certain each one would leave Raf begging. "You and I are unexpected. Delightfully so. But I want more." He raised himself up and leaned forward, hands on the arms of Raf's chair. A byproduct of that movement was Raf opening space between his legs, into which Silvan slipped easily. "A new agreement. So we don't lose focus on the opening, but we don't drive each other to distraction because we can't touch."

And he let his hand hover over Raf's thigh.

"You said just talking." He hadn't touched Raf and yet the man looked wild.

"I said no further than what we'd already gone. And admittedly, we touched quite a bit back outside the restaurant." Silvan smirked. "Just didn't want you to think I put out so easily."

Raf's hand was there, on his, pushing it down until he had a firm thigh under his palm. Something in the other man seemed to settle under Silvan's touch and oh the possibilities that opened up. Silvan felt a tingle of anticipation ripple through him. "So you're saying you *used to* put out easily."

"I gave it the old college try every now and then."

"You're funny."

"I know." Daring, he slid his hand a little higher and watched Raf's eyes flash. "And since I don't put out that easily, I thought we'd find another middle ground. It's only a few weeks to the opening. We should wait until then." And to hammer the point home, Silvan guided Raf's other hand to his face. Raf immediately took the cue, letting his fingers skate over Silvan's jaw. He wanted this moment to have impact; a boulder of desire and recognition through their orderly worlds. That's what Raf was for him. "When was the last time the thought of physical intimacy made you shiver? Where the mere thought of what you were *waiting* to experience was almost as exciting as that thing itself?"

Surprised delight danced over Raf's face and he leaned in more. His scent, rich cinnamon and plummy wine, made Silvan sigh a little. "You are...dangerous, Mr. Diedrich. And you came up with that idea rather quickly. I'm tempted to wonder if you weren't thinking of that all along."

"It wasn't fully realized until we kissed but I've had a crumb of it in my mind for a while. Then the thought of waiting to touch you again wouldn't do."

Raf's fingers slid into the hair behind Silvan's ear. Against his own will, Silvan's eyes drifted shut, his lips parting. "And I take it *older and wiser* isn't part of the game here."

"I'd say *more experienced* in certain realms." Again, Silvan's hand slid higher. Raf bit his lip but it didn't fully stifle his groan. "I'm not usually the one on my knees."

"Oh *gods*." Before him, a picture of debauched beauty, Raf was begging to be tasted. Every inch of his body ached but Silvan needed permission. He wouldn't take until Raf was fully willing to give, and fully understood what Silvan could offer him. He stilled his hand on Raf's hip, even as the edge of Raf's sweater rose up. Silvan knew one little push would give him access. Raf took a moment to collect himself before saying "So we...wait to sleep together? That's what you're proposing."

"It's more than that. It lets us not avoid each other like a single touch might kill one of us."

"A comic book reference? Didn't take you for a nerd, Diedrich." But the quip didn't have its usual spice; likely because Raf was doing everything he could to keep from squirming under Silvan's hands. "And then that night, we decide if we want to keep going..."

"Exactly. We're not so pent up that we lose focus. We can keep doing this..." Silvan rubbed his cheek against Raf's smooth palm, wanting to purr in satisfaction at that simple touch. "And our patience is rewarded. If we want to go that route."

"And if not?"

"I think the original agreement ought to stand. If something changes for one or both of us, then we either remain colleagues or part as friends."

"A little difficult now, since we've kissed." Raf looked away, his mouth turning down. "At least it would be for me. You are..."

When the rest of the sentence didn't come, Silvan gently turned Raf's face back so they could look at each other. "I know. I feel like that with you, too. And there are things I want to share with you, show you, that I can only do if we're feeling this way by the gallery opening. I can promise you so many things, Raf." His fingertips found the hinge of Raf's jaw and the other man gave a pleased sigh. "And we can talk about that if this works out between us."

Raf's laugh was a little watery. "I think *if* left the realm of possibility a while ago. Fled to some remote part of my psyche." Slowly and with care, he let his hand drop from Silvan's face. "And if it's consent you're looking for, you have it. Unabashedly."

"Good. Thank you."

"You say that now. Wait until I shove you into the janitor's closet for an impromptu make out session."

Silvan leaned in, paused to read Raf's expression, then brushed his lips over Raf's. "I look forward to it."

"I didn't know you had a fondness for the scent of cleaning agents."

That earned Raf a gentle push so his back hit the chair and Silvan could take up space before him. Not climbing into his lap but close to it; perched on his knees and leaning against Raf's while Silvan put his hands on the armrests. He stared at Raf's slightly parted lips and flashing hazel eyes. "You don't have to deflect with me, Raf. *Raphael*. Never with me. I like your humor, your spark. Everything. All of it. But you don't have to be that chameleon around me. I hope you'll come to understand that. That I can earn your trust."

Raf's breath left him in a gust and then he was surging forward, mouth hot and eager on Silvan's. There was a whisper of the kiss they'd shared outside the restaurant, but Silvan could feel Raf practically vibrating under him. So Silvan kissed him hard, his tongue claiming Raf's, his teeth sharp once more in that lower lip. Raf's moan was the finest song and Silvan had to press himself against the chair's seat even more to keep his erection at bay. Hard to do when Raf's mouth was a delight and he kissed like a man who knew exactly what he enjoyed.

When Raf gasped and pulled away, Silvan sat back on his haunches and watched. He watched Raf run a trembling hand through his hair and put fingertips to his mouth. He watched Raf's chest heave as he fought for air. Then Silvan's gaze caught on Raf's and he found himself grinning, a twin expression to the one on the other man's face.

"You're going to ruin me," Raf whispered.

Silvan let his hands drift up Raf's thighs once more. "In due time."

Chapter Fifteen

"Holy shit."

"You can't tell my mother."

"Holy *shit*, Raf." Her tone sounded shocked, but Marianna's grin was wide and toothy. She looked fucking *delighted* at his confession, whispered underneath a bright orange patio umbrella while his mother was out of earshot. Not perhaps the most ideal time to mention he'd kissed Silvan - and more than once - but outside of Ambrose and Barrett, no one knew. And some part of him wanted to keep this thing between them secret, safe. And the other part wanted to scream it to the heavens, holding a stereo over his head while sappy songs played.

He shook his head and whispered, "You said the same thing when I first ran into Silvan. In your bar. And would you lower your voice?"

Marianna leaned in, blunt cut bob and dangling pearl earrings swinging. But she replied in a throaty whisper, "Okay fine. But Raf! Hell yeah, good for you."

He couldn't help but flush. It had been one very long Saturday since Silvan had left his house. The other man hadn't pushed or pressed for anything more and had left soon after completely wrecking Raf's nerves and self-control.

But, to his surprise - given what he knew of Silvan's endless patience - Silvan had taken initiative as Raf walked him to the door.

"I hope you don't mind," Silvan murmured as they said goodbye at Raf's front door. When Raf turned, a question on his lips, Silvan was there; staring down at him, hands gripping Raf's waist.

"Not at all." The smirk was hopefully making him look more confident than he felt. "A kiss goodbye, then? We've both got busy weekends with family."

"That's why I asked." Silvan guided Raf until his back hit his own front door.

He would NOT sound breathless. He wouldn't. "You seem to have a thing with me pressed up against hard surfaces. This is three times tonight, if you count that chair."

Silvan's breath ghosted over his ear. "I do. Count every time, that is. Because every time I count brings me closer to confessing what I want to do to you."

He would not groan.

Raf lost that battle a moment later, though the sound was more whimper than anything else. Silvan's body was the most delightful cage in which to be trapped. Raf felt alive, like he was soaring. "You can't say things like that," he sniped, only half meaning the vitriol. It was a defense mechanism.

Silvan's lips grazed the sensitive point of his pulse. Raf's hips twitched up, seeking. "Why not?"

Oh fuck. "Because you may be patient -"

"I assure you, for some things I am not."

He made some kind of strangled noise that sounded completely unsexy but Silvan didn't seem to care. He kept planting soft kisses along Raf's neck, turning him into putty. "All well and good but you are currently making me want to..."

There was a tongue now running along his neck and Raf thought he might black out from the sheer jolt of pleasure shocking his system. "Want to what?"

Whatever game Silvan was playing, it was doing a fine job of twisting Raf up inside. And he was enjoying every second of it. "You're teasing me," he gasped, unable to blurt out anything else. His cock was doing all the thinking for him at the present and bless Silvan for not moving away, but pressing more into him.

That comment made Silvan pull back and give him a steady stare, those baby blues unwavering. "Hmmm, actually I'm not. Teasing would be wearing my tightest pants to work and bending over at opportune times." With gentle fingers, he pushed Raf's hair off his forehead, twirling a lock of it around his finger before continuing. "I never did get an answer. Want to what, Raf?"

A thousand images flashed before him, many involving them intertwined, sweating, panting. And several of those had Raf naked and at Silvan's mercy and...well, wasn't that a thought. "It's two things, actually. Possibly opposed." When Silvan arched an eyebrow, he continued. "One involves me pushing you until you break." He tried for haughty but doubted he was pulling it off; not as horny as he was right now. "Something slightly scandalous. You under my desk."

The only sign of Silvan's approval was the flare of his nostrils and the hand in his hair tensing. "And the second one?"

"I'm the one under the desk."

Silvan fell into him, groaning, their hips colliding almost painfully. Silvan's erection pressed into the cut of Raf's hip and he thrust back blindly, chasing pleasure. He wanted Silvan to tear him apart and then piece him together. "You realize your little fantasy involves me being the one to break first." Then there were teeth in his earlobe and Raf arched, gasping, as he grabbed any part of Silvan he could. "We're going to have a little talk later, Raf. About boundaries and consent and how good I think you would look in satin. But for now..."

His grip on Raf's chin was gentle, but there was a command in Silvan's eyes he couldn't ignore. "So at work...like normal colleagues and all that?"

"I think that's a good idea. No need to have rumors flying around." Raf resisted the urge to rub his jaw into Silvan's hand. "But I won't say hands off all the time."

The smugness in Silvan's smile - as if he knew how he made Raf feel - was evident. "So, subtle."

"Yes." His knees were starting to give out, so badly did he want to prostrate himself before Silvan.

"Subtle is something I'm rather good at," Raf replied, voice tight with need.

Silvan's voice was sultry, silky in his ear. "I've noticed."

And then Silvan pushed away, tugging at his shirt collar and swiping his hair back from his face. It would have been fussy save for the satisfied smile he wore. Raf, meanwhile, knew he was a sweating, shivering wreck, flattened against his own front door for anyone to see if they passed by. Thank fuck he lived on the outskirts of town. Later, he would think of a dozen smartass things to say but what he managed was, "Make sure the satin matches my eyes."

Silvan paused, then threw back his head and laughed. "You are wonderful." This kiss was softer, sweeter than the one before, and left Raf clutching helplessly at Silvan's shirt. After Silvan left, Raf looked down at his palms and swore he saw the imprint of coat buttons denting his flesh.

"You'd better go." Raf didn't want him to, but at the same time Silvan had been right. Already the anticipation was sweeter than immediate satisfaction. It left him giddy.

"Good night, Raf."

"Good night."

"I'm still probably breaking like ten employment laws," Raf said with a glare.

Marianna shrugged. "I don't think Silvan would sue."

"Comforting!"

"Do you regret it?"

Raf paused, gaze going distant until Marianna was a blur in his periphery. His mother's little garden paradise had long been drained of summer color, but a few stubborn flowers clung to the warm afternoons. He'd been so busy with the galleries of late that he'd missed seeing the morning glories bloom; mostly because he hadn't been making coffee dates with his mom a priority. Francia hadn't minded, and he knew she meant every word even when his own excuses rang hollow in his ears.

Something like that hollowness settled in his chest now as he stared at the shriveled remains of morning glory vines. "No. Not at all. Actually, I'm privy to a bit of Silvan's personal life and he makes the whole hot single dad thing look easy. Like he's got it all figured out. I admire him, honestly."

Marianna took all of that in, inhaled, and then said, "And you want to get in his pants."

"Oh my god, Mar."

While his cousin cackled in the background, Raf got to his feet and went into the house. "Hey, Mom. Need a hand?" After a few seconds, he spotted Francia coming down the hall. "You okay?"

"Yes, yes. It's that damn toilet, sometimes it runs and runs and you gotta fiddle with it." She wiggled her fingers at him. "What was your cousin laughing about?"

He fought not to fidget. "Per usual, taking the piss. Doesn't matter. Do you want me to call a plumber?"

Francia batted at him as she passed. "No need."

"Mom."

"I'm serious, Raf. It's just a toilet."

He followed after her. "Yes, that could fracture or rupture or...whatever busted toilets do and then you've got toilet water trickling down the hall."

"Ooo, great band name." Camilla was suddenly at his elbow and Raf barely held back a startled noise.

"Jesus Christ, Cam." He put a hand on his chest. "And what's a great band name?"

"Toilet Water."

"Eugh."

His mother laughed. "Okay you two, outside. Shoo."

"You'd think we were dogs," Camilla muttered as they obeyed.

"I heard that, young one!"

When the four of them were settled outside with coffee and cake, Raf turned to his mother. "Are you busy this afternoon? I was wanting to go antiquing for some pieces for the opening. We haven't done that in forever."

Francia brightened. "Oh honey, I'd love to."

"Wonderful! I can help you clean up."

"But," his mother continued, "I've already got plans today. What about next weekend? Can you get away?"

Raf hid his disappointment by pulling out his phone to check the calendar. He needed to be at the gallery to receive the final exhibit shipments for the opening but St. Augustine had several funky little secondhand stores along with at least two proper antique shops.

After he and Francia made plans for the following Sunday, Camilla plopped down beside him and immediately - somehow, magically - folded their legs up in the chair. Learning forward, they said, "So. Antiquing. Still want to go today?"

Truth be told, Raf did. He was restless, itchy after his Friday night with Silvan. A part of him left on tenterhooks, just waiting. The other part of him intellectually understood that this tension, this push and pull, was part of their little dance now. They both felt comfortable enough to trust each other that much. And Raf was getting to see the control Silvan wielded wasn't just for work; everything about the man changed when they'd kissed. Gone was the flirty coyness, the verbal sparring. In its place was a man rippling with exactness. Commanding, commandeering.

Silvan had caught Raf in his trap and Raf had never been so happy to struggle, even if some of the struggling was just for show.

"Yes, absolutely."

"Sweet!" Once they said their goodbyes, Camilla trailed after Raf to his car. "You're driving, right? Your car's nicer."

He gave Camilla's utility truck a glance. "What's wrong with your truck?"

They shrugged. "I just like the way your car sounds. Sexy and shit."

He burst out laughing. "And since when do you go antiquing?"

Another shrug, but Raf saw Camilla curl inward a little at the end. It was strange seeing them suddenly self-conscious. "I need to switch things up at my place. I'm learning to lean into my goth, witchy side."

"And nothing says witch like hobnail milk glass."

"Don't underestimate my aesthetic." They paused to buckle their seatbelt. "And Milk Glass is almost as good of a band name as Toilet Water."

"Remind me again why I agreed to this?" But Raf had to smile at the way Camilla laughed, sounding a lot like Marianna.

The first two shops they visited were a complete bust. Raf was looking for anything that spoke to him for their after-hours show: carnival glass, antlers and bone, old frames, strange pottery. But while he dug and dug for hidden gems with no luck, somehow Camilla had managed to buy several pieces of clothing and walk out with a jaunty beret on their head.

"What?" they asked as the two of them walked across the street.

"I'm starting to wonder if you're magic," Raf replied lightly, tapping the beret. "I should take you antiquing more often."

"You should. Mar always says I'm some kind of good luck charm. And here, for you." From the big tote bag over their shoulder, Camilla pulled out a wrapped bundle and handed it over. "Thought it might go with what you were looking for in props for the Night Garden show."

They paused outside a dark storefront so Raf could unwrap it. Inside was a beautiful square terrarium capturing a butterfly in flight over a few small crystals bedecked in moss. Between the rocks lay a perfectly preserved dark red rose. "Kinda thought it was the vibe you were going for," Camilla explained as they pressed their back into the store window. "I think the owner thought it was junk but you can see someone made that by hand. I've tried to make something like it before but it fucking sucked and I didn't have the patience."

Raf nudged Camilla with his arm until they moved closer; close enough that he could wrap his arm around their thin shoulders. "You are, despite being a giant pain in my ass, bloody brilliant."

Camilla grinned. They'd painted their lips a dark plum today and Raf had long ago spotted the champagne highlighter along their cheekbones. Somehow this sprite of a human being, someone he'd watched grow up, still held on to a childlike wonder and energy. And in his experience, once Camilla was in your orbit, it was hard not to get swept up. He returned the grin. "Did you get anything for your new friend?"

"What?" But he caught the way their eyes widened in surprise.

"You don't fool me, Cam."

"I refuse to answer your question on the grounds of privacy."

"For you or her?"

Grumbling, they leaned into him. "And just when I think you should be too preoccupied, you still manage to see everything."

"Ha, no. Not everything. But considering your new friend is the daughter of my marketing manager..."

Camilla waggled their eyebrows. "Just your marketing manager? So that tension we all see is just an act?"

"Shut up." Raf ruffled the curls near their shoulder and they both pushed off the window. "Ready for more?"

Bonnie plopped on the couch beside Silvan. "So."

He gave her a sidelong glance. "Well, I'll give you credit. You waited longer than I thought you would."

She pointed her finger at him. "You made your choice, Dad."

"I did."

Bonnie frowned. "What, no objections? No 'Well, in fairness' deflection?"

He shrugged. "You're an adult. You make your choices, I make mine. And I will always put you first." He grabbed at her finger and wiggled it, making her laugh. "So ask."

That seemed to bring her up short. She turned on the sofa until her back was against the armrest and she could pull her knees up to her chest. Silvan could practically see the gears turning as his kid figured out how to approach his tangled little web of half-truths. He just hoped she wasn't hurt by his reluctance to tell her about being laid off. Everyone praised the way he didn't hold back from tough conversations with his child, but the older he got, the more he wondered if he'd been too forthcoming. Wasn't part of being a parent shielding your child from both ugly truths and inconveniences?

But it was too late to change all that now. And what mattered was that Bonnie was happy, healthy, and not completely pissed at him. The last part of that was self-serving but he'd seen Bonnie angry. More than angry; hurt, betrayed, confused. He'd been there during the tough teenage years when she was bullied for being *different*, for not conforming. His kid had never been a conformer and Silvan was quietly proud that she'd found her own way early on. But that didn't mean it had been easy.

So to look at her now and remember what had been, dredged up a sudden tightness in his chest. Silvan took up a spot against the other armrest and said, “I’m serious, Bon. Ask.

She blew out a hard breath. “Okay, okay. So what the hell happened at Longbeach?”

He told her the whole story, pausing only after he mentioned going to The Lash & Rose the night he’d been let go. “I met Raf there, which you knew,” he said, watching her expression shift into something calculated. “And uh…”

“You flirted with him.”

“Blunt. But yes.”

“So how do you go from flirting to getting a job?”

The urge to twist his family ring around his finger was strong. He always fussed with it when he was unsure of what to say. “Dumb luck? Honestly, I saw pretty quickly that Raf was doing something unique, something interesting, with his galleries. And I kind of knew who he was, or at least had heard of Ablaze. But when we were doing the interview, he had all these ideas. Brilliant things, really. And we simply…clicked.” Silvan glanced away, the tightness in his chest returning. “I’m sorry I didn’t tell you earlier. Some part of me thought I was protecting you from all that. I didn’t want you to worry about having your tuition paid. I know it was selfish, but you have enough going on.”

“Dad.” Bonnie practically launched herself at him. Her hug was warm and firm and it made him swallow hard even as he pressed his cheek into the top of her head. “You are the best. And also the worst sometimes. But you don’t have to protect me, okay?” She pulled back, eyes bright. “Hold on. I want to show you something.” When Bonnie came back from her room, she had a legal-sized envelope in hand, which she passed to him before sitting back down. As he pulled out the papers inside, she explained, “I applied for this work-study program. I really didn’t think I’d have a chance, but my advisor wrote a great recommendation letter and I was so nervous when I had to do this big presentation for the judges. But I *got in*, Dad!”

“Bon, holy shit.” Silvan skimmed the papers while reaching out for her hand. “This is incredible!”

She flushed, clearly pleased. “I didn’t want to say anything in case it didn’t work out but yeah. It’s going to be so great.”

His eyes caught on a few words at the bottom of one of the pages, where she had signed her consent to travel on behalf of the university. “Wait, this is in Ireland?”

“Yeah. The community we'll be working with wanted to start planning and the 'work' part of the program involves helping to build out community resources. I'll actually be ahead of the others in my degree program, since this is hands-on with actual engineers and city planners."

Silvan's mind reeled. He was immensely proud of her. He was also a little worried, but her traveling wasn't unusual. Every summer Bonnie and her friends would take off on road trips or fly to meet up with other friends in Canada or England. But now she'd be on her own, and not just across the country. The program she'd been accepted into was months long and over the holidays. He could feel himself frowning and immediately wiped the expression away. This wasn't about him at all. "You are...Jesus, Bon. I'm so, so proud of you."

He watched her eyes shimmer before she blinked away tears. "Thanks, Dad. I know I won't be here for Christmas but I couldn't say no to this. And I just found out about getting in and I wanted to surprise you-"

He held up a hand. "You don't have to explain, kid. It would be insane to not take the spot. You deserve this. You've worked so hard. I've seen it. Your mom has seen it." Silvan handed the envelope back to her. "Does she know?"

Bonnie shook her head. "I was going to tell her and Shaleena tomorrow when we go out for breakfast. You know how Mom likes to make a fuss."

"Better be prepared."

"I'm battening down the hatches now, promise."

Silvan returned her tight, warm hug and felt Bonnie sigh. "I'm so, so proud of you," he whispered. "I'm going to miss you like hell."

"I haven't trained you, with being across the country in one of the world's most rigorous programs?"

"Nope."

Bonnie scrunched her nose at him. "Guess we'll have to make sure we use the next weeks really well."

"Any time I have is yours."

That got him a grin. "Even with your hot boss demanding so much of you?"

"Ugh, Bon."

"You said you'd tell me everything!"

"You don't want to hear about your Dad's love life, do you?"

He knew he'd made a mistake when she lit up. "I knew it! I knew it when Raf drove you home and you two were looking at each other like it was a first date." Silvan let his head thunk back against the couch while she laughed, delighted. “But what about the whole employee-boss thing?”

Silvan looked anywhere but at her. Focusing on the nubby fabric of the couch was a good distraction. “We’re uh....figuring that out.” He remembered the way Raf had felt under his hands, his body as they were pressed against his front door.

His scent, the silk of his hair. The parting shot Raf had made, asking for satin that matched his eyes.

“We’re figuring it out,” he repeated.

Chapter Sixteen

Raf had expected tension in the air when he came into the gallery on Monday morning. As usual, Silvan was already there; somehow the man managed to beat him to work almost every day. He expected a sly look or a hasty, whispered promise as they passed by each other.

But when he walked in, tray of coffees from Steamy Indulgences in hand, Silvan was flipping through a stack of posters spread out over a table near the front desk. Raf did get a bright smile, the kind that made him suck in a deep breath. But whatever he had expected or anticipated was tucked away.

They had work to do, after all.

Relief coursed through him. Maybe they *could* do this. Work side by side even with their personal lives and attractions tangling together more and more by the day. "Mondays call for special coffee," he said as he walked up to Silvan. "What's all this?"

"Ideas. A lot of them." Silvan pulled out two posters, both for old gallery shows from the Tangine location. One was for a limited-time show as part of the city's summer festival, so the art had been all created using natural materials. Raf had never seen so many beautiful, strange sculptures made out of wheat, pebbles, dried lavender, and more. The other poster was for a masquerade fundraiser from Halloween two years ago. It was easily one of the best events they'd ever done, and they still got requests to do another. But it was a huge undertaking and had nearly wiped out the staff. "And look here."

Out came another set of posters. And another. "Oh," Raf said, leaning forward to pull the masquerade poster closer. "You're making a point."

Something flickered over Silvan's face. The only word Raf could come up with was *approval*. "I very much am. Look at how juxtaposed all these events are. You work in themes and foils, Raf, and I don't think it was done on purpose."

"Not at all." He sipped at his coffee and winced when the too-hot liquid splashed over his tongue. "Ouch."

"Coffee too hot?"

"Unfortunately. Best set it aside for now."

Silvan gently took the coffee from Raf and put his other hand on Raf's shoulder. "I'm sorry for not saying so when you walked in. I got absorbed in all this." The hand on his shoulder slid down, gliding over his bicep, then his forearm before Silvan continued. "But you always look better than the last time I saw you and I wanted you to know that. How attractive you are to me."

There was nothing about Silvan's touch that didn't scream longing, but Raf knew instantly the other man was assuring they had an out should someone see them like this. "Just a bit of lint" or "We thought he spilled coffee on his beautiful sweater". Innocent, simple things that could be brushed aside. It was smart and kind and way too canny all at the same time.

It was also subtle as hell.

"Is this subtle enough?" Silvan's tone was teasing but Raf saw concern in his eyes. Silvan wanted to get this right, too.

"Perfect." Daring, Raf ran his palm down Silvan's back, following the hard knobs of his spine. "Thank you."

"Of course."

And then they were back to the posters and trying to sip on scalding coffee. It's where they were thirty minutes later when Camilla bounced in wearing a bright yellow miniskirt, dark blue sweater, and chunky platform boots. Their hair was tied up high in a knot on their head, but a few curls sprang out around their face. "Oooo, what are you two doing?"

The wink Camilla gave Raf made him snort. "Behave, you."

"Never." They grabbed a coffee and slid behind their desk. "Oh, Raf, I found antlers and cool skulls for the tables for the Night Garden show!" Immediately they shoved their phone in Raf's face and started scrolling through pictures. "Dude's name is Jian and he's a licensed taxidermist."

Silvan looked like he wanted to palm his own forehead. "A taxidermist. Shit. I didn't even think of that."

Without missing a beat, Camilla pinned Raf with a pointed stare. "I need a raise, boss."

"On your yearly review," Raf fired back.

"That's in like...four months!"

"Calendars, those sneaky little bitches. Always keeping track of time."

"Anyways," Camilla said, breezing on like Raf hadn't been a smartass. "He can drop stuff off this Sunday morning. Then he's not available for a few more weeks."

Raf shook his head while Silvan said, "That seems too close to the shows."

"It is. We could fudge it some, given 'Night Garden' doesn't open until after 'The Science of Art'." Raf turned to Camilla. "Confirm this Sunday morning and I'll make it work."

As Camilla got on the phone, Silvan motioned Raf back to the other table and their stacks of posters. "I can be here Sunday morning," Silvan said, fingers idly tapping the masquerade poster. "If that's all right."

Raf shrugged. "You're sweet, but I already am meeting my mother here to handle the afternoon drop-off of the last exhibits for the opening. I'll just get some work done."

"Or you could enjoy your Sunday morning without having to worry," Silvan replied. Something *snapped* in his voice, some quiet command that sent a thrill down Raf's spine.

But he wasn't one to bend quite so easily. "Or you could enjoy your Sunday morning, maybe with your daughter, and let your boss work in peace."

He moved barely an inch, but Raf felt the vibration of Silvan's voice in his ear. "Is that what you truly want, Raf?"

That made Raf's throat go tight. Maybe he should take Silvan's suggestion. "No," he finally said in a rush of breath. "Honestly, having a Sunday morning to myself sounds like a week's vacation in Tahiti."

That fierce expression melted. "I thought that might be the case."

With a glance back to Camilla, Raf dared to edge closer. "You know me frighteningly well already."

"I know the type. I was that type for a long time. Stubborn, overworked perfectionist wanting to triple check every detail. Take your Sunday morning, Raf." Blue eyes sparkled at him. "Give me instructions and I'll follow them to the letter. Promise."

"Do you expect a reward for such...good behavior?"

"Not unless you wish to give one. Then I'll happily accept."

Camilla snapped their fingers at them. "Hey, we're all good. Loading dock all right, boss?"

Raf smoothed down his shirt front with his palms and threw Silvan a small smile before going to Camilla's side. "Let me talk to him."

Raf took a sip of his latte before leaning on the pier railing. "How often do we come back to this spot?"

"Quite a bit. Is that a bad thing?"

Raf smiled over Silvan, who looked as relaxed as a man could be when a breeze was ruffling his hair and sending steam from his own cup to fog his sunglasses. The day was bright and clear and from this little vantage point, they could watch the ocean stretch out for miles. A vast expanse of blue glittering in the midday sun, broken only by the bobbing of a few fishing boats further down the coast. "Not a bit, handsome."

It was always fun watching Silvan accept Raf's compliments. With his dark aviator glasses and navy peacoat, the man looked good enough to eat already. But the little smirk on Silvan's face was quickly becoming one of Raf's favorite expressions. "That's good. I'm rather fond of this place." Silvan tapped the railing with a finger. "The view is spectacular and the company, as always, perfection."

"You're going to make me blush."

Silvan took a quick look around and then, content with what he saw, leaned into Raf. Raf loved this, too; Silvan's need for closeness. For touch. Subtlety was for work environments. Now, alone on what was becoming *their* pier, Raf indulged them both.

"Do you know how to blush?" Silvan teased, his breath ghosting over Raf's cheek.

Already Raf's heart was pounding. "You can't see my blush right now?"

Silvan leaned in closer still. The railing bit into Raf's palms but he was most certainly not moving right now. "Hmmm...maybe if you turn toward me."

"Flirt."

"Is it working?"

"Absolutely," Raf breathed before claiming Silvan's lips with his own. He kept his hands on the railing. If he touched Silvan now, things would quickly unravel. It wasn't that Raf felt tense every time Silvan was near - they'd never get *any* work done if that was an issue. But the man embodied temptation and all Raf could think about, from the moment they stepped outside the gallery for a break, was getting to do *this*. The simplest of affectionate touches. Silvan's lips slid over his and Raf let his eyes close. Felt the wind in his hair, reveled in Silvan's hand on the middle of his back.

"I've wanted to do that all day," Silvan confessed as they broke apart.

"Me, too."

Silvan hummed softly and pulled Raf closer. "And we've still got drinks, so the break can't be over just yet."

The sound of gulls overhead made Raf look up; a chance to admire all that blue around them. When he gazed back over the water, he noticed a boat heading their way. Boats went north and out, toward the places where bass and halibut were plentiful. They did not head toward the piers unless it was to use one of the few docks nearby. Something prickled at the back of Raf's neck. "Perhaps we should move." He gestured toward the boat closing in on them.

Silvan immediately plucked up their drinks and headed toward the boardwalk, Raf close on his heels. Raf chanced another glance at the boat and with a start, said, "You have to be kidding me."

"Raf?"

Raf swallowed hard but nudged Silvan forward. "Let's get to the boardwalk. And I'm going to apologize for what might be happening."

The boat diverted to the last open dock as they reached the surety of the wide expanse of walkway. "Raf! I can't believe you're out here." Decked out in a heavy coat and his usual scarf, Henry waved at them. The woman tying up the boat, Raf realized with a sinking heart, was likely Kate. She was a striking redhead with a long face and pointed chin. Raf could see why Henry liked her instantly, as her quick movements and keen, curious stare spoke volumes.

"You don't have to explain," Silvan said in his ear. "We can go if you want."

"Oh, I want. I want to very badly. But somehow I had a feeling this might happen. I have to keep this quick, I'm so sorry." The ocean air they'd been enjoying now felt bitter and desolate, putting a damper on their spot.

The texts had stopped soon after Raf had told Henry *no* that night in the backyard. Henry had never been pushy, not in all the years they'd known each other. But there had been a thrumming energy of sadness and regret in Henry's messages and now Raf realized it had been more genuine than he'd given it credit. He'd never brushed Henry off, but the contradiction between that night and Henry's current messages was apparent. And deeply frustrating.

"What do you need?" Silvan asked as he squeezed Raf's arm.

Raf looked up and saw nothing but concern as Silvan pushed his glasses up on his head. "It's an ex, kind of. We were never in a relationship but Henry would come over now and then."

"I get it."

Raf breathed a sigh of relief. Of course Silvan wouldn't judge. "Thank you. If you're okay staying, that might be helpful."

Another squeeze to his arm. "Anything."

"Raf!" Henry and the woman closed in on them and Raf gave a small wave. Silvan's presence was a solid wall behind him and Raf felt safe. He didn't fear Henry at all, but Raf wanted this completely behind him. Hadn't they said their goodbyes? Hadn't he been clear in his wishes to Henry? Had the man gone mad? The uncertainty of it made Raf's stomach churn.

Henry's eyes were clear and bright as he and the woman came to a stop before them. That smile on his face said one thing, but the way Henry's gaze kept flicking back to Silvan almost made Raf laugh. Which would have been completely, utterly inappropriate. But the urge was there. Thankfully, Silvan wasn't the possessive type (as hot as that might have been). "Henry," Raf said with a solemn nod.

"It's so good to see you," Henry said, voice warm with affection. "I thought that was you on the pier but wasn't sure until Kate moved the boat closer."

Kate, for her part, was watching Raf with a close, but not scrutinizing, curiosity. And as much as Raf and Henry hadn't been in a relationship, the energy of "when the exes meet" was strong. "Silvan and I take walks out to the pier on breaks during construction," Raf said smoothly. He wanted to put on an easy, but not affectated, front; conversational but gently dismissive. "And since we're nearly out of latte, we'll need to head back." He gestured to Silvan, who was hovering in his periphery. "Henry, Silvan."

Henry knew Raf would never be impolite, and he must have been counting on that as he reached for Silvan's hand. "And this is Kate," Henry said as the woman put her hand out to Raf.

"Nice to meet the man Henry speaks so fondly of," Kate replied. Her hand was warm but chapped and her voice was a melodic thing that reminded Raf of a jazz singer. All smoky lounges and glasses of bourbon while she crooned under a spotlight.

In the moment, Raf knew he was making a mistake. There was obviously tension in the air. He hated this. Hated that Henry wouldn't just ignore him, or maybe even give a small wave from the boat. Left to wonder if Raf had seen him or not. Why did this have to be so damned awkward and awful? So in a rare flicker of aggravation, Raf said, "Henry, you must know this isn't the choicest of situations. And Silvan and I need to get back to work. Whatever you're going to say, do you truly need an audience like this for it?"

Behind him, so close to his ear, Silvan's breathing deepened but the man made no other noise. Henry, however, looked shocked and when he turned to Kate, she was looking down at her feet.

Ah, so this was Henry's idea and he dragged his new lover into it. How terribly uncouth.

"I..I didn't put that much thought into it, Raf. I saw you and wanted to see how you are." Henry gave a helpless shrug. "Am I just supposed to stay away from you now?"

Raf let out a long breath through his nose. This wasn't good, any of it. And he feared anything else he said would make it worse. But the words spilled out anyways. "We were never together, Henry. And you are still my friend. You're important to me. But I think we owe it to each other to maintain some space." Raf reached back and was met with Silvan's warm hand slipping into his. "Henry said you were lovely," he said to Kate. "And I can only say that I genuinely hope you and he are being good to each other. I'm sorry you had to bear witness to our fumblings."

For his part, Henry looked utterly torn. But while Raf reached for Silvan in his moment of need, Henry didn't do the same to Kate. "Please, Raf. Just a few minutes."

Kate gave them all a tight smile. "I'll be in the boat," she said. "Good to meet you, Raf."

Raf fought not to raise his eyebrows at the tense line of Kate's spine, her curt nod to them. Clearly something was amiss in paradise, but it wasn't his business. "Two minutes," he said to Henry. "And just over there, by the ice cream stand. We really do need to get back." Raf let Henry begin to walk in the direction he'd chosen before turning fully back to Silvan. "I'm so, so sorry -"

"No apologies needed." Silvan was close but didn't touch him, and that was maybe the biggest relief in this entire debacle. He wasn't looking for a white knight; having Silvan near was more than enough to help soothe his nerves. "I'll head over to the other pier. Join me when you're ready?"

All right, perhaps a *little* possessiveness wasn't a bad thing. It warmed Raf to realize Silvan was keeping him in line of sight, even if the man was moving out of earshot. "Thank you."

"Anything for you."

"You big sap."

Silvan's chuckle rang in his ears. "I've been called worse."

When Silvan was several yards away, Raf slowly made the journey over to Henry. The ice cream stand was shut down for the season, but its worn, striped canopy was still standing. It provided a little shelter from the wind that had kicked up. "All right," Raf said. "Two minutes."

"Going to time me?"

"I might, if you don't get to the point."

Henry looked hurt and Raf kicked himself. He wasn't looking to start an argument, but he did want this over with. "Okay, fine. If you want quick, then...I miss you, okay. I miss getting your messages, I miss coming over, and I miss the way we were." Henry waved a hand in Silvan's direction. "He the new thing for you?"

Raf was going to get emotional whiplash at this point. He'd vacillated too much between confusion, embarrassment, and impatience. Now he was leaning towards anger. "*He*," Raf hissed, leaning in, "is my new marketing manager and a friend. And he has a name."

Henry gave an empty laugh. "Seems more than a friend, the way he was touching you."

"Don't you dare," Raf spat back. Oh, there was definitely anger welling in his chest. Even with the bitter wind, he felt his face flush. "This isn't you, Henry. Whatever is going on, it doesn't involve me. I gave you my answer, you told me to not contact you." Raf blinked and drew back. He hated getting angry, hated the way it loosened his tongue and made his heart pound. If he didn't settle down, there would be something to deeply regret later. "And you seem to be unable to abide by my wish to keep some distance between us after *you* texted *me* a few weeks after our split."

The color had drained out of Henry's face and he looked abashed now, as if his own behavior being called on the carpet wasn't something he'd expected. "I fucked up. I'm sorry."

Raf sniffed and crossed his arms. "That's a start."

"I didn't think...I was happy to see you again."

"Well, it led to this, so unless you've developed a sudden masochistic side, I'd say it was a bit of a cock up."

"Yeah."

They stared at each other, feeling the broken bits of their bond slowly disintegrate on the wind. Raf felt the loss, the stinging ache of it. They were never going to be more than lovers, and now he wondered if they could even be friends. "You'd best go back to Kate," Raf said finally, dropping his arms and stepping back.

"She's not..." Henry sighed but he didn't look back toward the boat. He kept his gaze firmly fixed on Raf. "She's not you. I miss you."

"You've said as much. But what you have isn't for me, darling."

"Why?"

Raf took another step back, wishing Silvan was closer; able to hold him, comfort him. But he could do this. Make a clean break, make it real for Henry. "Because it's not. And I need you to respect that. The Henry I know wouldn't cross boundaries." Another step back, another step away from the past and towards Silvan. He *could* do this. "Please respect my wishes. Take care, Henry."

Raf left Henry on the boardwalk, sullenly looking out to the ocean while standing under a pinstriped canopy. He jogged back to Silvan, who immediately curled him close. "Are you okay?"

"No." The tightness in Raf's throat only allowed that one word.

"What do you need?"

Raf shook his head and tugged on Silvan's hand. "To take my mind off of it."

"All right. But hey..." Silvan pulled them around a corner as they left the boardwalk for the cobblestoned sidewalks of St. Augustine's downtown. "Whatever you need. Anything. Just ask."

Raf threw his arms around Silvan and buried his face in the warmth of the other man's coat. Silvan's hug was a tight, comforting circle around him and now Raf felt like he could breathe. "Just this. Just for a moment."

Chapter Seventeen

"Give me the full three-sixty, Raf."

"Ambrose, my friend. My platonic soulmate above all others. I cannot let you see the full breadth of this abomination."

Beside Ambrose on the couch, Barrett paused with a bottle of beer halfway to his lips, then laughed. "It's a nice color, Raf. Suits your complexion."

Raf gave a little bow and a cheeky smile. "You are a doll, Barrett. But I'm afraid this jacket is several seasons out of fashion and cannot be abided by." He whipped off the dark teal jacket and tossed it on the bed. "Why am I being so indecisive about this?"

"Because it's a huge night and you want it to go right." Ambrose gave him a knowing look that practically pierced through the tablet screen. "And I know you, Raf. Your wardrobe is part of your aesthetic. You'll find the right piece, promise."

Raf mulled over his friend's assurances for a moment before saying, "You're right. Ugh, I'm so caught up in my head about all of this." He gave them a small smile. "And I want you both to enjoy your time here. That's important to me."

"Raf -"

He held up a hand. "I know, I know."

Barrett leaned closer to the camera, concern in his deep brown eyes. "Hey, Raf. I know it might not be my place but getting to see you and the new gallery is one of the highlights of this trip. It'll be good for me and Ambrose to get out of the woods-"

"And away from the mosquitos," Ambrose deadpanned. "Downside of the woods."

"That's what bug spray is for, babe," Barrett replied as he kissed the side of Ambrose's head.

"Still."

Raf chuckled. "I am also not a fan of mosquitos, which is why I live in a dry part of the west coast. We all make our choices." He sighed and plopped down on the bed between jackets haphazardly discarded. "All right well, I admit defeat. I will try very hard to not overly worry about all of this. But I eagerly await your presence."

Ambrose smiled, shifting into the curve of Barrett's arm. "You know we can't wait. Everything will turn out perfectly, Raf, because you're the one doing it. You've got this. If you feel panicky or just need to talk, call me, okay?"

"Or call me," Barrett offered. "Since Alpha tower fell, people are a little skittish in the woods of late. Lots of long, lonely hours in the truck."

"Aw, my poor forest ranger friend, all alone in the woods. Certainly you're not whiling away those hours *all* alone."

Ambrose threw his head back and laughed as Barrett went red in the face. "Don't know what you're talking about," he grumbled, no acid in his voice. "Ambrose sometimes calls me and we talk."

"Uh huh." Raf waggled his eyebrows. "Darlings, I hate to chat and run, but run I must. With any luck, I'll find something to wear when I'm out with my mother this afternoon."

"Say hi for me. I miss your mom," Ambrose said while Barrett waved goodbye. "Tell her for me?"

"Of course. Talk soon." He blew them a kiss and shut the video call app down. Surveying the wreck he'd made of his closet was suddenly depressing, so he quickly hung everything back up, grabbed his bag, and went out to his car. He'd be a little early to the gallery to get the afternoon shipment, and with any luck, Silvan would still be there. The two of them. Alone in the gallery.

All right, the loading dock wasn't exactly the sexiest setting, but he wasn't about to be choosy. They'd been so good, *mostly* keeping their hands to themselves, keeping their conversations *mostly* professional. Silvan had caught him once coming out of the storage room and quickly spun him around into a gentle kiss that certainly killed a few brain cells. But other than that one moment, they'd gone back to normal.

Mostly.

But the way his body hummed when Silvan was near was a tingling, thrilling thing that was starting to help Raf understand the delightful deviousness of Silvan's plan. Waiting - *anticipating* - made everything that much sweeter. He relished each brush of fingers, each smirk, every flirty little smile. Every knowing glance Silvan gave him, the ones where the blue of those eyes nearly sucked him in.

And now sitting in his car and staring up at his home, Raf realized he'd long been chasing something like the sensations that Silvan stoked in him. Even if they had no romantic or sexual attraction to each other, he would have wanted Silvan as a friend. The man was *smart* in a dryly witty kind of way. He was charming, sophisticated, worldly, and yet he knew his flaws. Silvan hadn't held back on admitting he was often too patient, too still, and that made others think he was indecisive or uncaring. "Something I'm always working on," he'd said over lunch the other day. "I never want to be one of those people who get to a certain age and simply stop caring about growing, learning, being better. Mostly being better to the people around me."

Silvan had a heart of gold and an artful soul and Raf wanted to spend all day talking to him. He wanted more stories from Silvan's ballet days in college, more stories about raising Bonnie, more about his travels during his gap years. He was deeply attracted to the man on so many levels. He'd been hesitant to "lay down roots" for so long; it had felt antithetical to the life he'd wanted to lead. Free-spirited, free-wheeling, always moving and doing. Raf had only recently considered slowing down and enjoying what he had. And now Silvan was in his life and things felt *right*.

Raf mulled over those thoughts as he drove to the gallery, the sun-dappled trees and curving roads leading into St. Augustine becoming a blur through his windshield. When he pulled into the lot behind the gallery, he spied Silvan's car and grinned before firing off a text.

From: Raf *I'm a little early but I'm here. Everything go all right?*

Immediately, Silvan began typing and seconds later, Raf had a reply.

From: Silvan *Come in and see for yourself. Loading dock door is open.*

Something bubbly rose up in his chest and he grinned, even as dark clouds gathered overhead. Raf quickly got out of his car and took only a moment to run his hand through his hair. He sucked in a deep breath and took the ramp up to the loading dock door. It wheeled up with a *snick* of gears and there was Silvan. Sweaty, disheveled, straw in his hair and dirt streaked on the right side of his face. He was wearing tight black athletic shorts and an equally tight, dark red muscle tank. And he was pulling a skull from a crate as Raf entered.

He looked *stunning*.

"I thought I'd start unpacking. Jian was more than generous with the pieces he loaned us," Silvan said, holding the skull aloft as Raf approached. "We're going to have plenty for set dressing."

But all Raf could spit out, through the fog of *how fucking good* Silvan looked was, "I didn't know you had any tattoos."

Silvan brightened, blue eyes flashing approvingly. *He likes being admired, even if he doesn't admit it with words*, Raf thought. *I'll be tucking that little morsel away for later.* "After my ballet stint, I decided to do some of the things I couldn't when dancing." He gestured to the swirling mass of intensely detailed roses, thorns, and birds on his right bicep. "Not the most original, I'll grant, but it's a part of my past."

The first splatters of rain hit Raf's back and he turned to push the gate down. "Leave it open." Raf glanced back and saw Silvan was now within arm's reach. "The cooler air will help. I'm a fucking mess."

"You're not." Raf let go of the gate handle to stand before Silvan. His hands hovered, wanting to touch; aching for it. He settled for plucking a piece of straw from those silvery-gray strands and tossing it to the floor. "I like seeing you like this," Raf said, voice gone hoarse from their sudden closeness. Raf always felt a little jumbled when Silvan was near, but something about *now* was flickering through him. Embers over dry brush. One spark was all it would take.

As Raf pulled his hand away, Silvan caught it. His thumb left a streak of something dark on the inside of Raf's wrist. "Is this on the table?"

Gods, his mouth was dry. "What?"

Silvan's smirk made him shiver. "Messy. On occasion, of course."

All he could do was nod. "If the mood is right. The setting."

"I wouldn't have it any other way."

Wind blew in cold autumn rain and set the metal gate banging in its track; a strange staccato in the wide, dark space in which they stood. But Raf's eyes were glued to Silvan. "Then show me messy."

Silvan's soft hum was the only warning he had. The other man advanced on him, his steps in time with the furious beat of Raf's heart, and his grip on Raf's wrist gentle but guiding. "I've not the proper setting for messy right now," Silvan purred in his ear as he wedged his knee between Raf's thighs before Raf's back hit the wall. Immediately, his hips twitched. Seeking. Chasing. "But I can show you a few things."

He drew Raf's arm up over his head, a questioning look on his face. Raf nodded quickly. "Please. I..."

"I need your words, Raf. Your permission."

Fuck, gods, shit. He was going to *perish* right here in his gallery's loading dock, hemmed in by a beautiful man who commanded every inch of his attention.

Commanded more than that. His attention, his desires, his very being. He wanted to please Silvan and receive pleasure in return. He wanted the satisfaction that would be written across the other man's face, from the sweat on his brow to kiss-bitten lips and feather-light touches that revered.

"Yes. Please." Raf was damn near close to begging. "You can pin my arms. I like it."

The calculation in Silvan's eyes was there, then gone. A second later Silvan was bringing up his other arm, gathering Raf's wrists up in one hand, and slotting their mouths together in a kiss that was far too gentle for the scalding bolt of desire shooting through him. The contrast of restraint with care left him groaning.

Silvan pulled back to study his face. "Are you all right? And I expect words. Always. Unless we've set up another flag system. Does that make sense?"

Raf tried hard not to whimper. "Yes," he whispered. "Gods, how did you know?"

"I read people pretty well. And it might be a cliche, but the ones in charge often like to be given the opportunity to let go of themselves for a bit. Let someone else do the directing. But a lot of those people prefer being scolded, humiliated even. I will not do that. So it can be hard to find someone with..." Silvan broke off to trail his free hand down Raf's chest. "With both strength and vulnerability, that loveliness that sings to me. You are remarkable, Raf."

Something caught in Raf's chest, making it impossible to swallow against the lump in his throat. He wanted to turn away, to break the hold Silvan had on him. But at the same time, he knew he was right where he belonged. Nothing - *no one* - had ever made him feel like this. Ambrose had said something similar about Barrett early on in their push-and-pull relationship and...gods, now he understood.

"You flatter me," he choked out, his fingers flexing in Silvan's grip.

"Maybe. But is it flattery if it's honest?"

He had to laugh, as tense as the sound was. "I'd rather you kiss me than flatter me."

That got him a smile before Silvan leaned in and captured his mouth once more. He was gentle still, careful, but the tongue flicking into his mouth was asking for permission. Permission Raf was ready to give. Silvan's scent filled his nostrils and he groaned. Despite the wind and rain and sweat, he could still smell the man's shampoo or soap, some citrusy thing that clung to his hair and skin.

The grip on Raf's wrists tightened and he gasped. "Too much?" Silvan asked, that concern firing once more.

"No. No. Not enough." Raf's head hit the wall, his body arching into Silvan's. Their chests and hips pressed together so closely that Raf could feel Silvan straining to keep his breathing even. He could feel everything, muscle and bone and the promise of Silvan's desire rubbing against him. "Please."

With clear regret, Silvan shook his head. "That involves a conversation you and I need to have. Over dinner, perhaps. Would you let me cook for you?"

"Yes. I would love that."

"So would I." Silvan kissed him again and now Raf understood. This man was a live wire of desire but he kept it tightly reigned in until he was allowed to unleash it. This kiss was dirty, messy, his tongue in Raf's mouth, his teeth skimming Raf's bottom lip. *The promise of a bite almost better than the bite itself.*

And then Silvan let Raf's hands drop and he wasted no time in grabbing, taking. Pushing his fingers into sweaty, knotted hair, sliding them under Silvan's tank top. Silvan's gasp was honest, left to ring in Raf's ears as his fingertips explored the flushed skin and hard muscle. Silvan fell into him, almost crushing him to the wall, one balled-up fist by Raf's ear. "God, Raf."

He had to smirk. "Too much?"

"You know the answer to that," Silvan snapped before running his tongue along Raf's jaw. "You know what you do to me."

Daring, more than he thought he ever would, Raf let his touch wander higher and higher still, until he found the hard nub of a nipple. Silvan hissed and threw his head back with a groan. "Sensitive. I love sensitive men." He could *feel* the tremble wracking Silvan's entire frame and it only made his heart beat faster. It made the desire in his veins pound through him, asking, begging, pleading. For anything, *everything* Silvan could offer him.

"Kiss me again," Raf whispered and immediately Silvan was there. Warm and alive and wanting. When Silvan kissed him for the third time, Raf's world tilted. Gone was the hot rush of lust, replaced with a sweeter ache that did nothing to help his cockstand go away. But he kissed Silvan back, his fingers twined into that silky hair. He was going to run his other hand up Silvan's arm, but Silvan caught it and intertwined their fingers.

The buzz in Raf's pocket broke the spell. "What the..." He pulled it out, silently cursing the damn device. "My mom's here. Shit."

Immediately Silvan was pulling away, straightening his shirt and then Raf's. Then his gaze dropped to the front of Raf's slacks. "Might want to duck into the bathroom first."

"Good point." Raf drafted a text to his mother, saying he'd be there in a moment. "Could you...I know that's not the best way to meet a parent but she doesn't know we're..." He gestured between them. "She knows who you are, just not the more intimate details.

"I understand, and I'll let her in." Silvan smiled before pushing Raf's hair back and letting his fingertips drift over Raf's ear. "I was serious before."

"About?"

Silvan's smile grew. "How remarkable you are."

While Raf took a moment in the restroom after texting his mother, Silvan went through the back hallways to the gallery's open main room. If he'd been younger, he would have been nervous to meet Raf's mother. But he was, instead, supremely curious about the woman who had raised such a beautiful, enticing man. He gave no real thought besides a passing one to his appearance; but enough to make him swing by the mirror in the coat check room and pick the straw from his hair. There was nothing to do about the dirt, unfortunately.

When Silvan got to the door between the gallery entrance and the vestibule, he spied a woman sitting on one of the cushioned benches. She was wearing a dark red faux fur coat, black slacks, and had a handbag slung across her tiny frame. Immediately he grinned. She certainly made an impression.

As he opened the door, she turned and slid her glasses down just enough so he could see her eyes. They were hazel, just like Raf's, and framed in perfect lashes. "Oh! Hello!" The woman rose to her feet and stuck out her hand. "You must be Silvan. I'm Francia, Raphael's mother."

Her voice was lightly accented, likely from years of integration in the country, but he could still hear the notes of Italian. Sometimes Raf slipped into Italian when he was frustrated and Silvan found it utterly charming.

Silvan shook her hand and ushered her inside. "It's very nice to meet you. Raf talks about you all the time." He smiled when she fidgeted a little at the kind words. The distraction of her movement caused his gaze to catch on the shadow that was approaching the building's front door, so he paused as curiosity got the better of him. The shadow was a man, tall and lithe, with dark hair and a rakish look to him. As the man drew closer, Silvan realized who it was and said to Francia, "Just a moment. Sometimes customers aren't sure when we're open."

"Of course." The smile she gave him was motherly, but he saw the hint of mischief in it. Undoubtedly where Raf got that same little smirk.

Now the man - Henry, it was in fact him - was hurrying forward and something about his stride sent up a red flag in Silvan's mind. Another flag went up when he caught the hungry look on the man's face, which was pale under his hood. "Sorry, we're not open yet," Silvan said, putting a hand out to stop the man. "We've got about five weeks to opening. I can get you a flyer if you'd like -"

"Is Raf here?" The man wiped rain off his cheeks and Silvan noticed his fingernails were bitten to the quick. "I need to talk to him. He won't return my calls."

"Again, apologies but we're not open." Silvan kept his voice pleasant but neutral even as concern blossomed in his stomach. Raf had given Silvan the rundown after the incident on the pier and his heart had hurt watching Raf struggle with the situation. He offered what he could and freely, and Raf had taken him up on the hugs and gentle touches. But it was clear to them both that Henry was an open-ended question; a lingering doubt.

One that had just shown up on the gallery's doorstep.

As Silvan closed the front door, the man shoved a foot in. Instantly Silvan sized the man up; he was shorter and leaner but had wide shoulders under his hooded jacket. "Is there going to be an issue here?"

"I just..." Henry waved his hands in the air. "I need to talk to him. To make sure we're done."

"And I need you to remove your foot from the door now, or I'm afraid I'll have to convince you it's for your own benefit." Silvan let his gaze narrow and he pulled himself up to his full height. "I won't ask again."

"What the hell?"

Raf came flying at them, anger twisting his divine features. It was like nothing Silvan had ever seen and his instincts told him to get out of the way, but his reason knew better. "Raf, I've got this."

"Henry, no. Just no." But Raf was *furious* and Silvan could only watch as Raf wedged himself between Silvan and the door and Henry. "We parted ways. You need to go live your life, with the choices you made. I told you that. I've told you that a thousand times."

"Raf, please...I miss you. Kate left me." Henry sniffed and shivered against the cold. "I just needed to be sure."

Something like lead settled in Silvan's stomach but he held firm to the door. The rain was making everything slick but he was determined to keep the handle in his grip. *The same grip that had pinned Raf's wrists to the wall not minutes earlier.* "Go, Henry. Just leave." Raf sounded defeated, deflated even, all the anger burnt out like a Roman candle. Bright, blinding, and then darkness and the scent of sulfur in the air. "This is borderline *stalking*. You need to stop. Please."

Silvan watched as the word *stalking* sank in. Henry's eyes went wide and he backed up instantly, hands in front of him. Silvan couldn't help but feel a pang of pity for the man. Raf was irresistible in a lot of ways, and he'd long suspected Henry had held out hope that Raf would want to come back, to be serious about something more permanent between them. "Oh god. Oh god. I'm so sorry. I didn't mean...I'm done. I promise. I won't contact you again. I would never, ever hurt you, Raf. I swear." Henry hung his head and slowly withdrew his foot. "Please be well, Raf. And I'm sorry."

Slouched against the rain, Henry walked away, disappearing into the dark afternoon.

Silvan had the door shut so fast it rattled and then he was ushering Raf back inside. Francia was watching them with concern but Raf was his focus. "Raf. Look at me." He wanted to touch the man's face, pull his gaze up so Silvan could look deeply into those hazel eyes and assess the damage for himself. But Francia was right there. So instead he put his hands on Raf's shoulders. "Are you all right?"

Raf shook his head, water droplets flying. Silvan then realized they were both drenched. "He's never been so persistent. I don't get it. I blocked him, but I warned him before I did it." Raf gave a shuddering sigh. "I think it's over. Finally. I feel for him, I truly do. but we were never, ever meant to be something long term. And I think he gets that now."

And Raf's steady stare sent a message, one just for him: *I've moved on. Trust me on that.*

Then Francia was there, handing them both handkerchiefs. "Oh, honey, I'm so sorry."

"I'm all right, Mom. I swear." Raf inhaled sharply and shook out his hands. Water dripped onto the floor. Silvan watched as Raf drew himself up, away from what just happened. Chameleon Raf was back, shielding Silvan and his mother from the worst of it. "Well, that was unexpected. I'm sorry you both had to witness that. We should do proper introductions. Mom, Silvan, very glad you both can meet. Silvan's been saving my hide these last few months and as you can see," and he pointed to the nearly finished flower waterfall above their heads, "he's got both vision and the wherewithal to see things through."

Silvan chuckled. "The waterfall was your idea, Raf. I remember a two a.m. phone call quite clearly."

That got him a little smile and some color on Raf's too-pale cheeks. "We can bicker about that later. Mom, would you like a tour before we set off?"

"Not before it's done, sweetheart. I want to see this place in its full glory." Francia gave her son's arm a squeeze but swiveled her head to stare hard at Silvan. "And I'm about to be rather rude here but why do you look familiar? I've been trying to figure it out."

Silvan tipped his head back slightly to give her another once-over. The little ping her appearance *had* sparked in his mind had been nagging at him. "Come to think of it, you do remind me of someone. Though to be honest, my memory's not what it used to be."

Francia said, "Join the club," at the same time Raf scoffed and replied, "I don't believe that." But Francia was adamant and said, "No, no. I do know you. It's been many years but...did you have blond hair when you were younger?"

"Mom!"

"What? I'm following a hunch!"

Silvan acquiesced, thoroughly charmed by this woman. "Actually, yes. Very pale blond, almost silver. Part of my Nordic heritage."

Now Raf looked utterly confused and more than a little embarrassed, but something kept ticking in the back of Silvan's mind. Francia was a striking woman in her early seventies, if he had to guess, and Raf had mentioned his mother was an artist. He tried to picture a younger version of Francia, her skin smoother, her hair black and lustrous.

"I'll be fucking damned," Francia whispered suddenly, coming right up to Silvan, her mouth agape. "You! You were the one!"

"Oh my god, Mom, what is going on?"

But Silvan was laughing and grinning and a moment later, so was Francia. "Would it be weird if we hugged?" she asked, expression hopeful.

"I certainly don't think so," he replied, barely able to eke out the last word before the tiny woman before him crushed his ribs in a hug.

"Okay, someone! Please tell me what's going on!" They both turned to see Raf staring at them as if they'd crashed through the ceiling. But their grins didn't subside. What a bizarre turn of events.

"Honey." Francia held out her hand to her son, which he took. "This is the man who bought my first painting all those years ago."

Chapter Eighteen

"I never got his name," Francia said as Raf gaped at them. "I think I was too busy being elated over my first sale, and to someone with such a cute baby."

The expression on Silvan's face seemed a mix of disbelief and joy. "I remember that. Bonnie was only about a year old, and it was hot and she was fussy. But she took one look at the painting and just...stopped. I also remember thinking her eyes couldn't get any bigger when she stared."

Raf didn't need to do the math in his head. It was the summer of his high school graduation and he'd been too busy partying to come home, thinking his mother's *little art show* wasn't special enough to fly back for.

He'd been a selfish prick. Most teenagers were at that age, but that didn't excuse his behavior. And it was behavior he'd apologized for many, many times; each time, his mother telling him she understood.

Guilt ripped through him, the rawness of it making him suck in a breath. It tangled messily with the nerves of seeing Henry again and left him feeling hollow.

"Honey?"

Now they were both looking at him with concern. Raf shook his head. "I'm simply...shocked." The little brush-aside fell from his lips easily, but it made Silvan narrow his eyes. Oh, he didn't like that stare.

Or maybe he did.

The question of the painting's location sat on his tongue. His mother, however, beat him to the punch. "Do you still have it?" Her hands were clasped in front of her now.

Silvan smiled. "I do. It's always hung in my daughter's bedroom. Even now."

Raf watched his mom grin and blink away tears. "I'm so honored. I can't even begin to tell you."

Silvan turned to Raf. "I debated including the painting in the files I sent in with my resume. But it felt a little too personal." He started back toward the loading dock. "Let me get my phone, I'll show you."

When he'd disappeared, Francia was there before him, grinning and crying. "Raf. How....what..."

"I have no idea." He was flabbergasted as well. But that guilt chewed at him hungrily. So he put his hands on his mother's shoulders and squeezed gently. "I should have been there. At your first show."

"Sweetheart, we've been over this."

"I know. I know." Raf let go of her shoulders so he could take her hands. "And I'm still so sorry, Mom. You mean the world to me. I was a dumbass kid -"

"Yes, you were." That brought him up short but Francia started laughing. "Every teenager doesn't know their head from their rear, darling. It's just part of growing up. You, my lovely son, are one of the kindest, most generous, most *sensitive* souls I've ever met." She let go of his hands to put her palms on his cheeks. "Let it go. We're here now. Enjoy it."

It was a simple painting of a misty beach shore where a lone boat was tied to a battered dock. The colors were dappled with light, as if the sun was trying to shine through the clouds covering the sky; the grass and cattails around the shore added depth and color to what could have been a washed-out palette. It was a contemplative, quiet piece and it had been his mother's first sale as a painter.

Below the image, Silvan had written a caption. *I bought this at an art fair over twenty years ago, and I remember the artist like it was yesterday. She was exuberant, bright and smiling with a knot of dark hair on top of her head and paint on her hands and cheek. I brought my very young daughter to the fair and she'd been cranky all day, but when we passed by this artist's stall, she stopped crying and stared. I took it as a sign to buy something. This painting hung in my daughter's nursery for years and remains in her bedroom to this day. A reminder of that time, that place; the sun and the warmth, the smell of spring grass, the sight of that kind artist cooing at my daughter and her excitement over her first sale.*

She's part of the memory of that day, and I'll never forget it or her. Art doesn't have to hang in a museum to be worthy of attention and love.

It was the one painting he didn't include in his resume packet to Raf. It had felt too personal, too real in a strange kind of way. Silvan had always tied that painting so closely to Bonnie and their relationship, and now he was face to face with the painter once again, all these years later.

Francia's smile was so soft, so heartwarming, Silvan nearly missed how red Raf's face was. "Thank you," she said, handing the phone back to Silvan. "Thank you for letting me see it again. Thank you for taking such good care of it and letting it be a part of your family."

"Yes, Silvan, I..." Raf trailed off. He saw Raf's long fingers twitch against his thigh, leaving him to wonder if Raf wanted to touch him or if it was a nervous gesture.

"No need to thank me, either of you. I loved the painting from the moment I saw it and it's been part of home ever since." He laughed, remembering all the times he'd carefully wrapped it for moves. "I think it's hung on walls in five places now. Always in Bonnie's room. I tried to put it in the family room once and she snatched it out of my hands and marched off with it."

That got him a laugh, one that broke through the sweetness and Raf's strange embarrassment. He would check in with Raf once his mother was out of earshot. "Well," Francia said with a squeeze to Silvan's arm, "that's the highlight of my year, I think. Thank you again, Silvan. You have no idea how much this all means." Her gaze turned canny. "I'll be outside waiting, Raf. I'm sure you have *business* to finish."

Raf moved toward her. "No, Mom, we can go -"

She waved him off. "Pish, it's fine. I've got another level of this mobile game Marianna introduced me to and I've been stuck there for a day." Francia waved to Silvan and left, a blur of red faux fur and dark hair.

"She's...a lot sometimes," Raf said once Francia was outside. "Shit. Sorry about all of that."

Now was his chance. With grace in his steps, Silvan pulled Raf down the other hallway into one of the spare offices. "You worry too much," he whispered as he pushed his fingers into that thick hair and let his thumbs trace over Raf's temples. "You worry about everyone and it makes me want to..." He took a deep inhale, curbing the curl of desire that immediately formed in his belly. There would be time for that later. "It makes me want to take care of you."

"She knows," Raf said as he stared up at Silvan. "I have no idea how. She didn't say anything but there was a look in her eyes."

"She's a parent, and a good one. Sometimes we just get it. Like how I know Bonnie and Camilla might be dancing around each other."

"I wondered." Raf paused, eyes fluttering shut. "It makes sense. There have been some little glances."

"There have." He pressed his thumb into Raf's lower lip just to feel the other man sharply inhale. "Now go. Before I keep you here."

Raf looked like he wanted to protest - or stay - but he finally nodded. "But you should go, too. Don't unpack all that on your own. That's what Monday is for."

"I promise I won't do much more. Just finish what I started. Boss."

Raf snorted. "Sure, take a dig at me now. I see how it is."

Silvan's kiss cut Raf off. It would never stop thrilling him how Raf melted when they kissed. It made the greedy, needy thing in him slide his hands down that lean back, stopping just before he was able to cup Raf's ass. The whine he got in return was reward enough for now.

"And I'm sorry about Henry," Raf said before he left, hazel eyes shadowed with regret. "It was not something I ever expected to happen."

Ah, yes. The former lover. It was no ding on Silvan's pride. "Not even a worry," he replied as he brushed his fingers over the back of Raf's left hand. "You've already met my ex and my daughter. I think whatever 'rules' there are to dealing with people's pasts don't really apply in many situations."

Silvan leaned in and kissed Raf's forehead, feeling both a sense of warm sentimentality and that slightly tilted view of the world that happened whenever Raf was near. It was like the man upset his very balance. "Go be with your mom."

"Thank you." Relief was palpable in Raf's voice. He squeezed Silvan's hand and then was gone, leaving Silvan with several crates full of skulls and an airy feeling in his chest, even as rain pounded on the windows.

"I feel like I'm having severe deja vu here," Raf muttered as he pushed through another rack of sub-par men's clothes. He'd never had such bad luck thrift shopping before that disaster of a trip with Camilla the previous weekend. And then now.

"What was that, dear?"

"Nothing. I'm being cantankerous."

Francia peered around the rack, the most innocent look on her face. "I would have thought you'd be over the moon. Given everything."

He narrowed his eyes. "Given...?"

"Oh, you know." She waved him off before pulling a silver sequined jumpsuit off the rack. "The gallery, the art. How attractive and sweet Silvan is."

"I knew it! I knew you could just...sense something." Raf sighed and scrubbed at his forehead with the heel of his palm. "How? Just tell me that."

Francia shrugged and wiggled the hanger on which the jumpsuit hung. The sequins danced in his vision. "I'm your mother. I know you better than almost anyone else, except maybe Ambrose. Darling, he's *perfect* for you." She grinned. "You always did have a thing for older men."

"Oh sweet Jesus," he groused, making her laugh. But he had to smile; his mom was having so much fun shopping and who was he to bust her over a bit of parental teasing? "I hate that you're so right. All the time."

"I've told you that for years, Raphael. Years."

"I know, I know."

They fussed about the racks for a bit longer, and Raf finally gave up and moved to the antique dresser full of scarves, ascots, handkerchiefs, and other little shiny, frilly bits of cloth. He had plenty of those things at home, tucked away neatly into drawers lined with velvet and smelling of cedar and cinnamon, but he had a *vision*. He knew exactly what he was looking for and barring a miracle at this point, he was doubting it could be found. And there was no time to have something custom made. Raf wanted something dark red, a maroon so rich it would appear black in certain lights. He wanted to pair it with just the right scarf, just the right set of slacks. Because that color, for some reason, spoke to him, reminding him of the decadent beauty of a single flower petal. A rose, maybe, as cliche as that might have been.

"Oh, what's this?"

Raf had his hand buried in one of the drawers, fingers grasping for what looked like a beautiful gold silk scarf, when his mother rushed toward him with a bundle of cloth in her arms.

It was a deep, dark red suit jacket and at a distance it looked to be wool. But as soon as Francia got close, Raf reached out. "Cashmere? How did you..." He stared at his mother, thrift store shopping queen that she was, and gently took the jacket from her. The collar and sleeves and bottom hem were decorated with shining gold beading. It was *beautiful.* "I don't want to know. It will spoil the magic or inflict some kind of curse on us both. This is *exactly* what I was looking for."

Francia ran her fingertips over the sleeve and they admired the way the fabric shone softly in the dull lights overhead. "I think you definitely need this, darling."

"Oh, I absolutely agree."

Raf immediately plucked up the scarf and draped it over the jacket. The unraveling threads at the cuffs and hem didn't bother him; he knew at least three people who could fix it up easily and put on new buttons. But when he flicked the jacket open to look at the lining, his mother said, "I actually saw that first."

The lining was, in a word, *stunning*. Soft, slippery silk dotted with tiny yellow and blue flowers, ones so small he had to put the jacket up to his face to see them properly. Raf pulled his mom into a side hug and kissed the top of her head. "My lucky charm, my muse, my best friend. I owe you dinner."

She chuckled. "I thought that was already happening."

"Then I owe you whatever you want off that menu."

"Done."

By the time they were done shopping, Raf was still floating on cloud nine, having the jacket in his possession. A silly thing, really, to get so hung up on a dream of how he wanted to look during this gallery opening. And he immediately knew why this one was so different.

Francia knew, too. "How excited is Ambrose for all this?" she asked as they lingered over dessert and coffee at a tiny French restaurant on the outskirts of the city.

Raf toyed with his cup handle, watching steam curl off the dark roast. "Beyond ecstatic. I'm honestly surprised he's been able to keep the thing a secret from Barrett. I thought his soul was going to leave his body when I showed him the final book."

"That's so sweet. I can't wait to meet Barrett, he sounds wonderful." Then she speared him with a keen gaze, the one that used to make him freeze up when he was younger. "So just tell me this and help calm your old mother's heart."

"You're not old."

"Just hear me out, dear." Francia leaned forward and kept him pinned with that stare. "It's not easy having someone you're dating also work for you. I might like what I see of Silvan, but your heart, and your livelihood, have to come first."

Raf didn't have to hear the unspoken. "I know, Mom."

"Yes, well, I'm not done. I just want to know - are you protected?"

That brought him up short. "What? Silvan and I have an agreement."

"A legal one?"

"He signed a non-compete."

"That's a good start. But any lawyer is going to tell you you're playing with fire."

He stared at her, mouth open slightly as his brain tried to rearrange itself. "I'm sorry, are you telling me *not* to date Silvan?"

"Are you dating?" The concern written all over Francia's face was making her dark green eyes deepen in color, and Raf swore softly. She swiped a hand over her cheek and he nabbed it on its way down to the tabletop.

"Mom." Worried, he rubbed the back of her hand with his thumb. "Mom. It's okay. I'm okay, I swear. Silvan's not going to ruin me. He readily signed the non-compete and if somehow...somehow whatever's between us doesn't work out, he'll leave the job. I don't want that, but I'm not completely idealistic either."

"Oh honey. I'm sorry. Your mom is being a little dramatic today."

"You're not. At all." Raf pulled her into as much of a hug as their little booth allowed. "I get it. Really."

Francia put her head on Raf's shoulder and sighed, but didn't say anything for a while. Silently, he pushed her coffee to her and picked up his cup, then held it out. "To my mother, who only ever wants the best for me. In life and love, as it were."

There was a bit of a wet glint left in her eyes, but his mom's smile was a balm to Raf's heart. "I love you, Raf."

"Love you, too." He sniffed then said, "All right, well this is far too many opposing emotions today, so I say we finish up here and find a bar."

Teasing, Francia gently smacked his forearm with her gloves. "My gods, who raised you?"

"Ah, you should meet her. Incredibly fierce woman, I wouldn't mess with her if it was my last stand. I'm afraid she fears none."

"Oh, you."

The autumn sun on Silvan's face felt good against the bite of crisp air coming off the ocean this morning. He had a few extra minutes and a stack of flyers for the opening, so he swung into Steamy Indulgences. Desiree was moving quickly behind the coffee bar while two other employees handled the cash and bussed tables.

"Ahoy there!" Desiree called out, waving at Silvan. "Just put 'em over there, honey! Whew, lordie, they went fast! I might be needing more next week."

"Just let me know when, Desiree." Silvan neatly stacked the flyers on a small bookshelf, next to the free pens and magnets he'd had made up a few weeks ago. People never thought about that "free swag" they picked up until it was on something they saw every day.

"Will do!" she sang back, sailing between machines like a dancer.

By the time he had left the cafe for the pier, Silvan was too busy contemplating designs for their spring shows (which of course Raf already had figured out for each gallery, or was asking for Silvan's help in completing) to notice much beyond the slow churn white-capped waves on the horizon. Coffee cup at his elbow, he made several sets of notes on his phone, occasionally looking up as gulls called overhead.

And then he started thinking about Raf. Specifically what he was going to cook on Friday night for their little dinner date. Though *dinner date* felt trite, considering that sounded as if they were strangers just testing the waters. Their dinner was a date, yes, one Raf had enthusiastically agreed to. And given what had transpired a few days ago in the loading dock - mostly an acknowledgement of Silvan's hunches about the man - he knew Raf wanted *something*.

So now the nerves were back. Vicious, nasty things swirling in the pit of his stomach and leaving Silvan to pace aimlessly as his mind tried to focus. It had been some time since he'd done any kind of negotiations with a partner. Trust wasn't easily built, and they'd have to work on it over time.

Time he hoped they'd have together.

But he needed to take things slow.

Maybe figuring out dinner was a good start. Roast chicken, perhaps. Silvan sat down at a small table near a cotton candy stand and sipped his coffee. Watching the waves made him feel less nervous.

A few minutes later, a figure slid into the seat opposite him and set their drink down.

"Darling." Silvan's brows couldn't climb any higher into his hairline as Becca observed him carefully before taking a sip of her drink. "Oh, don't be surprised. This isn't the first time I've found you like this."

"Agreed, though this is rather...odd." He gave his ex the same careful inspection and noted the big, dark glasses, the slightly frizzy hair. "Are you wearing a sweatshirt?"

"Let's not broadcast my athleisure wear to the entire boardwalk," she hissed. "Silvan, please."

"All right, all right." He held up a placating hand. "What's going on? You seem...off."

Becca hmphed and leaned back in her chair but kept her right hand tight around her cup. "What, all of a sudden I can't decide to get a cup of coffee near the ocean?"

"While wearing a black tracksuit. And massive glasses, the same ones you've said time and again make your face look ridiculous." He motioned to her. "Take those off."

"What? No. It's bright out."

"Agreed again, but Becca." Silvan put that hand on hers. "If something's going on, I need to know."

Becca drummed her nails on the table for a moment, then with a sigh, slid her glasses down. The skin around her eyes was slightly puffy and red, but there was no wetness on her cheeks. "It was stupid fight. But Shaleena hasn't called me in a day and won't answer my texts. It's never been like this." Becca's voice caught on her last few words and Silvan's heart broke. Bonnie had been quite young when they'd separated; they'd never married but considered their relationship like a marriage. But taking care of a child and having deep fondness for each other wasn't a replacement for love. When they realized they'd drifted apart, Becca had come to him with a list of questions in hand. Brutally honest ones, the ones he'd been hiding from for months.

And they'd agreed that equal co-parenting was best. At first. But then Becca's job demanded more and more travel and then Silvan was keeping Bonnie almost every week straight through. They agreed again, but this time for Silvan to be primary on everything concerning Bonnie. They never hid what was going on, and had Bonnie voice her opinions from the early stages. Home was with him, and her mother was the high-flying, loving, but often absent influence in the background of their daughter's life.

All that was to say he'd seen Becca at her best and her worst, as she had seen him. But he'd never seen her quite so sad, or small, before.

"Becca. What do you want to do?"

His ex shook her head, managing to keep the anguish in her voice in check. But Silvan heard it wobble. "I don't know, other than I want her to come back so I know she's not dead in a ditch somewhere. Then we can figure it out."

He needed to get to work, but he needed to make sure Becca was going to be okay. But caution stayed his hand as he reached for his phone. Yes, his and Raf's lives were already enmeshed in some ways, but unlike his encounter with Raf's mother, this would be forced. By his doing. And no matter how ex she was, Becca was still that, and Bonnie's mother.

Silvan sighed. "I need to head to work, but do you want to take a peek inside? You should see the waterfall, it's gorgeous."

Becca froze mid-sip, then slowly swallowed and put her cup down. "That seems very much like a bad idea, Silvan. The show's not open to the public yet."

"You're not *public*. You're my friend, and our child's mother."

Something like hope glimmered in Becca's eyes but her tone was airy as she said, "You should check with your boss first, darling. I refuse to be the cause of work issues for you."

Oh, Becca. Always looking out for him in her own way.

> **To Raf:** *I'm just getting coffee and Becca's here. She's got a good eye for window and set dressing if you want to run that one alcove by her. No pressure.*

The reply came back immediately

> **To Silvan:** *Absolutely bring her. I need all the eyes I can get at this point.*

If Raf thought the request odd, he made no inference.

"Come on," Silvan said, standing and extending an arm to her.

"Wait, really?" Becca got to her feet, coffee in hand, and looped her arm through his. "Well, that's a surprise. Your boss is a generous man."

"You don't have to be coy, Becca."

"What?"

Silvan rolled his eyes behind his sunglasses. "All right, fine. But I give you this one opportunity to take a strip off my hide and I want you to remember that *you* were the one who refused."

Becca didn't answer except to give him a wide smile.

When they got to the loading dock at Ablaze, the door was wide open and some people Silvan recognized from Arie's crew were moving out the old crates and packing materials. They waved to Silvan, who waved back, before steering Becca through the back hallways, then turning sharp left to a set of double doors.

"Hang here for a moment," Silvan said. "I'll go get Raf."

Becca settled on a wide, low bench and waved him off. "Yes, yes."

"Be right back."

He saw her smile as he walked away and wondered if just being in the gallery was helping take her mind off things. He took another hallway to where the offices were located. Raf was in his office, pen in hand, seated behind his desk. He looked good enough to *eat*, with all that silver running up his ears and square black glasses perched on his perfect nose. There was a bit of stubble around Raf's jaw and Silvan nearly gaped at the sight, then his cock decided that stubble would feel *very good* against his skin. Sheer desire coursed through him, angry at being denied for so long.

Silvan didn't knock, simply entered the room, shut the door, and marched behind the desk. With a swift yank, he had Raf up by the lapels and was crushing their mouths together. Raf made a muffled noise of surprise but opened to him immediately. Eager, willing, warm.

He spun them, shoved Raf into the wall, and hemmed him in. His hands were pressed into the wall above Raf's head and for once, Silvan used his height to his advantage. The knee he wedged between muscled thighs got him another yelp, then a moan.

"You are....the kindest, sweetest man," Silvan murmured against Raf's mouth. Raf made a soft noise of pleasure and *fuck,* it sounded so good. Curling into Silvan's ears and wrapping around his brain and making him want to *take*. "I'm going to *ruin you* when the time is right."

Raf gasped, balling his fists tighter into the back of Silvan's coat. "Promise?"

"Absolutely."

Then Raf gave him a shove, nothing more than a playful push, and Silvan let it carry him back. "You are going to be the death of me," Raf panted. He paused, scanning the room. "My pen is clear over there."

Silvan looked to where Raf was pointing, saw the pen near the wastebasket on the opposite side of the room, and laughed. "Whoops."

"Whoops? Whoops?" Raf advanced on him, snagging Silvan's hands and pulling him in for a kiss. "Whoops is all you have to say, hmm?"

"Guilty as charged." But he let Raf lead this time and savored the sweetness of his mouth before they broke the kiss.

"Okay, well, good morning to you, too." But Raf's tone was teasing even as he pulled back to straighten his jacket and push his hair out of his face. "Now, you and I have a full day ahead, and apparently you brought a visitor."

"I did. Thank you for that, truly."

"Absolutely. I meant that. You said she was a set dresser for the big department stores for a long time and that's the kind of eye I need right now."

"My usual retainer is eight thousand dollars, but I'll waive it this time."

Silvan and Raf both froze, then Silvan shook his head. "Becca, you can come in."

"Are you sure? I hate to interrupt."

"You were just eavesdropping," he shot back, making sure to grin so Raf understood all was well. It could take some time to get used to their dynamic, a mix of constant playful exasperation and gentle fondness. But Raf seemed to understand because he nodded and opened the door.

Becca was settled on the bench against the opposite wall and grinning like a fiend. "So, Raf, we meet again with Silvan in the middle. Really, there's no buffer needed. I don't bite."

"Ah, but what if the buffer isn't for me?" Raf raised an eyebrow in challenge.

That got him a genuine smile, no playfulness about it. Now her expression was pure admiration. "Game recognizes game, Mr. Lutz. Now come show me this set that needs dressing."

Silvan trailed in their wake, already trying to figure out how to tell Bonnie this story without her calling him a liar.

Chapter Nineteen

The only thing more nerve wracking than trying to ensure his gallery opening's success was staring him in the face. Silvan's closed front door, a bright turquoise against the pine forest surrounding his home, felt like a wall. Which, it was physically but Raf felt the metaphorical barrier, too. Silvan had asked him over for dinner and a "conversation", and while intellectually Raf knew what that meant, emotionally he was quivering.

Anticipation, perhaps. Nerves, most certainly. But this also felt like a solid step forward for the both of them, and that had some part of him - the free-wheeling, high-flying, never-tied-to-anyone - was wanting to flee.

It was a ridiculous notion, Raf thought as he stared at the door through his car's windshield. Ridiculous to have any part of him wanting to sprout wings and take off, away from something that would challenge him on so many levels. But Silvan had already done that over and over again. And this was simply a step in the right direction. He wasn't scared of new things, but the unknown in this particular scenario left him jittery.

Silvan had said *negotiations* and Raf realized that had never been a part of his arrangements with other partners. Henry wasn't someone he wanted to think about right now, but he'd also been the closest. Henry would ask what he wanted, Raf would tell him, and that usually meant he got pressed into the mattress and catered to. Not a bad way to spend a night, not in the least. But something *darker* lingered in the bright blue of Silvan's eyes and that unspoken promise left him shivering.

Anticipation was exactly what he was feeling.

The door opened as Raf exited his car, bottle of wine and sleeve of bright white peonies in hand. Silvan had said this was casual. Raf took that to mean a little flirty, maybe even a bit sultry. So he'd paired a black jumpsuit (three buttons open, of course) with a thin green tank top and all the necklaces he could layer without looking gaudy.

He was spectacularly underdressed.

"You're welcome to stand there gaping, but it's getting a bit chilly."

Silvan was a picture in grays and blues, from the tight jeans to the loose v-neck sweater to the thin scarf around his neck. It was the most relaxed Raf had ever seen the man, and all of his wit and charm fled his mind. Surely that was the reason why he said, "That scarf is incredibly gay."

Silvan's little chuckle settled in his bones. "It really is, isn't it?" He ran a delicate hand over the fluttering end of the scarf, fingertips tracing the tassels. "It was a drunk purchase many years ago and I can't let it go. I think it's technically vintage now."

Vintage or not, Raf wasted no time in stepping up to Silvan and tugging on the scarf to reel him in. He held back on a kiss hello, however, to whisper, "The scarf, the sweater, all of it works so well I nearly forgot my words. But hello."

"Hello to you, too." Silvan reached up to touch the medallion Raf always wore. "You brought me flowers?"

"I did." Raf angled his head, teasing. His heart was beating hard but in excited anticipation now, any lingering doubts gone. How could he doubt anything other than the solid warmth of the man who was so close? "Though I'm afraid they come with a toll."

Something sparked in Silvan's eyes moments before he closed what little distance lay between them. His kiss was soft, easy, almost comforting. It took Raf's nerves away in the simple press of lips against his. He wanted to sink into it, into Silvan. "Toll paid?" Silvan asked when they broke apart.

"I think it's sufficient." Raf couldn't resist kissing his cheek. "For now."

Silvan ushered him inside, pushing the door shut against a sudden burst of wind, and took the wine and flowers off Raf so he could shrug out of his coat. "I don't know what I was expecting, but this somehow matches exactly what I was picturing," Raf said as he looked around. The house was a standard Cape Cod on the outside, but inside was a fascinating miasma of clean lines, gleaming surfaces, and cozy comforts. Silvan has a few of the more classic seaside touches, from shells and sea glass in jars to a gorgeous driftwood and glass coffee table. But Raf spotted the thick throws in chunky knits, the family photographs subtly displayed, and the slightly messy stacks of books. The entire place had a lived in, homey feel and it instantly set him at ease.

"I figured cleaning up too much might be a little unrealistic," Silvan explained as he led Raf from the living room to the open, airy kitchen smelling of herbs and roast chicken. Raf's stomach growled in response. "I do live here, after all. And currently have a twenty year old college student in residence." Silvan chuckled and held out a hand to pull Raf near when Raf's eyes widened slightly. "She's out with Camilla. I think attraction is in the air."

"Well, we both knew it," Raf said as Silvan pressed close.

"We did." Silvan tipped Raf's chin up with a finger. "May I?"

"You need permission?"

"Always."

Raf caught Silvan's lips with his own and decided then to take his time. Many of their physical touches had been subtle, secretive, or rushed. And even though Silvan's whispered confession from the loading dock rang in his ears...

You are remarkable

Remarkable

...he wanted to pay back that sweet earnestness, that dark voice laced with desire. Raf wanted to watch Silvan fall apart slowly, to know once again he was affecting the man in the same kind of way. Never mind that it was a massive ego boost; Raf *needed* to know he was pleasing, satisfying to Silvan in the same way Silvan seemed to find him.

So he took it slow. He relearned the shape of Silvan's lips, felt the tiny nick in the corner of the upper one, the plush velvet of the bottom one. His tongue did as much exploring as his hands, desperate to map everything, feel everything. Silvan's breath caught as Raf skimmed his palms down heaving sides and he swore he felt the other man stumble, just a little, as he bumped them into the kitchen counter.

"Distracting," Silvan murmured, letting his own lips slide over Raf's jaw. The hands at his waist, so chaste a moment ago, suddenly gripped Raf's clothes. There was tension was so thick between that them it nearly took Raf's knees out. "So lovely."

"Keep talking like that..."

"What?"

Raf shook his head and took the tiniest step back. "Don't want dinner to burn, do we?"

Silvan stared at him hard, then laughed. "Just when I think I have you figured out."

"I am full of surprises."

One eyebrow went up. "I have no doubt."

Dinner turned out to be an exquisite roast chicken with new potatoes and salad. Silvan called it *humble* but Raf's mouth was watering before it was pulled from the oven. "You have a different calling in another life, I think," Raf said as he speared a potato on his fork. "This is incredible."

"I'm glad you like it." Silvan eyed him over the rim of his wine glass. "I was afraid it was too simple."

"Absolutely not. Classics are just that for a reason." Raf looked at the plants spilling from every shelf and nook in the kitchen. "And you get to use what you've already put work into, all the herbs."

"They brighten the place up. Certainly makes everything feel more at home. Some of them are going on a decade old at this point." Silvan frowned for a moment then shook it off. "It's still quiet here, though. Some days it's too much."

Raf reached for him then, easing his hand along the counter until he could grab Silvan's. "You put up a good front but you don't have to be alone, you know."

"You're here now."

"I am."

"And that brings up a question." Something mischievous glimmered in Silvan's eyes and Raf was entranced. "How do you feel about cats?"

"Unexpected but I'll play along." Raf grinned. "I actually quite like cats. I considered adopting one a while back and then decided that was for after the gallery opening."

Silvan laughed. "You'll probably be saying that for a while now, as often as you open new ones."

"I'm afraid not." He'd never said this out loud and yet it somehow felt right, sitting here with Silvan over dinner, talking about cats. More than cats - they were talking about the future. "This is the last one." Silvan's face was instantly a picture of confused bewilderment and Raf shrugged. "St. Augustine was always the unattainable. Space was too expensive, it had a market I couldn't figure out how to crack for the longest time. And at some point I want to be able to take two weeks to go to...anywhere other than up and down the coast. And to do that, I need to know the galleries are all in good hands while I'm gone."

Silvan slowly set down his fork. "You've built your empire, and now you want to enjoy it."

Raf snorted. "*Empire* feels a tad exaggerated."

"I don't think so. Look at what you've done, Raf. You bring art to these communities. You bring in artists who need that chance, or a second one. You educate, inform. Culture and beauty flourish in the wake of whatever you touch."

Silvan's words were a punch to his heart. That had been the goal for so long and until recently, he'd felt like it was slipping away from him. It made sense that St. Augustine was the last gallery in the line up, that the two opening shows were going back to his roots.

"How do you do that?" Raf whispered, watching as Silvan pushed their empty plates away and turned on his stool to face him. "I assume your beautiful phrasings got you top marks in marketing school or what have you."

It was Silvan's turn to snort. "Actually, I was going to be a dancer but I wrecked my knee on a hiking trip."

"I still partially can't believe you were a ballet dancer."

Silvan got to his feet, as graceful as anything Raf had ever seen, and held out his hand. "Care to see?"

He absolutely did.

"I had no idea ballet was so incredibly erotic."

"Now you do." Silvan couldn't help but feel rather pleased with himself, especially given the slightly stunned look on Raf's face. "It's not always about the leotards."

"Clearly." Raf was staring at a photo of Silvan at twenty-two years old playing Puck in a ballet version of *A Midsummer Night's Dream*. "I'm now regretting never going to the ballet."

Silvan caught Raf by the chin, gently tipping his face up until they could stare directly at each other. "I'll take you some time. They're not all dusty old shows, and now that you understand how beautiful it is..." He leaned in close, close enough that another two inches would bring their mouths together.

Raf immediately bent to his will, just as Silvan had been hoping. The younger man was pliable but not too much, and Raf seemed to enjoy the occasional lingering suggestion as much as he did direct contact. "I have this particular fantasy," Raf said softly as Silvan pulled back. "It involves tuxedos and a night at the theater."

"I like where this is going. And since we're headed in that direction, perhaps we should talk."

Silvan was desperate to not let his nerves show. It wasn't just the fact that he hadn't broached this with many partners in the past. This was *Raf*. Something deep in his bones curled up in satisfaction at everything Raf offered, but he could sense it tasting the air like a snake. Curious, adaptive, ready.

"I'm not looking for a cataloging of your fantasies or anything," Silvan said, trying to lighten things a little to start. Raf was shifting on the couch, fingers fluttering on his thigh. "But you and I seem to have interlocking interests. I can start, if it's easier."

"Please," Raf breathed out, giving him an embarrassed smile. "I feel like a slack-jawed teenager again and might need to lean on your uh...expertise for a moment."

"Give yourself some grace, Raf. You know what you want. But we're taught that voicing such things is dirty or should remain a secret. So I'll try to make this as simple as possible."

Gods, he'd gone over this again and again in his head, but having Raf so near was spinning him out of focus. Silvan took a deep breath and leveled his gaze at the truly beautiful man sitting so close. "I like giving," he said firmly but not unkindly. "I like making my partners feel as though they're the sole focus of my attention, because they are. They should be." Gently, so gently, he put his hand on top of Raf's. "The biggest key to my satisfaction is watching an exhausted partner smile and then fall asleep, limp and sated, in my arms. Knowing I did that, that what I was able to make happen, that I could be so pleasing is an *incredible* high." Silvan cocked his head and gave Raf a look he hoped registered. "Does that make sense?"

He watched the bob of Raf's throat as the other man swallowed hard. "It does."

"Does that sound like something you'd be interested in?"

"My god, yes." Then Raf's hazel eyes shot wide and he scrambled to say, "Sorry, I didn't mean to sound so eager."

"You're more than fine." Silvan had to lean in, to breathe Raf in and catch cinnamon on the air. He could already feel that alien, tingling sensation that would soon beg to be slaked on someone's taste, their skin. "May I kiss you? I feel like that's the transition to the next bit of conversation."

"Consent."

"Always. That will never change."

Raf melted into him. "Please."

Silvan kept the kiss soft and brief; a tease not just for him, but for Raf, too. More than a tease - a promise. But Raf looked stunned after Silvan pulled away and the thing in his gut coiled tighter, satisfied. "Tell me something," he murmured, pushing Raf's hair back so he could better trace his cheek. "You liked it when I pinned your wrists."

"Yes."

"But it didn't hurt."

"No." Raf was quick to shake his head. "I'm not a fan of pain. Or, mostly."

"I'll need that explained, Raf. These are hard limits we need to set, even if there's nothing we're doing about it now."

Raf shifted in his seat. His nerves must be settling in. It was natural in someone who wasn't as experienced with things like boundaries, but there was no way Silvan would fly blind into any physical aspect of any relationship. But especially not this one. "No lasting pain. Or...no bruises, no smacking on the face."

"All right." He squeezed Raf's hand. "I'm hearing that you like things a little rough, perhaps?"

Raf nodded again. "I enjoy being manhandled a little. Smacks on the ass, that kind of thing."

"Pinned down."

That got him a whimper, but Silvan didn't think Raf was fully aware he'd made a sound. "Yes. God. Fuck. I don't know why that's so hot."

"It doesn't matter. If you like it, and your partner agrees, and it's not hurting anyone...then it doesn't matter. As long as we're on the same page."

Slowly and with great care, Silvan went down the line: hair pulling was a yes; biting was okay as long as it didn't break the skin; no blood or bodily fluids outside what one would encounter normally during sex. They'd both get tested in the next few weeks and swap results. And since neither of them were interested in multiple partners, now or in the future, they'd only need that one test. Silvan hadn't been entirely sure if Raf would be amenable to monogamy, but the weighted look Raf gave him, along with a firm *Yes*, was more than enough.

Praise, not punishment, was a big thing for both of them. Silvan had never taken joy in humiliating a partner (he'd tried it once and had felt so disgusting afterwards he never did it again). And once he explained the stoplight system and Raf had given him a safe word, Silvan was finally able to relax. To tease just a little. And that's when he found out Raf was more than amenable to being tied down and teased, blown, even fucked. Toys would be on a case by case basis, and Silvan figured they could tuck that away for later.

Because he wanted a *later* very badly. And from the way Raf was staring at him, he did as well.

"I honestly thought it would be more....I don't know, scary?" Raf was laughing, leaning into Silvan in relief.

"I can go get a clipboard if you want to make it more official."

"Oh please no. I wouldn't dare impugn."

Silvan stared at Raf. Examining. "How do you feel, honestly?"

Raf shook his head so his hair fell into his eyes once more. It made Silvan's fingers itch. He stared at Silvan for a long moment before saying, "Safe. As though I know for a fact you won't do anything I don't want, and anything I do want you'll also enjoy."

"Thoroughly and completely." Silvan was torn between ecstatic and turned on and they warred within him. Every inch of his body felt *alive*. "You enjoy receiving, and giving is the one thing I'm very, *very* good at. But all of this is to say, if we do move forward..."

"If?"

"If. I have to say that because for all our talk tonight, we could be horribly incompatible in bed."

"I refuse to believe that. Impossible."

"Stranger things, Raf." Silvan walked his fingers up Raf's thigh, felt the other man tense. The coiled thing in him could sense the tension building once again. "I also had a thought about that. The night of the opening is fast approaching. We'll likely both be exhausted." He gestured to the living room. "You could stay here and we could approach our little...arrangement in the morning. Making any decisions like that on adrenaline and lack of sleep doesn't seem wise."

Raf's gaze scraped over him and for once, Silvan couldn't read his expression. The next thing he knew, he had a very eager Raf in his lap and an erection pressing into his hip. "You beautiful man," Raf murmured in his ear while he pulled at Silvan's hair, drawing his head back. "Yes. Yes to all of it."

Raf sucked a wet, hot path down his neck and Silvan arched into him, groaning. Rougher than he meant to, he drew Raf's face up by the jaw and kissed him. Hard. Yearning. Desperate for the taste of him on his tongue. The kiss lasted forever and not long enough and soon Raf was pulling away, his breath coming in hard, hot pants. "Dear god. You're some kind of...nymph sent to torture me."

Silvan could only chuckle and run his hands up and down Raf's back. "How do you think I feel?"

Raf squirmed, purposefully driving his hips down and making Silvan moan. "It's almost like I can tell."

"Hush, you."

"Make me."

Something *greedy* rose up in him at Raf's playful challenge, so their next kiss was everything Silvan wanted to show. Desire and promises unspoken but for a whisper against Raf's mouth as the man above him sighed in satisfaction.

When they broke apart again, Raf was glassy-eyed, his lips swollen a little. Silvan wanted to preen. "So...what was that before?"

"Hmmm?"

"Something about a cat."

Silvan grinned. "I thought we could end the night with a bit less tension and more fuzzy cuteness."

"Oh, do tell."

"Have you been to the cat cafe in town?"

Raf turned in a slow circle, taking in the soothing scents of tea and sugar in the air and the sight of a few dozen cats lounging, playing, and stalking across the tile floor of the cafe. A brown tabby walked right up to him and promptly headbutted his shin. "I do love a bold soul," he said as he knelt to let the cat sniff his hand. The cat's collar said *Frank* and he laughed. "Do they all have human names?"

Silvan was being playfully swatted at by a tiny calico kitten, so he scooped it up and scratched its head. The kitten was so small that its collar and tag looked like a kid playing dress up. "This one is Sherbert, so I guess not." Gently, he put the kitten back down but Sherbert was having none of it. It whined, high and quiet, and he picked it up once more.

Raf stood as Frank walked away, moving closer to give Sherbert a chin scratch. "I think you've been claimed."

"She is very cute," Silvan conceded, "but a kitten would be too much right now. With me gone all the time, I think an older cat would be best."

"Sleep all day, beg for food when you get home, then sleep again but likely on your bed. Not a bad way to spend one's existence."

Silvan chuckled and gently moved Sherbert to Raf so he could go over to the counter to order. The cafe was quiet in the evening, just a few couples enjoying drinks and playing with cats, so Raf picked a spot in the far corner, giving them a view of the entire space. Sherbert made a tiny rumpled sound and he looked down to see the kitten pulling on the pocket of his jumpsuit. "Well, why not?" he whispered and put the kitten in his pocket. She immediately closed her eyes. Behind him, he heard Silvan laugh and he waved him off. "Shush. I can't help it. She's tiny."

"You look adorable," Silvan said with a wink before turning to the woman behind the counter.

Raf tried not to blush.

Sherbert was snoring against him when Silvan came over with their teas and scones. As he settled into the booth, another cat jumped up to join them. "Well, hello," Silvan said as it sat on the table and blinked at them with its one eye. "Mozart? What a lovely name."

One of the cafe workers, a young man with long blond hair, paused as he passed by and said, "Oh hey, Mozart likes you! She's awful picky about people. Like most cats." He pointed to Sherbert sound asleep in Raf's pocket. "I think you two have been chosen."

Raf tried not to let panic show on his face as he said, "I really can't handle a kitten right now. Maybe ever."

The young man smiled. "Well, no worries. This one won't last long. The kittens always get picked first." He held out his hand and Raf carefully gave him Sherbert. She barely made a sound as she was placed in a nearby cat bed. "But poor Mozart's been here a bit. People think a one-eyed cat going on double digits isn't fun." He scratched Mozart between the ears and she began to purr. "But she's really just a big softie."

Raf watched Silvan hold his hand out, which Mozart promptly sniffed, licked, then batted at. "I feel very much like I've been selected for a rare club," he mused while Mozart rubbed her cheek into his palm. "I might be in trouble here."

"She seems rather sweet. Are you considering it?"

Silvan sighed and leaned back into the booth. Mozart had gotten distracted by another cat buzzing by and took after them. "Perhaps. I really do think I'd like having a cat around but it's..." He trailed off and Raf saw doubt creep over his face. "I'm not sure, to be honest. It's not the only thing weighing on me."

Raf put a hand on his knee and squeezed. "Do you want to talk about it?"

"Not now. Not on our first date."

"All right." Raf sipped his tea and Silvan did the same. "So, I'm very curious about this whole ballet thing. You can't show me something like that photograph and not pique my interest."

Silvan relaxed instantly. "I would love to tell you about it. The abridged version for now, unless we wind up here all night."

Raf snuggled closer. "I can think of worse things."

Chapter Twenty

Two nights before the gallery opening

"You look a little green, Raf."

"I'm fine."

"You sure?" Camilla leaned in closer. "Hey Arie, does he look green to you?"

"Muppet green or swamp green?" Arie yelled back, managing to keep track of their conversation while finishing the pulley system for the rotunda waterfall.

Raf swatted limply at Camilla while they gazed up at him. "Like pea soup green."

"I need a drink," he muttered, much to Camilla's delight. "If you're done speculating on the state of my face, could you make sure all the set pieces are in place in the blue room?"

Camilla instantly straightened, all humor gone from their expression. "You got it." They snatched up a tablet and took off, stiletto boots clicking on the floor as they disappeared.

"I'm surprised you're letting anyone in there at this point." Raf looked up to see Silvan smiling gently at him.

"Honestly, if I look at it one more time, I'll just fuss with everything again. Camilla's got a good eye for detail. If something is out of place, they'll take care of it."

"Magnanimous of you."

"You tease but at this point..." Raf sighed and leaned on the front desk counter. "At this point I'm ready to be done, collapsed in bed."

Silvan moved closer, aware of all the people bustling back and forth. "I promise only the softest sheets for us both."

Raf wanted so badly to reach for him. "Silvan..."

"All right, we're ready!" Arie ran over and pulled a remote from her pocket. "Now or never, Raf."

Oh gods, please work, Raf thought as he stared at the remote she was offering. "All right, let's get everyone together! If you all could stand over here with Silvan and I, we're going to give this a try."

Silvan put a hand on his shoulder. "You've got this."

Heart in his throat, Raf watched Arie's crew, all of his gallery employees, and a few special guests shuffle into the wide open space and look up at the rotunda display. Every gallery opening had a special "preview" a few nights before; a kind of dress rehearsal and a way for Raf to give his thanks to those who worked so hard to make the opening happen. Tonight was a little more terrifying than normal, however. The waterfall rigging had been tricky and Arie's assurances that it would work only stemmed his anxiety to a certain extent. And Raf felt as though, no matter which way he turned, there was another issue to pop up, another thing to wrangle. He could feel that tightness in his chest, the kind that wouldn't fade until he either managed to push it away, or completely broke down. And he didn't have time for the latter.

Raf looked over the crowd and caught his mother's eye, then Marianna's, and with a nod to them, said, "All right, well. Everyone is here, so I suppose I should say something before you all eat and drink too much." He paused, his perfectly rehearsed words fleeing his mind as if chased by the boogeyman.

Silvan's hand on his shoulder tightened. "You've got this," he said so only Raf would hear. "You do."

"Thank you." Raf cleared his throat and gestured to the immense waterfall of flowers above their heads. "I'll keep this short. Thank you for being here. For all your hard work. For sticking with me even when I stared blankly into space or asked nonsense questions. For helping build something that gives back. Ablaze has always been about local art and creation, imagination and beauty. And we've certainly never done anything like this." He pointed to the ceiling, to the incredible rigging above their heads. "Arie, are we ready?"

Arie gave him a thumb's up. "Might as well give it a whirl."

"It's gonna be great, Raf!" Desiree yelled from somewhere to his left.

Raf pressed the bottom button on the remote and waited. There was a slight churning noise in the air, then a grinding. He held his breath. Who needed to breathe, anyways?

"It's opening!" Camilla said, clutching the tablet to their chest. "Look!"

They were right. The massive red, purple, and pink parade float petals that housed the more intricate, delicate structure of the piece were slowly peeling apart from each other. Four large segments made up the entire display and as if on cue (more like Arie's incredible programming skills), they opened. Flowers and greenery spilled down from thirty feet above; a veritable *waterfall* of beauty raining down on them. The waterfall was a mix of real and artificial flowers and leaves, each piece held in place by wire so thin it was nearly invisible. The natural pieces would be replaced every few days, generously harvested and provided by the local conservatory. The conservatory would take back everything as it decayed and use it for compost. The art pieces mixed in with the real greenery had been created by many hands, and their names were proudly displayed on a nearby plaque. Many of the artists were in the audience now, gasping and pointing as the piece they'd donated to unfurled before their very eyes.

"So far so good," Raf said, getting a few laughs. "Now the final part." The confused looks he got in return made him grin. "You can thank my new marketing manager for the idea. Silvan, do you want to say anything?"

Silvan was quick, immediately stepping forward to say, "Just that art needs to breathe, and I thought it only right that this piece be the center of the gallery opening, but a good reminder to all of us. Art doesn't have to be earth-shattering to be important or inspiring. Sometimes it simply needs to breathe."

Raf hit the top button.

And slowly the lines of flowers rippled, one set at a time. As if breathing.

"Holy shit," Arie said for all to hear. "It worked!"

Raf shot her an astonished look. "That's not exactly inspiring confidence, Arie."

She shrugged, grinning. "What can I say? I operate with extreme positivity up until the moment someone hits a button."

Above them, the waterfall of flowers undulated gently.

The evening flew by, a blur of people and food and wine and hearty congratulations. Silvan felt as though he didn't have enough time to thoroughly, earnestly thank every single person, but he tried. Raf had long been pulled from his side but every time he looked, the man appeared in his element. Chameleon Raphael was back, sliding from person to person with a grace Silvan couldn't help but admire.

"I think you got the better end of the deal," Marianna said as she hopped up on the low wall next to him. "And are we supposed to be sitting up here?"

"Probably not," he replied. It had been nice to catch up with her over the evening and now, as the crowd thinned and cars pulled out of the lot, he felt like he could breathe once more. "And, the better end of what deal?"

"You getting laid off from your old job. I mean, it's their loss. And mine, quite frankly." She tipped her glass at him. "Unless you've got room for some freelance work."

"Ah, sadly not. And my new boss is a bit of a stickler. Made me sign an iron-clad non-compete."

"Sucks for me."

"Indeed."

Marianna swirled the last bit of wine in her glass and stared out over the gallery. "So you know I have to do this, right?"

Silvan tried to suppress his smile as he said, "Ah, am I about to get *the talk*?"

"You bet your ass you are." She pointed at him, red lacquered fingernails glinting in the light overhead. "Do not fuck with him. I don't give a hoot who you are or how old you are or whatever. That's my cousin. I know people."

Silvan was a little taken aback by her tone, but he did understand. Marianna was never someone he'd want to get on the bad side of, so her metaphorical - and honestly, physical - claws coming out wasn't a total shock. When they'd worked together, she'd always had a particular vision and could be stubborn if he'd made other suggestions. What he saw now was born out of love and it was hard to deny that. Especially not when he'd spotted Bonnie and Camilla dancing around each other during the course of the evening. "I understand."

"I'm serious, Silvan. I will eat you alive."

Now he had to chuckle. "I'm afraid cannibalism is on my list of hard stops, so I think you're good."

Marianna snorted, threw back the rest of her wine, and hopped down from the wall. "Okay then. See you later." And then she was gone, bounding over to Arie and a few of the artists, leaving Silvan to shake his head. Becca must have seen the opening, because after a moment she was next to him, handing Silvan a glass of water.

"Do I look dehydrated?" he teased.

"More like you just got reprimanded by that stunning woman who is...Raf's family, I take it?"

"Correct." He stared down at Becca in her polished, stylish black suit. "New suit? I don't recognize that one."

"Shaleena picked it out for me."

"It's lovely. Was it an apology gift?"

Becca shrugged as if it was no big thing to fuss over, but he saw her expression flicker. "Something like that. Honestly, it was just a misunderstanding, like I told you before. It happens with every couple."

Silvan was silent for a moment, curious if his ex would continue to talk. Becca didn't have many tells but when she was uncertain or nervous, sometimes her words got away from her. She'd called him the other night to thank him again for pulling her together after her fight with Shaleena, but she hadn't given over many details. It wasn't his business anyways and as much as he liked Shaleena, he'd always be in Becca's corner. They'd arrived together tonight, all smiles and linked arms, but Silvan could sense tension.

"It does. I'm glad you're feeling better," he said, keeping his tone mild. No need to poke another bear after Raf's cousin. "So, what did you think of the preview?"

"I think you're very lucky." Becca craned her neck to look up at him. "This space, these people...they're all here because they believe in a vision. One your boss started and carries with him. I think it's incredible, Silvan, and I can tell you're happy." Becca reached out to pat his knee. "You deserve it, darling."

"That means a lot, Becca."

"Of course." From the corner of the room, Silvan saw Raf break out of a small group of artists and begin to head his way. "I better let you get back to it," Becca said. "Congratulations again, Silvan."

And then she was gone and Raf was striding over. There was a bounce in the other man's step and a big smile on his face, but Silvan could see that same smile drooping at the corners. *He must be exhausted, but he's doing well not showing it*. Still, concern flared in his chest. "The man of the hour has found a chance to break away, I see," Silvan teased gently. "You should hop up here, the vantage point is better."

"Hmm, well, if it's good enough for my marketing manager..." Raf easily took up space to Silvan's left; not quite leaning into him but close. Close enough to let Silvan feel his warmth. It made him want to bundle Raf up and take him home, take care of him.

Then take him apart and do it all over again.

Soon. Very soon.

"Would it be awful if I just slipped away now?" Raf asked. "To be rather blunt, this was far more taxing than I realized it would be."

"I don't think anyone would feel it was out of line, and if they did..."

"Would you defend my honor?"

"Absolutely." He nudged Raf with his shoulder. "You know I used to fence. Was rather good at it, I must say."

"Why am I not surprised?" Raf leaned in, hazel eyes flashing. That look went straight to Silvan's gut. "Ballet dancer, fencer, genius marketer. Good father." He moved in another inch. "Good man."

"What are you doing?" Silvan whispered, well aware they were out in the open. He didn't object but he'd been careful because Raf had asked him to be.

"I've thanked everyone for their part tonight. Except for you." Gods, he was close and Silvan *wanted*. "Though, admittedly, the way I wish to thank you is for you only."

"You don't care that anyone can see us?"

"Not now."

"Raf." Silvan wanted to reach out but for once, had no idea what to do in the moment. "Don't do something you'll regret."

"Why would I regret this?" Those eyes flashed again and Silvan understood. Some hurdle had been leapt over tonight and for Raf, this was the next step. "I don't..." He paused and leaned back. "You're being cautious. For me."

"Because we'd been so careful before -"

Raf didn't pause this time. He pressed his lips to Silvan's, palming the back of his head with a steady hand. Raf kept the kiss gentle, the kind of softness Silvan had come to associate with Raf being Raf - giving, sweet, kind.

And then Raf let his tongue tease at Silvan's bottom lip and he remembered the other side of the man he was kissing. The darker, needier, *receptive* side. The mere thought of it made Silvan clench his hand into a fist, to prevent him from doing something untoward in full view of others.

"Let them talk," Raf whispered against his mouth, as if he'd plucked that thought from Silvan's head. "For once, I don't care."

"At least no one is making noises at us," Silvan retorted, getting a laugh out of Raf.

"I honestly thought Camilla would." They both turned, searching for the aforementioned assistant, and found them standing near Bonnie. They were both so absorbed in their conversation that Silvan was pretty sure his daughter hadn't just seen him kissing his boss. "Oh. Never mind."

"Seconded."

Raf's eyebrows went up and he stifled a laugh with his hand. "Those two are going to be trouble. Better prepare yourself."

"Bonnie's life is her own. I'm not here to tell my adult daughter what to do."

"Well, I am here to tell my adult son what to do, for just a moment." Francia slipped in front of them, her grin wide. "I knew it, by the way."

"Mom."

"Well, then don't kiss your beau in front of everyone!" she retorted.

"I need to go hide now," Raf moaned, mostly for show. Though Silvan did catch a bit of pink highlighting Raf's sharp cheekbones.

"Anyways, I wanted to say goodbye. Marianna drove us over and we're both tired." Francia stared up at her son and Silvan knew the look she wore was one of parental pride and adoration. "You really outdid yourself, dear. This is incredible. And the blue room? Ambrose and Barrett will be over the moon."

"I hope so. I really do. This has to go right." Raf hopped down from the wall and pulled his mother into a big hug. "Thank you for being here tonight." He turned to Silvan, his arm still around Francia. "I'm gonna walk her out. Wait for me?"

"Of course." Silvan stepped back to give them some room, but Francia tugged on his sleeve and then roped him into a hug.

"Get used to it," she said as Silvan shot Raf a bewildered look. "We're huggers."

"Now you're stuck," Raf said as he eyed Silvan over his mother's head.

"I'm okay with stuck," he replied.

The day before the gallery opening

"You two look great on camera," the reporter said as she straightened her jacket. "Are all your opening night tickets sold out?"

Silvan nodded. "I'm afraid so."

"Too bad. Your phones are going to be ringing off the hook after this."

"She sounds confident," Raf muttered to Silvan when the reporter turned away.

Silvan nodded but he was looking at the crowd that had slowly been gathering behind the news van. "I don't think she's wrong, Raf. Camilla's been handling the phones but we must have gotten forty emails just this morning inquiring about tickets." Raf pulled a face and Silvan chuckled before continuing. "And I've had to tell many people that the 'Night Garden' show is for adults only. Not my favorite conversation to have on a Friday morning."

His plan worked because his words made Raf laugh and popped the bubble of nervous air around them. "I'm sure we'll scandalize someone at some point during that show." He gave Silvan a smile that left him feeling a tad floaty.

The reporter bustled back over and had the station tech check the mics on both of them. "It'll be pre-recorded so if you need a moment, or mess up, just wave a hand and we'll do it over. But time is short, gentlemen, so not too much in the way of mistakes."

The cameraman counted down and then the reporter launched into her spiel. Silvan had walked Raf through what to expect, how to hold himself. *You have a tendency to fidget, Raf, and as much as I enjoy your wandering fingers, we'll want to save that for later. Off camera*. Thankfully Raf was, as Silvan had expected, an attentive student.

And very pliable. And enjoyed being rewarded.

Silvan had lobbed softball questions at him when they practiced this morning and when Raf got nervous, it was so simple to promise the man a kiss for every time he answered something with that calm, cool air he knew Raf possessed.

You've got this. You do. Everything about you shines, Raf. People flock to you because you're honest and genuine and you see the world in a beautiful, bold way. Show them that.

Beside him, Raf inhaled deeply, straightened his shoulders, and as the camera swiveled to them, gave the reporter a big smile. "Welcome to Ablaze St. Augustine, everyone. We're so happy to have you here."

"Well, thank you for that incredibly kind welcome. Raphael, you've taken an old building and breathed new life into downtown St. Augustine. But this isn't the first art gallery for you, is it?"

"It's not, Kayla. This gallery is the fifth, and final, gallery under the Ablaze name. Setting up in St. Augustine has been a dream of mine for years and I'm over the moon to finally have the opportunity to give more room for the arts in this incredible city."

Silvan watched the exchange closely, silently proud that he'd been able to accurately predict the kind of questions the reporter would send Raf's way. He was hitting every one of them back to her with ease, and it was a rare chance to watch the man in action. Silvan had no doubt that viewers would be leaning closer to their monitors as they watched, pulled to Raf's glow like moths.

And then the reporter turned to him. "So you're the new marketing manager for the galleries, Silvan. How has it been working with Raf and Ablaze? My understanding is you were working with a big firm until recently."

Oh shit. Silvan gave her a beatific, innocent smile. "I was, but this opportunity was too good to pass up. I've always been a patron of the arts, and in my youth I was a ballet dancer. I saw this as a chance to work for something truly worth it, for a place and a group of people who understand how important art is to both community and our everyday lives." Silvan gestured to the street beyond, where years ago street artists had painted on the sides of the buildings for charity. "It's everywhere we look. Art is the beating heart of our civilization, our humanity." And then he looked at Raf, who was staring at him with the most expressive eyes; as if he was staring directly into Silvan's heart. "What Raf and Ablaze and all the artists are doing here is special. And I'll support that any way I can, no matter what."

Even the reporter seemed caught off guard by the passion in Silvan's voice, and while he was busy beating himself up for slipping, Raf said, "I got very lucky finding Silvan. Any work that requires passion also requires dedication, and everyone here has that in spades."

"I can certainly tell." Kayla regained her focus and began to pepper them with questions about the artists and the themes of both shows. Raf was quick to remind viewers that the shows were sold out but an online viewing would be available at the end of the month for a one-time charitable donation to the artist workshops they were setting up for the winter season.

"One last question for both of you. What would you say to anyone who thinks arts funding is better spent somewhere else? We've had a few city council members express concern that local funding shouldn't skew so heavily to the arts. Do you have any feedback for them?"

Raf looked to him, nodded, and then said, "Honestly, someone who doesn't see the value in art - how it educates, entertains, informs, how it pushes us, can change our views - is welcome here anytime. I'll happily give them a private tour, let them sit in on our classes, have them talk to the artists, especially the kids we see come in after school. If that can't change their mind, I daresay they have no heart."

"I couldn't have said it better," Silvan replied, aching to reach out to Raf.

Kayla turned back to the camera. "Bold statement from the owner of Ablaze galleries, but I don't think he's wrong. Tickets are sold out for the big opening shows but keep an eye on ablazegalleries.com for their upcoming show calendar."

After they said their goodbyes to the reporting crew, Silvan nearly dragged Raf inside. He did his best to make it look casual, but everything in him was *screaming* for contact.

"Office," Raf said, voice shaking. "I need to sit down."

So Silvan waited until they were safely, privately closed off in Raf's office before sinking to his knees and running his hands up Raf's thighs. "You brilliant man, you were perfect," he breathed, clutching Raf's hands in his own. "More than perfect."

"No such thing," Raf said, voice weak. "Oh gods, that was terrifying." He slumped in his seat and closed his eyes. "Really?"

"Really what?"

Hazel eyes flew open to lock on him. "I really did all right?"

Silvan was slowly untangling the brilliant knot that was Raf bit by bit. And this moment only solidified a theory he had - that Raf occasionally needed blunt honesty, without flowery phrases or high-handed praise. When it was work, or something he valued, Raf wanted to hear things clearly.

"You did a truly great job." Silvan laced their fingers together, drawing a sigh from Raf. "I don't know that I could have coached you any better, and I don't know that you could improve on what you just did. I am completely, utterly impressed."

"Wow. Okay. I was not ready for that. Remind me to occasionally forgo the extreme honesty."

"Too much?"

Raf shuddered. "No, I'm just not used to your brand of it. Yet."

Silvan stayed quiet, watching Raf closely. He took a few moments to breathe, to let his gaze fall over the man who had upended his life so thoroughly. He was used to being cautious in matters of the heart, especially because for so long he'd been too busy to do much other than a few dinners here and there. But desire and sex hadn't factored into any of that. And now Silvan had a passionate, beautiful, intelligent man who, for whatever reason, found him to be important. It was a bit of a mindfuck.

Finally, Silvan spoke up. "And I have to admit I'm not used to any of this. What is between you and me is...well, suffice to say I consider myself lucky, horny, and just a little scared."

Raf burst into laughter. "*Oh my god, Silvan.*"

But he was laughing, too; so much he had to pull his hand away to wipe his eyes. "No one ever used that particular line on you?"

Raf coughed and shook his head. "You. Holy shit. That was incredible."

"I am, on occasion, quite funny. I just take time warming up."

The next thing he knew, Silvan was pulled forward into a kiss that *scorched*. He felt the wild urge to check his eyebrows, but Raf's tongue and lips and *fuck*, his teeth were staking a claim. Silvan fell forward even more and braced his hands on the back of the chair while Raf kissed the breath from him. That very kiss that turned his insides molten made him also want to never let Raf go.

It was so soon to fall like this.

He didn't care.

Chapter Twenty-One

The gallery opening

The text from Judy read: "*For the new patron of the arts in St. Augustine. You should arrive in style to your own gallery opening. Break a leg, Raf. I'll see you there.*" And it arrived ten minutes ahead of the limo now parked in his driveway.

Raf rang Judy instead of texting her back. "This is far too kind, Judy."

"Not at all. It's a plush ride, and now you can arrive at both the gallery and back home in style."

"Ah, so if there's a change in plans..."

"Just tell the driver. She'll take you where you want to go." Then Judy laughed softly. "So the rumors are true."

"Judy."

"Not a word, darling. I'm happy for you. He's a catch. Your Silvan's been quite the talk around town, particularly with some of the older singles."

"I'm hanging up now, Judy. Thank you again for the limo."

Judy's laugh rang in his ears for a moment, then he called Silvan. "So it turns out I have a limo tonight. Care for a pickup?"

"As long as you're in the backseat with an overnight bag."

"I can one thousand percent guarantee it."

"Reaching for the stars so early."

Raf smiled, leaning into the sound of Silvan's voice. So calm, so collected. It helped smooth his own nerves down a little. He would be nervous until fifteen minutes before opening, then the evening would fly by and he'd turn around at midnight or one a.m., exhausted but happy. It was the come down during the few days afterwards that was always tough. It was like walking through a fog.

But this was the final time. The home stretch. Part of him felt like grieving, just a little, but the rest was elated. With this final gallery opening, his life had changed drastically. It hadn't been the intention, of course, but here he was, staring at a pristine white limo he wouldn't be riding in alone.

Silvan certainly hadn't been part of the plan.

Raf grinned, grabbed his things, and got into the vehicle. The driver was a young woman in her twenties with big brown eyes and an easy smile. "Where to?"

Raf gave her the address for Silvan's house and settled back. They cruised out of the suburbs and onto the coastal highway. The sun was largely blocked by the tinted windows but Raf soaked in what warmth came through. The glint of his jewelry caught in his periphery and a naughty little thought crept into his mind. He could blame it on nervous energy - for the opening, for what would come later. He could also blame it on wanting to tease Silvan, just a little.

But as he swiftly undid the buttons on his shirt and tossed the scarf over his shoulder, a little thrill went down his spine. He held his phone up, angled it just so, and took several pictures. Dithering over the "perfect" one wasn't worth his worry, or brain space, right now, so he chose one and sent it over to Silvan.

> **From: Raf** *I'm leaning into my own sense of artistry ahead of tonight's big event. Do you like the way I captured the sunlight streaming in?*

He bit his lip and waited for the reply.

Silvan had just finished a call with the cat cafe when his phone lit up. With barely a glance to the device, he thumbed over the screen to pull up the message but his attention was still locked on the pictures of Mozart that had been emailed over. It hadn't taken long for him to decide that Mozart was a good fit for him - older, easy-going, in need of a home. In the mad scramble days before the gallery opening, he'd asked Bonnie to pick up all the needed supplies and she had, like he'd figured, gone overboard. But since she'd had fun picking out toys and scratchers and a glittery collar - and spending his money instead of her own

- he couldn't fault her. It was exciting, a new being in a house that had been empty save for him for so long. Mozart would be coming home on Monday and he wanted to be prepared.

He closed his laptop with a sigh and picked up his phone. The text from Raf was innocuous. The photo, less so.

That fucking tease, he thought, blood instantly heating. The glint of several necklaces - including the chain on which he wore that *lira* piece - should have been the focus. But Raf's skin glowed in the late afternoon sun. It made Silvan's mouth water, the sight of all that skin and dark, curling chest hair framed by a peacock-paisley shirt and hint of dark red jacket. He wanted to *unwind* Raf from all of it, peel the pieces from his body and worship every bit of skin revealed.

This was going to be a long night.

From: Silvan *If your intention is to ruin me, you win. I cannot resist you.*

From: Raf *As long as it's gentle. I've never wanted to be ruined so badly. Promise me the jacket will survive, I'm quite fond of it.*

Silvan shifted in his seat. The stirrings of desire were flaring to life hot and fast and he did not need to worry about an erection right now.

From: Silvan *I would never rip anything from you without permission.*

From: Raf *I'm giving it. Explicitly.*

From: Silvan *How close are you?*

From: Raf *Five minutes, maybe six.*

The crunch of tires on his drive a few minutes later made his heart kick up a notch, but he made sure he had his things before stepping outside to meet the car. The back door of the limo opened and a bejeweled hand beckoned Silvan into its dark, cool confines.

Silvan didn't hardly have the door shut before he heard Raf say, "Drive, please. To the gallery." And then there were lips on his, eager. Almost demanding.

"Did you rile yourself up?" Silvan teased between hot, slick kisses. Raf's hands didn't wander much beyond squeezing Silvan's thighs, but it was enough.

"Incredibly," Raf murmured against his mouth. "Everything is beyond the pale tonight. The opening. You." He pulled back and gave Silvan's suit the once-over. "This suit. This decadent, beautiful thing the color of ice. You look *amazing*."

"We make quite the pair." Silvan let his fingers tangle in the tassels of Raf's scarf instead of that thick, dark hair. It wouldn't do to get rumpled before the night even started. Raf laid his hand over Silvan's and brought them to rest on his chest.

He'd left two buttons undone.

"Three buttons is a bit of a slut move," Raf said, voice dark with promises Silvan intended to ensure he kept.

"The scandal," he replied.

The temptation to tell the limo driver to turn back, take them back, was quelled only by the buzz of Raf's phone. "I think that's our cue for business," Raf said.

"Pleasure later."

Raf kissed him once more and Silvan heard the unspoken promise in it. "I can't wait.

There was too much to do and never enough time. Raf felt like his head would burst from all the dashing about he did over the next two hours. But none of it would have been finished if it hadn't been for Silvan and Camilla and April and everyone else who offered their help.

He'd barely had a chance to talk to April face to face over the last several weeks, as she floated from gallery to gallery handling clients, and now she was three feet away and beaming at him. "You're gonna have people breaking down the doors," she said as he approached.

"I thought I saw you sparkling from afar," he said, matching her smile. "Those earrings are killer."

April thumbed at the bright blue crystal hoops. "Not too much, I hope. I was wanting to match the walls."

"They're gorgeous. You look fantastic." He held her at arm's length and gave her sleeveless white power suit and teased afro the once-over. "I do admire your bravery for the white suit but you look fantastic."

"That's why white wine exists, Raf."

"Touché."

She linked her arm in his and guided him over to the blue room. "I thought you might want to do a walk-through before Ambrose and Barrett arrive."

Raf's head swam. His best friend and forest ranger, teddy bear boyfriend would be let in with the other VIP ticket-holders soon. *Excited* didn't cover how glad he was going to be to see them both. With a certain kind of quiet reverence, he put his hands on the doors and pushed in.

The room was as Raf remembered, full of life and color splashed against bright white and dark navy. The center of the room held a four-sided, free-standing display, impossible to miss as you walked in. The front-facing wall displayed a collage of soft watercolors and charcoal sketches, from the elegant drape of wisteria vines to a whimsical spread of larkspur and buttercups. He'd selected this set of prints as an invitation, a way of welcoming everyone into a space that held art from a very special person. He'd never met Perry, but the man had been the catalyst for Ambrose and Barrett meeting. In some way, he'd also kept them together. Perry's death at the beginning of the previous year had changed Barrett's life, and then Ambrose's. It felt only right to honor the memory of the man at the heart of that seismic shift.

"You think they'll like it?" April asked as they followed the path around the room, gazing at the canvases.

Raf went over to the table where the books featuring Perry's art were displayed. "I think they'll love it," he said quietly, letting his hand drift over the cover of the top book. "I haven't thanked you enough, April, and I'm so sorry about that. I think I'll have a lot of mea culpas to ask for when all of this is said and done."

When April didn't speak for a long set of moments, Raf looked her way. She was studying the canvas in front of them, her eyes glued to the spray of multi-hued wildflowers. The canvas was long and wide, perfectly placed at eye level; the goal was to let viewers sink into the art, hopefully so much that they could place themselves in that field and let the rest of the world drop away.

"There's nothing to apologize for, Raf. I've been through three gallery openings with you, I know the score." She turned to face him, her expression deadly serious. "Is this really the last one? It feels too final."

He shook his head, a bittersweet taste rising in the back of his throat. "It is. I was going to have a sit down with all of you after this weekend."

"Good. And thanks."

"Of course."

She sighed and crossed her arms. "It's a little sad, gotta admit. But I get it." And then she spread her arms wide and said, "Look at this. This is incredible."

"It is."

When Raf handed her a copy of the book, it was with that same reverence with which he'd opened the doors. "Best get in on the first print run, my friend."

That got him a grin. "Oh, I already snatched one up. It's my bonus for working my ass off for you these last several years."

"You get a yearly bonus!"

"I know. But I wanted the book."

They were both chuckling when the door to the room opened and Silvan stuck his head in. "Thirty minutes, Raf."

Oh sweet Jesus and Zeus and whoever else. Raf smoothed down his lapels, then his scarf, and then pulled Silvan inside. "I'm gonna leave you two," April said, slipping away with a shit-eating grin plastered to her sharp features.

When she was gone, Raf busied himself by fussing with Silvan's dark blue pocket square. "Do you need anything?" Silvan asked, voice soft, like he didn't want to disturb the peace of the room or break the moment. He had Raf by the elbows and that blue gaze was checking him over. All of the sultriness and teasing from earlier was gone. This was Silvan showing concern and care and the kindness of it made Raf's heart melt.

"I'm okay. Really. My nerves usually vanish when we're close to time." Raf paused, staring up at Silvan, hoping his expression could convey the things he couldn't form into words. Everything had led up until tonight - every email, phone call, frantic practicing for an interview while locked away in his office, every new idea and old one. He'd been living and breathing this opening for more than eighteen months and now to finally have it happen...to know it was the last one...

Raf was sure he'd be overcome with bittersweet happiness were it not for Silvan. Standing in front of him in an ice blue suit, hair perfectly mussed, his hands warm, his touch comforting.

"I'm really okay," Raf repeated, leaning in and staring hard into Silvan's eyes, seeking permission. When he got it in the form of a smile and head nod, Raf kissed him. "I'm just really glad you're here."

"Me, too."

"Who could have known what our chance encounter would bring."

Silvan's hands were now on his face, tugging him up into another kiss. "I don't want to think about what would have happened otherwise."

The doors were waiting to open with a nod from Raf. Silvan's stomach fluttered with nerves, but this was the plan. Let the VIP ticket holders in, let them get drinks and food, let them wander in the massive main hall and admire the breathing flowers over their heads. Then let Raf give a speech, open all the other doors, and truly begin the night.

His job was to keep an eye out for Raf's friend, Ambrose. He'd seen plenty of pictures, and given the man had bright auburn hair, he figured it'd be an easy task. But when the doors finally yawned open and Raf darted off (he left behind a kiss to Silvan's cheek) to help Camilla guide people inside, the crowd became an excited, civilized *crush*. No one was causing a scene, but everyone was pushing a little to get inside, see everything, experience the event. And that made him swell with pride.

They'd actually pulled this off. More than pulled it off, accomplished it almost flawlessly. He thought it *had* been flawless but he also knew Raf would reject such an idea. *Nothing is flawless, Silvan darling. Best we can do is slightly flawed but fashionable.*

Silvan wanted to move to get a better vantage point from the top of the ramp that led to a small walkway and one of the currently closed rooms, but the collective gasp of the crowd stopped him in his tracks. The first ones with their tickets scanned were just catching sight of the flower waterfall. There was a burst of pride in his chest, a fuzzy warm feeling of accomplishment as those entering stared up in awe. As Silvan watched the crowd react, he caught Arie's eye as she stood with some of her crew, watching the same spectacle unfold. Arie gave him a wink and a wave; the wave he returned with a smile of his own.

Slowly the crowd spread out, everyone heading for whichever art piece called to them first. There were few who wandered to the bar, but he did see a tall man with auburn hair on the arm of an equally tall man in a blue suit. Picking his way across the crowd was easy when he had a keycard to get through the back hallways and skip all that mess.

He popped out near the bar and headed over to Ambrose and Barrett. "Good to see some faces I recognize, even if we've not formally met." Silvan thrust out his hand. "Silvan Diedrich, I'm Raf's marketing manager."

Gray eyes scraped over him, instantly poking his exterior for weakness. Raf's best friend was, as Raf had explained, a *discerning man* who would - discreetly - want to make sure he could measure up. Raf tried to apologize for Ambrose's protectiveness, but Silvan knew where it was coming from. Love - that bright, bursting, high and the dedication and respect that powered it - wasn't something he'd stand in the way of. "Ambrose," the man said. "Good to finally meet you, Silvan."

The man beside Ambrose had a bright grin in a dark beard and the stature of someone who was used to being the tallest, broadest one in the room. But his eyes were kind and it was easy to picture Barrett in a forest ranger uniform, guiding hikers or setting up trail markers. "I'm Barrett. And this is..." He took the beer bottle Ambrose handed him and widened his motion with it. "Incredible. I'll be complimenting Raf all night."

"He won't blush," Ambrose said with a chuckle. "At least not in public. You'll have to work hard, Barrett."

Barrett shrugged his mountainous shoulders. "I think I've got his number."

Ambrose's single eyebrow lift, accompanied by Barrett's booming laugh, made Silvan smile. "I'm going to fetch Raf, if you'll wait here?"

Ambrose nodded but Barrett leaned in to whisper, "Don't tell Raf I said that."

"Absolutely not. I'm not a fan of digging graves for other people."

That got him a snort from Ambrose. "Smart man. I see why Raf likes you."

Silvan disappeared into the crowd with a nod and almost immediately caught sight of Raf, who he snagged by the hand. "By the bar."

Raf sighed happily. "You're the best." And with a swift kiss to Silvan's cheek, he was off again and there was a cry of delight seconds later. Raf was going to take Ambrose and Barrett into the blue room, where Perry's drawings were displayed. That left Silvan to mind the shop, so to speak, so he floated in and out of the crowd, trying to discreetly take pictures for a social media livestream. They'd hired a photographer for the good shots, but what he wanted was the unscripted looks of awe, the heads leaning together in close conversation, the glint of sequins and beads and glass.

He was lining up a great shot of Judy and a few other *very* well-dressed guests in conversation when a warm hand wrapped around his left shoulder. "Hey, Dad."

"Hey, kid." Silvan snapped the picture, then immediately turned and pulled Bonnie into a hug. "So, what do you think?"

"I have no words. Really." Bonnie was in a stunning dark green velvet dress, the boatneck dip of fabric showing off her tattoos and the necklace he'd bought her for her eighteenth birthday. "I mean that thing is just wild but seeing this place full of people having a good time..."

Bonnie trailed off but Silvan understood. That warm feeling of accomplishment still sat in his chest, but the look on Bonnie's face, the hum of the crowd, the snippets of conversation, the wine flowing...all of it added up to something the word *proud* couldn't even begin to describe.

Silvan decided to revel in it. He put his arm around his daughter and said, "Let's stroll. Raf's going to open the doors to all the rooms soon and I can get us in the easy way."

Bonnie gasped. "Using your power as an employee for evil already, Dad?"

"Yes, absolutely." He gazed down at her as they began to walk to the western wing of the gallery. "You look great, by the way. Is that dress new?"

Bonnie squirmed under his arm. "New by the way of vintage. I, uh, went shopping with Camilla last week and they magically found this on the bottom of a pile of items the shop had just gotten in."

"It's like it was made for you. You look beautiful."

Bonnie went silent for a moment. When she peered up at him, Silvan sucked in a breath. Those blue eyes were so like his own, and Bonnie was far more fierce and independent than he remembered being at that age. But in this moment, she was his daughter. And apparently his daughter was a bit nervous, because she said, "So me and Camilla. We're just getting to know each other. But they're cool."

He had to bite back a smile. "Just cool?"

"Dad."

"I'm asking, it's not an interrogation."

"I could give you shit about dating your *boss*."

Silvan kissed the top of her head. "Shit-slinging is for later. Let's enjoy this."

"Barrett. My friend. I do need to be able to breathe."

"Breathing's overrated, Raf," Ambrose shot back, his voice near Raf's right ear.

Raf was basically pulled from Barrett's arms into Ambrose's. His best friend, his platonic soulmate and truest confidant, embraced him tightly. Something caught in his throat but he pushed it down, unwilling to cry. Not yet, anyways. When Ambrose let him go, Barrett refused to relinquish his grip. "You have no idea what this means. None."

Ah, damn. Raf's eyes burned. "I'm glad you like it. It needed to be right, for your friend. For you."

"It's perfect." Unashamed, Barrett was blinking away tears of his own, and Raf could see Ambrose's gray eyes shimmer as he stared at his boyfriend. "I...can we have a minute?"

"Absolutely." With a last squeeze to Barrett's arm, Raf left them in the blue room. His head felt fuzzy, his heart too full, and when he walked back out into the main gallery space, he feared he'd be overwhelmed. But Silvan was there, steady hands and blue eyes and a glass of water in hand.

"Come sit for a second." The command in Silvan's voice, however gentle, still sent a shiver of *something* down Raf's spine. He let Silvan guide him into one of the gallery's back hallways to an unused office.

He sank into the chair while Silvan perched on the edge of the desk. Raf wanted to gulp the water down but took a moment to rest the cool glass against his forehead. "You remembered," he said quietly, his eyes closed. "Thank you."

When he looked up, Silvan was staring steadily at him, gaze assessing. "Of course. You did ask me to pull you away if I thought you looked overwhelmed."

"And you did, so now I'm thanking you." Raf took one last gulp of water and then, with no preamble, shot to his feet and reeled Silvan in. Hands joined, Raf dragged them down his chest. Sitting and ruminating wouldn't help him. Action would. And his entire being yearned for one more stolen moment with Silvan before the night wore deep into the late hours and he was too exhausted to do even this. "Be grounded with me. One more time."

Raf moved their hands lower, until the bottom of Silvan's palm brushed his belt. He hissed in response but it died as soon as he saw the darkness in Silvan's eyes, the intense, focused stare. Silvan pushed him - gently, but with enough force to carry Raf back a few steps.

Another push. Another few steps.

One more. This push more firm, with something like a snarl on Silvan's face. A jolt of desire arced through Raf. A bit of silver hair fell over Silvan's forehead and Raf reached up to brush it away, only to have his hand grabbed. Pinned to the wall. The rest of him hemmed in by a gorgeous man in an immaculate suit whose body and mind and spirit called to him in a way that knocked all sense from Raf's head. "You remembered," Raf breathed, fighting against the urge to squirm in pleasure.

"I remember everything about you," Silvan said, leaning in and down. Letting his breath ghost over Raf's lips. "And tonight I've watched you. So confident, so strong, so brilliant. Everyone watches you when you're near and yet..." Warm lips pressed into the thin skin below his ear, directly over his pulse. He had no control over how his breathing hitched, that single touch making him groan in delight. "I know whose bed you'll be in tonight. Tomorrow morning."

This *possessiveness*, playful but prideful, firm yet not unbending, was going to drive Raf up the fucking wall. And the bastard knew it, because the next thing Raf knew, Silvan was kissing down his neck. Everything in him heated past the boiling point of *wanting*. He was damn close to begging by now.

"This is...is what you wanted, isn't it?" Raf asked. The blunt edge of fucking *teeth* skimmed over the curve of his shoulder as Silvan pushed his shirt out of the way.

"What did I want?" Fingers were now in his hair, pulling. Making Raf tip his head back, bare his throat.

"Me. Desperate."

"Right on both counts," Silvan growled. "I want you, and I'm determined you'll be desperate before I even have you naked. *I promise you that.*"

They had to go. They had to get back.

All Raf wanted was to drop to his knees.

Silvan's lips left Raf's neck and found his mouth instead. The kiss bit, it claimed, it made Raf whimper and strain against Silvan's hold while the tongue in his mouth took its time. While the man holding him, pinning him, kissing him like he wanted to take a bit of Raf's soul with every touch.

"We have to go back." Silvan's voice was a whisper now.

Words Raf didn't want to hear, and yet they were the blunt anvil of truth crashing through his haze of lust. "I know."

Silvan leaned back to study him carefully, blue eyes narrowed as he inspected Raf's face. "You are remarkable."

Raf reached up to run the pad of his index finger over the corner of Silvan's mouth. "So are you."

"Gather round, everyone! I swear I'll be quick."

Raf stood on a small stage above the crowd, microphone in hand, and smiled as everyone slowly quieted and turned toward him. Silvan watched from the back of the room, leaning against a far wall and as out of sight as possible. This was Raf's moment, and he wasn't about to spoil anything.

"Ah yes, there's my lovely audience." Raf could command a room by just standing in it, but give him a beautiful set of clothes, a microphone, and hair mussed on the edge of sexy bedhead, and everyone stopped what they were doing to watch. Silvan knew the appeal; not ten minutes before he'd had Raf pinned to a wall in a dark office and had given serious contemplation to taking him right there.

Raf's smile was bright. Proud. "Well, here we are. For some of you, those of you who have been here from the start, you've been with me through three or four or even five openings." Raf pointed to the right side of the room, where Camilla and April stood with Raf's family. "Those lovely beings there are my lifers, apparently. Stuck with me through the end times." He grinned wider and Silvan watched so many in the crowd smile in return. His Raf was enigmatic, alluring. "They know, should the end times involve zombies, they have permission to eat me first. It's a courtesy thing, after all they've done for me. A terrible joke, but it stands nonetheless."

"I think you're too stringy!" Marianna called out.

"And I'm vegan so..." Camilla got a round of laughter out of it.

"Look at that," Raf drawled. "Such dedication." He paused and walked closer to the edge of the stage. Posture straightened, shoulders back, wide hazel eyes scanning the crowd. "You are all here for the fifth gallery opening under the Ablaze family. You're here for the art, the free food and wine, and hopefully to donate something to what I'm proud to announce is our new Community Art Network. A meeting place for artists looking to learn, to trade information, to find clients, and the realization of a dream I had many years ago. Art education in schools is waning, and it's my hope we can revive it under the CAN. Your ticket costs tonight feed into that fund, and of course we will happily take your incredibly kind, generous donations."

Raf held up a hand, smile dropping to be replaced by a more serious expression. "So to not keep you all waiting any longer in anticipation, the moment I'm done here, you'll have full reign of the gallery. All of the doors will be opened and you can explore at will. I encourage you to check the blue room to your left. It contains the artwork of a very special man who captured the delicate, wild beauty of the east coast through his careful eye for detail and genuine love for the outdoors. The art books are incredibly limited quantity, so if you don't get one and want a copy, please see Camilla at the desk. They'll handle your order for you. Take your time. Look at everything on display. Talk to the artists. Take pictures. Remember this."

"And so here we are. Another gallery opening." Raf paused, looked around, and caught Silvan's eye. "The final one." A few people gasped and there were some murmurs. "I know. I made the decision a long time ago and while I'd love to have more, it's simply not in the cards. So you are here on a very special night, never to be repeated in this particular fashion. And this would have never happened had it not been for the incredible work of our staff and volunteers, our community partners, and yes, even those pesky politicians we all take umbrage with from time to time."

Raf went down the line, his words perfectly thoughtful and funny, from thanking Arie and Desiree and teasing Camilla about being able to handle ten phone lines to the sweet endearments for his mother. Silvan saw a few people swipe quickly at their eyes. "And finally, if you've not met him, that incredibly handsome man in the back in the ice blue suit is Silvan, our new marketing manager at Ablaze. Without him, none of this would have worked out. His vision got us over the last few hurdles, and his dedication saw us through to the end. To this. So if you'll toast with me. One more opening. One more exciting, special night." Raf raised his glass high and found Silvan's eyes once more. "For the sake of art and creation and imagination. For the love that goes into everything around us. And for the sweat and tears and genuine, unadulterated *love* poured into every inch of it."

Behind them, over their heads in the rotunda, the flower waterfall breathed slowly. In and out. In and out.

Living, moving art.

Chapter Twenty-Two

Midnight approached, and with every minute that ticked by, Raf could feel his energy draining. Many of the guests and artists had left, leaving behind the big spenders looking to purchase pieces (including Judy, which shocked no one) and Raf's family and friends. He helped Camilla get paperwork sorted while the others chatted near the blue room. Barrett still looked a little stunned after the big reveal of Perry's art, but Raf knew Ambrose would keep him steady until they could both collapse back at the seaside bungalow Raf had rented for them. And thankfully, Silvan was engaging Barrett in conversation; from the hand motions, Raf could only guess it was about fishing.

Ambrose wandered over to him just as Francia snagged his arm when he stepped away from the desk. "You were amazing," she said quietly, her face buried in his shoulder. "I'm so proud of you. I know I say that all the time."

"I'll never get tired of hearing it," Raf admitted, grinning down at her. "Did you enjoy the night?"

"I did. Incredible. Just incredible. And I can't wait to see the Night Garden show in a few weeks."

He groaned, the sound exaggerated so she'd smack him on the arm. When it worked, he had to laugh. "I don't know, Mom. There's some naughty things in that show."

Francia rolled her eyes. "Please. As if I've never seen naked bodies before. You weren't miraculously conceived, you know."

"I have so little desire to even think about discussing that, now or...ever," he said, steering her toward the little group she'd broken away from. "Absolutely not." When Ambrose gave him a questioning look, Raf shrugged. "My mother being her usual self."

"Well, I like her usual self."

"Suck up," Raf shot back.

"Boys." Francia might not have been actually scolding them, but her tone worked just fine. They both snapped to attention, and Francia looked rather pleased. "Ah, I still have 'Mom voice'. Good to know."

Barrett and Silvan wandered over, as did Bonnie and Camilla. Becca and Shaleena had made a quick appearance early on before leaving for a red-eye to Italy. "Our chance to get reestablished with each other," Becca had said to both Raf and Silvan on their way out. Raf hoped it would work out for them. He knew how much Silvan cared for his ex and her well-being, so it mattered to him, too.

And wasn't that a wild thought? That already he was in the deep end and learning how to swim without ever putting on the safety gear.

As Bonnie took up a spot near his left shoulder, Raf smiled at her. "Did you have a good evening?"

"I really did. Thanks for inviting me." Bonnie was beaming, and Raf didn't miss how close she and Camilla were standing next to each other. The way Camilla's fingers twitched, as if wanting to take Bonnie's hand. They would be trouble. The good kind, but still trouble.

"A final word, if I may," Raf said, pulling everyone's focus once more. He usually enjoyed being the center of attention, but with exhaustion dogging his footsteps, he wanted to do this now. "I'll keep this short and sweet." He took the time to look at every person in their little group. "I love you all. None of this would have happened without you. So before I go on too much and get sappy and have to dig for tissues in Camilla's desk..."

"Pretty sure that's theft, boss," they shot back, thick eyebrows wiggling in delight.

"Take it up with the head of the gallery," he replied evenly, and that got them laughing. Which, of course, had been the goal. "I love you all. I'll say it as much as I need to in order to make that sink in. Never once have you done anything but stand by me, the galleries, the artists. You worked your asses off, you saved mine time and again, and this has always been about so much more than displaying canvases on a wall." Raf gestured wide, staring at the art surrounding them. "We are in a very special place, filled with passion and emotion. That's what art is, after all. Imagination and passion and emotion molded in clay or dashed across paper, strung up on wire. The ultimate show of making something out of nothing. Art is beauty, it's culture, it's our very humanity. I cannot thank you enough for making so many dreams come true."

Arie was the first to break, crushing Raf in a hug that threatened his ribcage. There were hugs and kisses on the cheek, Barrett accidentally tickling Raf's nose with his beard, and Ambrose holding his dearest friend close. His mother hugging him once more, then Marianna, while Desiree called him "honey darling" and told him how proud she was. Bonnie even gave him a hug, which left him staring after her as she stepped back and Silvan materialized before him. "I'm staying at Camilla's," he heard Bonnie say. "I'd crash at Mom's but it's weird when there's no one around."

"Not to drop eaves but I'm assuming Camilla told you about their cat," Raf said, catching Camilla by the arm. "Cam?"

"What? Yeah, of course! You gotta get entry approved by Shrimp." They shrugged, their thick sweater falling off one shoulder. "Bonnie knows."

Silvan looked baffled. "You have a cat named Shrimp?"

"Yeah! She's the best." They curled close to Bonnie and batted their eyes at Silvan. "She's also old and grouchy."

"Extremely grouchy. Age has only made it worse." Marianna sidled up to them, eyes glittering. "Everyone looks to be on their way out. Anything left to do, Raf?"

He shook his head. "Not a thing. Go home. Rest."

"Until weekend brunch, that is," Francia said. She pointed at him and Silvan. "You get a pass. Just this once."

"My magnanimous mother, everyone." But Raf kissed her cheek and gave her a final hug before watching her and Marianna leave. Bonnie and Camilla were next, walking out arm in arm and leaving Silvan to chuckle and shake his head. Arie wandered out with Desiree on her heels, the two of them headed across the street to the little corner cocktail place.

When Ambrose and Barrett stepped up to say goodbye, Barrett was clutching a copy of Perry's book to his chest. His mouth opened a few times, then he squished Raf into another man-eating hug. "I'm really glad to know you," Barrett said, voice gruff, but Raf heard the ends of his words tremble.

He was swooped from Barrett to Ambrose, his friend's familiar warmth comforting and making him sigh. And then they were saying goodbye before walking out into the night.

Silvan draped an arm over his shoulders, leaning close so he could take ahold of Raf's chin between his thumb and forefinger. "Now we're alone. And in desperate need of sleep."

His stomach rumbled. "And food. I didn't eat at all tonight."

"I've got that handled, don't worry."

"It didn't even cross my mind otherwise." With a playful nip to Silvan's fingers, Raf leaned in as well. "Take me home?"

Silvan stared at him. "Is that your answer on our agreement?"

"Yes. Absolutely." Saying it out loud felt *good*. He hadn't really doubted this was where they would land, but he wanted to hear it from Silvan. "And you?"

Silvan pressed his forehead into Raf's, gathering him close. "Somehow, I knew it all along."

"Knew what?"

"Knew you'd step into my life and change it for the better. So, yes."

The limo was waiting, as were chilled bottles of champagne and water and tiny chocolates. As soon as they were settled in the back seat, Raf reached for the chocolate in the middle of the tray and popped it into his mouth. Cherry exploded on his tongue and he sighed happily. "There's always a cherry one in the middle," he explained as Silvan eyed the tray. "Apologies, but I just...*wanted it*."

"Take what you want. I won't stop you."

Raf hummed as if in thought, when really the noise was to distract from the way he shivered. *Anticipation, indeed*. "Should we take the champagne inside?" he asked, letting his fingers dance lightly over Silvan's thigh. Those pants were tight enough that he could feel a ridge of muscle jump under his touch.

"Probably a good idea." Silvan was watching him closely, as if he could read Raf's mind.

Raf knew he looked tired. There was no helping it after such an evening. But he didn't want Silvan to think he was *too* tired. The smudge of chocolate on his thumb gave him ideas. "I think I want this," he said quietly, smearing the chocolate on Silvan's lower lip, then leaning in to lick it away. He was *this close* to crawling into Silvan's lap, with the way the other man was gripping his arm, palming the back of his head. Kissing him with such intense focus. Raf leaned in to brace himself on the seat back, freeing his other hand. The hand that was now sliding down Silvan's chest and tracing over the curve of a hip.

"Fuck." Silvan tore away from their kiss to tip his head back, breathing hard. "You make temptation look like the best thing in the world. Gods."

"Good to know I have an effect," he replied, mouth now against the hinge of Silvan's jaw. The hand in Raf's hair tightened.

"An *effect*?" Silvan was melted into the seat, leaving room for Raf to press against him more. "Never thought you to be one for understatement, Raf."

"I'm not. But I'll note that I am following instructions." Raf leaned back and gave Silvan a wicked grin. "*Your* instructions, handsome. I can't wait to see what plans you have for us."

Silvan was quick, Raf had to give him that. He found himself hauled into Silvan's lap and kissed *hard*; the kind of kiss that left him dizzy, with a buzz of energy under his skin, begging for release. His cock certainly had release in mind as well.

The intercom buzzed. "We're five minutes away from your destination. Do you have any other stops to make tonight?"

Silvan was determined to get Raf's jacket off, so Raf struggled to reach the speaker. "No, we're good. Thank you."

"Have a good night."

"You, too." Raf gasped at the slide of fingers on his chest. "Fuck, you're sneaky."

Silvan's grip was tight as he hauled Raf back. That touch - commanding, needy - sent a thrill down his spine. But those blue eyes were wide, focused, and Raf thought about swooning. "I have wanted to get my hands on you since Judy's brunch," Silvan growled in his ear. They were pressed so tightly against each other that Raf could only squirm. "Do you know I got myself off thinking about you?"

"*Shit.*" Silvan had an iron grip on him, his right hand sliding under Raf's jacket and up his back while the left was holding onto his hip. Raf really wanted him to move that left hand in a few inches but Silvan seemed determined to keep him here. Pinned in place. Staring down.

Silvan nuzzled against him, pressing kisses along his breastbone. It felt *so good*, unlike any other touch he'd ever had the pleasure to experience. "That night when you texted me about the rotunda display."

Raf's laugh left him in a gust of breath. "That's why you were awake at some ungodly hour in the morning?"

"Insomnia. It happens on occasion." Silvan grinned up at him and Raf released the seat to run his palm along Silvan's jaw. "But I thought about you and your eyes and how much I wanted to put you on your knees and keep you there."

Something crackled in Raf's vision. Like staring directly at a firework. Or the fucking sun. "I'd go willingly, you know."

"I do."

The limo came to a stop. Raf didn't wait for the driver to open the door. He nabbed the champagne bottle from the little holder and practically dragged Silvan from the car, the both of them laughing. All he wanted to do was strip off their fine clothes and drink champagne in bed with Silvan, knowing no matter what they did tonight or tomorrow, all that he wanted was to be with this glorious, beautiful man.

"I could get used to this," Raf said, pressing up behind Silvan as he unlocked his front door. "Alone. In the dark. With you so close."

"One problem with that," Silvan replied as he got them inside and turned on a lamp. "I want to see you. I've spent months staring at you, not able to touch you the way I've dreamt of." He closed the distance between them and took the champagne bottle from Raf, set it aside. "I know we're both exhausted. We've earned it. Tonight..." Silvan's expression flickered, something vulnerable flitting over his face and it made Raf's heart jump in his chest. "Tonight I just want to touch you. Any way you want. Everything else can wait."

The way Raf kissed him now meant something he didn't quite have the words for. But Silvan was warm and receptive, opening to him so sweetly it made Raf want to clutch and cling, to wrap his limbs around Silvan and never let go. "Yes, anything."

"We'll take our time."

"It's all I want."

With gentle hands, Silvan pushed him to the bathroom. "Get changed, shower if you want to. I'll get our food." But instead of letting him go, Silvan drew him close. "You must know I adore you. Beyond anything physical. You...speak to me in a way I've never experienced. It makes me want more, all the time."

He would *not* go weak at Silvan's words, but it was a close thing. "You are incredible," he breathed. The other words - smart, sexy, sweet things he wanted to murmur into Silvan's ear - left him. He stared up into Silvan's blue eyes and saw something there that meant more than any words either of them could produce.

Silvan took out the tray of cheese and fruit he'd prepared beforehand, then took the slow cooker off "warm" to reheat the food. He'd asked Bonnie to start it before she left for the opening, knowing he'd not have time for it otherwise. On the lid of the slow cooker was a sticky note. She'd drawn a heart and a devil face. Laughing, he pinned the note to the fridge with a magnet. With wine and water out on the counter, Silvan texted Raf to start without him if he got to the kitchen first.

The shower kicked on and that was his cue to head to the loft to change. The suit would need dry cleaning but he made sure to hang it up and tuck it back into the bag. Moving through those little necessities gave Silvan something to focus on outside of Raf in his house.

He glanced at the bed, perfectly made in shades of blue and teal. Blew out a breath. Then slipped into the master bath to comb his hair and change. Tonight wasn't for *too* much, and he'd made sure to shower that morning. But right now he wanted to ensure what Raf wanted *happened*. While climbing into bed to let their hands and mouths wander sounded heavenly, nothing could be done on an empty stomach. And he'd seen the label on the champagne; Judy hadn't skimped at all. They were going to get tipsy off twenty-year bubbly.

The thought had crossed his mind to drag out some satin pajamas from his drawers, but that felt like too much for a lowkey celebration. And boxers felt a little too *familiar*. So Silvan went with simple black joggers and a gray v-neck shirt, the kind of clothes that got softer with each laundry day. After the delicious weight of his suit, this felt like wearing almost nothing. It was freeing, easier somehow. The last little bit of weight of the night released from his shoulders.

(The hair he only mussed because combing it made him look too hard at a no-longer even hairline and Raf had liked it a little messy.)

When he went downstairs, Raf had the champagne bottle held aloft as he peered at the label. "Do you know how much this bottle goes for?"

"I...hmmm. Yes?"

One dark eyebrow arched. "You do. Or...you *do*?"

"Honestly, I just have a decent guess." Silvan put his hand out and Raf instantly took it. "I'm a little distracted at the moment."

"Too much?" Raf cocked a hip and Silvan got an eyeful of upper thigh. "It's a little decadent compared to what I sleep in, but not too far off the mark."

The rose pink satin shorts and tight black tank top were all Silvan could see. Focus on. Think about. All the bottled desire for this man in front of him came roaring back. With a swift yank, he had an armful of delighted Raf, and when Silvan kissed him, Raf's noise of surprise turned into a moan.

When they broke apart, Raf looked as dazed as Silvan felt. "Asked and answered. Well."

Silvan kissed his cheek before drawing him over to the small spread. "It's not fancy but I thought it might be welcome."

Raf sniffed the air. "Is that..."

"Homemade lobster bisque."

This groan was the sound of a different kind of hunger. "I'm going to do something drastic. Like stick a straw in your slow cooker and start slurping. How did you know?"

"Let's start with a bowl and if that's not enough, I'll find you a straw."

"My hero."

"And I asked Camilla. They were very helpful." Raf groaned again, the sound aggrieved. "I promise it was only about your favorite foods and not digging for family secrets." He gave Raf a coy look. "Still your hero?"

Raf hauled him in by the collar and kissed him. "Yes."

When their food was ladled out into bowls and piled high on plates, Silvan held out the champagne. "Do you want to do the honors?"

Raf was already perched on a stool at the kitchen island, eyes glued to his bowl. "I will never deny a beautiful man the opportunity to pour me champagne."

It seemed Raf's wit and charm had returned, even after the long night he'd had. Silvan shook his head with a chuckle. "Then open it we shall." He swiftly unwrapped the foil and wire cage from the cork, then held the bottle aloft, gazing into the dark green glass. Then into Raf's hazel eyes. "On three?"

"Yes, please."

"One, two..." Silvan grasped the cork and pulled. The *pop* exploded in his eardrums and then there was foam spilling over his hand.

Raf was giving him a wide-eyed look when he brought the bottle and two glasses over to the counter. "Might want to clean that off," he said, voice suddenly dark.

It took him a moment to understand and then Silvan smirked. "I really wasn't going for the sexual innuendo. Truly."

"Uh huh."

He poured for them both, pushing Raf's glass at him then leaning in to claim a kiss. "Eat, please."

Raf practically inhaled the first few spoonfuls of bisque, eyes fluttering shut in obvious pleasure. Silvan watched him, ensuring his contentment before digging in himself. It *was* good bisque and every time he made it, there was a spark of satisfaction watching people enjoy it so much. It was that same look on Raf's face now and Silvan was entranced.

"A toast," Raf said a few minutes later as he pushed his bowl away and refilled their glasses.

"To...?"

Raf tipped his chin up and strands of wavy hair fell away from his eyes. "To learning how to enjoy each other."

Smart, beautiful man. "To learning how to enjoy each other," Silvan repeated as he raised his glass.

Raf leaned in to steal a kiss, then clinked their glasses together. That high, crystalline note felt like a promise.

When the leftovers were packed away and the champagne was drained, Silvan silently held out a hand, then led Raf upstairs. "It's lovely," Raf said as he looked around Silvan's bedroom. "I didn't get to come up here last time."

"Wait until you see it in the morning. The sun hits just right and if it's a clear day, the ocean sparkles." Leaning against the wall, he watched Raf wander. Silvan felt it important to put a little space between them; there would be no pressure from him in any matter involving them in bed together. And watching Raf move through his space was giving him a vicarious thrill. The first thing Raf did was stop, take in the room, and then head to the bank of east-facing windows, not caring it was pitch black outside.

And as Raf moved into the middle of the room once more, he ran a hand over the bed's white oak footboard. Smirked. Then slipped onto the bed with a dancer's grace and spread his legs wide.

"An invitation?" Silvan asked as he pushed away from the wall.

"An invitation. A question. A proposal."

That smirk grew wider and Silvan nearly groaned. He hated the term *bratty bottom* but goddamn if Raf wasn't fitting that to a T. That tight black tank top strained across Raf's pecs and his tiny satin shorts weren't hiding an inch of his erection. Raf wanted him close *now* and yet Silvan was shivering in delight from holding back a little. Taking his time to approach the gorgeous man now leaning back on his elbows on Silvan's bed, staring at him with hot expectation.

"Ask me your question. Give me your proposal," Silvan said as he stalked toward Raf. "And I'll consider the invitation. But only if we're on the same page."

"Hmm...all right. Proposal first, since the question relies on that answer." Raf crooked a finger at him. "But I won't do anything without a kiss."

"You drive a hard bargain."

"The worst."

Silvan laid down beside Raf and propped his head up on his fist. "A kiss."

Raf looked at home on his bed, on his sheets. Beside him. So close. Smelling like the aloe soap from the downstairs shower and the fizzy pop of champagne. "Please."

Silvan leaned down, teasing. "Ah, now you're getting it."

Black eyelashes fluttered, hazel eyes scraping down Silvan's body. "Please."

Silvan braced himself on his forearms, leaning down just enough to brush his lips over Raf's pout. "How's that?"

"A fucking crime against humanity and my ego, that's what it is."

Raf shut up the second Silvan kissed him again, but he felt those long, agile fingers gripping his shoulders, digging in. He kept their kiss lazy, almost too slow, but he wanted to see how Raf withstood a little more teasing. With every touch, every kiss, they were drawing and redrawing the little lines that formed into bigger, bolder boundaries. And Silvan wanted to learn; to imprint every twitch, every gasp, every indent from a finger into his being.

But Raf had been right. All of that needed to start with a kiss.

"Devil," Raf whispered when they broke apart. "Gorgeous devil of a man."

But he had Raf now, pinned below him (beneath or below him, it didn't matter because having Raf trapped and squirming was quickly becoming a favorite), and slightly mussed. Silvan let his touch glide down Raf's chest and listened to the music of his groan before tugging at his tank top. "Take this off."

"That was actually in my proposal."

"Taking your shirt off?"

"Getting as naked as we want."

"And your question?"

A deft hand was now in his hair, dragging him down for another kiss. Silvan could see the promise of it written all over Raf's face. "If you'd let me touch you. More than this. I want to learn you, know you."

He let out a soft moan before kissing Raf again. It was impossible to ignore the flash of warmth through his body or, as they kissed and their hands wandered, the solidness of the man below him. When Raf squirmed, Silvan shifted away enough to grab the hem of his tank top and yank it up. "Fucking finally," he growled, not waiting for Raf to pull the garment off before sliding his hands up Raf's chest. Raf practically yelped in response, earning him a laugh while the tank top was thrown to the floor. "Ticklish?"

"No!"

"You are." Silvan gentled his touch, not wanting to provoke. Not now, not like this. "But I won't, I swear." Instead, he leaned down and pressed a kiss just above Raf's navel, listening to the way the man sighed, feeling how he went limp instantly. "Better?"

"Much."

Raf's fingers in his hair. The feel of his skin against Silvan's lips. The twitching of Raf's hips, how his thighs tightened around Silvan's ribs. He could lose himself like this; senses overwhelmed, his head buzzing. He wanted to stay here, linger in this feeling, roll around with it (and Raf) and not let go.

And while he worked his way up Raf's chest, his kisses and touches soft, the man below him shivered and gasped. "Devil," Raf whispered again, waiting until Silvan was petting his chest hair to haul him up by the arms and kiss him. "You're making me crazy."

"Is this okay?" He peered up at Raf. "Too much?"

Raf's breathing hitched. "It's perfect. I'm so turned on I can't see straight and yet..." Hips shifted against his own and Silvan bit back on a groan. "I'm good here. Just like this."

"There's nothing wrong with slow. And we're both exhausted."

A wicked spark lit up Raf's eyes. "Ah, age has caught up with you, I see."

Silvan licked the side of his neck in response and Raf melted beneath him once more. But they were laughing. Touching. Kissing. Taking their time. Making sure it was right. And Silvan had never felt so safe, so at ease with someone before. Not since Becca.

"This old man has a few tricks left," he finally said. "But it is late."

"Mmmm, it is." Raf opened his arms and Silvan fell into them. They shifted around until Raf was curled on his side, his legs tangled with Silvan's and one arm flung over his chest. Silence lay still in the air. Silvan breathed it in.

"Please don't think I don't want you." Raf's voice was quiet but worry lay under every syllable.

"Raf."

"Apologies." Raf lifted his head. "I worry too much."

"You do." Silvan leaned down to brush their lips together. "I never worried. If anything, I should be the one worried. But I'm not." He let his touch linger on Raf's side, heart thundering in his ears. How could he make Raf see how he felt, make him understand? Pushing those fears aside got easier as he went along in life, but doubt was a lingering, hungering thing that never rested. "You make me want in a way I've never felt before. It's...exciting. Enticing. A little scary. And, as it turns out, getting older doesn't mean this part of my life is over. I wasn't expecting you at all." Silvan tipped Raf's face up with two fingers under his chin. "But I'm so glad you're here."

Raf swallowed hard, the click of it audible in the silence around them. Understanding softened his expression. "I don't want to be anywhere else."

Chapter Twenty-Three

"Silvan."

"Mmmph."

Raf nuzzled closer, tightening his arm over Silvan's chest. "Does that noise mean you're awake?"

"Mmmph."

Raf held back a snicker and shifted again. Nothing like waking with an erection as you were pressed into someone you were desperate for. He barely had to open his eyes to know the sun hadn't yet risen. There was something about the darkness that held comfort. It also helped being curled into Silvan's side, their bodies pressed tightly to one another.

His arm was going a tad numb, but he figured that was the price to pay.

"Silvan."

A restless stirring, and then, "Please tell me it's not two in the morning."

"Guessing more like five."

"Ugh."

"Yes. Agreed."

Finally, Silvan stirred properly and Raf figured he'd move to get more comfortable. Instead, he was pulled even closer as Silvan rested his cheek on top of Raf's head. And it was lovely and wonderful, being so close. So warm and comfortable, his entire body at ease.

Except for the restlessness under his skin. Like an itch he couldn't scratch. Raf shifted again, trying to keep from pressing his erection into Silvan's hip. He didn't want the man to think Raf was desperate or anything; nor was he willing to break this blanket of sleepy silence. The darkness began to pull at him, welcoming him back into the land of exhaustion. If he would stay still, quiet his mind, slow his breathing, then it would all be fine. The itch could be scratched later.

His mind - and his libido - had other ideas when Silvan sighed and the arm looped around his chest moved. More specifically, the hand resting against his back slid south. Raf's breath caught.

Silvan made a pleased little sound that went straight to Raf's cock and everything came roaring back with bared teeth and naked desire. "I'm surprised we lasted this long," Silvan said, his breath stirring Raf's hair. That little thing nearly made Raf's eyes roll back in his head. His skin felt like it was on *fire* and he clawed at Silvan, desperate for more.

And then Silvan said, "Are you sure?"

Silvan wouldn't if Raf didn't want it. *Want him*. Even now at some ungodly hour, in the pre-dawn darkness with grogginess clinging to their minds, Silvan wanted to be sure.

"Yes." Raf pressed against him, lips skimming over Silvan's jaw. That got him a breathy groan, and then Silvan was rolling them, pushing Raf into the mattress and sliding a knee between his thighs. He happily took Silvan's weight, shoving his hands into thick silver hair. "Gods. Fuck."

"I've a question for you," Silvan murmured against his skin, lips and tongue leaving tingling in their wake as they made their way down his neck.

"I might have one braincell left."

The bed shifted, and then there was a hand on his cock. Squeezing. Raf moaned. "Or two."

"Fucking tease."

Silvan's laugh slipped over him. Raf was quickly learning new things about his wants and desires, trapped here under Silvan's weight, being fondled and kissed in the dark. He'd always enjoyed seeing lovers in all their glory, because they were always beautiful. Sometimes it took a bit of gentle coaxing to make them understand he didn't care about moles or wrinkles or stretch marks. *People* were beautiful, in all their fascinating ways; they were art. Living, breathing art. But now, Raf *wanted,* and he wanted what they each desired to be coiled around each other, beginnings and endings undefined and not necessary.

He didn't need light to know Silvan desired, too.

Raf reached up to touch, to caress, and Silvan sighed. "Gorgeous thing. How could I resist?"

"Silvan. Please."

"You remembered."

Raf yanked Silvan's head up to stare at him. "Is this the part where I get demanding and you tell me you're going to take your time?"

"No. I want what you want. So tell me."

The simplest question. And Raf had a simple answer. "Fuck me."

He expected something. Anything. Anything different from a thumb being pressed into his lower lip, then fingertips trailing down his throat. "My way or yours?"

"Dangerous question." Raf licked his lips, catching the tip of Silvan's thumb. All the humor dropped from Silvan's face and now, *now* Raf had what he wanted. "You're so controlled all the time. I want *you*. Take me."

The next question didn't bely the trembling in Silvan's fingers as they slowly slid under Raf's thighs. It was a velvet whisper against his ear. "How hard?"

Fuck.

The jolt of pleasure through him was almost too much. This man - devil that he was - shook something loose inside him. The only thing Raf could think to do was stretch his arms out and push on Silvan's hands with his own. He widened the vee of his legs, opening to Silvan, as they pushed. He wasn't sure Silvan was completely in control of himself when the man ground down on him, sliding their erections together. Sparks danced before his eyes.

Silvan understood. *Thank fuck.*

But he didn't move from atop Raf. His hands slid down, down more until he was cupping Raf's ass and raising his hips just enough to give him room to thrust down. Raf wanted to howl his pleasure but kept it back enough to only groan.

"No. Let me hear you." Silvan kissed him hard. Drew back. Kissed him again. "I want to know how it feels. Because this, right now? Feels so goddamned good and I can only imagine how it'll feel when I'm inside you."

"Fuck." It was a weak whimper but Silvan seemed pleased, nipping at his lips again before sliding down Raf's body. He was quick now with his kisses, peppering Raf's chest, tongue gliding across his skin. But he was carefully thorough, not lingering too long in any one spot and if Raf squirmed, Silvan quickly moved away. "You remembered."

Silvan gazed up at him from where he rested his chin on Raf's stomach. "I did. Of course I did. Your pleasure is mine, which means I will never do anything on purpose that you don't like." He snaked a hand free, reaching for Raf and twisting their fingers together. "As hot as this is, if you told me no, we'd move on to something else or stop completely. I never want you to simply lay back and take it."

Raf heard him now. Really heard him. If their conversation prior about boundaries and stops was real, this was an anvil through his reality. "It might take me some time to fully understand," Raf managed to say, tongue feeling too big for his mouth. His body jarred between the warring sensations of desire and pushing through his mushy gray matter to really hear Silvan. "But I'll tell you. I promise."

Those blue eyes studied him. They blazed in the fiery red line that burst onto the horizon outside the window and Raf never wanted to look away. "Good. I'm glad. Everything is negotiable." He squeezed Raf's fingers. "Do you still want this?"

Raf arched against him, squeezing back. "Yes, *please*."

That naughty little smirk was back and Raf was so happy to see it. It made his stomach tremble in anticipation. "Can I feel you?"

"Oh my *god*, Silvan."

Silvan laughed but his tone was deadly serious after a moment. "Yes or no. That's all I need."

"God fuck *yes*."

Silvan made a pleased sound. Then with no preamble, yanked Raf's shorts down until he could pull them free and toss them aside. Raf thought he'd feel vulnerable, maybe too much, in this moment. But what he felt was *power*. Silvan stared at him, raw lust written all over his feline features. He wanted to preen.

"You are beautiful." Silvan ran his hands up the insides of Raf's thighs. "I've thought about this so much."

"So much that you jerked yourself off to it," Raf shot back. Some part of his brain was clearly working even if most of it was consumed with the fire in his veins.

"No. That was to the idea of you under me, tied down and *screaming for it*."

"Fuck. Fuck. Silvan, clothes off. Please."

Raf shoved at what he could reach, desperate for the slide of skin against his own. But Silvan had other ideas. "Not yet." There was a dangerous gleam in the man's eye, right before he began kissing the inside of Raf's right thigh. "Behave."

Raf flopped back down. But he kept his grip on Silvan's fingers, holding on tight.

"Let me hear you, Raf."

Raf whimpered at that. "I have to be able to put a thought together to make noise."

"Then I'm not doing it right."

Teeth. There were *teeth* scraping along his sensitive skin and he bucked. Silvan laid a heavy arm across his hips. Pinning him. Raf groaned Silvan's name and got a chuckle in response. "Bastard."

"Better." More teeth, their edges barely making an indent but still there. Then Silvan switched to open mouthed kisses, moving higher. Squeezing Raf's hand, grounding him while the rest of his body lit up from the inside. "But I'm afraid I need more."

The kisses and little bites slipped higher and higher and Raf was certain he was going to explode. The teasing was overstimulating him in all the right ways but the edges were knife-sharp, razor-fine, and Raf wanted to run right into them. "Silvan. *Please.*"

"I won't make you beg any more." He gave one last kiss to the inside of Raf's knee. "As much as I enjoy the sound of it. Like honey in my ears."

And then Silvan wrapped his hand around the base of Raf's sorely neglected cock. Raf keened, arched like his back had been blown out, and the only thing keeping him tethered was the grip Silvan had on his hand. Words tumbled from him, unintelligible and *loud*, interspersed with moans that seemed to only drive Silvan forward, egging him on. That hand worked him over, twisting, stroking, occasionally pausing so he could catch his breath, then dragging more moans and cries from the very bottom of his soul.

"Fuck. Fuck. Silvan. I can't..."

Silvan slowed his hand, those eyes so, *so* dark as they stared right through him. "Now, like this? Or do you want to wait?"

"Wait. Please. I need you." Raf tugged helplessly at Silvan's shirt. Silvan gave him one last stroke, smearing drops of precome into his skin. He was a lump of mindless pleasure. Desperate. "*I want you in me.*"

"Jesus Christ." Silvan's shell broke and now, now Raf could see the wantonness on his face. He felt matched now, not so outclassed by Silvan's calm demeanor. And there was no denying the erection tenting his pants. Silvan shed his clothes and came back to Raf after diverting into a bedside table for lube. And for the first time since he'd known the man, Silvan hesitated. "How do you want me?"

Feverish, lust-soaked images flooded his mind but his body decided for him. Raf flipped onto his stomach, getting to all fours, and then looked at Silvan over his shoulder. "Like this. Just...I need you against me."

Silvan's face crumpled, desire written over those arches and planes like it was meant to be there all along. Raf's ego would later stroke itself off to that expression, but now it only heated his blood that much more. "Anything you want."

And with Silvan pressed to him, their skin slick and hands wandering, the kiss they shared felt right all over again. Every kiss was right but this one made his brain stutter to a halt. Silvan was stroking his skin, whispering sweet little words of encouragement into his ear, his chest plastered to Raf's back. When a hand squeezed his ass and he moaned in delight, Silvan couldn't seem to hold back anymore. "Want you. Gods, Raf."

His fingers were gentle as they explored his crease, the cool tackiness of the lube fading away into sheer pleasure. Raf grabbed for the headboard. Silvan touched him gently. And the breath left his lungs.

"Christ." Silvan dropped his forehead to Raf's shoulder, the pressure of it another point of grounding. Otherwise he'd be a balloon on a windy spring day. That finger sank in and Raf willed himself to relax even more. Everything ached and burned and *sang* in him and he never, ever wanted it to stop. "Are you okay?"

"Yes," Raf hissed out. His grip made the headboard creak. "Please keep going. Don't stop."

Silvan's prep was thorough. Slow, but thorough. Raf was reduced to mindless, throbbing need and he couldn't stop his whines and moans if he'd tried. They spilled from him as he panted and swore. And when he was ready - truly ready, not an overeager virgin forcing himself to accommodate someone else - Raf tipped his head back and was met with Silvan's temple pressing into his. "Take me."

He was so careful. So sweet. Pressing kisses to Raf's shoulder, hands holding him steady as Silvan buried himself in Raf's body. They rocked together, the rhythm faltering until Raf reached back, fumbling, finally able to draw Silvan's hand up to join his on the headboard. Their other hands clasped together on the mattress.

Silvan's breath hot in his ear.

The sweat building, making them slip.

The way they fit together.

The way Silvan's body moved with his.

How Silvan kissed him, stroked him, fucked him.

And Raf's world exploded.

Chapter Twenty-Four

Two weeks later, the opening of the Night Garden show

"I thought you might be the one to hit the spotlight."

Raf looked around. Back to Silvan. Around again. Then realization settled in. "You clean up nicely," he purred, slinking forward, gaze hot on Silvan's tuxedo. "But I seem to be missing...everyone."

"I asked them to give us a minute." Silvan held out a dark red rose as Raf approached. "Just long enough."

There was a naughty smile on his lover's face. "Hmm. So not long *enough* you're telling me?"

He held out a hand, which Raf took, and tucked the rose behind his ear. "Given our marathon sessions, not nearly enough."

Raf practically molded his body to Silvan's as he wrapped his arms around Silvan's shoulders. "Then hello."

"Hello."

Raf liked it when Silvan initiated things, but tonight he knew Raf would be in a particular mood. Maybe it was the power of suggestion, staring at raw, primal pieces of art mixed in with the heady scent of orchids on loan from the conservatory. Maybe their time together, dotted with long afternoon beach walks and the slide of satin over Raf's body, was helping Raf relax more.

Maybe it was because they fit so well together.

Whatever it was that had Raf so pliable in his arms was to be commended. No one could adapt their thinking overnight, but these last few weeks had seen a change in Raf's panicked perfectionism. He hid it well, but was slowly, carefully learning to let others help him, and Silvan knew that was tough.

"I'm proud of you," Silvan said softly between gentle kisses, the kind that left his knees feeling watery. Raf's fingers tightened on his shoulders, so Silvan kept talking, kept kissing him. "I know how hard it is to let people help. But I hope you're doing all right with..."

Raf pulled back to look at him. "With?"

"Everything. It's been a hectic few weeks, not counting everything leading up to these shows." The way Raf was staring at him was melting his heart, so Silvan gently put a hand on his cheek. "And then us. I know I check in and we're both learning how to communicate with each other."

"But this is different," Raf replied.

"It's different." Silvan's chest tightened, like a lead band squeezing his lungs, his ribs. His heart.

Raf managed words where Silvan's fled him. "I never expected you," he replied, mirroring Silvan's touch to his face. "I'm so glad, for once, my planning couldn't anticipate something."

That made him laugh. "See? We're learning."

"Oh? And what have you learned, Mr. Diedrich?"

Tease. "More than I can tell you. But I'll start with this."

Silvan kissed him again and when Raf took control of it from him, he surrendered.

When they broke apart, Silvan handed him the remote he'd stored safely in his jacket pocket. "Ready?"

Raf looked around at all the pieces lit up by their own spotlights, then nodded. Together they turned to face *Dual Sisters*, the only piece not alight from above or below. The artist had stopped by earlier in the day to double check everything, and then draped the piece in a sheer black veil. The veil made it so you had to lean in and really *look* at the piece, and it was a simple but ingenious way of making guests of the show slow down.

And when it was lit from underneath, the entire thing had a haunting air about it that sent delightful chills down Silvan's spine. Chills he felt even now, before Raf hit the button for the spotlight.

"One more big night," Raf said as he leaned his head on Silvan's shoulder.

Silvan kissed the top of his head. "We'll make it wonderful."

"It already is."

The light came on. The veil fluttered. And as they stared at the piece - the one that had brought them together - Raf sighed and tightened his arm around Silvan's waist. "Thank you," Raf said quietly.

"Hey." When Raf looked up, Silvan put two fingers under his chin and smiled down at him before leaning in and brushing their lips together. "Remarkable man."

"Devil." Raf smirked at him, eyes traveling over Silvan's body. "In a very nice tuxedo."

"I remembered."

Raf froze. Then laughed, the sound loud and echoing through the space. "Well, lucky me."

"Hard to forget that little confession."

Raf gave a playful shiver and leaned into him more. "Then lucky me when we get back to your place. Just maybe remember to keep Mozart out of the bedroom this time."

"She thought the fabric was something to play with. Can you blame her?"

Raf's groan made him chuckle. "At least it wasn't the good satin ties. Does she need more toys?"

"Absolutely not, that cat is completely spoiled already."

"Not the only one who is spoiled."

"You or me?"

"Both of us I'm afraid, my darling."

One month later

"Hide!" Camilla was frantically waving at everyone in the room. "Seriously, get down! Marianna's bringing her right now!"

Raf slid into place between Camilla and Silvan. He was flushed from running around with last-minute preparations and didn't want to be out of breath when his mother walked in the door. He took several big gulps of air, then breathed out hard. "You okay?" Camilla whispered.

"Yes. Sorry. Excited and nervous all at the same time."

Silvan squeezed his arm. "It looks amazing. She's going to be thrilled."

"Oh my god," Camilla moaned softly. "Silvan. Hush."

Watching Silvan smile apologetically at Camilla's order nearly made Raf laugh. But his phone buzzed with a text from Marianna and they were out of time.

The bell they put up over the door specifically for this dinged, and on three, the room exploded in a joint cheer of "Happy birthday!". The look on his mother's face was exactly what he'd been hoping for. Surprise. Elation. Love.

Francia put her hands over her mouth and stared, wide-eyed, at everyone gathered in the gallery. "What...how..."

Raf was immediately at her side, Silvan and Camilla trailing in his wake. "Happy birthday, Mom." And very gently, he turned her to the left where a row of covered easels awaited them. Friends and family stepped forward and whipped the covers away.

And his mom burst into tears.

Raf had been expecting such a reaction, but seeing his mother cry before his very eyes forced him to suck in a few more deep breaths. If he started crying, he'd never recover.

"Raf..." Francia turned to him, bright tears tracking down her face, hands shaking. "What..."

"All those canvases in your attic deserve to be seen," he explained. "So Marianna and Camilla and everyone here made it happen."

"How long have you been planning this?" She was still staring wide-eyed at the display of her own art in front of her, but drying her tears with the handkerchief Raf handed her seemed to calm her some.

Raf shrugged. "All that matters is you like it. Do you?"

"I love it." Francia moved toward the row of art; her art, long buried in the attic and now lovingly restored and framed. But soon she drifted to the one easel off to the side, anticipation making her fingers tremble. "Is this..."

Silvan was right there, lending them both soft, warm smiles and a steady gaze. "It seemed only right," he said before whipping off the cover to reveal that painting. That first painting, the one that had sold at an art faire all those years ago and had hung in Silvan's home for decades. "It deserves to be seen by more than just a few people."

Everyone was silent as Francia ran her fingers over the frame. Raf felt an arm around his shoulders. "You did good," Marianna whispered. "She's going to remember this forever."

He had no words. He looked at his cousin, then at Camilla before holding an arm out to them. They came immediately, squeezing Raf's side hard. And they watched as Francia embraced Silvan tightly, her silent tears dropping onto his sleeve. Raf watched those blue eyes close and his heart clenched.

After a few moments, his mother and Silvan broke apart, and then she was sliding into their little group hug, laughing and crying and so happy. It was all he'd ever wanted for her birthday. For her. For the woman who had raised him all on her own and had given him so much.

"I love you. Happy birthday," Raf said into her hair.

Francia sniffled and looked up at him, her hands on his face and adoration in her eyes. "You. My brilliant, beautiful son. I love you so much. Thank you."

It took a few moments for the tears to stop, but slowly they got Francia over to the tables full of food and gifts and Raf listened to her half-hearted protests about the party being "too much". He knew she was enjoying every minute.

"You okay?"

Raf turned as Silvan came back to him. "Yes. Shaky, admittedly, but yes. I knew it would be a gut punch but..." He pulled Silvan into a tight hug and breathed him in. "Still, I think she's happy."

Silvan's chuckle was warm and it helped settle his nerves. "More than happy. Elated. She had no idea this was happening and now look at her. Your mom is an incredible person."

"Oh, I am well aware." Raf tipped his head up in invitation. "So are you."

Another chuckle. "I thought I was a devil."

"You can be both."

"Thank you for that."

He snorted. "Devil man. Lovely man that you are." He slid his palm along Silvan's jaw, unable to stop the smile spreading over his face. "And I'm so happy."

There was no hesitation in Silvan's voice as he said, "So am I. Thank you for letting me be a part of this."

"Today? Of course."

Silvan's kiss was soft, sweet. A promise to both of them. "All of it. Today, the opening, being in your life." Blue eyes stared into his and the arms around him tightened. "Remarkable man."

Tears threatened once more, but Raf shook them off. "I adore you," he whispered. "You've changed my life."

"And you mine."

Raf returned that promise Silvan had silently made in his kiss with a smile of his own. "Then lucky us."

About The Author

Halli Starling (she/they) is a queer author, librarian, gamer, editor, and nerd. *A Brighter, Darker Art* is her fifth book. Her work can be found on hallistarlingbooks.com and she's on Twitter and Instagram @hallistarling.

Lightning Source UK Ltd.
Milton Keynes UK
UKHW021953020223
416405UK00022B/96/J